STRIFE'S COST

STEVE RZASA

STRIFE'S COST
by Steve Rzasa

ISBN: 978-1-64709-016-6

Cover design by Dmitry Borodin

Randall Ritnour, Art Director

Published by
Kgruppe, LLC
Lincoln, Nebraska

Kgruppe 2nd Edition 2025

Visit our website for
sneak previews, updates, new projects.

www.Takamo.com

TAKAMO

TA'KA'MO (High Radnian, Radnia—Central continent from TAI (Universe) and KHA'MO (ebb and flow) 1. Gestalt, the wholeness of the universe. 2. History. 3. Conflict.

VOL. 234, FILE 451 – SEPAL'S UNABRIDGED GALACTIC DICTIONARY

What is Takamo?

Takamo started as a massive multiplayer science fiction play-by-mail game in the early 1980s. It had a newsletter where players and staff published descriptions and stories about their interstellar empires. That generated spin off publications for fan fiction and stories rooted in Takamo lore. Over the years, the worldbuilding took on a life of its own and became a library of collected works developed over four decades.

In 2014, Kevin J. Anderson and Wordfire Press published the first Takamo novel, Empire's Rift by Steve Rzasa. Takamo is a science fiction imprint with over twenty titles by various authors, all based in the shared Takamo universe.

I like to think of Takamo is the ancient language of space. Any moment in the Takamo timeline is one part of the whole – a single star point in this complex, limitless, gestalt universe. Takamo stories are set in a historical timeline spanning half a million years. They are penned by different authors in a shared universe with a collective destiny. This book is a part of that universe.

Want to know more? Visit www.takamo.com

PROLOGUE

August 2679

The Sanctuary of the Revered Barad was one of the oldest houses of worship in the Briddarri Kingdom, dating four millennia and housing some of the most ancient relics of sacred history. Six towers of weathered white stone topped with obsidian domes stood like sentinels around a central pavilion, its crumbling walls reinforced with modern guardstone and covered with a transparent dome. From the sky, a riot of colors formed by tapestries, weapons, and manuscripts on display in the pavilion provided the only relief from stark black and white.

To Lira Lin Reen, it was like gazing on a tiny flower in the midst of a barren meadow.

Such a beautiful sight.

Even more beautiful with the knowledge the humdrum artifacts sheltered a certain rare gemstone worth millions.

Lira adjusted her wrist scanner. The gel's progress was so sluggish; she wanted to reach in and give it a shove. Numbers ticked down. Hurry along, come on!

She got the green lights she craved. The gel's chemical reaction to the circuitry took hold as planned. It slowed the operating system at such a level that she could interfere with the case without fear of activating the alarms. Worst case scenario, the security system would see the slowdown as something to be flagged for later maintenance.

Lira reached for the latches holding the plas-glass case down and stopped to tap her left shoulder three times with the first two fingers of her right hand—the Briddarri gesture for luck.

The latch clicked as loud as weapons fire to her ears, but nothing happened.

Not pausing to rejoice, she flipped the rest of the latches in rapid succession and eased the case back on its hinges. The Seerrstone brightened in response to her motion. She was amazed by its warmth, even through the filigree wrapping.

A klaxon screamed.

Red lights pulsed.

What? How? She tucked the gem into her pocket and ran for the center of the room.

Too late. The guard came on the run, a burly Briddarri male in a drab tan jumpsuit, but there was nothing drab about the stunpole in his hands. A meter long, its top third crackled with electricity. A good poke from that and Lira's body would go as limp as a child's *riddadd*, a floppy puppet.

The pair of drones hovering with him didn't improve her chances. Each one was the size of her head, a flattened diamond with two dangling pincers. Air rippled around their tiny jets.

She tapped her wrist unit. The suit responded in reverse of its usual camouflage tactics, brightening until she was a gleaming white figure sprinting toward the guard. The visor protected her eyes, but it was enough of a glare to make them water.

The guard covered his face and cried out.

Lira grabbed the handle end of the stunpole, using it as leverage, and swept his feet from under him, a move made simpler by his forward momentum. As he dropped, she wrenched the stunpole away. Pain shot up her arms. His grasp was stronger than she'd anticipated.

He hit the floor with the sound of a sack of food being dropped.

The drones gave no warning, no demand to submit. They swept in and reached for her with arms that elongated to three times their standard length.

Lira spun out of their reach, tucking into a roll, and when she came up, she bashed the first drone across its flank with the stunpole.

Sparks exploded. The drone went completely dead, its engines sputtering. It crashed against a plas-glass case, leaving a virry scuttler's web of cracks.

The second drone pivoted in midair and slashed at her with those spindly arms. A claw cut across her suit, severing fabric and the woven circuitry. The effect was instantaneous: Lira's blinding light doused, and her suit turned a plain charcoal. It ignored the surroundings, as useless as if she'd worn the guard's plain jumpsuit.

Lira stabbed the stunpole into the cluster of optical domes on the drone's front half, smashing them to bits.

By now the guard was up and grabbed her about the waist. She put an elbow to his nose, cracking bone and spraying bright green blood. A quick jab with the stunpole left him twitching on the stone floor.

Shouts, and more footsteps.

The blasted grav-harness better still be operational.

Lira leaped straight up, and let the anti-gravity shoot her into the air. She scraped her already raw shoulder against the hole cut through the transparent ceiling, and then she was out, wind whipping around her, cold air biting the wound.

A shuttle banked overhead, spotlight illuminating her in a circle of harsh white.

Farrudd. That route was cut. But she never went into a place without at least four more ways out.

She twisted onto her side and shot out past the towers. Didn't matter if she set off all the rest of the alarms now, and as she passed through the security grid, that's exactly what happened.

Then she was out, in the black night, with water roaring from the falls all around her. She dove down the wall of spray, every sound drowned out.

Only thing she could hear was her own laughter.

***

A week later, she walked into the central park of Gira, capital city of Dorraddin Prime.

Ramper trees were in full bloom, showering everything and everyone with pale yellow blossoms. Couples giggled and swept them at each other.

Lira walked softly, blending with the crowds and individuals dressed in springtime clothing. The cut on her shoulder was healed, and she bared both to the sun's caress in a flowing yellow blouse. If she stayed out long enough, she might get a deeper verdant tone to her skin.

There was a single bench along this path, a walkway of tan stones. She sat on it and started reading her scroll.

Soon the surface of the bench was coated in blossoms. She brushed several from beside her, as if making room for another person, and brushed the rest off her striped skirt.

The transceiver on her index finger adhered to a blossom and spun off into the air, propelling itself on minuscule fans built from the molecular level up.

The message would get to its recipient, and they'd know the job was a success. Seven days and no one had followed her. No one had made any sign that they knew she'd stolen the Seerrstone.

Two more weeks, and she'd be rich. Well, richer.

"Lira Lin Reen?"

A young couple stood by her. She was shorter than him, and both had matching blue and brown hair—such was the fad among couples these days. He seemed too ugly for her, with his stockier than usual build and way too tall body.

It was in that instant she realized they were both stern-faced, absent any sign of ardor for each other.

She was on her feet and flipping backward over the bench when the stun pulse from behind hit her. Lira slapped hard to the grass, face down in the blossoms.

Impossible. How had she so badly miscalculated? How had they gotten her?

They put binders on her wrists, which Lira could barely feel. "You are hereby detained by the Bureau for Law and Discipline," the woman said. "For the theft of state property. Your rights as a citizen of the Briddarri Kingdom have been frozen. Your ancestors are hereby shamed."

She didn't panic. She kept her cool, even when they dragged her to her feet and slammed the handles of stun-rods into her gut. Pain wouldn't matter.

The others were watching. They'd know and spread the word. Blue Kitt would survive.

CHAPTER ONE

April 2681

C aptain Taggart Wester dodged getting his starfighter blown up by three seconds with a half klick to spare.

A pair of Naplian missiles streaked by the underside of his SF-107, and he'd swear before a combat review commission to whoever would listen he could feel the heat of their exhaust through the hull plating.

He grinned. One-eyes weren't going to get the drop on him today.

Tag punched the thruster controls for his Warhawk, spinning the fighter as it hurtled along. The Naplian fighter, all sharp wings and admirable curves, was too far back to open fire with its energy weapons—those pulses dissipated at the edges of their range.

That was the bonus of relying on the underpowered railguns slung on the centerline of the Warhawk. Yes, they didn't pack nearly as much punch over fighter-to-fighter brawls as the Naplian energy bursts, but, thanks to elementary physics, the projectiles would keep on going unless gravity altered their courses, or an obstacle forced them to unleash their insane kinetic energy.

Tag was betting on the second option.

Targeting sensors bracketed the Naplian fighter with a double-outlined red diamond. Tag punched the firing key.

It was simple, really. Electromagnets inside the railgun's barrel accelerated tungsten projectiles at hypervelocities. Even without their diamond coating, the bullets would tear through anything in their path.

The Naplian pilot wasn't an idiot. He'd apparently fought long enough in the two-year invasion of Terran space to know how nasty railguns were close up. His fighter slipped back and forth along its pursuit trajectory, particle weapon flashing green blasts as it picked off the incoming projectiles.

Good. Had him distracted.

Tag's comm chirped. "Bronze Leader here. Two, this isn't a hot time for a tactical discussion."

"Lead, this is Two. I was merely inquiring if you needed my assistance."

"Nah, you know me, Princess. I can handle a lone One-eye." Although, he was rapidly cycling through his ammo reserve for the railgun. How many missiles did he have left? Three of his six RS-18s were gone. The Naplian's quick closure, however, precluded launching an antimatter warhead this close.

"Very good, Captain." A red blip vanished from the tactical display, showing his wingman was clear of enemy ships for the moment—a rare blank black spot in the swirling melee of enemy and allied markers. "Take care of his missiles."

"Yeah, I know, they haven't detonated." The targeting computer was kind enough to keep track of them, two arrows streaking away. Right into the cluster of asteroids up ahead. There were more than fifty, spaced apart at intervals of several tens of thousands of klicks. Near enough to represent a significant navigational hazard to starfighters moving at thousands of klicks per second.

More green flashes. The Naplian was closing. Was he really going to hound Tag into the field? Probably thought he was dealing with a single Terran pilot who was crazy enough to pose a danger to the rest of the Naplian's squadron.

Probably true. Tag had already blasted two of his buddies.

He punched the thrusters, boosting up into an arc. It pushed him "up" relative to the top of the Naplian fighter, even as Tag hurtled along backwards with his bottom facing the nearest asteroid. Tag cut the railguns and opened up with blasts from the Briddarri plasma projector pod dangling from the underside of his Warhawk. The recoil made everything shudder so bad his teeth rattled. Three shots and the energy weapon had to recharge. But those bursts passed near enough to the Naplian to make him alter his course.

Right into the gravitational pull of the asteroid.

The two missiles the Naplian had intended for Tag came ripping around the asteroid, dragged along by its gravity enough to give them the appearance of stray Saarno foxes. The comparison struck

Tag with a pang of homesickness. Sure, there were probably plenty of Saarno foxes left on his homeworld of Baedecker Four, but there was no way he'd be seeing either the place or the animal any time soon.

It was headquarters for the Naplian occupation forces along the Terran front lines of this blasted war.

The missiles quickly veered toward the Naplian. Tag knew he only had seconds before the rudimentary AI aboard both figured out their new target was, in fact, a Naplian friendly.

So, he used the next round of plasma bursts to good effect.

The three-shot barrage ignited the antimatter warheads of both missiles. One sec, a Naplian and his two missiles presented themselves as shiny specks racing toward embrace above a big space rock reminiscent of a lump of charcoal. Next, a brilliant white flash, so intense Tag's nav computer tamped down the visual input. When it cleared, the asteroid was missing a sizeable chunk.

Tag blew out a breath. "I'm clear, Princess. Sorry to have to run so far from the party."

"It's preferable to you being atomized, Tag."

He chuckled. She talked as if they were having a quiet cup of tea in the pilot country mess hall aboard TSS *Confiance*, their ship, and home base. It didn't matter she'd engaged another fighter and was chasing it down with her railguns.

The rest of his squadron was spread across a sphere of local space six million klicks in diameter, along with the heavy fighter-bombers of Halberd squadron. Tag's starfighters were tasked with keeping the escort squadron of Naplians busy, while Halberd's AF-32G Raiders pounded at the shields of a Naplian corvette. The ship, with its slender hull and broad jump sails, reminded Tag of a Jendu swan, though it wasn't white and tan, but an iridescent gray streaked with carbon scoring where weapons fire had penetrated the shields.

Jendu swans. Again with Baedecker memories. He shook his head and accelerated to join Princess.

Whatever Naplian fighters weren't destroyed were damaged, left drifting in space. Tag wasn't so concerned about their welfare. Commodore Sobban Ram wanted prisoners for interrogation. Naplians would have vaporized Terran escape pods and disabled fighters.

"Captain, the freighters are trying to slip the net."

"Roger that, Two." Right. The reason for the escort corvette and fighters—a Naplian mining complex, huge beast of a ship, lumbering along on its sublight drives. They'd have to be careful with this one. Tag switched channels on his communications systems. "Bronze Leader to Halberd."

"Halberd Lead." The voice was terse and full of gravel. "You mind? We're busy."

They were indeed. The escort corvette's shields wavered under a barrage of antimatter missiles, rippling and sparking along the starboard flanks. "And a fine job of kicking their rears, sir. But the freighter looks to be boosting."

Halberd Lead swore. "Where's *Confiance*?"

"Ten minutes out by ripwave, tussling with a destroyer last I heard."

"All right, then, the freighter's all yours. Cripple her engines. And for stars' sake, watch the fuel tanks. That thing's loaded down with enough serjaum and weapons to blow everything to atoms."

"That'd rankle Commodore Ram," Tag said. "Relax, I'm on it. Bronze Lead out."

On it. Yeah, easier said than done. Halberd Lead wasn't joking. Not only was the mining complex hauling serjaum ore to a Naplian depot on the front lines of the Terran incursion, but it was carrying replacement particle weapons and missiles. Prime tech. Tag wanted Terran hands on it as badly as the brass above. "Bronze Leader to all units. Target the mining complex. Disabling fire only, repeat, disabling fire only. Two, you're with me for the engines. Six? Take Five and your flight after their point defense weapons."

Affirmatives overlapped. Princess braked to match Tag's course, and together they swept in on the mining complex with Bronze Three and Four. Two more quartets of Tag's Warhawks blasted ahead, battering the mining complex with railgun projectiles and, when available, Briddarri plasma projectors. Only half the squadron was equipped with those.

Tag lined up the sights on his plasma weapon. Better some than none, he mused, and let fly a three-shot burst.

Princess did the same, a split second after him, and their shots hit home. The complex's shields shuddered under the impact.

Meanwhile, the other eight fighters traded fire with the complex. Green energy blasts peppered space, filling the darkness with so many flashes of light, Tag wondered if he'd underestimated this opponent.

"Counting six turrets dorsal, six ventral, and two along each side," Princess said.

"Roger." Tag glanced at the sensor data his console picked up from her report. The first two flights of his squadron knocked down most of the ventral turrets in short order, but Bronze Eight picked up a blast that ripped through its port wing. His wingman, Bronze Seven, moved to cover him. "Watch those turrets, boys and girls. Our One-eye pals aren't playing nice."

"Sir, energy readings indicate the complex is powering up its version of ripwave for a short jump."

"Give the plasma projector another go when it recharges. Three and Four, boys, I want you to spread out and concentrate railgun fire on the weakest points your scanners can find, copy?"

"Copy that, Bronze Leader, but I've got a missile locked and racked for—"

"Negative. Under no circumstances are you to engage with missiles. Novafire, use your brains for a microsec! You light off an AM warhead, or even a low-level disabler, you could ignite the entire drive assembly. That's no problem if we want to cut their supply chain, but the Commodore wants this package delivered intact."

"Yes, sir. Sorry, sir."

"Never apologize for taking initiative, Three." Tag fired off another blast from the plasma weapon, but he hadn't waited long enough for the full recharge. All he got was a double shot. He scowled. His memories dredged up the ghostly sound of his old radar intercept operator, Ichiro "Scrape" Sakawa chuckling—most likely at the irony. Tag Wester, advocating restraint?

Yeah, well, command was far different than running targets in a two-seat fighter-bomber.

And Scrape was dead, his neck broken, of all things.

Tag couldn't help but magnify the image, like a targeting scope on maximum amplification, as he pressed home his attack with the

Warhawk's railguns.

"Those dorsal cannons are not going to let up because you charge at them, Tag," Princess said.

Tag burned straight in for the weakest portion of the complex's shields, highlighted in flashing red by his scanners. The Naplian's weapons fire bracketed space all around him, but Tag set the Warhawk on evasive twists and thruster slides. She staggered in and out of her flight path, while maintaining the fast approach.

Fast approach. Tag grinned. Okay, so he'd warned the impatient rookies among his squadron about overkill, but maybe there was a way to up the ante without destroying the mining complex.

"Princess, you with me?" It was a rhetorical question; her Warhawk unloaded round after round of tungsten bullets from less than 100 klicks away. His cockpit canopy magnified the image of the arrowhead-shaped fighter, its front flashing white. "I got an idea."

Princess exhaled.

"Problem?" A near miss jolted the Warhawk.

"Only, every time you say that, Captain, I wonder if I should signal *Confiance* and have them forward my last will and testament to my kin."

He chuckled. "Doubt it. When I give the mark, flip and burn for full acceleration with your sublight drives."

"Ah. Clever."

"I know, right? Thanks."

The mining complex was twisting over in a slow roll. Its ventral guns were gone, and its captain must have decided the eight fighters attacking the damaged side of the ship's hull were a greater threat. Which was good for Tag, because it meant the captain had also decided Tag's flight of four wasn't as bad a nuisance.

Well, he'd see about that.

With the energy blasts tapering off, and the complex growing huge in his visual display, Tag kept an eye on the proximity indicator. "Give it a few more seconds, Princess."

"Standing by."

Almost … almost … "Go!"

In unison, the Warhawks flipped and ignited their sublight drives. The radiation output was of a magnitude far worse than what the Briddarri plasma weapons could manage, and while not of pinpoint accuracy like the railguns, the drives battered the weak portions of the Naplian's aft shields. The damaged section overloaded, flashed with a spray of sparks that expanded like a blooming flower in slow motion, and vanished.

"Bronze Three and Four, mark that gap and fire!"

Streams of white-hot railgun projectiles cut through space. Tag, now facing back the way he'd come, watched the display out the top of his canopy. His and Princess's Warhawks sped along, engines dormant and angled "down" at the mining complex. The shots were surgical, severing relays and puncturing hull plating.

Nothing exploded, thankfully, but Tag's scanners told him, in typically understated form, when the deed had been done; the aft section of the mining complex glowed red.

"Ripwave generator's offline," Princess said. "Power's cut to their jump sails. Best they can manage is maneuvering thrusters, Captain."

"Yes!" Tag thumped his console. Then, remembering he was squadron commander and not just an ace pilot, he toggled the all-squadron signal. "Nice work, boys and girls, our target's dead in the water. Finish stripping her weapons, and we'll have this one wrapped up neat for Commodore Ram."

Tinny cheers echoed across the comm, even from the crippled Bronze Eight. The Naplian's energy blasts slackened as the Warhawks took out each gun turret. They might still have a fight on their hands if the captain wanted to chew up the fighters in hopes of the corvette coming to his rescue, but …

Light flashed a long way off. Tag smiled at the display. TSS *Confiance* had come to the party and made it in much faster time than the ten minutes Tag had anticipated. The sight of the 300-meter *Monsoon*-class heavy cruiser, and the knowledge of its loads of firepower, buoyed Tag's spirits as much as it must have sapped his Naplian opponents'. The mining complex finally stopped shooting altogether. Tag's comm line blinked with a hail from the Naplian captain.

Surrender.

His heart wanted to burst from his chest. Best of all, none of his people were dead. That one's for you, Scrape.

***

Confiance wasn't alone. A flotilla of four gunboats orbited the heavy cruiser, tiny 90-meter vessels with big sublight engines for their size. Ugly brutes, small as they were, with triangular prism hulls only 12 meters on each side. Railgun turrets sprouted from several surfaces, and a single pulsed particle cannon of capital ship caliber was shoved down the centerline.

"Odd for local patrollers to be out this far in the Great Desert Rift." Princess's voice registered the same confusion Tag felt.

"Yeah. Not like *Confiance* needs the help against an escort and a destroyer. They're easy enough pickings for a heavy cruiser. Maybe the fleet's stretched thin enough they have to pull the smaller ships into the broader fight. All those gunboats have jump drives and ripwave generators, anyway."

Tag led the squadron back to *Confiance*'s main hangar, a huge expanse which the fighters accessed via landing tunnels on the port and starboard sides. Only after all the rest were dragged in on autopilot by Flight Ops, and finally the damaged Bronze Seven was pulled aboard, did Tag give up control of his Warhawk. Tag glanced up at the curved supports overhead as the fighter floated down the tunnel, thinking of his own ribcage, which he was sure had some bruises.

The landing tunnel dumped him inside *Confiance*'s main hangar. A catchfield caught hold of the Warhawk and shunted it into an alcove just large enough for the arrowhead-shaped fighter. The rest of Bronze Squadron was tucked in, two rows of six, stacked one atop the other. Halberd Squadron's Raiders flitted in through the starboard landing tunnel, taking up their berths on the opposite side. The rest of the space was filled with assault shuttles for armored jump troopers and cargo craft.

Tag doffed his helmet as soon as the canopy popped open. The hangar stank of ozone, lubricants, and sweat, the latter of which Tag had no one to blame but himself. His white and black Colonial Defense Force AES pilot's jumpsuit was equipped with life support and air scrubbers, but in the heat of battle those systems were hard-pressed to keep up with human stink.

Tag ran a hand through dark brown hair. Princess had teased him about a supposed streak of gray, but he couldn't find it. He chalked it up to a trick of lighting.

"Good shooting out there, Captain." First Lieutenant Naomi Wyss was tall enough Tag couldn't quite believe she was comfortable in a Warhawk's tight confines, but her slender body moved with the grace of a dancer every step she took. Her complexion was dusky, and her eyes green, making them stand out like emeralds against the black of her hair and white of her jumpsuit.

"Thanks." Tag slapped her on the shoulder. "You weren't too shabby yourself. Two more kills for your Warhawk."

"Every fighter I obliterate is one less Naplian trying to take our stars."

Sometimes he wished she had a little more spark to her—like her former wingman, Chasm, or Cage or Daft or Big Sue. He had to stop thinking like that. Such thoughts became a litany of dead pilots.

They'd lost many, in three years, with not much to show.

"Captain Wester." Another woman spoke his name, and she didn't ask a question—this was an order. Commander Allison Vollan might have been shorter than both Tag and Princess by a good half meter, but she was first officer of *Confiance*.

Tag saluted. "Ma'am."

"Nice work roping in the mining complex."

Tag stayed stiffly at attention but slid Princess a wink. The latter managed to restrain herself to a mild quirk of the corner of her mouth. "Thank you, ma'am. Always happy to kick some more One-eyes down the black hole, if you catch my ripwave."

"That I do." Vollan crossed her arms, not appearing the least amused. Her skin was so pale and her hair such a straw blonde they reflected every flashing light in the hangar bay. She watched him with eyes like glittering blue stars. "Commodore Ram happens to agree. He and his guests want to see you upstairs, though, for something that could hurt them more than the loss of one munitions and fuel ship."

"Of course. Right away." Tag tugged at his flight suit. "But it's best for all concerned if I strip off this thing. Bad as it smells I doubt it's good for anything more than incineration."

"Belay that. Upstairs means immediately, Captain. I'll take you myself." Tag swore. Princess edged a few centimeters away.

He followed Vollan out, keenly aware of every eyeball and robotic optic port trained his direction. Bridge brass didn't frequent the hangar, and when they dragged someone out, it wasn't for a pat on the back and a glass of Crown & Scepter rum.

Tag kept his expression neutral. Ah, well. Wouldn't be the first time he got dragged before his superiors for running his engines too hot.

Bottom line, he still got the job done.

***

The commodore's office was up a deck and behind the bridge, with a transparent section of bulkhead allowing Ram to keep an eye on operations. The room was typical Navy fare—a big box, edges truncated, done up in gray and black metals and composites. A half-dozen chairs of silver tubing were arrayed around a plas-glass table. Holograms swirled in a bowl-shaped depression at the center, a clustering of stars Tag recognized—their operational corner of the Great Desert Rift. *Confiance* and other Terran fleet elements were in the lower galactic "southeast" corner of the Rift, about fifty sectors from Baedecker. Van Sutton Naval Base, their stronghold on the Terran side of the border, was a couple sectors nearer, but it was still weeks away. The Naplian incursion was marked in a long red stripe slashing several sectors wide through the Rift and jutting into Terran space, like a big old thumb in the eye of collective humanity. Tag noted with grim satisfaction there were chunks dug out of that thumb where CDF and the Briddarri had taken some pretty big bites in the past few years.

It wasn't enough to push them back, not yet.

Ram was seated at his desk, with two men standing nearby. The desk was an antique, made from mahogany, and added the only warm colors to the room. Its surface, a rich wood grain polished to a shine, was decorated with a pot of violets and a smattering of holo images. The people in those images looked an awful lot like Sobban Ram—tall, slender, deep brown skin. Ram's hair was streaked through with gray, what little there was remaining.

"Captain Wester. Do come in. I am pleased you can join us." Ram rose from his chair. Tag snapped off another salute, very much realizing it wasn't nearly as sharp as Commander Vollan's.

"Commodore."

"There's no need to be so stiff about this, Captain. Our discussion here is something Navy regulations do not cover, and I trust that makes it more to your liking."

Tag frowned. He didn't know how to answer that one and was about to say so to the Commodore when one of the two men faced him.

"Tim!" Tag rushed the officer and pumped his hand with a furious handshake. "Novafire, but it's good to see you."

Commander Timothy Ess smiled, pushing up the corners of a mustache and beard groomed with laserlike precision. Tim's hair was golden blond, cropped short, and he wore the same blue jumpsuit of the Terran Navy as Vollan and Ram. "Good to see family this deep out in space, Tag. You've been busy from what I hear."

Tag shrugged. "Nah, wasn't much trouble. Just a small Naplian convoy."

"What about the hornet's nest you kicked over at Govanvi?"

"That? Ah. Yeah, the One-eyes don't take it kindly when you scuttle one of their battlecruisers before it's had a chance to launch."

Tag realized everyone was watching him, Ram and Vollan included. The other guy now faced him, a bald fellow with tanned skin and a blank stare Tag found as bothersome as a missile lock. He wore a uniform and rank identical to Tim's and Vollan's, the three silver stripes glinting under the low lights of the office.

"Captain Wester, there can be no arguing your record in our campaign against the Naplians," Ram said. "For three years you've led Bronze Squadron with increasing aplomb, earning commendations at a faster rate than you've gathered demerits."

Tag scratched at the back of his neck. "Yes, sir. Thanks. I think." Vollan shook her head.

Not impressed? Well, Tag was never overly fond of her, either.

Ram, however, pursed his lips, as if mulling over new information or holding back a smirk. "Yes. It seems your notoriety, for good or ill, has worked its way up the chain of command. You've caught the eye of Terran Intelligence in particular, and their Briddarri compatriots."

"TI drag you all the way out here, Tim?" Tag asked.

"My flotilla's been on escort duty and deployed in some raids along the fringes of the Rift—though with the Naplian invasion, there's hardly a need to be distinct about where the Rift begins and the Terran boundaries end." Tim scowled. "Like you, Tag, I've been pressed into their service."

"Pressed?" Tag cocked an eyebrow. "Hang on. Is this a transfer?"

"Of a sort, though it is completely voluntary." Ram steepled his fingers, forming a pyramid above his desk. "Your brother-in-law has brought us a potential avenue of hurting the Naplians and putting paid to their goals in this region. We simply want to know if you're interested in serving outside your normal role, for a short duration."

Tag searched everyone's faces, even Tim's, but no one gave anything away. Something about the situation didn't feel right. There was also the matter of the guy standing off to the side of Ram's desk, bald as a billiard cue, and utterly unruffled. Why was no one talking to him? Why wasn't he saying anything?

Ram must have picked up on Tag's deliberation because he flicked his gaze to the right. "Perhaps Mr. Ashteo can better address the matter."

"Thank you, Commodore." The voice was smooth, with a slight Terran accent that indicated the man hailed from the core planets. He pronounced every vowel and consonant without error.

"Captain Wester, Terran Intelligence would like to enlist you for this mission, during which you would temporarily rescind your CDF commission and command of your squadron. You would be, for all intents and purposes, resigned, though I am assured the process can be painlessly reversed."

It sounded like a joke, but Tag wasn't paying close attention. Those unnerving brown eyes, lacking visible imperfection, bothered him. So, he counted. Ten seconds went by, and the man blinked again. Ten seconds more, and the same.

Added together with all the clues, it came to one answer only. Tag opted to test it. He yanked his comm unit from his belt and flung at Commodore Ram.

The bald man snatched it in midair before anyone could flinch. And he did it without taking his gaze off Tag.

"Well, isn't this fun." Tag sneered. "You're trying to pack me off my squadron in the care of an android spy."

CHAPTER TWO

Commander Vollan stood between Tag and the android. "Remember your place, Mister. This is the commodore's office, not an ale tavern on Rittorno Seven."

"I'd sure rather be there now than drink any of his swill." He pointed a finger at the android. "You can tell TI I'm not palling around with wires-for-brains. I'll stick to blasting One-eye starfighters."

"He has a name, Tag," Tim said. "This is Dyson Ashteo."

"No. Wrong answer." Tag glared at the 'bot. "What's your designation?"

"Commander Ess is correct in stating—"

"I said, give me your designation, 'bot."

The bland voice cut off. Ashteo set Tag's comm down on the desk, with a soft *clink*. "I am an FR66 model."

"Not a fifty-seven?"

"The same basic structures, both physically and mentally, are present, though my series is much more adaptable to espionage uses than any other."

Tag's fists unclenched—and that was when he realized he'd even had them clenched.

"Tag, I understand your anger, but Dyson isn't one of them." Tim placed a hand on his shoulder. "If he were, do you think I'd be out here with him?"

"No, I guess not."

"Then you'd better explain, Mister, before you get written up again," Vollan snapped.

"Commander …" Ram held up a hand as if to forestall any further argument. "Captain Wester's family has prior history with some of the more advanced androids. Specifically, those involved in the Call Moon incident."

Vollan glanced at him. "But that's been a century."

"Not Call Moon." Tag tamped down the anger boiling up in him. He had to let off steam, but not in front of his superiors. "TSS *Hermes*. The mutiny."

"I see." Ram became solemn. "I would suggest, Captain Wester, that you put history into perspective. Those were difficult times for both man and machine. Things have smoothed considerably since, and Mr. Ashteo has every bit the right to serve Terra as you do."

"Yes, sir." Outwardly, he kept his expression placid. Inwardly, he saw what he knew was true from that history—the deaths of five of his family line, five Westers whose demise left a gaping hole in the family tree.

"Very good. Mr. Ashteo?"

"Thank you, Commodore." Ashteo stepped past Tag to the desk. He smelled, oddly enough, of mild sweat and some kind of deodorant. Did he really stink? Like a flesh and blood human? Novafire, was that even real flesh Tag saw? "I have taken the liberty of uploading relevant data for this assignment."

Ashteo touched the control panel for the holographic display. The stars swirled faster and zoomed out to an arrangement Tag found more familiar.

"The Union of Planets," Ashteo said. "One of the many offshoot human empires which have sprung up throughout the galaxy in the last seven centuries of interstellar expansion. Following the culmination of the First Consular War, the treaty gave the Northern Alliance administrative control over the Union in exchange for handing over the seized Lost Worlds to Terran occupation. Sources indicate the NA was thoroughly disappointed with this trade."

"Small wonder," Tim said. "The Union was never a prosperous nation. It sure isn't now."

"As I was saying, disappointment was the prevalent emotion," Ashteo said. "So much so that by the time of the Second Consular War, the NA abandoned it completely. No one was left in control. Pirates and criminals seized key systems, enslaving citizens, but a collection of intellectuals, together with several business guilds, managed to evict them. The bloodshed was horrific. Millions died."

What would you care about bloodshed? Tag kept the thought locked away. "Where's the Union at now? Doesn't sound like a place I'd want to tour on vacation."

"Stable, but only just." Ashteo swept a hand through the hologram. Lights flashed red along the edges of the Great Desert Rift, near the Union border. "The main Naplian force has left them be, concentrating on the drive into Baedecker and the fifty-light-year deep thrust into Terran space. Only through the efforts of Commodore Ram and Admiral Tatsura has our stronghold at Van Sutton Naval Base and in the surrounding sectors remained secure. What this means, however, is the Union has resisted all diplomatic efforts to join in the war."

"And you want them in."

"The more guns we can bring to the fight, the better chance we have of winning," Tim said. "It's why the Briddarri sought us out for their Grand Alliance."

"Yeah, well, we haven't joined that party yet."

"It's a matter of time and diplomacy. Don't forget, without them, Baedecker would have been a rout."

"It was. We lost my homeworld, remember? Me and my sister and my father, along with millions of other people, are refugees."

"That isn't what I meant, Tag."

"I get it, Tim. I really do. It's numbers." Tag gestured aft vaguely. "But the Briddarri? I'm not kidding myself. They talk a good game, but they don't share much tech with their so-called allies."

"Don't kid yourself, Wester," Vollan said. "Without Briddarri warships, the Naplians would have overrun most of our systems by now."

Tag folded his arms but didn't argue the point any further.

Ashteo waited throughout the exchange, not speaking until it was clear the matter was settled—or settled enough for him. Tag considered it still open for debate. "The Leadership Board, as their governing officers are called, has built up a strong fleet in the past fifty years. While not enough to compete for territory on a galactic scale, their force has made short work of pirates within Union boundaries. It is our hope this fleet can be used to cut through the tenuous supply lines the Naplians have stretched across the Rift."

"It sounds logical," Ram said. "However, in my experience logical doesn't equate with simple in all circumstances. There must be some complication; hence, your arrival here, seeking Captain Wester's help."

"The complication is thus: The Leadership Board is firmly committed to neutrality. The scars of their past conflicts run deep; everyone mourns lost ancestors." Ashteo glanced at Tag.

At least the Leadership didn't have to stand face-to-face with one of the kind that tried to chop some blasted big branches off their family tree.

"There is a competing faction of businesspeople who have quietly amassed their own ships and mercenaries. This opposition, the Riven Cabal, presents itself in public as a minority political party, while their shadowy arm foments dissent on all Union worlds it can reach. They are enough to keep the Leadership occupied and provide them with an excuse to expend resources which could otherwise be put to better use preparing the Union for war."

"Terran Intelligence has identified a most vital goal: to infiltrate the Leadership and gain access to data we know to be in existence, data which will force the Union to enter the war on our side."

Tag snorted.

"Something to add, Captain Wester?" Ram asked.

"No amount of scandal's bad enough to force a whole government to declare war, especially not against a juggernaut like the Naplians," Tag said. "It'd have to be one novafired mess. What about the Union people? Are they pro- or anti-war?"

"From what we can ascertain, the populace, in general, are fearful of the Naplian advances but unwilling to fight," Ashteo said. "Yet."

Tag paced around the holographic map. "And these Cabal guys, the Riven. They've got to figure into your plans somehow, right?"

"The Cabal, while prone to using unsavory methods to achieve their ends, do have the underworld connections which will prove ... advantageous to recovering the data."

"Okay. So ..." Tag ticked off items on his fingers, compiling a list as much for himself as for those gathered in Ram's office. "You know there's this secret data. You know you can find people bad enough to help you grab it. Do you know where it is?"

Ashteo held his blink for far longer than ten seconds. "The

information about its location is unclear."

"I'm going to translate that as a big 'No,' then." Tag shook his head. "Tim, you could have saved a lot of time and fuel not dragging this 'bot out here."

"He isn't a 'bot, Tag," Tim said. "He's an operative with Terran Intelligence."

"Makes him a double oxymoron."

"It makes him a man who, when his bosses snap their fingers, we jump." Tim's neck and cheeks reddened. He scowled. "Blast it all. We've come for your help."

"Yeah, everybody keeps saying that, but nobody's got the reactor strong enough to spit out what exactly I'm supposed to do! You want me to stuff the 'bot into the rear seat of a Raider and fly it all the way to Union space?"

"No, Captain," Ashteo said. "We want you to steal the data."

Tag blinked, any and all snide commentary deleted from his mind.

"Let me be more precise. You and I, with the assistance of an agent provided by the Briddarri, will infiltrate Union space. Disguising myself should be simple. My features can be altered to withstand facial recognition, and my body is constructed in such a manner to baffle scans."

"The Briddarri know the trick, too," Tim said. "They can pass off one of their own as human. Word was they had one running around Baedecker Four, up to and through the takeover."

"Your notoriety, while it has spread among Terran military members, is known to the Union of Planets—specifically, through business dealings with your father, Antiny Wester."

"So what kind of disguise do I get?" Tag asked.

"None. You shall be Taggart Wester, recently resigned CDF pilot, who now represents Cavill Aerospace Limited. You are interested in establishing contracts for new starfighter production for the Terran war effort, inside Union space."

Cavill Aero? The name was familiar, but Tag was baffled as to where he'd heard it. "Okay. So, I'm me, and you're—what, my assistant?"

"Yes."

Tag smirked. "Must be rough, having to subordinate that big AI brain of yours to a lowly human."

Ashteo didn't smile. "Needs must, Captain."

Ram cleared his throat. "Captain Wester, as was previously indicated, we will establish your resignation and discharge the veneer of legitimacy. If you do this, you'll be cut off from CDF. Officially."

"And unofficially, Commodore? Where do I stand if the sky fills with bogeys?"

"I won't leave one of my officers without support. You have my word, by all I hold sacred."

Pretty good stuff, coming from Ram. Tag nodded. Something else bothered him, though. Something about Tim's presence in all this. "Did Father put you up to this?"

Ess's mustache twitched. "He knew Terran Intelligence wanted you, and while they were busy arguing about the best way to approach, he suggested I be the one to make contact by bringing Dyson out this far."

Tag shook his head but couldn't find fault with Father's actions. "He's shrewd, the old man, but I don't love him any less for it. He knew I'd do anything to help us win the war." Tag looked at Ashteo. "I suppose you'll tell me Father knew about the 'bot, too."

"He did."

Leave it to Father to set aside an old family vendetta where the needs of all Terrans were concerned. Funny Tag couldn't do it as readily. He still suppressed the urge to zap the 'bot with an electromagnetic pulse and break him down part by part. "If I agree to this, I want my command back. Not just any Warhawk. Bronze Squadron."

"Done," Ram said.

"And if you and I are working together, I'm calling the shots," Tag said to Ashteo.

"Unacceptable." Ashteo wiped the hologram blank. "I am the authorized operative. You will serve under my command."

"In your dreams," Tag said. "Though I hear you don't. Dream, that is. So, in your data review, then."

Ashteo's face was just as placid as a frozen lake, impermeable. Tag took it as a personal challenge to irk him—if an android could be irked.

"Gentlemen, I suggest you consider partnership, if the mission has any hope of succeeding," Ram said. "Otherwise I doubt TI will be happy with either of you."

"Of course. A partnership can be effective." Ashteo stuck out his hand, smooth and poised as any human offering a shake.

Tag took the proffered hand. He squeezed hard against the measured grip and was surprised when it did not crush his digits in a vise.

"Good." Ram must have been more tense about the arrangement than he let on, because he sagged into his chair like a landing skid's hydraulics with a leak. "Very pleased this is all settled. Commander, let's attend to the bridge while our guests sort out the details. I understand we have quite the bounty from Captain Wester's capture."

Vollan gave Tag what he took to be a rather critical look, because he'd seen it at least a dozen times in the past few years, right before getting written up. Tag just winked and grinned. He remembered to add on a salute. "Ma'am."

She left at Ram's side, without further word.

Tim chuckled. "Got to say, you haven't lost the Wester edge, even with combat and command experience under your belt."

Tag shrugged. "Old habits and all that. But before we dig into this any deeper, I have to know something I didn't want the brass around to hear me ask."

"By all means."

"Why me? Of all people, Wester connections aside, why the fighter jock?"

It was Ashteo who answered. "Because, Captain, of precisely the nerve you showed in both your recent seizure of the Naplian ship—and your unwillingness to let things such as regulations bind your course of action."

"So … because I'm rash?"

"And a touch cocky," Tim said.

"Thanks."

Ashteo nodded. "Both words suffice."

***

Tag had only a couple hours to tender his resignation, however impermanent it may wind up, and gather his belongings. He didn't have much—some souvenirs from the more exotic worlds he'd visited, holo cubes of messages from friends now far dispersed throughout the Terran fleets. Three sets of civilian clothes, for whenever he had a chance at shore leave. Not that he'd had much call to use those.

In the end, it amounted to a single duffel bag's worth, which he carried over his shoulder. Princess met him at the airlock. "Any special instructions, Captain?"

"Keep our boys and girls alive, Naomi," Tag said. "You're squadron commander in my absence. I've already spoken to Colonel Chok about getting you a reserve pilot to fill out the twelfth plane."

"I see. Will our rookie take the controls of your Warhawk?"

Tag laughed. "Over my atomized body. But you already knew that much."

She smiled. "Good luck to you, Tag. I'll put you first in my prayers tonight."

"Aw, no need for a special fuss." Tag's cheeks heated. He had nothing of the sort to offer back to her. Princess likely spent more time visiting the shipboard chaplain than any officer. "But thanks all the same."

He crossed the airlock to Tim's lead gunboat, TSS *Greyfox*. The connecting tube was only twenty meters long and devoid of gravity, so Tag pushed off from the frame of *Confiance*'s outer airlock hatch and soared along. For a few seconds he was his own starfighter, weightless, experiencing a feeling of complete joy bolstered by the tube's transparency. Stars shone all around, and Tag twisted along his vector, setting himself into a spin. From here he could not only see the scarred hull of the gunboat but also the seemingly unending expanse of the heavy cruiser, looming over him like the greatest skyscrapers of Vossberg City back on Baedecker Four.

His homesickness was tempered by the knowledge for a short leg of his journey, he'd be traveling with Tim aboard. Though not as his cabin mate.

"Our space is limited, as you can imagine." Tim returned the salute of a skinny ensign who tucked himself into the alcove of a closed hatch. There was room enough for Tim and Tag to pass by single file, but little else. Tag was certain he'd get his bag permanently wedged between the bulkheads if he moved wrong.

The corridors were all the same: pale gray bulkheads, black metal deck grating with openings large enough for Tag to glimpse the reds and blues and yellows of conduits streaming underfoot. They were headed forward of the Combat Information Center, and from what Tag knew of these gunboats he was salivating at the chance to peek into the cramped CIC. Like a fighter's cockpit, magnified three or four times, with room for a handful of people.

Instead, Tim stopped outside an open hatch, its access panel glowing green with the words "Auxiliary Cabin 3." He gestured as if he were a valet 'bot. "Your accommodations, Captain."

"Mighty fine digs, Captain." Tag made sure to return the honorific. Tim was a commander and led the flotilla, but he was captain of *Greyfox*. Theoretically, he also counted as a Commodore, since he was in charge of four ships, but the designation didn't apply to gunboats. More like a squadron leader in that respect.

"You'd better give it a thorough investigation before you rate us five stars."

He was right. Tag cataloged it quickly: four bunks, two atop each other on the left and right sides of the cabin, with a semi-transparent partition on the far wall. Must be the head, Tag surmised. Next to it, a small workspace was folded down and had a chair set at it. Storage lockers were arranged in trios, underneath each of the four bunks. The lights were dim and pale blue. The colors, even the sheets and pillows, matched everything he'd seen thus far aboard *Greyfox*.

Only thing he didn't find agreeable about the cabin was the android sitting at the desk.

***

Ashteo turned and rose from the chair, with as fluid a motion as a man doing calisthenics. "Captain. Welcome."

"Ashteo."

"I would suggest, for the duration of this mission, we abstain from formal titles, as you are resigned from CDF."

"Fine by me." Tag tossed his bag onto the bunk. "You go by Dyson?"

"I do. And your preference is ..."

For you to shut your circuit-filled trap, Tag thought, but it was hardly a notion that'd help them pull this off. He thought about making the 'bot call him Taggart, but just as quickly decided against it. No sense in having someone sounding like Father along for this excursion, or it would get real old, real fast. "Tag."

"Understood, Tag."

Tag heard a noise that could have been a chuckle, but when he checked the open hatch, Tim stood there as stiffly as always. There was a remnant of a smile beneath his mustache. "I'll leave you to it. We jump in one hour."

"Which system?"

Tim opened his mouth, but Dyson spoke before he did. "The coordinates of the staging area are classified information, as I am sure you both understand. It is necessary to operational security they remain such."

Tag frowned. "No problem. I'll just make up a location in my head and pretend that's where we're going. Thanks anyway, Tim."

"I'll leave you two to get settled in," Tim said. "If you need anything, use the comm panel to get ahold of the ship's steward. Link's programmed in."

Tag soon regretted his absence. Dyson went back to work on— well, whatever it was he had going on his scroll. The device was rolled out flat across the desk. Two holograms wavered from the emitter, one showing a raft of information which must have been encoded, because Tag couldn't make any more sense out of the jumbled letters and numbers than a refueling drone could make of a Warhawk's nav console. The other hologram projected a pretty blue and white planet, obviously Terran type, but with far more ocean coverage than Tag had seen. It reminded him of Govanvi, a world not 100 light-years from his present location. Bronze Squadron had scouted out a Naplian forward communications array, hidden among the tall, spiky coral islands of endless seas, and blasted it to grit. Govanvi was also the last time he'd had shore leave—eight months ago, a three-day rest after an arduous stretch of the campaign.

He could almost smell the salt water and feel the hot sand. "That our destination, or is it classified, too?"

"This is Kayna Two, capital world of the Union of Planets, and yes, it is our destination."

Dyson did not look up from his data streams. "Population 500 million, grouped mostly in the cities on the continent."

"The continent?" Though now Tag saw Kayna did indeed have only one huge landmass, taking up about a sixth of the world's surface area. Hundreds of island chains followed it as the holographic planet spun, like pups trailing their mother. "Right. Got it. Anything else I need to know about it?"

"All the relevant information is in a data packet which you will find on your scroll."

Tag untucked the unit from his pocket. A quick squeeze of the thick cylinder loosened the display fabric into a flopping sheet. Tag snapped it, and the sheet solidified. Yeah, there was a message waiting for him, along with a sizeable attachment. He parsed the relevant data, but no big surprise, it was boring demographic and geological stuff. "Wow. Okay, this is amazingly dull. Have you ever been there?"

Dyson turned and placed his hands on his knees. "Kayna Two?"

"Yeah."

"Once, years ago, to surveil. Again, four months ago, in preparation for this assignment."

"And?"

"And ... what?"

"What's it like?"

"All the relevant information—"

"Is in this dull packet, blah blah." Tag dropped into his bunk and propped his feet up on his bag. Man. Like sleeping on a Raider's wing. "I mean, what did it feel like? How were the people?"

"The people were ... people. I have all their customs programmed

into a secondary adaptation module. As for what did it feel like ...'"
Dyson shrugged, and though he looked eerily human when he did it,
Tag thought he could discern a pause midway through. Or maybe his
focus on Dyson being an android got in the way. "I have no reference
point."

Tag shook his head. "How in space you expect to fit in with
humans when you can't small talk about a place is beyond me."

"I have excellent experience faking such interactions."

"I'll believe that when I see it." Tag put his head back against the
pillow—which he thought was thinner than his scroll—and kept on
reading his packet. With any luck, he'd sleep through the jump.

***

Greyfox and the rest of the flotilla wound up in a star system Tag
thought to be the perfect waypoint, in that it was already teeming
with ships.

It was a white dwarf eighty light-years from the Union border,
and another 240 from Terran space, inside a stretch of the Great
Desert Rift called the Atharzon Dunes. For someone like Tag, who'd
earned his wings flying training missions over actual sand dunes
back on Baedecker Four, the description seemed ridiculous, but he
understood the rationale. Space for dozens of light-years around the
star system was swathed in the ruddy orange of a thick, dark nebula.

"Sheridan Post is neutral ground for all manner of traders and
pirates," Tim said. "It's astride the widest corridor of clear space
through the Dunes. Makes it a whole lot simpler on the nav systems
and shortens jump times by a good forty-eight hours in most
directions."

"I can see why it's popular." From his vantage point standing
behind Tim's command chair in *Greyfox*'s CIC, Tag's view of the
holographic tactical display made it clear. He counted at least sixty
ships, maybe more, with a handful jumping in or out every few
minutes. Five orbital stations of varying design—some incorporating
familiar human elements, others as alien to him as the Naplians were
—formed the nexus of the activity.

"Helm, take us to the following coordinates, one-quarter
ripwave." Tim swiped a long series of numbers from a blue list of data
hovering over the arm of his chair. He dropped it into a green column,

where it promptly dissolved. "Keep it casual. Tactical, remind all turrets and tubes we aren't hunting on this run, so have the guns manned accordingly."

"Aye, Captain." The two men sat up front and another two at the opposite end of the CIC, within five meters of each other. That was it: five officers, plus the navigational computer and targeting sensors, ran the ship from here. Tim's chair sported a desk-sized console which doubled as the main communications system. Behind Tag was the hatch which led back to the rest of the ship, down its spine; ahead was another hatch opening into the firing controls for the pulse cannon.

"Any idea who our buddies are?" Tag asked.

"Besides Briddarri? No. They're due in about ten minutes."

Tag spotted a pair of Rutak warcruisers at the fringes of the largest space station. "They get all types out here."

"That's for certain."

"How come I never heard of it? Sheridan Post—it's a human name."

"Sort of. It was started by the Rutak, who named it Shurr' Eidaan. The common name came from the human trade companies that moved in, figuring they couldn't be bothered using the Rutak designation."

Tag smirked. "Or maybe they were just sticking their thumbs in the Rutak's eyes."

Tim shrugged. "Could be. Not the best idea, if you ask me. The Rutak can be just as rough as the Naplians. Fortunately, they aren't any friendlier with the One-eyes than we are."

Greyfox zipped around the edges of the gathered ships, her companions maintaining a loose diamond formation. Their ripwave generators helped them cover millions of klicks in a couple minutes, and when they cut them, they were clustered near the surface of a lumpy planetoid ninety klicks long. Tag saw they weren't the only ships so secreted throughout the system; *Greyfox* must have a superb set of sensors, to pick up the fluctuations of ripwave generators and the flare of sublight drives peeking from behind scattered astral bodies.

Within seconds of taking up orbit, a flash of light heralded the arrival of their contact. Tag whistled.

The Briddarri battleship hung in space with all the subtlety of a pulse cannon ready to fire. The blip on the nav display dutifully listed her specs, but it was the visual feed projected on a pair of display screens which gave true sense to the battleship's size. It was far larger than even TSS *Confiance* and its class of Terran heavy cruisers; next to *Greyfox* and her kin it was a monster. Tag shook his head.

"What?" Tim asked.

"Just reminding myself for the umpteenth time in three years I'm glad the Briddarri are fighting against the Naplians, not on the same side."

Tim nodded, eyes wide at the same sight. "She's the *Night's Claw*. Transport for the third member of your party."

"I am glad they arrived on schedule."

Tag had to steel himself not to jump at the unexpected voice. Dyson must have entered through the hatch behind them, though when he'd made his approach, Tag couldn't say. The android might make a half-decent pilot if he could pull the same stunt on an unsuspecting Naplian fighter. "The Briddarri sent somebody to us on a battleship? Sounds like a high-ranking player."

Dyson's eyebrow rose. "The person in question is exactly the opposite. If you would please join me at the primary airlock, Tag."

They walked the short distance, Tag following after him, squeezing past military personnel en route. Halfway down the spine, they picked up a pair of young, tall men, in Navy blues augmented by black body armor and helmets with opaque visors. Each carried a Wolf Arsenal PAK SG-12F submachine gun. Tag recognized the compact weapons as the threat they were—and the threat they anticipated because no one wanted to be on the receiving end of the 100 flechettes in the magazine.

The guards didn't seem to surprise Dyson, who motioned them to either side of the airlock once they arrived. A green light flashed above the lock, and the hatch slid open.

Four Briddarri crowded in. Three were officers of their navy, clad in the slate gray Tag had come to expect. They were short, thick as fuel tanks, though the one who was obviously in command stood a few centimeters taller. Which meant he came up to Tag's nose. He had thick black hair, a large but well-groomed beard, and locked onto Dyson and Tag with eyes the color of sand.

The fourth person was nothing like them. For starters, she was a woman—a Briddarri female. Tag had never seen one before; apparently, their leadership didn't let the ladies serve, at least on the advance forces which had shown up deep in Terran space. But she didn't look like military type anyway. Not with the smirk permanently laser-etched onto thick emerald lips, the color of which made her skin all the paler. The guys had a hue two shades darker.

Scrape, Tag's lost wingman, would have used a word like celadon, or mint.

Everything about her stance, from the way her arms swayed as she walked with hands secured in magnetic binders, to the sashay of long, slender legs Tag figured belonged more to a dancer, broadcast defiance. Her hair flowed long and loose over her shoulders—half black, and half a brilliant neon blue.

But the eyes froze him—gold. Tiny silver flecks around the pupils. She stood close enough for perfume to waft over him.

"Captain Taggart Wester, may I introduce Lira Lin Reen," Dyson said. "She will assist us in our mission."

"Yeah?" Tag hooked his thumbs in his jumpsuit pockets. "What're her credentials? We've already got the ace pilot and the intelligence operative."

"Master thief." Her voice was cultured, a singer's. Each word rang clear.

Tag must have appeared confused to all gathered, because the lead guy with the beard grumbled, "She's Blue Kitt."

"Blue Kitt. *The* Blue Kitt? The one who stole the Anchor Diadem? The one who gave up the Riash Amal Hoard because a hovertram caught fire outside the museum, and rescued those people instead?"

She shrugged. "It was there for the taking eight months later, anyway." Tag grinned. Maybe this mission wouldn't be so bad after all.

CHAPTER THREE

November 2679

T he white light above the door flashed red, accompanied by a harsh buzzer.

Lira sighed. Time for another round of interrogation. She set down the flims-book, atop her stack of six others. No electronics for her. Not even a simple scroll. She got physical reading materials; she assumed because her captors didn't want her fashioning a device she could use for escape.

A surprisingly smart precaution.

"Prisoner, stand ready," the guard's voice growled from the other side of the door. Sounded like Harro. He was all right, as far as the guards went. Lots of bluster, little bite.

Lira rubbed absentmindedly at a lump on her arm.

She stood in the center of her cell, with her hands behind her head. Lira could have touched both sides if she wanted, though the cell was twice as long as its width. The single shelf bed was tucked into an alcove of the wall, and the toilet at the back, in plain view of the window gap. Otherwise, the cell walls and floor were bare taupe guardstone.

Metal scraped. Brown eyes peered in through the window gap, its armor sheath slid aside.

Yes, Harro. Lira smiled and winked.

The door locks banged as they disengaged, and it slid aside. Such a horrendous squealing, every time. Of course, it only opened once every few weeks. They didn't let Lira out much.

Harro came in first, checking her all over for … what? Lira knew they couldn't expect her to have brought in weapons or gear. It was demeaning, meant to break her spirits, but she laughed in her head. It was a game. They wanted her to break; she refused to even bend.

Since she had the information they wanted, it made her the winner.

"What's on our agenda today, Harro?" Lira asked. "Is Inspector Ferrd going to ask the same questions, like he does every week? Or do I get an early Barraddrid Day present in the form of more creative inquiry?"

"Shut your mouth, *vurr*." Ah, yes. The Briddarri insult meaning "shamed." Wouldn't be a good day unless she heard it. After two months, it became like an insect's buzz in the background. Obnoxious, but tolerable.

The man who entered next was not Inspector Ferrd. He was one hundred percent military—a commander, judging by the braids on his tan navy uniform. He had brown hair with three lines shaved into the sides, above his ears. "Lira Lin Reen. The Blue Kitt. Guard, leave us."

Harro sent outside? Lira kept her smile steady, but this was new. Inspector Ferrd wasn't nearly as confident. But this man radiated something. Tension. Order.

Harro was out in a ripwave and sealed the hatch behind him. That blasted squeal again … "Are you an admirer, Commander?"

"You've refused to tell anyone about Blue Kitt."

"I am Blue Kitt." She sat down on the bunk. He didn't protest or demand she stand up.

Interesting. "Were you expecting a formal resume?"

"Don't play me for the fool. Unlike that idiot Ferrd, I'm not interested in criminal prosecution. I know Blue Kitt has existed for a century, making you only the latest to use the name. I also know that means you have help."

"Sorry, Commander, I work alone."

"Really." He broke his ramrod posture to lean against the wall, a smirk creasing his craggy features. "Is that why the Seerrstone has vanished?"

"Must have been misplaced." More than likely, her compatriots had whisked it off-world and sold it. She'd get her cut. Whenever she got out of here. Wherever here was, because she knew she'd made three jumps to get to this prison. That put it near the fringes of Briddarri space, or even into Audrian. "Let's be simple. Who are you, and what do you want?"

"Commander Ortan Olt Burrak."

"BLD?"

"Law and Discipline?" Burrak snorted. "No. Not at all. You insult me. My position is Forecasting, with the Espionage Directorate."

Oh. Not just naval information, then, about depots and starships and weapons. The Direct only focused on the big picture. Grand strategy. Curious they'd pick her.

"As I said, I'm not interested in your past work. I'm interested in your skills. You have broken into and out of some of the most secure places in the kingdom. Desecrated the sacred memories of our most vaunted warriors in the process."

"Oh, are your kind still sore about the Chieftain's Belt?" Lira smiled. "I did use twine to keep the antique breeches from falling down so the poor statue wouldn't be … debriefed."

This was the part where Burrak would try to strike her, and Lira would put her fingers through his eyes.

But he just stood there, impassive. Infuriating. So unlike the guards. She would have to watch her words. "All right, Commander, what in particular about my work interests you?"

"All of it. I have need of someone of your ill repute to conduct a mission for the glory of the kingdom, a mission far from here."

"Glory of the kingdom? Please." Lira wrinkled her nose. "That's hardly incentive to someone locked up in this pit."

"I understand more tangible rewards would better suit you. That is why the Admiralty has authorized me to seek your pardon and release."

That got her attention. Once free from here, she'd disappear again. "I see. What do you need stolen?"

"Information."

"Ah, my favorite." Not as lovely as art or jewels, and not as easy to find use for as money, but information was so easily transported. Such a great deal of wealth in such a tiny, invisible space. "What kind of information?"

"The kind that tips the scales of war in our favor. While you've been locked aboard, the Naplians slipped through the Great Desert Rift and attacked the Terrans."

A slip. He said "aboard," not inside. So, her prison cell was on a prison vessel, or asteroid.

One with a destination, perhaps? "Terrans. A human nation? What could they have to offer?"

"Serjaum. It doesn't matter now. What matters is our fleets have brought the Terrans alongside the Grand Alliance, and they have proven brave warriors."

"What does this have to do with a proposed job?"

"If you agree, we'll have you out of here and fully informed within the day." If she agreed?

"I take it there is a penalty if I don't comply."

"No penalty—none beyond what you've earned. You rot here."

"As delightful as it sounds, I'm more inclined to take you up on your offer."

"I would imagine so. But let me make something clear." Burrak rapped his knuckles on the door. It rumbled and squealed open. Harro stood outside. "If you walk out, and agreed to serve the kingdom, we will honor our end of the bargain upon success."

"Not that it's likely—because it's never yet happened—but what if I fail?" Lira stood and walked over to the commander. She saw Harro twitch, as if he was preparing to zap her with the stun-rod, so she stopped short of the commander. "I like to know all options on the table."

"If you fail, you will be killed," Burrak said.

Well, then. "Glad we understand each other." She walked out the door.

***

April 2681

Lira had almost backed out when they told her she'd actually have to work with the humans.

Humans? Really? The species were a galactic infestation. Oh, they didn't personally bother her, but please … such a fractious and unruly bunch of humanoids.

Hmm. Funny how their term for any race resembling their own bled over into the languages of the galaxy, after centuries of their influence. It didn't matter one asteroid fragment what Burrak said they'd done against the Naplians. Lots of tiny allies had gotten sucked into the war. Few of them remained—and if they did, they were Briddarri protectorates.

She wore one of her own jumpsuits, form-fitting bright blue with black sleeves, shoulders, and chest. It was one of three they'd saved. She'd picked it because it left little room to breathe—always an advantage when dealing with Briddarri warrior men.

But these humans—not what she expected. The bald one was quiet, appearing lost in thought, though his eyes caught every action in the room. Even when she resumed pulling at the wirelink of her binders, his gaze seemed to see her. He made no move to interfere, however.

And the other one. Now, he was a warrior. A pilot. Even if she hadn't seen the wings pinned to his jumpsuit, she recognized it in the way he moved—a curious fluidity, as if he were still behind the controls of a starfighter. There was also the attitude—grinning, expression as sly as a Yander hound, supremely at ease with everything around him. Also very much appreciative of her jumpsuit, but not distracted like her guards.

Even as she assessed him, the grin faded. "Hang on. Blue Kitt? No way."

"That is what the data says." Lira had the wirelink. If she could sever it, she'd drop the binder. A nice trick, a reminder of who was in charge here.

"Look, my father told me tales of the Blue Kitt from when he was in school, and there isn't a chance you're old enough to have been him. He always said 'him,' and those stories had to be from thirty years ago. So, unless Briddarri ladies age differently than the guys ..."

She laughed. "Well done, human. Most of your kind don't catch on so quickly."

"Keep quiet," Burrak said. "Captain Wester, I apologize for her lack of tact. I am Commander Ortan Olt Burrak. It is an honor to meet you."

He bowed, the ridiculous deep bow of a warrior showing deference to another. For this human? Wester. She had nothing on the name, until she put "father" along with it. Taggart Wester, and Antiny. Baedecker Four and the Briddarri intervention that helped rescue a planet's population. The Naplians still gained a foothold, but the Grand Alliance gained an informal partner.

Wester accepted the bow with a nod, and a bit of uncertainty. "I'm doing what needs to be done, Commander. The Naplians took my home, so I'm here to kick them back to theirs."

"Very good. Don't let the likes of the prisoner dissuade us from the mission at hand."

"I'll keep an eye on her."

Not a close enough one. Lira broke the wirelink, and tugged on the binders—

Hands latched onto her wrists. The grip was strong enough to make her gasp. She looked up into cool, brown eyes, unblinking.

"Our third member seems anxious to join our group," he said. "Perhaps your precautions were unnecessary, Commander."

Burrak muttered an apology, but Lira wasn't listening. Just who were these humans?

Wester chuckled. "Probably you can unlock her. She's not going to run off."

The brown-eyed man released her. "Dyson Ashteo, Terran Intelligence. I apologize if I have done you any harm, Miss Reen."

Such manners. "Thank you. No damage done. And you may call me Lira." Dyson gave a polite half bow.

Wester stuck forth a hand. "Tag Wester. Captain, CDF. Ace pilot."

Lira matched the shake. "Tag, charmed. Ace pilot? Modesty is not part of your skill set."

"Hey, no boast. Anybody who's shot down five bogies is considered an ace."

"From what I gather, especially Commander Burrak's reaction, your total is greater."

"By a bit." If he puffed out his chest any further, he'd burst the seams of his jumpsuit. "So, Commander, I take it you're bringing Lira to us."

"Yes. I am rid of her for now." Burrak leaned in. "Remember your place, and your orders."

Orders. Yes, she remembered. She also remembered the deprivation and abuse in her dank cell. "Of course, Commander." Lira patted his cheek. "Do have a pleasant voyage back to the kingdom. I hope you don't run into any One-eyes on the way."

Burrak swept back down the airlock tunnel with his guards. "Nice guy." Tag rolled his eyes. "You okay?"

Why would she be otherwise? As if the human cared what would happen to her one way or another at the completion of their assignment.

Still ... "As I said, no damage."

Tag nodded. "Okay then."

The three of them stood there, with the most awkward silence Lira had ever experienced.

It was worth waiting through, to determine who was in charge of this mission.

Finally, the man called Dyson gestured down the corridor. "If you please, we must make arrangements with Commander Ess for our transport to the Union."

Ah. This one led.

As they walked, though, Lira saw the flash of not just irritation, but outright anger, across Tag's face. It vanished within a second. Trouble between the two men, perhaps. She could file that away if it proved to her advantage.

***

Tag wasn't surprised they had to pick up a civilian transport to get into Union space. They could hardly stroll up to the capital in a Terran gunboat.

But man, this ride.

He stood with his duffel bag slung over his shoulder. The uniform was gone, replaced by a red shirt, gray trousers, brown boots, and his most comfortable, thread-worn jacket—tan with brown elbow patches. The whole outfit was rundown and put him at ease.

The ship in the hangar was rundown, too, and inspired in him the exact opposite feeling.

A Cago Cavebat 171. Wow. Talk about antique. In some journal or another, he'd read it had been discontinued the same year Antiny Wester had entered university training. It was a lumpen, squat transport, akin to a smashed boot wearing wings. Sure, the wings were wide, folding aero-wings designed for decent atmospheric maneuverability, and the sublight engines looked good and strong, but what a piece of junk.

The hangar in which she sat on bowed landing skids wasn't any better. It was hewn straight from the sickly gray rock of the planetoid the gunboats orbited. By the rough cuts and jagged edges, not to mention heaps of shattered rock piled in corners, it had been blasted out rather than laser cut. A shiny film sealed it good and airtight, or so Tag hoped. Other than the airlock through which they'd entered, the hanger contained a large hatch for the Cavebat to exit, a long row of refueling tanks, loading equipment, and cargo containers. Everything was a variation on rusted metal, beaten rock, and battered plastics.

"You look ill," Lira said.

"Huh? No, not ill." Tag straightened his posture. "This thing isn't in its prime."

"Didn't your people build it?"

"My people?"

"Humans."

Tag frowned. "Some human without a lick of sense of how to make a decent aircraft, yeah, but nobody I'd ever buy a glass of rum."

Lira lifted her chin. "I suppose all that matters is how well you handle it."

She walked up the ramp, and Tag had to admit, he enjoyed every step. When he didn't want to dump her out the nearest airlock.

"I trust this vessel is within your handling capabilities," Dyson said.

"Really? Listen, I could fly a bucket out of a gravity well if you strapped a ramjet and ripwave generator to it. But this ..." Tag waved his finger, as if he could conjure a substitute, preferably something more streamlined and less liable to falling apart. "This is embarrassing."

"The external appearance is meant to deceive."

Tag didn't understand what he meant until he followed Dyson up the ship's ramp, down a narrow, rust-streaked corridor past two sleeping alcoves, and into the cockpit. The viewport was reinforced plas-glass, offering a broad view for atmospheric handling.

And the control board, while grimy on the surface, was state of the art. Tag whistled. He dumped his duffel on deck plates, one of which popped in protest. "I haven't seen a sensor package this good since the Raider updates. Are those holos five-scalable? Okay, the engine output scale can't be right."

"Everything is assembled according to my specifications," Dyson said. "The vessel's sublight and ripwave velocities have been upgraded by a factor of thirty percent. Fuel efficiency is doubled. Weapons and—"

"She's armed?"

"There is a railgun stowed in a forward ventral compartment, as well as a six-missile launcher aft." Dyson gestured at a blank portion of the control board, a square with chipped grey paint.

Tag grinned. He flipped over the square. Yeah, definitely military grade targeting and firing systems. "You had TI put all this in?"

"I did. I felt it was necessary for both our safety and the success of the mission. It has been command-coded to you and me; the necessary pilot's access is listed in your scroll."

Tag punched in the code. Power surged through the ship, a thrum that settled down into a steady vibration he felt clear up through his boots. She was ready.

"I suggest you stow your belongings and prepare Miss Reen for departure," Dyson said.

"I suggest you're right," Tag said. "What's her name?"

"Her name?"

"Ship's designation."

"Civilian registry, CR-82834-311." Dyson paused. "*Olivia Vy.*"

Tag nodded. "Good name for a civvie ship. Pretty, too. *Vy*, huh? I think we're going to get along real well."

It took him and Dyson some time to get *Olivia Vy* loaded with cargo. Dyson didn't mention what was in the containers, and Tag didn't ask. He noted a pungent aroma wafting from one, some kind of spice like he'd smelled and tasted at restaurants in the Neo-Cajun quarter of Vossberg City, the capital of Baedecker Four. But since his android overseer didn't see fit to share what they were hauling, other than to say it was needed to trade, he didn't figure it was worth his bother.

Lira did not help with the loading. Big surprise. Tag doubted she'd ever done any real work, besides stealing other people's stuff. Of course, that was why all three of them were going on this mission in the first place. Still, Tag checked his duffel bag and personal belongings twice before shoving what he could fit in tiny storage lockers next to the first bunk.

That's when he realized there were only two.

He rapped on the frame of another alcove. Lira lounged on the mattress, legs stretched out. Stretched *way* out. "Hey, got a question."

"And I may supply an answer, if you're lucky and not boring." She didn't bother looking up from the blue holo text projected from her scroll.

"There's only two bunks on this boat."

"Math is a strong suit of Terrans, as well, is it?"

Novafire. If she didn't watch her mouth … "Look, do you expect me and the 'bot to share? You've obviously staked this one out for yourself."

Lira glanced at him, appearing intrigued. Rather, she had an expression Tag recognized from cats hunting. Eagerness. "He's artificial? I should have seen it sooner. That does explain a great deal about his behavior. My guess, Tag, is he doesn't require anything upon which to rest his weary android head."

Blast. Why hadn't Tag thought of that? He'd been too frustrated by the whipsaw reversals of seeing this dumpy ship, then finding out it was actually modified to fly right, and *then* finding out there were only two bunks for three people. Maybe he'd imagined some other sleeping arrangement, forgetting Dyson wasn't a real person. He shook his head. "Good point. Well, you'd better get up to the cockpit and strap in—unless you have any special passenger requests."

"None I can think of. Yet." She smiled and rearranged her legs.

***

They did not depart until several hours after both the Briddarri battleship and Tim's four-ship flotilla had left Sheridan Post. Lira did join them in the cockpit, taking a small jump seat with red cushions Dyson affixed to the bulkhead next to the hatch. Dyson himself took up the co-pilot's chair next to Tag.

"Okay, then." The hatch yawned ahead, a huge mouth full of brilliant stars. Tag eased the drive controls. "Here we go."

Olivia Vy shuddered, and for a moment Tag wondered if she'd collapse as he attempted take off. But she was off the landing pad and hurtling through the hatch before he had a chance to finish the worry.

He stifled a whoop. She could move, just like Dyson claimed. It felt like flying a double-sized Raider, though her agility was on par. There were so many thruster banks hidden across her spaceframe Tag could put her through the same spins and rolls as his first fighter-bomber.

Scrape, you'd eat your sensor console if you could fly with me on this thing.

"Perhaps some restraint is advisable," Dyson said. "We do not need to advertise our advantage."

"Relax. We're out in the middle of nowhere, and I doubt we're the only ship among the schools swimming around Sheridan Post that has modifications of an illegal variety." Tag grinned over his shoulder. "How's the ride so far?"

Lira's smile was a shaky imitation of the normal bold. "Good. Nice ship."

"Ah, you guys are no fun." Tag leveled out *Vy*—well, level to the ecliptic plane of the solar system, anyway—and spun up the jump drive. She was only good for a few jumps before she'd have to have the core recharged, which would take a couple of days. "How far to Kayna Two?"

"Ten sectors." A swirling display of stars filled the air in front of Dyson. It was as finely detailed a hologram as Tag had ever seen, and as he watched from the corner of his eye, Dyson reduced magnification from a sector of a city grid out to their intended route from the Great Desert Rift into Union of Planets space. "With the required stops, it should take us approximately nine days."

Tag nodded. A week and change. Not too shabby. If he wanted to sneak back to Baedecker for a glimpse of the old homestead it was a month and a half away. "That work for you, Lady Blue Kitt?"

Lira scowled. She seemed to have regained some of her color—well, a bolder shade of her pale green, anyway. "Nine days aboard with two humans? I have spent worse times in transit. The Briddarri prison ship wasn't exactly a luxury liner."

"Good enough."

"Navigational beacon acquired for the neighboring sector," Dyson said. "The jump drive is fully charged and ready."

Tag reached for the controls. Rankled as he was to have the 'bot flying co-pilot, there was no denying Dyson's efficiency. That is why the Navy placed a premium on them—why their mutinies were so galling. "Prepare for jump."

***

Vy completed the first jump right on schedule, nineteen hours later. Tag jerked awake at the dinging sound of the nav computer's arrival notice. Just like the ovens at the governor's compound on Baedecker Four. He half expected to smell biscuits cooking and hear gravy bubbling.

Instead he squinted through bleary eyes at a starry field. Yep, smack in the middle of nowhere. Nothing but a nav beacon which they'd used to get this far.

"The jump went without incident." Dyson sat there, as alert as when they'd left.

Tag mopped his face. He'd caught a nap back in the bunk, but on the first leg of a mission like this, with his adrenaline running full throttle, sleep was evasive. "Thanks. I got it." He pulled up his own copy of the nav display, a duplicate of Dyson's. As he did, something flickered on the array. Tag frowned. "You see that?"

"I did not detect a variance." Dyson, however, was consulting the fuel readouts and engine power levels.

Tag shunted aside the live scans and pulled up the record of the last few seconds. He played it back.

Nothing.

But he was sure he'd seen something, a reading.

It could be a gravitational anomaly. Telling himself so didn't make it more convincing. He was used to flying on instinct, feeling the approach of trouble before he could see it.

Tag had a feeling there was another ship out there, shadowing them.

CHAPTER FOUR

Elden Silva led the charge into the Naplian outpost, without fear for his safety. Not long ago, in terms of human years, he would have been sick with anxiety, though equally determined.

Now he stomped across the deck plates, his clawed feet leaving jagged depressions, as green flashes from Furta energy rifles caromed off an armored body designed to inflict the greatest terror on his opponents.

There were a dozen Naplian soldiers tucked into the dark hallway. Body armor, mottled blue, shifted colors and rippled in texture as it tried to blend with the surroundings. That adjustment stopped the instant Elden drove a thick, silver blade through the chest of the nearest Naplian. Yellow blood splashed across the deck.

"Ziura!" The soldier who shouted the imprecation backpedaled, his uniform in tatters.

He fired wildly with his rifle, blasts spattering off bulkheads.

Elden knew the Ffawe curse by now. *Devastators.* Is that what he'd become? Consul of the Northern Alliance, heir to a failed rebellion against Terran masters.

A dead man wreaking havoc on the powers that took everything from him.

A swipe with his claws severed the head of a second Naplian, and he slapped aside a third's rifle. The weapon crumpled under the impact, emitting sparks and smoke.

The Naplian soldier's single eye, the iris a bright green, stared wide—wider than usual for a Naplian, and surely their species' equivalent of a human's fearful gaze. Elden saw himself in a tiny reflection, a towering cybernetic form of sharp angles, navy blue paint job so dark it was near black, twin optical ports glowing red like hot coals on a campfire.

The smell of smoked meat filtered through his senses, a leftover from when his olfactory nerves connected his mind to a working nose. Truppen had no need to smell—the host of sensors implanted all through his body could identify any scent, whether benign or hazardous—but ghostly memories plagued him. This one was easy to identify. Saarno fox, the abundant animal he had survived upon when he was temporarily a refugee in the tunnels of Vossberg City on Baedecker Four. His faithful companion Franklin Goetz had caught and cooked them, when lack of rations brought the refugees to near starvation levels.

Him, and Marney Wester.

With a static-filled grunt, Elden skewered the Naplian soldier.

Twenty seconds later, they were all dead. Truppen gave no quarter. Not where the One-eyes were concerned.

Goetz lived on in a cybernetic form similar to Elden's, though it was a metallic gray like the other six on this mission with him and Elden. The headpiece was more rounded, like a trooper's helmet, and it bore no indication of rank. There was no need for exterior adornment that might tip off the enemy to a vital target, not when the Truppen were all interlinked.

"Sir, base is secure." Goetz's voice was still a subdued symphony of words, though with an artificial edge. "Nordall and Bates are making sure all comms are shut down. We should have all the data transferred and supplies rounded up within the half hour."

Goetz rattled off the information with as little inflection as he'd managed when he was flesh and blood. But the rusty coloring of the sides of his headpiece were testament to the man's surviving, if dry, sense of humor. After all, he'd been a redhead. Elden would have allowed himself a smile, if he still had facial muscles. "Good work. The scans did not show any Naplian vessels within a few hours' travel of the outpost, but it's best to be cautious."

Goetz nudged the broken Furta rifle. "You charge headlong into a dozen Ffawe warriors, and you get to tell me about caution?"

Elden shook his head. The red glow from his optical ports acted as a flashlight in the dim hall. Funny he should still think that way, when he relied on a combination of visual input, infrared readings, and bioscans. "Your concern is touching, as always, but these One-eyes hardly posed such a threat. They lacked heavy weaponry."

"Doesn't mean you're invulnerable, or less reckless. Fernandez got himself ripped in half by railguns a month ago. Lachton and Isaacs and Riofsky all lost their heads—and for us, that's the end of the deal, for good."

"Very well, Goetz. Next time I will remain on the lander and you seven can assault the target. I will think fondly of you while I have my joints serviced. Now go make certain the data's not corrupted."

Goetz tromped down the corridor, muttering darkly and shaking his head.

Elden waited until he was gone before running a full diagnostic. It was evident to even the naked human eye he'd taken damage; one couldn't miss the plate-sized carbon scoring across his chest and torso from energy bursts. The diagnostics revealed the damage went deeper—ionization had disabled a backup power source for his lower servos. If he'd taken a bad hit below his waist, he'd have been unable to walk. Fit only to crawl about until his men could drag him to safety.

It was galling, but Elden had only himself to fault. He was never raised a soldier.

Ideologically, yes, he'd fought for the cause of Northern Alliance independence, but politics and pressure had been his bailiwick. Goetz was the kind of man trained in all arts martial since his youth; it was only because of his guidance Elden wasn't dead these past three years of Truppen soldiering.

The emergency lighting changed color to white and brightened. The main corridor was hewn straight from the black and gray rock of the minor planetoid it inhabited. Behind Elden were the shattered remains of the main airlock; four hatches led off either side ahead. Thankfully the corridor had been constructed wide to allow loading robots and easy cargo passage, or else the Truppen would have had great difficulty traversing. The normal height of the ceiling forced Elden to crouch, as it was.

And yet eight crouching, cramped Truppen were plenty to cut through twelve Naplian soldiers as if they were made of silk.

Elden joined Goetz, Nordall, and Bates in the command center, a hexagonal chamber thirty meters across. From there four more corridors branched off. Nordall and Bates were each hunkered near a console, unmoving as statues. Lights flickered across their cybernetic faces, in tandem with lights on each control surface.

"They're getting in. It's encrypted, but nothing they haven't cracked before." Goetz folded his arms, claws clacking against the armor. A railgun bobbed on his shoulder, the weapon painted with white circles on its out-facing side, one for each Naplian base or ship taken. There were a lot. "We'll be ready to transmit in four minutes. Their estimate, not mine."

"I will take them at their word. Where's Rett?"

Goetz snorted; a noise even more filled with derision when laced through with digitalization. "Off poking through the rest of the base. Straying from the objective. Again."

"By himself?"

Goetz shrugged. Apparently, his concern for Truppen taking unnecessary risks did not extend to Rett. "Corridor Bravo."

Elden followed indicators to a corridor marked on the map provided by Briddarri Naval Intelligence. It was only a rough outline, based on crude sensor data, but it was close enough to reality to gain them access to the base. No sign of Naplians down there. Unsurprising, given the outpost's entire complement met them in force at the airlock after the breach.

"Elden! Hey, you've got to see this." Everett Lind crouched awkwardly over an open hatch in the deck. His armor was a slimmer unit, same color as the rest of Elden's octant, though he had green painted in a wide band above his optical ports. Of all the Truppen under Elden's command—and frankly, of all the Truppen he'd ever encountered—Rett was the only Briddarri who'd undergone the transfer process.

He was also the reason Elden was in this form. Since it was a choice between being a dead human or a living cyborg, the latter wasn't so bad.

"Whatever the One-eyes were up to on this rock, they were pulling a lot of data." Rett hooked a claw around a cable and pulled it up. It was twenty centimeters across, and when Rett sliced it open, the wiring inside was so dense Elden had to use his high-definition sensors to distinguish one strand from the other. "A feed like this has to have a major grid attached at the other end."

"Have you backtraced it? Any idea where the installation is?"

"No, but I figure it's on the surface—only it's disguised, because I sure didn't catch anything when we shot a probe around the planetoid prior to the attack."

"It would have to draw a significant amount of power, too. See if you can track the origin of the data, converging with a major power drain. Once we get back to the lander, we'll take a spin around and destroy it."

Elden was halfway down the corridor when Rett caught up with him. "Ah, that isn't what Admiral Ergen had in mind, you know."

"Ergen tasked us with taking this outpost and dumping its sensor data," Elden said. "I am not leaving a shard behind for the Naplians to use against us."

"The admiral's keen on having the base intact. You know, for the Briddarri to use."

"And then what?" Elden rounded on him. His cyborg form was the same height as Rett's, but the Briddarri man had been an undercover operative for the Espionage Directorate. Physical intimidation and command presence were only things he'd received, never dealt. "Leave it staffed by Briddarri soldiers whom the Naplians can wipe out once they learn the base has fallen into enemy hands? Would you have me leave this base a soak for casualties while there are bigger battles to fight? No."

Elden didn't wait for a response, and by the time they both returned to the command center, Rett had found a power systems console. "Got the location of the sensors." Rett's tone was much less collegial than a moment before. "A hundred klicks northeast from this outpost."

"Good. Feed the coordinates to the lander pilots." Elden joined Goetz and transferred the data he'd gathered from Rett into his former bodyguard's information systems.

"New target?" Goetz asked.

"As part of our exit plan, yes. Do we have everything here?"

"We will in a bit."

"Good. Rett, access the primary power systems and bypass the safety protocols. I want this place slagged when we're gone."

"Yes, sir," Rett said.

Goetz glanced at Elden. <Difference of opinion?> The message came through a private link between the two.

<One which I will have to bring up with Admiral Ergen, yet again.>

"Greenbloods," Goetz muttered aloud.

***

Elden's office aboard the troop transport *Hessian* was a simple, unadorned room. There was a central dais from which he had access to multiple data ports, and huge holographic repeaters. While true he didn't need visual input to review reports, Elden was still tied to fleshly habits. He had to see, and not just in his mind's eye.

Other than that, the chamber contained a rest station, an alcove set into the bulkhead designed to recharge and refurbish the Truppen body. When he was done with the after-action analysis from the outpost raid, he'd promised himself an hour of nanite scrubbing along the servos and artificial musculature of his frame.

The hologram spread out before him showed the extent of Truppen raids in a triangular region formed by the Naplian gash through the Great Desert Rift, the southernmost border of Union of Planets space, and the northwestern frontier of Terran space. *Hessian* was the command transport for all the Truppen forces, tens of thousands of cybernetic soldiers fighting the Naplians. Seven more transports and their escorts spread out; smaller craft dispersed the Truppen beyond those, extending their reach. Red diamonds indicated engagements fought. There were more than sixty, and Elden pulled the data down from every single one.

Line after line of text and sensor readings flowed into his awareness. It took all his training in Truppen form to not cry out. Too much. Too fast. He willed himself to focus on what he was looking for, a singular objective. Gradually, the data slowed, trickling into neat lines. He sorted by locations, by scan results, even by date and time.

The correlation was clear.

The hatch to his office opened. Goetz stood on the other side of the hologram, waiting at parade rest, arms held behind him.

Elden saved and filed the analysis, pushing it aside from his awareness. It hovered behind his thoughts, a bird waiting there in the branches. "What is it?"

"Problem, sir, and given your latest hobby thought I'd better tell you straight off: Major Faisal's unit's gone missing."

"Blast."

"Yeah. Two octants, Special Operations team. Went out on assignment to a supposed Naplian resupply depot, escorted by a Briddarri corvette. Never came back."

This was one of the times Elden wished he still had the facial muscles to allow a frown. "I don't understand. Faisal sent me coded communications not a week ago, indicating they'd eliminated the base. Sector GDR71, correct?"

"Yes, sir."

Elden dug for the communique as they spoke. He cross-referenced it with one of the many red diamonds on his map. "It fits the pattern, you realize."

Goetz nodded. "Faisal was due to check in at predetermined coordinates on his return route. He missed all of them."

"That's unlike him. Faisal would rather have his headpiece detached and get hooked up to a nav console as backup than be that sloppy."

Goetz stood silently.

Elden left his circle of displays and triggered a control on the bulkhead behind. A section big enough to admit four Truppen slid open, revealing the bulk of the Briddarri task force in this region of the Rift. Dozens of warships cruised along, some tiny specks against the orange-purple of the swirling Yalten Nebula, others near enough to be identifiable—such as Admiral Ergen's flagship, *Winter Scourge*. The nebula provided ideal visual and sensor cover from which the fleet could launch attacks along the Naplian advance column.

It also meant Elden was tied to it with a short leash. Legions of Truppen under his command, and he still had to hop-skip every time the Briddarri called.

"You still think we can chalk these up to nav errors or jump drive failures?" Goetz asked.

"Of course not. Look at this." Elden shared the updated analysis across their link, coded to the private encryption only they shared.

"Hmph. Faisal makes the third disappearance."

"Yes. The coordinates suggest a trail."

"Okay, then, when do we follow it?"

Elden chuckled. Despite all their physical changes, Goetz remained Goetz. Ready for action, every moment. "It is no longer that simple. There is a chain of command."

"Only if we let the Greenbloods tell us what to do."

"Oh, I know. We're an allied body, neither Terran nor Briddarri. But Ergen has made it very clear about who he expects to answer to whom."

Elden's console beeped. The communications light flashed.

"Speak of the devil," Goetz muttered.

Elden answered the call in the standard display mode he knew the admiral favored, giving Ergen a half-person view of his Truppen frame. "Admiral. What can we do for you?"

Admiral Sett San Ergen was losing the battle with early onset Briddarri baldness, tufts of gray hair surrounding a shiny green pate. It appeared as if the hair had given up and retreated to his upper lip, where the bushy moustache had, against all Elden thought possible, thickened.

Ergen's gut and muscles bulged against a slate gray uniform, bedecked with gold braids and white rank cuffs. It helped immensely that he was taller and bigger than all the rest of his men, outstripping even most humans. "No pleasantries, Consul Selva. What's with your inability to do what I ask? You were supposed to secure us the outpost, not blow it up!"

Goetz remained behind the display, where Ergen couldn't see him, and thus the latter missed the former's red-eyed glare.

"We had this discussion, Admiral. I denied the Naplians a forward base and a sensor post."

"And denied us one, too!"

Elden shrugged. "Such are the fortunes of war."

"If I didn't know better, I'd say you were ignoring my orders."

"Let us be clear—I either agree with or disagree with your operational plans. I do not take orders from you, Admiral. It would be best to keep that in mind, lest you want us to rearrange our allegiance."

Ergen looked mad enough to chew his moustache, but the storm on his expression passed.

He snorted. "You've got a backbone, that's for sure. No wonder you Truppen boys make good warriors. All right, Selva, I'll let it slide —this time. You're getting a packet on a new target. Try not to blow it to bits this time, will you?"

"Of course, Admiral."

"That's a good lad. Ergen out."

As soon as the link was cut, Goetz grumbled, "Rett's becoming a nuisance."

"Becoming? He's been that since he was transferred into Truppen form." Elden drummed his claws against the console. "Ergen didn't ask about the missing units."

"You've told him?"

"It isn't exactly a secret, Goetz. I've chalked them all up to the aforementioned malfunctions. But if this keeps up, he's going to investigate. Which is why I agree with your recommendation: we'd best follow this trail."

"Good to hear."

Elden's links came alive with the mission packet Ergen sent. "Pass the word to Colonel Diaz. I want two octants, selected men for a special assignment. Fold them alongside another dozen octants for the raid. We'll take advantage of our next strike to set out on our own."

"What'll you tell Admiral Ergen?"

Elden glanced over his shoulder, at the huge battleship cruising in the distance. "The truth. My men are lost, and I'm going to find them."

***

Admiral Gussan Va'Kur Erassia raised his single eyebrow at the report streaming across his desk. Outpost Naravond Eleven, destroyed. Power core overload. Sensor station wiped out by orbital strike.

Blasted *ziura*.

"You can see my concern, reflected in these incidents." The

Naplian officer standing in the middle of his office was cast in holographic shadow, the communications beamed across hundreds of light-years with nary a couple of seconds' lag time. Even the brief delay did nothing to reduce the sheer presence the man carried.

Erassia had no illusions Admiral Tir Ad'Andra Daviont was anything but in charge.

He wore the same black and burnished orange of a Naplian Fleet officer as Erassia, and even the same rank insignia: twin silver suns on either shoulder. But Daviont was in command of the advance into vermin space, pushing aside the *shirish* as he scraped serjaum from the star system his forces had seized as their advance headquarters.

Erassia's job was to make certain the serjaum found its way along the Naplian corridor to all the Fleet's forces. "I trust, Admiral Daviont, that your concern does not make you doubt my ability or fervor. Your shipments have been safely escorted, by and large. These attacks have not weakened my resolve to serve the emperors and supply their glorious forces."

"Do not blind your eye to the *ziura*, Admiral. Their appearance on the human world Baedecker cost me many fine officers—even those of command rank."

Erassia bobbed his head. He'd blind himself rather than fail Daviont. "Yes, Admiral, I understand, and that is why our special forces are now deployed. The *ziurathal* are created from our finest soldiers, utilizing the latest intelligence we have on the Devastators. They are more than a match."

"They had better be. What are your plans for dealing with the Terran resistance in the Rift?"

Erassia smothered a grimace before it could pass narrow lips. His eye had a pale orange iris, and his gray skin was flushed with too much yellow up and down a slender neck. A sure sign he was nervous. "I have deployed strike teams and destroyer flotillas to hunt down and destroy them. Rest assured, we will protect the shipments of arms and serjaum, for the expansion of Naplia will remain the goal of every Ffawe under my command."

Daviont nodded. "Report when you have dealt with the problem. If I have to peel off one of my squadrons to clean up your mess, because you are blinking instead of fighting, the results will be dire."

His hologram dissolved in a spray of light.

Erassia sagged against his chair. Confounded two-eyes! If he could wipe the galaxy of them with a swipe of his hand, just as he cleared away the morass of holographic readouts floating above his desk, by the sacred Emperors he'd do it!

Rather than dwell on the fear he felt closing in on all sides, he took a walk.

***

His flagship, the battlecruiser *Fulnax*, was teeming with activity as officers, crew, and robots prepared her for yet another battle. Erassia's scroll informed him a Terran flotilla had been spotted not far from the system they called Sheridan Post—and the heavy cruiser TSS *Confiance* was among the assembled vessels.

Erassia scowled. Even if they jumped this second, it would take nearly thirty-six hours to cross the two sectors. By then, who knew where the accursed *shirish* vessel would be? He had a standing bounty for promotion to whichever captain brought him a hull shard.

He pushed aside all the stressful thoughts when he reached *Fulnax*'s hangar bay. The massive chamber was ribbed like a *naprial*'s chest, though far more slightly in gleaming metals and plastics. Erassia passed the lines of claw-winged fighters, the hulking bombers, and the insectoid landing craft. He wanted something else.

His *ziurathal*.

Erassia's eye widened when he saw them standing ready inside one of the armory cabins. Hulking battle armor suits, not much taller than the average Naplian, but a hunkered down, four-legged collection of weaponry. Each one's front hatch was open. Inside, he could see a saddle with shock webbing arrayed around a tiny compartment, one just large enough to accommodate a Ffawe.

"Admiral." A young officer, more thickly built than Erassia, saluted. Major Zet Ki'Lan Gandraad wore the bright yellow jumpsuit assigned to the *ziurathal*, some of the color dimmed by thick gray armor. His skin was pale gray to the point of being chalky, and his eye was a dark brown near black. Far more arresting was the black and red slash tattooed from his eyebrow up over the top of his head, and down the backside to his neck.

"Major Gandraad. Your company is impressive." And this was the best understatement Erassia could manage. The spindly-legged machines sent a chill throughout him. Ascended Masters, show favor on your soldiers and look kindly upon these beasts!

"Thank you, sir. A few more modifications and I am confident we'll be ready for a field test."

"Might I have a demonstration now?"

"Of course, Admiral." Gandraad snapped off orders at several soldiers and technicians.

He strapped himself into the nearest mech and let the webbing tie him down. Holograms glowed white and red in the dark confines of the interior, until the closing hatch cut him off from Erassia's view.

The *ziurathal's* exterior was blank of anything resembling a face, with only jagged armor plating to give a sense of its features. Still, Erassia imagined it glowered at him.

Four legs clattered across the deck, the machine bobbing along. A pair of Furta XRD mounted energy rifles hung from cables, one on either side, and short, clawed arms were held in close to the body.

At the far end of the room, someone had set up a broken and captured Truppen body. No headpiece—the blasted things self-destructed, rather than have that crucial technology be claimed for Naplia's glory. For all their crudity, the humans had come up with a simple, brute-force cybernetic being capable of unleashing tremendous damage.

Erassia was no fanatic. He harbored no superstitions that these Truppen were anything but man-made machines, and as such, were as fallible as the beings who built them.

The *ziurathal* scuttled at the Truppen. Energy bursts targeted weak points, severing connective cables and ripping apart servos. At a meter away, the claws tucked into the sides of the Naplian mech lashed out. They flowed on extruded tendrils, slashing through the air like *iriatta* vines caught in storm winds. Claws punctured the armor. The tendrils followed, and where they burrowed, the Truppen's body bulged.

Within moments, the *ziura* carcass was limp, its arms severed, and its mechanical innards spilled out across the deck.

Cheers went up from the crew observing the test. Fervent cheers, Erassia recognized—adulation of those who believed these were the Devastators come to threaten the existence of the Naplian Empire.

Erassia masked his disgust. They were never going to win this war if the feeble-minded continued their quivering. Hence his *ziurathal*.

Major Gandraad dismounted the mech. His face was slick with perspiration, and his eye sharp. "Our company is ready for action, Admiral. I promise you we will take space back from the *ziura*."

"Very good, Major. Very good, indeed." Erassia saluted. Gandraad saluted back. More cheers went up.

Erassia let the celebration continue. Why not? Morale needed boosting. His certainly among them.

Now to find a suitable target.

CHAPTER FIVE

Kayna Two was as pretty as advertised.

The blue sphere filled *Vy's* viewport, the continent a sprawling patch of dark forests, sweeping orange deserts, and glittering yellow plains. Tag spotted tiny glittering points flitting back and forth among the hundreds of large islands and their miniature offspring. Busy world. He couldn't make much of the cities, since this was the dayside.

"Terran vessel, this is Commercial Orbital Tracking." The voice was sullen, robotic, and sounded of scratching metal plates. *"We have you on our sensors. Your identification is confirmed. State your purpose of visit."*

Tag opened his mouth, but Dyson's words filled the air. "Good day, Tracking. This is Dyson Astor, trade rep for Cavill Aerospace Limited. I'm bringing my tidings and wares to your lovely world for the Interstellar Tech Expo. You should have the registration data for myself and my assistants."

Assistants? Tag scowled. And since when could the android sound like he was chatting with a pal over coffee after a sortie?

Lira stood behind him, hands on the back of his chair. Her breath brushed the back of his neck. "My, hasn't he become sociable."

"Would've made nine days pass a lot faster if he'd practiced sooner," Tag muttered.

"Registration confirmed for Dyson Astor, Taggart Wester, and Lira Lon Raddock."

"Raddock," Lira murmured. "One of the larger clans, mostly mercantile caste, who live on the Briddarri frontiers farthest from the capital."

"Handy cover," Tag whispered.

Dyson gave them both a dull look, which Tag supposed was his normal expression for "Will you two idiots please be quiet?"

"Proceed to Checkpoint Home Alpha. We will inspect your vessel and once finished, grant clearance to Atterissage."

"Thanks, Tracking. *Olivia Vy* out." The instant Dyson cut the signal his face resumed its usual mask. "Please follow the approach vector provided, Tag."

"You got it. But, leave it to me to ask the obvious—aren't they going to be a tad irked when they scan the pile of weaponry stashed in our belly?"

"Terran Intelligence has adequately prepared for such a contingency. Their scans will not penetrate the hull. More than that, they will receive false readings which indicate normal cargo such as luggage and foodstuffs."

"Oh. Check."

***

Commercial Orbital Tracking was a station one klick long, sitting in geosynchronous orbit about 200 klicks up over Kayna Two's equator. Tag found the long, tapered shape familiar, and couldn't peg why until he brought *Vy* over the axis and saw the full ovoid. The thing was a giant white seashell, complete with a seam running along one side as if it were the mouth ready to open. As they neared, he spotted more black lines, dozens of rows of yellow lights, and silver sprays of antennae. Sensor posts jutted from both ends, and sunlight shimmered across solar absorption panels that rippled in the sun's winds.

The console chirped at him. Tracking prompted Tag to relinquish control for the duration of the scan process, which Tag did—and sweated the whole thirty seconds. If something was going to go wrong, this would be when it would happen. He let his hands drift over the ripwave triggers. First sign of trouble, he could spin them up and blast out of here.

The console chirped again. Done.

"Olivia Vy, this is Tracking. Scans are complete. Results have been posted to your account. Thank you for your cooperation. Please follow Descent Route Two into the city."

"Roger that, Tracking, thanks a bunch," Dyson said.

As Tag slipped *Vy* through the clouds, he said, "You know, you could stay more pleasant the whole time instead of switching back into 'bot mode."

"Perhaps I find it a tedious use of my processing capability." Dyson expanded a holographic map of the planet. A hexagonal city grid filled the view.

Tag scowled.

"I think he handles sarcasm well enough, don't you?" Lira patted Tag's shoulder.

***

Tag followed the coordinates down an invisible arc into a sky suffused with a violet hue. His route afforded them a great view of skyhooks, huge dome-topped stations hanging in low orbit. There were six of them, each one busy with small-craft traffic and visited by at least a half-dozen civilian vessels. He swore a Denaxa Starman was docked at the nearest one and craned his neck for a better look at the huge luxury yacht, its hull a gleaming gold blade against starry blackness.

Each skyhook was tethered to the surface by a glittering cable anchored to one of the six corners of Atterissage. The capital city sat on a broad, grassy plain, itself pale yellow streaked through with rusty red brush. The precision impressed Tag—the hexagon gave the appearance someone had dropped the city, all twenty-four klicks across, smack into the middle of nothing. Indeed, the coordinates Dyson shared from the nav computer told him it was in the geographic center of the planet's sole continent.

For all her clunky appearance, *Vy* performed pretty well in the atmosphere. Not as smoothly as she cruised in space, mind, but Tag expected that—hull shape mattered way more down in the air than in vacuum. So, he accepted the bumps and jolts. Dyson glanced at the structural integrity indicators more than a few times, making Tag wonder just how sturdy *Vy* was, but otherwise didn't say a word about Tag's flying.

Lira, though, didn't mince.

"I swear I could drop down softer with a grav-harness," she snapped. "You call yourself an ace pilot?"

Tag spotted an avian, a huge condor, riding a thermal not a few meters from his portside. He tucked *Vy* into that thermal and let her jump over it with a tremendous surge that pushed him into the seat.

57

Lira swore and gripped the sides of her seat.

"Sorry, missed your last comment." Tag leveled out, and then winked at Lira.

She didn't say anything more.

Tracking directed them to land at the hexagonal pad in Corner One, the upper left angle of Atterissage's boundary, oriented to the northwest. The pad was several klicks across, and Tag couldn't begin to catalog all the craft parked across it. He set *Vy* down with a tremor and a thump; no more than ten seconds later, a diplomatic ketch with Stelltron markings alighted at the next zone, thirty meters away.

"Okay, we're down and done." Tag started locking systems and powering *Vy* off. "Where to?"

Dyson handed him and Lira each a scroll. "These will provide you with possible locations TI has determined for the data storage. Both have been coded to respond to your touch; however, when someone else tries to access them, they will be routed into a front which shows only personal and commercial data one would expect from visitors to a technology symposium."

"Right. Fake scrolls." Tag opened his and was impressed by the detailed map which unfolded. Ten white diamonds were speckled across it. Quite a lot of possibilities.

"So, you really don't have any idea where our target is stashed away," Lira said.

"The ten possible locations include all six skyhooks and four commercial airfields. Once we are near enough to the target information, these scrolls will help pinpoint and extract the database we need."

"How do we know which database? These places have to be absolutely overflowing with backup systems for storage and review."

"Did you not study the information regarding the Union of Planet's economic development and technological status?"

Tag rolled his eyes. "Other than the parts about aerospace industry, which are the only things I give a fully loaded railgun about, no. I had plenty of boredom without using the stuff you loaded as an aid."

"Pity. You would have learned about the crystalline lattice the Union has developed for securing sensitive data." Dyson flicked his scroll. A holographic object floated above it, reminding Tag of several large snowflakes molded together into a structure small enough to fit inside his palm.

"It's lovely." Lira's voice was soft. She brushed her fingers through the edges of the hologram. "They create these?"

"The more accurate description would be they grew them. Each is unique; a work of art unto itself. But each is also kept separate from any hardwired network and has no way of being accessed through signals. Encryption is made doubly difficult by the crystalline structure, which alters itself every few days."

"We have to find one jeweled storage box," Tag said, "in one of ten locations. Six of which are skyhooks floating at the edge of space."

"The crystals emit a peculiar, low-level mix of radiation, one which these scrolls are adapted to recognize." Dyson wiped the hologram away. "Unfortunately, these ten locations are all the guidance TI was able to provide us."

"I understand." Lira sighed. "Well, it would be best to start looking."

"Yes. I concur. We shall attend the Expo. Whatever contacts we need, every corporation with a skyhook will be present."

"This Expo—you said it was tech." Tag spread his arms. "I take it that's where I come in."

"Of course, Tag. The primary focus of the symposium is aerospace advancements, as you've already studied."

Tag grinned. "You should have led with that."

***

They passed customs with no bother, and Dyson secured an open-topped automated transport into the heart of Atterissage. The air carried a cloying scent that tickled the inside of Tag's nose. Fortunately, the ozone scent of ship engines and tang of transferred fuel masked some of it. Tag gathered it'd be worse out on the surrounding plains.

Their transport was full of eight other people headed to the expo, males and females of various human and humanoid nationalities. Lira struck up a conversation with a handsome young man who wore robes of the Depran League's traders. Tag, meanwhile, memorized the buildings they passed and the intersections they crossed as if they were interplanetary obstacles. He wanted a clean route back to Corner One, and *Vy.*

"The skyhooks are each owned by a separate corporation," Dyson said. "Stelltron has a presence here, as does the Molnsa Trade Guild."

"Man. That's a lot of money." Tag looked up at the skyhooks. They were tiny, so many klicks up through the atmosphere, like lost balloons, but even being down here and knowing what they were impressed him. "Don't suppose Western Rim's got one."

Dyson arched an eyebrow. "Hardly. Stelltron has made its practice to keep their new competitors as far away from events like these as possible. At any rate, none of the skyhooks are owned by the Union government."

"Oh. So, no luck on them being the location we need, right?"

"Do not discount them based on outward appearances. All these corporations have a vested interest in Union commerce. If they can provide services to the government, they will, provided it serves their interests."

"I'll bet."

The transport rounded a corner, rolling down a broad avenue lined with tall, skinny trees. Their trunks were white and their leaves yellow, but Tag's interest waned in a half second when he saw the huge structure looming beyond.

The Interstellar Technology Expo took up four by four city blocks at the dead center of Atterissage, underneath a gigantic dome that rippled with the air currents. It arced hundreds of meters overhead, transparent to the violet sky in some portions and sheathed in solar panels in others. The transport followed a separate road which branched off the avenue, right up to and inside an entry ramp. It queued up behind four more transports.

Security was tight. Men and women in bold purple jumpsuits and black vests managed a stream of visitors, ushering them like fish along a line which never paused. Tag submitted to a bioscan, had his belongings checked and stored, and received a chit to reclaim them from a secure locker when his visit was concluded for the day.

If the scanners happened to notice Dyson was an android, they must not have cared, because he went through without a fuss.

Tag caught up with Lira in the line. "How was your seating buddy?"

"Quite charming. He knows several restaurants we might find appealing."

"That's it?"

Lira smiled. "He also was quite forthcoming about the Iriada Limited skyhook. As in, he works in it."

"He told you that?"

"No, I noticed his service pin, on his left lapel." Lira opened her right palm. "This pin."

Sure enough, slender green fingers cupped a silver pin, round like a crescent moon with a red sun hanging off.

"You swiped it off his neck?" Tag glanced around for the man. He was several meters back, having a heated discussion with security personnel and a blonde woman whose face was turning several shades of crimson.

"*Shhh.*" Lira reached up and captured his chin. She turned him to face her and winked. "He doesn't know I took it."

"Doubtful, since you were sitting right next to him."

"And the blonde woman from Laterad was behind him, with her purse open on the floor, between her feet. When I took his lapel pin, I also relieved him of his communications device and planted it."

Voices rose in strident argument. Tag hazarded one last look. Sure enough, a security officer pulled something small and gold from the woman's purse, even as she shook her head, blonde tresses scattering like parted clouds.

"Wow. Okay, remind me to check all my pockets if I sit next to you."

Lira laughed. "I will take that as a compliment."

"This lapel pin—I take it the thing does more than look pretty?"

"It should literally open doors."

"You going to tell Dyson this?"

"Of course. Whatever helps us pinpoint our target."

The three of them joined up at the main mezzanine, overlooking the exhibits floor. Tag wished right then he was insanely rich, because he saw at least four starfighters he wanted to buy. If he was as handy a thief as Lira, he would have tried stuffing one under his shirt.

Kybers, Talon-Fives, Sixwings, Uhlans, sleek delta-winged planes, sharp-angled deep space fighters, solid black interceptors—he goggled at the collection.

"You see now why your expertise was required," Dyson said.

Tag nodded. "You want me to go talk to these guys? See if anyone knows anything?"

"More specifically, you need to obtain an invitation to one of the corporate skyhooks or airfields in Atterissage."

***

Tag clapped his hands. "Consider it done."

The largest crowd had gathered around the starfighters fielded by the Union of Planets itself, or rather, the aerospace corporations thereof. Seven models were spread across an area of neon red carpeting the same size as a soccer field. Tag doubted he could kick a ball without hitting a wing, even if said field was in a zero-gravity environment.

Those seven models were fielded by three companies, one of which was Pallas Industries. Pallas was a Union corporation, specializing in defense technology and information systems. Hmm. It also owned not just one of the six skyhooks around Atterissage, but one of the commercial airfields as well. Sounded like a good place to start.

He parked himself at the Pallas circle, in which three of the fighters were arranged nose-to-nose in triangular formation. The celebrity was by far the SSF-90 Sunsaber, a big, flat starfighter with broad delta wings and a fin protruding from each aft wing surface. She was a two-seater, Tag noted, though she was halfway in size between a Warhawk and a Raider. This model was painted matte gray. There wasn't a seam visible.

"Quite the eye-catcher, no?" A tall man in a white suit just as immaculate as the plane's fuselage stood by him. He had slicked black hair and four lines shaved into the sides above his ears. Tag could have used his moustache to lubricate the servos in a Warhawk, it was so slathered with product.

"Yeah, sure is."

"The Sunsaber has a ripwave rating of three point eight, twenty percent greater than the comparable fighters in its class. Eight hardpoints, capable of carrying a fighter-bomber's full bombload without the accompanying drag in atmo. And she boasts two twelve-centimeter laser turrets for point defense."

"Two? Nice. But that has to put a drain on the core."

"Pallas's proprietary core technology reduces drawdown by ten percent."

Tag nodded. "Now that's worth the price tag."

The man held out a hand. "Ranif Leroux."

"Tag Wester."

"Wester? Surely not the Captain Wester of Baedecker fame."

"Wouldn't say fame but ..." Tag grinned. "You've got him."

"What brings you out here? With the war on I'd have thought you would be hard-pressed to escape the front lines."

"Private citizen." Tag flipped up his nametag, complete with Cavill Aerospace Limited logo and—to help authenticate his story—ID number. Tag didn't know who all at Cavill Aero was in on the Terran Intelligence plan, and didn't much care, so long as his fake ID held up. So far, so good. "Doing some shopping for private concerns."

If Leroux formed any opinions of what Tag meant by his deliberately vague statement, he didn't let them show on his face. Instead he kept his smile, as broad as the Sunsaber's wings, fixed. "Very good, very good. You need only ask, and Pallas is at your service. We're honored to have someone of your skill level here at our expo."

Leroux toured Tag around the other fighters, all of which were impressive with their improvements to ripwave velocity, armament, and shield efficiency. None of them tugged at Tag's desire to fly like the Sunsaber. It was a plane he knew Scrape would have loved, especially if the sensor mix was as fine-tuned as Leroux claimed.

"She will read the hairs off the backside of a sea-gnat at five klicks and categorize them by size, largest to smallest," Leroux said. "I'm sensing you have a certain affinity for her."

"Can't lie, Ranif, if I were going to spend Cavill credits right here and now, this would be the prize I'd take home." Tag patted the wing. He didn't have to fake his affection. "But, as my father would say, you can't truly know a machine's abilities unless you test it yourself."

Antiny Wester never said such a thing, but it sounded good to Tag, and must have to Ranif. At the mention of "father," his eyes took on a greater gleam, which Tag marked up to either avarice or envy. "I would never argue with a man as esteemed as Antiny Wester. He displays great sense. Let's arrange a test flight. Tomorrow morning, 0700, at Velo Field."

"That'd be great."

"We'll have one of our best as your co-pilot, to sit in the RIO's spot."

"Actually, my colleague would be perfect for that role." Tag wasn't about to ruin a perfectly good chance to scan the Pallas airfield—and hopefully the skyhook—network with some company lackey riding behind him.

"If that is your preference, we will certainly accommodate." Leroux gave a short bow, with a flourish of his right hand. He stayed in the position for a couple of seconds, long enough Tag wondered if he was stuck, or in need of a med scanner.

Must be local custom. Tag mimicked the stance as best he could. Only then did Leroux rise.

"If you'll speak with Ms. Hadar, she will make the necessary arrangements." Leroux beamed. "Thank you again, Mr. Wester, for the opportunity to showcase our finest space superiority fighter to you. I promise you won't be disappointed."

He was gone amongst a throng of other men and women clustered about the Sunsaber. Tag was about to ask him who Ms. Hadar was and where she could be found when a gorgeous woman in a black dress, with glittering jewelry twirling about her neck, approached. "Captain Wester?"

"Mr. Wester. Out of service, you know." Tag grinned.

"Amari Hadar." Her skin was caramel, her hair long and equally as black as her dress, though with a yellow luminescence Tag guessed must be caused by dermal implants. The jewelry didn't touch her body at all—held aloft with a tiny anti-grav projector? "I will need your contact information."

"Of course." As Tag synced his scroll with hers, he glanced about for Lira. Wait a sec … "You know, I haven't gotten the full tour of this place, besides your boss showing off his favorite fighter. And I'm fantastic company."

She smiled. "I would imagine so, and yes, I'd be delighted."

"All right, then. You're my wingman." Tag offered his arm.

She took it and began listing off the benefits of all things Pallas. Didn't stop Tag from worrying about where his new colleague had vanished to.

Ah. Let the 'bot fret about her.

***

Lira mingled with the Iriada crowd, all of whom were far more intrigued by the latest advancements in holoprojectors. The centerpiece model was the size of a chair yet dazzled everyone with a scale representation of the Kayna star system, incorporating real-time scan data of the local orbits.

She noticed Tag leave with the human female on his arm, as if she were his prize—or perhaps he was hers. The woman had the body language Lira would have employed to get her way when she was after a particular bauble. It reminded her of her actions with the guard she'd bribed.

That had turned out well, even though the Briddarri had caught up with her afterward.

Lira shook her head. If human males were as susceptible as she'd heard—and as she'd just seen Tag demonstrate—this assignment would be simple.

Certainly no one would mind if she borrowed a scroll from one of the Iriada reps, a woman wearing too much makeup and cheap perfume.

The woman was too busy entertaining a trio of businessmen who were either enthralled by her sales pitch or struck numb by the stench of her. Lira wove her way between the group, toward the back of the exhibit partitions, where a black doorway reflected her image back to her. She did not look like she belonged at Iriada, but with the lapel pin in place at her collar, the door whisked open with nary a complaint.

How lovely. She appreciated when things went according to plan.

Inside, a drab, taupe corridor wound in a curve past several open doorways. She heard voices in the one ahead and on the right, followed by footsteps. Lira entered the one to the left and doused the light strips. She pressed against the wall, just inside the frame.

Two men walked by. She glimpsed silver devices tucked behind their ears, tiny lights flashing. One of them murmured into a black cylinder affixed to a tall collar. He wore the same blue and gray jumpsuit as his companion, with matching caps.

Security. They were sharp and alert, in stark contrast to the vacuum-brained woman trying to woo buyers. But they were also gone, through the door in a burst of sound from the expo floor.

Lira exhaled. She checked her surroundings, not bothering to bring lights back up. One advantage of being Briddarri—her night vision was markedly better than most humanoids'.

There was nothing of interest in this room. Only boxes and stacked chairs lined two walls. Storage.

She slipped into the corridor and down to the next room. Her wrist sensor—thank the stars those navy dunces had actually returned it to her—pinged in the presence of a scanner unit mounted on the ceiling, complete with camera. Lira smiled. Well, it wouldn't see much of her. She adjusted her wrist unit.

The scanner went dead, every light winking out.

Lira only had a couple of minutes before the malfunction righted itself. The next room was a break area, with crumbs scattered across a white table of cheap, chipped material and empty drink bottles abandoned by a sink.

The next room—much better.

Four consoles, each one equipped with a holoprojector equal to the massive one on display on the expo floor. The room was big enough to accommodate dozens of people, yet seemed expressly used for only those four. It was the same taupe as the rest of the rooms and the corridor. Spiky green cacti of a writhing variety Lira had never seen before stood guard in each corner.

She used her wrist sensor to force a connection between her scroll and the nearest console. The results were promising: Iriada did have huge data storage facilities aboard their skyhook, yet she couldn't tell from this system what level of encryption was involved, or even who had access to the facilities. If the crystals were present, she'd have to give this readout to Dyson for interpretation—the mass of information meant nothing to her.

Lira did know vaults, and security meant for valuables. She marked a half dozen of those aboard the Iriada skyhook.

Even if that location proved a bust as far as the data was concerned, she could still make it worth her while, perhaps enough to let her slip Briddarri bonds.

Whatever else she hoped to find was cut short by the buzzing of the timer on her wrist. A minute and ten remaining. Lira copied every bit of data she could fit onto her scroll, then made for the door.

She forced herself to walk at a swift but unconcerned pace. It was all about body language—portraying that she had somewhere to be, while simultaneously maintaining a façade that insisted she didn't care.

The door at the end of the corridor opened. A tall Audrian male carried a clear container with a mixed batch of circuitry inside. He wore a technician's coveralls and seemed puzzled by her appearance. Wide oval eyes set high atop a head she found misshapen and similar to Naplian biology squinted. "Can I help you?"

"You already are, by being a gentleman and holding the door." Lira slid by him, though she made sure to keep the distance narrow enough her body brushed his. Fascinating how whatever inquiry he had in mind vaporized, and she imagined she could see it happen.

Males. No matter the species.

Tag was nowhere to be seen, but she did come across Dyson. The intelligence officer was chatting amiably with a short, rotund Golduk male who showed off six kinds of navigational sensor upgrades, one module held in each tentacle.

Lira perused a stand of jewelry with embedded scroll functions until Dyson extricated himself. "Did you make a choice of the six?"

"I purchased this year's Molnsa model." Dyson's voice retained some of its faked lilt. For show to casual observers, Lira assumed. "I was able to plant a nanite on our salesman in the process, which will activate inside their skyhook. Assuming it enters their facility undetected."

"Terran Intelligence does not impress me thus far," Lira said. "Shouldn't you have known the data storage's precise location prior to our arrival?"

"We have sent previous assets, all robotic. None reported back."

"Someone knows we're interested."

"The probability is greater that these corporations are geared toward eliminating electronic and robotic infiltration," Dyson said. "Hence our use of Humint."

"Human intelligence." Lira laughed. She patted Dyson's cheek. It was much warmer than she'd anticipated, and she swore she felt a pulse beneath the flesh. "The two of us discussing human intelligence strikes me as darkly funny."

He considered this, those dark eyes keenly aware. "Your point is well taken."

Tag chose that moment to reappear, looking as reinvigorated as if he'd finished a run. "Getting quite the show here, aren't we? Find anything useful?"

"Possibilities at Iriada," Lira said. "And Molnsa."

"Good deal. I'm taking us out for a spin at Pallas tomorrow morning. Dyson, you bring along your scanners and we'll see what we can scrounge up."

Dyson nodded. "Pallas is nearest to the Iriada skyhook, and we can scan other targets nearby—subtly, of course."

"Of course." Tag winked at them. "You're about to gain firsthand knowledge of a fighter's backseat."

CHAPTER SIX

The toxic atmosphere of Planet 5240-Beta was so thick Elden had to set his sensors at their greatest resolution, and even then, he could only penetrate the swirling orange morass a klick in any direction.

Muffled screams from Naplian energy blasts accosted him from all sides. Each one lit up the dense fog so brightly it was difficult to pinpoint the location of each firefight, at least visually. Elden's targeting systems worked overtime, trying to differentiate approaching enemy from distant snipers.

When the mechs emerged from the gloom, he was convinced this target was a bad idea.

They were unlike any of the Naplian crawlers he'd seen before —small, lumpen, carried aloft on four legs. Each one scuttled apart from the main group so fast he'd have sworn they were fleeing.

But no, it was a charge, straight into the jaws of the Truppen advance.

"Engage by pairs!" Elden's octant split up on cue, with Goetz taking his familiar post at Elden's side. Across the battlefield—as far as his IFF could pick up the signals from Truppen armor—his soldiers paired off from their units of eight.

There were a lot of new red lights on his display.

Elden dispatched a regular Naplian soldier who appeared seemingly out of nowhere, his body armor having taken on ruddy orange hues identical to the atmosphere. The disguise didn't stop Elden's sensors from picking up the infrared difference, nor did it protect him from the railgun flechettes that shredded his torso.

Goetz dodged fire from twin guns mounted on the nearest mech and drove into it with all the subtlety of a demolition 'bot knocking down a building. The mech stabbed at him with spindly claws, each one whipping out on vine-like arms, but Goetz wormed out of the way, suffering only scratches to his shoulders. He stabbed deep into the thing's backside with his claws, sending out a spray of sparks.

The mech pivoted and came for Elden. He fired on it, damaging one of its weapons, but it closed on his position about twice as fast as he'd anticipated. A slash from its arms opened a gap in Elden's armor, along the left side of his torso. Damage control systems flashed red across his view, and streams of data pushed alongside his internal vision. Nanites were en route to stabilize and repair. Already his body was working to fix itself. It was an odd sensation, sustaining injury without pain.

It only made him more determined to slay his opponent.

Elden disengaged with a long jump backwards and to his right, while firing a discarded Furta energy rifle. Whatever these new mechs were designed to do, they were not invulnerable, for several of his shots severed one of the claw-arms. Clearly, they were built for speed; by the time Elden landed, the mech was right on top of his position.

This time, he was better prepared, and ducked around flailing claws. Energy blasts sloughed off the armor on his right shoulder, eliciting another flurry of alarms. Elden mentally obliterated all of them and ripped the energy weapon off the mech's shoulder with both hands. Then he swept it like a cudgel underfoot, making the thing stumble.

He tossed the gun aside and stabbed deep with both claws into a gap in the armor. Sparks sprayed all over—and his blades retracted with yellow blood dripping from them.

Goetz ripped the front off. It was a canopy, and inside sat the Naplian pilot, dead from his wounds. He wore a bright yellow suit and environmental mask with air supply.

"Never seen one of these," Goetz said. "Their mechs are usually dumb AI. Not nearly as quick."

"Those are definitely not occupied units." Elden made sure his scanners picked up every inch of the mech's controls.

Then the power readings spiked into crimson.

"Back up!" Goetz thudded into Elden and lifted him away in a dizzying jump.

The mech exploded; its power core's discharge detonating every last weapon it held in a blinding flash. When the pair landed, all Elden saw was a swirl of black smoke amidst the orange fog, with a burnt crater at the bottom.

"So much for actionable intelligence," he murmured. "Did you get anything?"

"Basic scans. There may be enough."

Elden's displays showed the battle spreading out to the northeast and southwest from his coordinates, but the atmosphere interfered so badly with his readings that several times the display glitched out entirely, every symbol for every friend and foe disappearing. Reports crackled across his communications link, overlapping and filtered only by his tactical systems.

"Where's Colonel Diaz's unit?" he asked Goetz. "They aren't responding to my signals."

"I'll check." Goetz went silent, presumably while communicating with Truppen in the area. Meantime Elden kept his weapons ready, unable to see who was fighting whom but hearing signs of battle all around.

"Got nothing," Goetz said. "But their last fix was eight klicks south-southwest."

"Follow me."

Together they bound toward Diaz's last known location, interceding as needed in the pockets of fighting they came across. Three Truppen were dead, with five comrades prodding at the smoldering remains of a quartet of the new Naplian mechs that had killed them. Behind a farther ridge, they found an octant spread across a basin in twos, fighting with a half dozen of the beasts. Goetz came down on the nearest mech with a flying leap, severing its gun mounts.

Suddenly the mechs withdrew, disappearing into the fog.

"Regroup with Octant One-Six two klicks over the rise," Elden said. "I'm sending you their coordinates. Do not pursue these One-eye machines. We have no idea how many more may be waiting."

"Yes, sir." The Truppen leapt up over the ridge, melting away.

"Diaz and his men should have secured the fuel supplies by now," Goetz said.

Elden nodded. "Should have. If these new mechs proved as dangerous to them as they were to us ..."

When they reached the coordinates, they found only destruction.

The fuel depot had indeed been ransacked. Serjaum processing machinery lay wrecked, alongside a tunnel reaching deep below the planet's surface. Automated extraction carts, all silvery gray and stained with reddish-brown dirt, sat in a silent line. There were still serjaum containers sitting undamaged by a makeshift tarmac of blast-hardened soil, but everything else had been shot through, ripped apart, or bombed.

There were also plenty of dead Naplians. None of the mechs, none that Elden and Goetz could find. None of their self-destruct craters, either. Only a half-dozen soldiers, their bodies already coated with a fine layer of orange particulate deposited by the fog.

Elden signaled to Diaz and his men. No response.

Goetz trod farther, to the opposite end of the mining camp. "Tracks here, inbound. Probably where Diaz and the boys attacked— looks like fast jumps."

"It also matches the direction of fire." Elden's targeting systems reconstructed the camp, based on existing debris and scan intelligence the Briddarri had provided prior to the raid. "But not all of it. See these blast points here, and those craters?"

Goetz made a noise that sounded like metal grinding. "From above."

Elden ran scans across the tarmac. Residual ions. "Sublight drive. Something landed nearby, recently."

"Can't imagine why we never saw it, in all this muck," Goetz muttered. "Worst part is, I can't find any exit tracks for Truppen. Like Diaz came in, and never left."

Elden recorded every bit of the site. Diaz and his men, just gone. Like the others. Could the Naplians have abducted them? It seemed improbable, even with their new mechs. Diaz had two octants, sixteen Truppen, including himself. A powerful electromagnetic pulse could theoretically disable them all, but Elden had never encountered one that could penetrate Truppen hardware, short of a nuclear blast.

Where were his men? What happened to the Naplians?

<This doesn't bode well for our private mission,> Elden said.

<No kidding. We'd better link up with the rest. I'll signal the

transports, let them know we've got the serjaum Ergen wanted.>

<Do that. I have someone whose ear I need to bend.>

Their raiding party consisted of 112 Truppen in 14 octants. By the appointed time of the rendezvous, after it was confirmed all remaining Naplians had either been killed, fled, or in the case of the new mechs obliterated themselves, Elden had seventy. A thirty-three percent casualty rate, not counting the damaged. He clenched his fists, claws scratching the inside of his palms. It was the worst death rate his men had suffered under his command in two years.

It was unacceptable.

"What's going on?" Rett bounded to a halt at the edge of the mining camp. "You boys sure did pound this place. Transports are coming down. Admiral Ergen's so happy you nabbed this stuff he cracked open a new case of cigars."

"Let me show you something." Elden took Rett to the edge of the camp, where Goetz crouched by the Truppen tracks supposedly made by Colonel Diaz and his men. "This is where our Truppen attacked. Look around this camp and tell me what you see."

It took thirty seconds for Rett to catch up to them in terms of site analysis and the conclusions they drew. "Oh. Ah, I don't see where they bugged out."

"They didn't leave this area. Not as far as we can tell." Elden pointed to the landing field. "At least, not by land."

"There weren't supposed to be any landing craft in the region," Rett said. "Intelligence says—"

"Intelligence has been unable to explain why I have lost three units of Truppen," Elden snapped. "Intelligence says it forwards my inquiries up the chain of command, yet I never hear anything in return. Intelligence is stonewalling me, Rett. Do you have any idea why?"

"Look, I get it, you're upset—"

Goetz put a clawed hand on Rett's shoulder, like two people having a friendly reunion. His other hand prodded dangerously close to a seam in Rett's armor. <The Consul is concerned. I'm upset.>

Rett stood as frozen as if he'd been deactivated.

<I know something's wrong,> Elden sent to him. <My men are

vanishing, and every time I strive for an explanation, I'm met with nothing but excuses, misdirection, and indifference. Tell me why that is.>

<I ... I don't know. I don't know.> Outwardly, Rett didn't change his stance, but the link between him, Elden, and Goetz crackled with his anxiety. <I don't ... okay, the admiral knows something is wrong. I get the sense when I talk to him. But he won't say whether he knows what it is, or whether the One-eyes are involved.>

<You've asked him about the missing soldiers?>

<A couple of times. He says there's a lead. Maybe.>

<This lead wouldn't happen to have coordinates, would it?>

Rett switched back over to his speakers. "The transport's coming. We should get the serjaum ready to move."

But he couldn't move, because Goetz held him in a grip so firm Elden could see the dents on Rett's armor. "Rett, if you have information, then as your commander I require it."

"Hey, wait a sec. I'm with Briddarri Espionage Directorate, and—"

"That was your former life. Whatever ties you had to the Briddarri as Everett Lind, the spy, are severed. You're Rett, the Truppen, and as such far more admired by your warrior people than you had been as a reviled spy. But you're Truppen, first and foremost. That means you serve me. I don't care one novafired bit what Admiral Ergen demands of you. My demands outweigh his. Know this—if you refuse my orders, you'll find yourself as scrap for the repair of better men. Braver men."

Rett's arms developed a tremor that most techs would chalk up to neural interface malfunction, but Elden knew it was fear. He had been harsh with the man, yes, and perhaps unfairly so; he had served loyally both the Truppen and Briddarri during the long campaign against the Naplians. But Elden had lost too many people he valued— too many friends—to let a man influenced by other powers stop the recovery of his lost soldiers.

"I can get them for you," Rett said. "They're stashed away in a secure portion of my memory. I don't even know precisely what directory—I have to run several decryption sequences just to find it. We're talking a couple of hours."

"Good. You can do that as we jump from the system."

"But … Admiral Ergen. He'll be here for the rendezvous."

"And with any luck, we'll be on our way out of the system when he arrives." Elden turned and faced the camp. Truppen lined up stacks of serjaum containers in neat rows alongside the tarmac. A steady thrum rose in the air, the sound of the landing craft drawing near. "Goetz, secure one of the arriving landers for us, and signal *Hessian*. We're uploading a new destination."

Goetz gave Rett a shove. "Come on, Greenblood. You're part of the hunt."

***

Tag expected the Sunsaber to be good. How could it not be? It was a test model for potential buyers, one they fully expected a credentialed pilot to take for a joyride—or proving flight, he should have said—without a single hiccup. Pallas would provide the absolute best model in their inventory so that a single trip around Atterissage would convince the buyer to shell out for a squadron or two.

But man, when he brought her to a hover and kicked in the ionic fusion engines, she launched like a missile targeted on a Naplian's tail.

The g-forces punched Tag deep into his suit, and only the nano-mesh of his Pallas-brand flight suit kept him from passing out. He was breathless, his heart banging off his ribs, sensations the clinical part of his brain would catalog as problems. Now this was flying!

He whooped and spun the Sunsaber twice on its axis.

"I would suggest we return to a level trajectory," Dyson said from the RIO's seat. "Our hosts may not be pleased if we damage their property."

"Damage their property?" Tag snorted and spun the starfighter twice more just to tick him off. "Please. I could spin this plane through a canyon upside down while combing my hair and pouring a glass of Crown & Scepter without scratching the wingtips."

"A highly doubtful outcome to an outlandish proposition."

Tag shook his head. There they were, shooting through gauzy purple skies with the Kaynan sun hovering low on the morning horizon, and the whole of Atterissage laid out like a shiny new control board below them, and Dyson sounded as dulled by the experience as if he were awaiting a system reboot. This was an aircraft so new, there were still manufacturer's stickers on the cockpit plas-glass. Some of the control surfaces were even polished!

Sure glad he wasn't a 'bot.

It made Tag wonder if this had been the attitude of the mutinous androids aboard TSS *Hermes*, a hundred years ago—cold, unfeeling automatons just as self-aware as a man, yet willing to butcher their commanding officers on a whim. "Tell you what. When we land, why don't you shine up my boots and hang my clothes straight? Make yourself useful, like a good 'bot should."

It was the cruelest thing he could think of in the spur of the moment, yet whether it had any effect on Dyson, he couldn't figure. There were exactly five seconds of silence, then the android said, "Put us into a wide loop so I can engage the primary sensors. This falls within the checklist of activities Pallas expects of us. Once we are within range, I can filter the data through my scroll and search for any evidence of data storage facilities capable of containing the information we seek."

Fair enough. Tag leveled out above a cluster of low clouds, and banked right, the wingtip cutting through water vapor. He continued upward in a spiral, bringing them far beyond the boundaries of Atterissage, and ascending nearer to the Pallas skyhook. There were a handful of other high-performance vehicles out, taking leisurely test runs around the city. With nothing but vast open plains dotted by tiny blue-green lakes for klicks out to the horizon, the region around the city was perfect for the demonstrations. Tag itched to drop the Sunsaber to ground level and kick up spray across those lakes, but he guessed Dyson would just mope about it.

Targeting sensors lit up as the Pallas skyhook entered weapons range. The Sunsaber didn't carry any bombs, missiles, or even ammunition for its railgun, and the lasers were disconnected from their power source. The scanner's resolution impressed Tag. Even his Warhawk wouldn't latch on this fast. "Okay, got a huge bogey for you."

"Thank you." A moment later, an unfamiliar data stream trickled across the edge of Tag's display. "Accessing sensor reports. Running analysis."

"That's an awfully big place. You sure you can find a tiny crystal unit inside?"

"The Union Leadership is fond of large, heavily secured data storage compounds," Dyson said, "But they rarely have the expertise to operate such. If any of the skyhooks do indeed possess such a facility, it will draw significant power off the station's supply, and will also emit a particular energy signature for its security systems, both physical and virtual. As I have also previously stated, the crystal itself gives off a peculiar radiation. The combination of these factors should pinpoint its location."

"Could've just said 'yes' and I'd have been happy," Tag muttered.

The Sunsaber bounced, as if she'd hit a rough patch of clear air. It wasn't anything disconcerting to Tag, but he checked the airflow scanners for any indication of turbulence. None he could see. No matter. Air pockets formed and made rides rough. It happened.

"Scans are almost complete," Dyson said. "A pass around the Iriada facility would be most appreciated."

Tag expanded his loop, making as if he were testing the Sunsaber's acceleration capabilities. He grinned. No problem faking that one. The fighter leapt ahead, with the agility of a Warhawk but the steady flight pattern of a Raider. "I tell you, Dyson, if we were really on a purchase mission, I would absolutely grab up a squadron of these beauties and tell Commodore Ram to start training pilots immediately. I bet the weapons loadout could completely spank anything the One-eyes threw our way."

"I am sure your assessment is correct. Please direct the scanners at the Iriada station."

"What, you're done already?"

"The scroll has amassed the data it needs, yes. The analysis will take a few minutes more."

"Okay then, Skipper." Tag broke away from the Pallas skyhook, sparing a long look at the dome-topped station. Like a graceful, shining version of a mushroom, it hovered where the purple skies faded to the midnight of space. A long, slender passenger liner made a slow approach, tiny bursts from maneuvering thrusters sparkling like the stars themselves. The Iriada skyhook was a dozen kilometers away, a smaller, broader dome with far more antennae and towers dangling from its underside.

He brought them as close as he could for a detailed scan while remaining outside the proximity sphere marked in red lines across the displays. A small, two-seater patrol craft circled lazily overhead, like a diamond skate riding the shallow waves off Triadon Bay on Baedecker Four. Twin engines glowed bright at the aft end of the diamond. It was white, with Iriada corporate logos stamped on the underside of the wings.

"That will suffice. Running scans now."

"If we do find it, let me be the first to ask the obvious—how in the bottom of a black hole are we going to get the lattice out of there?"

"The actual extraction falls within Ms. Reen's purview," Dyson said. "You and I will be outside the skyhook, facilitating her entry and exit."

"Check. So, we're the wheelmen."

"Wheelmen?"

"Sure. Getaway drivers."

He could see the frown crease Dyson's otherwise expressionless face in the reflection on the canopy. "Most likely an aerial effort will be required, though a ground infiltration can be possible if—"

"Never mind. Forget it."

"Captain Wester, this mission will proceed with greater efficiency if you will refrain from succumbing to your hostility toward my kind."

"You think?" Tag scowled. "Your kind are the ones who killed a bunch of my people—my family, years ago. That isn't something Westers let go of."

"You are referring to the TSS *Hermes* incident."

"Incident? Mutiny and massacre, those are the nouns you want. Android crew killed the officers and took the ship!"

"Even if there were extenuating circumstances—"

"For the murder of my great-grandparents? Their brothers and sisters?" Tag snapped off into a roll, spinning the Sunsaber away, not even caring if the 'bot got his blasted scans.

Dyson was silent for a long spell. Finally, he said, "Since I am merely ten years old from my date of manufacture and initialization, you cannot hold me guilty for actions committed by those who are, in a manner of speaking, my ancestors."

Tag didn't have any comeback. Instead he leveled the starfighter on a return course to the landing pads.

The Sunsaber lurched again. Only this time, the nav displays winked out, then returned to full brightness.

"Did you also experience a malfunction?"

"I'll say." Tag's sensors showed no rough air, not even when he checked the area through which he'd just flown. He lowered his airspeed, and ran a third scan—

The engines died.

He'd forgotten how much noise the constant rumble of a starfighter's engines made in flight. Pilots got used to it, folding it alongside myriad background sounds. But when it was gone, it was jarring. Silence, except for the wind rushing by and the beeps of the instrumentation.

"This is disconcerting," Dyson said.

"Yeah, a bit!" Already their altitude was dropping, as the Sunsaber's aerodynamic body rode the air currents down. Tag fumbled for the emergency restart, flipping two panels up and punching both switches at the same time.

Nothing.

"Blast it." He queued up an all-bands signal. "Mayday, Mayday, this is Pallas Test Flight Echo, we have suffered full engine shutdown, repeat, full engine shutdown. Restart is unresponsive. Request rescue craft at the following coordinates."

Tag shuffled their nav heading into the signal and sent it. Or rather, he tried to. "Communications systems are showing inoperative," Dyson said. "My sensor network has similarly failed."

"Then we'd better bail before this thing gets sucked into a spin." Tag toggled a red lever by his right leg.

Again, nothing.

Kick me in the face and call me a One-eye, Tag thought. He'd heard of individual systems bonking out, or even a total power failure, but the eject lever was wired directly into explosive charges and a dormant miniature thruster bank. It had nothing to do with main power—completely separate network of the fighter's computers!

Not a normal malfunction.

The control stick still responded, but without thrusters or engines, he was waggling the ailerons of a boulder with wings. The Sunsaber dropped faster, losing hundreds of feet with every second. "I need the specs on this thing."

"One moment."

"Don't really have one, but sure, take your time!"

Dyson passed his scroll ahead, and it landed in Tag's lap. Good enough. The diagrams showed exactly how the fighter was wired together, where all the command routes were. Tag needed something to jump-start the engines, because whatever controls he pushed and prodded refused to do their jobs.

But he couldn't relinquish control. His arms ached with the strain of maneuvering the starfighter, bereft of computer-aided guidance. Without nav, his guesses were all that was going to get them down in one piece. "Listen, I need you to follow my directions. I've got to get some maneuvering thrusters back, or we're going to make a very big, very burnt hole on the plains. Got me?"

"Indeed I do."

"Okay. Your left hand, panel in front of your knee. Remove it."

Tag realized belatedly that neither he nor Dyson had tools to unbolt said hatch, but he heard a squeal of plastics, then something cracked. "It is open," Dyson said.

Here's hoping they wouldn't need to close it. "Right. You should see six sets of circuits, each with a different color. Any lights running?"

"No. All are inactive."

Blast. "Remove the yellow one—carefully."

"A moment."

Wind roared by, ever louder, and they dove at a steep angle through a cloud bank. Tag got a way too detailed look at the grassy plains. There were a couple of big lakes nearby, double the size of most of the rest of the glassy ponds. If he could hit the right current ...

"It is out."

"Got a long set of wires trailing it?"

"Correct."

"Okay. Patch it into the wiring at the base of your console, on the right side. There should be a long, black cable marked with red and white hash marks, locked down by brackets."

"It is sealed in, and unable to be accessed."

"Well, pull the blasted brackets up and patch it in!"

The seconds ticked by, g-forces pressing Tag into his seat, black squeezing at the corners of his vision, his breath reduced to gasps. His head felt full of foam. But he could still see that lake, the one he'd picked as a target. If he couldn't get the Sunsaber righted, they'd fall short by twenty klicks.

Tag heard electricity arc and smelled something burnt. "Task accomplished."

"Yes!" He pounded the control panel for the dorsal thrusters.

The Sunsaber put its nose up, kicked high by a tremendous force that rattled the cockpit.

When it subsided, he could see the shimmering aquamarine surface of a lake. "Hang on!" he cried.

The water rushed up at them, and Tag braked with the fighter's control surfaces as much as he could muster. The back end slapped water, bounced high, and slapped down again. Twice more. Then the belly and nose dug a furrow in the water as easily as an auto-tiller through soil.

Tag let go of the stick of what was now, essentially, a boat.

The starfighter ceased its headlong rush, dragged to a stop. Water seeped into the cockpit, rising up several centimeters around Tag's shoes. He fumbled with his straps, released himself from their grasp, and pounded futilely on the plas-glass canopy. Figures. He'd managed a miraculous landing, only to drown in a coffin made of one of the best starfighters in the galaxy.

The canopy shattered as if it were targeted by a railgun. A tremendous grip yanked him out through the broken top, and into the water. He submerged, everything around him cool and wet. He blinked, trying to see in the glassy glow. The Sunsaber, its back broken, sank underneath him.

When he surfaced, and struggled for air, he found he was treading water next to Dyson. "That was an excellent landing, Tag, considering the negative factors involved."

Tag shook his head and blew water from his face. Off on the horizon, a pair of rescue craft approached, tiny and white like distant gulls, except with flashing lights.

"Only negative factor I'm worried about," Tag said, "is who just tried to kill us."

CHAPTER SEVEN

Tag stood under the heat vents of the bathroom at their hotel suite and let the rush of hot air dry him off. Hair, face, clothing—even down to his skivvies—it blasted the moisture away. He'd doffed his boots at the edge of the tile floor. Lira's insistence he not track anything any farther than the front door was obnoxious, but he was so drained he was in no mood to argue.

The bathroom was huge, with a shower, tub, two sinks, and mirrors everywhere. Tag flashed himself a grin and tousled his hair. Not bad. But this place, with white and sandstone tiles all over, wasn't his style. Give him plain old bulkheads and he'd be a happy pilot.

The main sitting area of the suite was double the size, with couches and reclining chairs of the finest leathers scattered about. Tag dropped into one black seat, rubbing his hands across the arms. Felt more like scales than the real deal. "Must not have cows on this planet," he muttered.

"All the major herbivorous species of Kayna Two are reptilian." Dyson sat on the couch nearest the floor-to-ceiling windows, apparently oblivious to the sprawling cityscape of spires and pyramids reflecting purple light skyward. The expo canopy rose in the distance. A pair of four-winged lizards with serrated teeth soared by the balcony beyond the windows, tussling over something small and hairy.

Dyson had his nose almost literally buried in three holograms, each one a morass of digits and symbols. Good luck figuring what it meant. Probably child's writing for a 'bot.

"I would like to hear that you were successful on your joyride." Lira approached from the kitchenette adjacent to the bathroom, bearing two glasses of frothy blue liquid. Gold ribbons twisted inside the drinks with each step she took.

"Joyride? We almost drowned!" Tag accepted a glass. Smelled like the inside of a greenhouse—flowery. "Thanks. Well, okay, so I almost drowned."

"Dyson prevented that. Good for you." She gave Dyson a peck on the cheek.

"Programmed reflex." Dyson swiped aside a raft of data. "The flight did, as it happens, prove successful. Look at this."

Lira sat on the arm of the couch. Tag admired the way she lounged there, and the casual attitude about her, from the way she draped one arm behind Dyson to the way she sipped her drink. He shook his head and sipped his own drink. Gotta clear my head—but blast, that blue stuff was sour. Like sucking on a lime. "What is this?"

"Eleret. Some of the finest Briddarri champagne."

"A little early to celebrate. We just finished breakfast."

Lira smirked. "No meal should be without eleret, whether you're a warrior or a thief. Now, Dyson, please continue."

"Of course. Tag's piloting managed to bring us close enough to both the Iriada and Pallas skyhooks to confirm radiation consistent with the crystal in both."

Managed? Tag groaned. "Great. Narrowed it down from two to two. Tell me there's more good news related to us almost smashing a test fighter into the ground."

Dyson glanced at him. "The good news, as you put it, is Iriada contains secure vaults most likely to contain the crystalline lattice."

Lira couldn't have looked any happier if Dyson had just announced they were throwing her a party. "Perfect! It should be easy enough to infiltrate the Iriada skyhook from its base. The pin I procured will allow me inside."

"You mean us," Tag said.

"I mean me, or perhaps my language skills are not up to par for explaining myself to humans. You may be a skilled pilot, Tag, but you can't simply walk into a facility like that. Everything about you screams military."

"It is why he was given no false background for this mission," Dyson said. "I concur with Ms. Reen."

"You concur—now wait a novafired second." Tag jabbed a thumb into his chest. "I am the pilot, you've got that right, and I say it makes way more sense to get Lira inside with a flyby."

Lira sighed. "Any craft would be spotted from klicks away."

"Not *Vy*. I got to looking under her hood, to borrow from ancient Terra wordplay." Tag smiled. "Dyson, you want to clue her in, or should I?"

Dyson appeared hesitant, or at least, his blinks lasted longer than usual. "That aspect of *Olivia Vy*'s capabilities is classified. I am not authorized to divulge it."

"Since I already did the divulging, it doesn't matter. Anyway, Lira, our less than fancy-looking ride has a clouder." Tag felt a jolt of anticipation saying the words, or maybe it was whatever passed for alcohol in the eleret taking effect.

Lira's eyes widened. "Not possible. Those are theoretical."

"Not on our boat. Of course, I have no idea if it works."

"It functions properly," Dyson said. "Though I caution its use as a last resort."

"I'd use it for a first resort," Tag said. "Why bother with a complex route inside when we can smash and grab from the top, by going completely invisible to not only sensors but biological eyes, too?"

"My way is quieter and leaves you two in a position to back me up." Lira folded her arms. Her glass was empty. How'd he miss her draining it?

"I think you're forgetting you're not in charge."

"I think you're forgetting neither are you."

Dyson continued perusing his data. He didn't say anything to either of them. Tag cleared his throat.

"As I stated aboard *Confiance*, I am the TI operative and thusly should be in command of this operation." Dyson's tone was the same, but the words came out faster, clipped. "Your insistence reduced said role to a partnership with a carbon. So, I will simply say Ms. Reen's option makes the most sense, and I offer my support for it."

Tag nearly missed the last portion of his statement, because one word stayed on his sensors. "Carbon?"

Dyson deactivated the data. He faced Tag, hands set on his knees. "It is the emotional equivalent of your ''bot' usage."

"You pile of parts," Tag growled. "We almost got ourselves killed in a sabotaged starfighter because of this stupid mission! I was perfectly happy vaporizing Naplians and defending Terran space, but no! We have to go traipsing off into backwater stars for a bunch of info—we don't even know what it says!—to convince a people who don't want to go to war that they should do it."

"Your temper is a liability to this mission," Dyson said. "If necessary, I will remove you from it."

"Just like your kind removed my kin?" Tag dropped his glass. The last half of his eleret splatted on the cream carpet. He stood up. "Come on and remove me."

"Boys, please, you're being ridiculous." Lira was in front of him. She pressed a hand to his chest and smiled. "Tag, you're rightly upset someone apparently tried to kill you."

"A fact Pallas representatives have yet to conclusively prove," Dyson said. "Though I have to say the odds of such a catastrophic systems failure occurring on a starfighter as advanced as the Sunsaber are extremely low."

"And Dyson, you are, of course, being very cautious about what is a sensitive intelligence operation."

Whether it was her hand warming him, or the eleret, or some combination with her voice, Tag's ire subsided.

"Let's try this—we'll approach Iriada tonight, and we'll both get up to the skyhook. Have ourselves a look around." She winked at Tag. "With some modifications to our attire, of course. Dyson?"

The android made a face, as if he were processing that question harder than the rest. Tag hoped he froze a relay. "I have brought along the necessary equipment to make significant identity alterations, though they were not my first choice."

"I believe we've moved on from that."

"Very well. I assume you are eager to investigate because of the reception planned for this evening?"

"Correct."

"Reception?" Tag frowned. "You want to go to a party?"

"One available to all staff and guests of Iriada," Lira said. "And one to which we can gain entry, if Dyson's skills are up to par."

"The collar pin which you appropriated will not be difficult to modify. As for the identity alterations ..." Dyson made eye contact with Tag. "What is your opinion of felines?"

"Felines."

"Some humans have a deep-seated resentment of the species."

Tag shrugged. "Never had a cat before."

Dyson nodded. "Then you should adapt well."

As soon as he showed off the specifications, Tag wished he'd said the opposite.

***

Admiral Erassia took in the losses among the *ziurathal* with three-fingered hands clasped behind his back. The stench of machine oils, burnt plastics, and dried blood suffused the air in the company's barracks off *Fulnax*'s hangar bay. There was no talking, no jibes, no arguments or chuckling; the only sounds were the hiss of plasma torches as they reinforced armor plating or cut apart damaged segments.

Erassia kept his single, unyielding eye fixed on the scene. The remnants of his once-proud strike force—battered, beaten, minus two dozen dead and wounded. And the serjaum depot they'd fought the Truppen for in enemy hands. By most accounts, a failure. One he planned to keep as far from Admiral Daviont's eye as possible.

Yet, the *ziurathal* killed or damaged two score of the Devastators. Never before in one-to-one combat had this been achieved. Not even the armored units with their tanks and their mechs had managed to inflict such pain.

Perhaps the Ascended Masters were pleased with his votive, after all.

Major Gandraad was himself bloodied. His eye was swollen, black and purple flesh squeezing its sides, and his neck stained dark yellow from a cut the medics had already sealed. He stood stiffly by his mech, the machine as scarred as its rider. "Admiral, we failed."

"Nonsense. You took more Devastators than you lost. Name to me one unit of soldiers in this war who has accomplished the same." Erassia paused and pivoted so he might meet the somber gazes of all assembled. "None. You've achieved a great triumph. Our comrades gave up their lives to secure it, so the *ziura* might be turned away."

He received no cheers, only weary nods and a few scattered grins. Their bravado was tempered by bloodshed and death. Erassia considered it a valuable lesson. He had many more *ziurathal* in production, and countless loyal Ffawe training to operate them. The remnants of the first company were now his veterans, the ones who had faced the Truppen eyes front. They would be the diamond core of his forces.

First, though, he had to strike a greater blow at the *ziura*. He had to find the one who caused the greatest turmoil among Naplian forces than had been ever seen.

The cursed human *maranat*.

Erassia gestured to Gandraad to follow him. They walked among the bustle of the starfighters and their deck crews. Weapons were recharged, planes refueled, new missiles primed and loaded. Erassia kept his head near to Gandraad so they could hear each other above the steady drumbeat of activity. "The trans-light pulse. Were you able to secure it?"

"Yes, Admiral. I hid it myself, among the serjaum containers at the camp, per your orders."

"I take it the technicians found a way around the difficulty of it possibly being discarded."

"The nanites are programmed to leave the container in search of metals with the same composition as Truppen armor, and once there form the trans-light pulse."

"Good. Any indication the enemy is aware of its presence?" Gandraad shook his head.

"Then we're receiving a clear signal."

"Intermittent, sir, but yes—it continues to move as if it were in transit. Our estimate is the vessel aboard which it's secreted has made several combat jumps."

"Very good. As soon as they cease their movements, triangulate a destination. Meanwhile I will give orders for our squadron to travel along the route already taken."

"Yes, Admiral."

Erassia stopped by a Jarra Fol starfighter. He ran his long fingers down a curved forewing. The plane reminded him of a double-edged blade, one used for fending off multiple enemies. He was pleased to see a half-dozen blue circles painted underneath the canopy seam. The pilot had made ace status, in killing six Terran opponents. "Tell me, Major. Did you see him there? The Consul."

Gandraad stared off at the bulkhead. His mouth was pressed shut in a tiny, thin line, a comforting sight compared to the huge, gaping maw of humankind. Erassia pushed the image from his mind, disgusted at the two-eyed vermin. It took him a moment to realize Gandraad had not answered his question.

"Major? Respond."

"Apologies, Admiral. I … I thought I would react with more ferocity, more bravery, when I saw the one called Consul Selva."

A shudder made Erassia's neck twitch. "Continue."

"He is just as our Denic spies indicated, and as the records of the Baedecker victory tell us—a valiant, reckless fighter with the blood of many Ffawe on his claws. He and his companion faced even the *ziurathal* without fear, attacking as a pair, lacking support." Gandraad straightened his neck even longer. "I have word at least two of our squads fled at his appearance, not wishing to be eternally damned if he were to slay them."

"This is not some *yirian* demon of the old myths," Erassia said. "This is a human vermin, a *shirish*, bearing the same two-eyed weaknesses of its species. Don't forget how they abandoned their planet to our rule, and how we've pushed them back from their frontiers with each passing week."

Gandraad nodded, but Erassia sensed his hesitation, his lack of complete agreement—and couldn't blame the younger officer. Daviont's incursion had cost the Fleet dozens of warships and thousands of Ffawe souls. There was talk the emperors considered sacking him—or worse—if the serjaum supply that cost so much blood to secure ever dried up. Small wonder Daviont had pressed Erassia to hold the lines through the Great Desert Rift.

Despite casting the humans as cowardly, he knew better. And so did Erassia. But talking about the enemy's bravery, their willingness to throw themselves at overwhelming forces in hopes of saving their companions, was not the best way to improve morale.

"Elden Selva was a human man, one who was an enemy of the very government we fight," Erassia continued.

"Word is, he was *maranat*," Gandraad said. "He knew our custom and followed it. Even the magistrates at Baedecker Four approved.

Doesn't that mean he fulfils the prophecy of the Devastators? That they are the ones who will bring down the empire?"

"Enough!" Erassia snapped. "You keep such traitorous thoughts confined to your darkest dreams, or I'll likewise keep you confined to a brig to face court-martial."

Gandraad did not back down. "Isn't it true, sir, that the *ziura* would have wiped out our ground forces if they hadn't withdrawn?"

"No." Not if I had been there, in command. No disrespect to Admiral Daviont—Erassia would never speak ill of him. But it didn't mean he didn't find fault with the man's strategy, or his trust in General Falloram, reportedly the ground forces commander. Falloram was an idiot; oppressing the populace only to create an armed insurrection and draw the ire of the *ziura*.

Erassia would have turned the city to slag from orbit and been done with it. "Our men let fear weaken them. They shied from their duty and closed their eye to victory. Not us."

"Yes, sir." Gandraad nodded.

"We will trace Selva and his Truppen across every system in the Great Desert Rift if we have to and search every rock from here to conquered Audrian space. When we find his forces—all of them—you and the *ziurathal* will be ready for him. We will win this war."

"Admiral, I believe it, but … how?"

Erassia waved his hand back towards the assembled mechs and their crews. "The same way you kill the sailserpent that has crawled into your boat and latched onto your leg—you cut off its head."

***

Three years ago, Elden would have found Admiral Ergen's presence intimidating. His bulk and his height no doubt helped him maintain a physical dominion over his forces. Elden had yet to meet any Briddarri who matched him, even among the armored soldiers.

Standing there receiving his verbal abuse while in Truppen form, however, it was all Elden could do to hold back laughter.

"Leave? I don't remember approving any blasted requests for a holiday!" Ergen puffed acrid blue smoke from a cigar he was rapidly chewing into oblivion. "In case your sensors are malfunctioning, this is a war, not a pleasure cruise."

"What I'm proposing is nothing of the sort." Elden hated being here. His plan had turned out to have spectacularly bad timing. No sooner had the Truppen boarded *Hessian* and plotted a course out of the system of their last raid than *Winter Scourge* had jumped into the system. There was no option but to board and converse with Ergen once he was informed of Elden's outward-bound trajectory.

For one thing, he wasn't entirely sure the admiral wouldn't shoot him out of space.

"Like a sun's core it is," Ergen grumbled. "You want to leave my fleet without its primary strike team, all for the sake of some hunch."

"This isn't a hunch. I have scores of men missing."

"No. You have casualties. If they're gone, it's either because the One-eyes got them, or their jump drive computers miscalculated and dumped them down a singularity." Ergen took a long draw from his cigar stub, blew the smoke out across Elden's office, then smashed it against the bulkhead. A skitter 'bot appeared underfoot, sucking up the embers and ashes from the deck. "Face it, Consul: this happens in war."

"No one has proven these men have died," Elden said. "I am searching for them."

"Not without leave."

"I do not require your leave, Admiral." This argument again. Fine. He would have it, but not for long. "*Hessian* is prepared to depart. Our jump coordinates are set."

"And what coordinates would those be?"

Elden didn't look at Rett, who stood halfway between them, but sent him a link. <Keep your vocalizer off.> "For purposes of operational security, they will remain undisclosed. I'm sure you understand."

Ergen jabbed a finger at him. "Understand this, Consul. The brass isn't as patient as I am. They're not going to let you continue freelance. Eventually you'll sign on to our chain of command."

"Like stars we will," Goetz muttered. "We'd take rank from the Terrans first."

"Why? Because you were human?" Ergen chuckled. "Please. The Terrans are as scared of you as the Naplians—possibly more, because they fought a long war against Truppen soldiers. No, I take that back.

They're not as scared as the Naplians, because they actually beat you. Ground down your defenses and forced you to surrender."

Goetz took a step forward, clawed foot scraping the metal deck plates, but Elden stopped him with a hand to the chest. He knew what Ergen was attempting—guilt. Too bad for him the leader of the Truppen was already consumed by a different kind of guilt, the kind accrued from too many times failing his men.

"We're leaving formation, Admiral," Elden said. "We'll meet up with you when this mission is complete, but not a microsecond sooner. I'll not abandon loyal Truppen to the depths of space. One way or another, I will determine their fates. Is that clear?"

Ergen's face flushed a deeper green. Elden could hear his teeth grinding, and his sensors recorded an alarming spike in both blood pressure and heart rate. It took the admiral a few moments to calm himself. "All right, you do that. Go out there and waste your fuel on men who are dead. I'm sure we can muddle along without our vaunted Truppen warriors for a few weeks, or more. We can always call in your pal General Baessler if we get in a pinch."

Elden doubted Erich Baessler would come running with his cruisers if Ergen whistled. "I understood *Prinz Eitel* was at least a month from our current position."

"Could be. That was a while ago. Coordinates I had put her nearer, on a classified action against the Naplians' supply routes." Ergen grinned. "Sorry, but I can't share those with you. Operational security."

***

Enough of this. "Admiral, I believe our conference is concluded. Goetz, please escort our guest to the airlock." Elden manipulated the brightness level of his optical ports, making them gleam. "The one connected to his ship, you understand."

"Sure do, Consul." Goetz poked Ergen in the side of his arm with a claw. "After you, Admiral."

Ergen glared at them, his look lingering longest on Rett. "Keep in mind where your allegiance lies, Consul—and you too, Lind."

"Of course, sir, yes, sir." Rett saluted, his clawed hand banging off his headpiece with a *clunk*.

Ergen stormed through the hatch, Briddarri curses ringing off the corridor quite some time after he'd departed, with Goetz on his six.

Rett sagged. "That went well."

"Admiral Ergen did have a point." Elden leaned in close to Rett and let his targeting sensors settle on the former Briddarri spy—an action Rett's systems would definitely register. "About allegiances. We should all be aware of ours."

Rett's headpiece bobbed.

"Join me on the bridge," Elden said. "For the jump and whatever lies beyond."

***

The jump took them to what was actually the first of several waypoints, stretching over the intervening parsecs and four days. After six stops in odd places—a radiation-free corridor of a nebula, the blazing hot edges of a double star's coronae, the swirling rings of a gas giant that would make something like Saturn seem a tiny pebble —*Hessian* jumped to the fifth orbit of a cool dwarf star.

Hessian ripwaved in, taking ten hours to cover the distance. The outer system was empty of debris, except for errant cometary fragments. "Scans show only three planets," Goetz said. "The giant with eight moons we saw on the way in, a sun-blasted rock that's probably close to melting, and a habitable world."

"How habitable?" At this distance, the planet was a brown disc the size of a coin. Its sun wasn't much more than a dull red ember.

"Barely. But it's got metallic readings off the charts. Indications of heavy mining activity in both hemispheres, most of it automated."

"Orbital traffic?"

"None to speak of. Handful of communications and weather-scanning satellites ..." Goetz expanded a readout near the planet's lone moon. A spread of red dots grew larger, until they filled an area a meter across. "Debris field."

"Get as much detail on it as you can. Launch a probe if you have to. Ripwave us in closer." Elden faced Rett. "Well? Any more information you can share with us?"

Rett shrugged. "I don't know anything except these coordinates were the ones Admiral Ergen had in his databanks. He could have noticed my entry—he could have altered them after the fact."

"Ergen doesn't strike me as being that clever," Elden said. "Give me a hailing signal to the surface."

Rett complied, and the link came alive in Elden's displays. "This is Consul Elden Selva of the transport vessel *Hessian*, to any inhabitants of the planet below. Please respond. We are on a search and retrieval mission. Any information you have for us could be helpful."

Silence over the link. "Getting some comm activity on the surface," Rett said. "Coded. Looks pretty high-grade ... and Terran. Definitely military origin. Hey, this is the same stuff I saw the Colonial Defense using on Baedecker."

That made Elden pause before he could repeat his message. What would CDF be doing out this far? There was nothing of strategic value. Neither the Naplians nor the Grand Alliance had laid claim to the system. There had been no recorded battles.

Unless the mining concerns had turned up something valuable, and the debris near the moon was a silent testament to a recent scuffle.

"Sir, whatever craft was destroyed was definitely one of ours," Goetz said. "Prelim metallurgy dropped enough hints—she's of Northern Alliance manufacture, probably on a frame bought off the Reittians. But I'm getting results on more than one vessel. See this trail? Definitely from a Naplian destroyer."

"Bring us into a broad orbit," Elden said. "Prep countermeasures. Shields charged and angled for deflection and maximum absorption."

"Energy surge!" Rett said. "Three of them, twenty klicks from the largest settlement! I've got incoming projectiles accelerating at— blast, they're cruising!"

"Evasive maneuvers!" Elden snapped. "Track and fire!"

Red lines stabbed out from the hologram of the planet. Each one was a track of hypervelocity projectiles, swarms capable of piercing the toughest hulls. Elden was sure *Hessian*'s shields could deflect them, and her armor was up to par with most warships, thanks to a Briddarri upgrade. But he felt much more at ease when *Hessian* moved clear. Goetz had the helmsmen trained well.

The pair of Truppen at the firing consoles bracketed each swarm with particle cannon. White flashes streaked across the hologram, immolating the projectiles. Fewer than a handful made it through the barrage, the remnants barreling onward to the outer edges of the solar system, where they'd drift forever.

"Surface installation, this is *Hessian*," Elden said. "Do not fire again or you will be fired upon. We have bombardment weaponry capable of destroying your ground turrets."

Goetz gave him a mechanical thumbs-up.

"Signal your response. We seek only information and have not come to do battle—"

"Elden Selva. I should have guessed you'd show up here, eventually." The voice was garbled by software meant to disguise identity, though Elden was reminded of the raspy Audrian speech. "We'll allow you to land a shuttle with six men, no more. Follow the coordinates we're sending. And refrain from trans-light calls. You're being monitored."

"Novafire," Goetz muttered.

The sensor board lit up with contacts, up until then hidden between the debris. Armed pickets, automated drone ships sitting quietly in the vacuum. *Hessian* informed Elden that each of the six vessels was armed with a dozen medium-range torpedoes and a handful of long-range torpedoes, not to mention a Naplian energy cannon and CDF-issue railgun.

Who in sun's glare were these people?

"We accept. *Hessian* out." Elden killed the transmission and stored the coordinates as they flowed in from whomever was sending planetside. "Goetz, Rett, you're with me."

"I knew he was going to say that," Rett muttered.

***

No one shot at them, scanned them, or otherwise accosted them on the flight down. The sky was burnished as if in perpetual sunset, even though the system's star was high overhead. It was probably twice the size Elden would have expected.

"Welcoming party," Goetz said.

True to his understated nature, Goetz made it seem as if a mining foreman and a handful of techs were waiting at the edge of a jet-blasted circle of brown stone. Instead, hundreds of people thronged, all of them armed—even the handful of youth Elden spotted, who barely topped the adults' shoulders. Most were dark-skinned humans, though a handful of Audrians were mixed in, oval eyes closed to tiny slits to protect against the dust kicked aloft by the lander's arrival.

There were also four mechs arrayed around the zone, one at each corner.

When they disembarked, Elden's sensors revealed the mechs were actually old CDF jump armor, reconfigured as autonomous units. Each was painted some mix of gray and white and brown, with an unfamiliar emblem on their arms—black stripes on a red band. A trio of human men, each topping two meters, stood in the Truppens' path.

The leader was tall, clean-shaven, with dark hair transitioning to gray. He wore a red shirt with bare shoulders. His vest was midnight black, and his trousers a digital camouflage pattern matching the surrounding terrain.

He held a Naplian Furta energy rifle. So did a few other people, but Elden also cataloged CDF issue rifles, most notable M36s. Brand new, still bearing packing labels, and gleaming freshly cleaned. Several men behind him had Naplian combat armor strapped to their chests, queued up to the standard mottled blue hue the armor took on when not adapting to the visible environment.

And humans weren't the only creatures bristling for a fight. Four dogs flanked the man, their barks approaching fever pitch. Goetz muttered something about <fleas> through the shared link. Elden's databases dutifully identified two border collies, an elkhound, and a red heeler, none of whom seemed fond of Truppen.

"Scout! Ace! Star! Smokey!" The leader snapped off their names like a drill sergeant calling his soldiers to attention. It had the intended effect, because the dogs lapsed into muffled growling. "Never mind them. State your business, 'bot."

"I believe I already did," Elden said. "When we spoke in orbit. You are in command here, I take it?"

The tall guardian smirked. "Dave Nolte, FFEG Mining. I'm the elected representative to offworlders, but I am not in command. You want her." He jerked a thumb over his shoulder.

The crowd made an aisle neatly ordered enough for royalty, admitting a slender woman who strode toward them with a dark brown cloak flowing in the breeze. Auburn hair slid across her face and shoulders, but she paid it no mind. She wore black boots, the same camouflaged trousers, and a stained, forest green work shirt. The M36 slung over her shoulder was as new as the rest held by the crowd, as was the pair of Ubinth DK-40 pistols secured in waist holsters. Bits of armor, black and white, were cobbled together over her outfit. Too late, Elden realized many in the crowd had the same armor. Then he recognized its source.

It was all CDF leftovers.

The woman's beauty left him speechless. It had, for more than a decade. Without consciously commanding it, Elden called up a memory from three years prior: his clawed fingers gently touching her cheek.

"Elden Selva." Marney Wester smiled, blue eyes the brightest color amongst the assembled. Freckles bunched up across her cheeks. "Welcome to one of my worlds."

CHAPTER EIGHT

The mining settlement was a crude affair. The largest buildings were constructed from deep space shipping containers, long boxes with rounded edges half buried in the dirt. Ratty scrub grass, every blade sickly yellow and spotted brown, crept up the sides.

Marney led their contingent into one of the containers, a dark gray one five rows back from the landing area and two columns from the center of the settlement. Other than the chipped paint proclaiming its origin as a Molnsa trade unit, it looked identical to its neighbors.

Inside, though, was a veritable military command center.

Three holographic displays lit the interior with the same ambiance as a VR theater. Eight men and women were crowded around the consoles, reviewing streams of data falling as constantly as the rain that Elden thought the arid planet needed. All wore the same red shirts as the leader, minus the vest. Weapons were stacked in the corners—SAAR railguns, SMGs, M36s, an array of pistols from dozens of manufacturers, and a row of Naplian guns.

Goetz prodded a metal chair with his foot. It squeaked and tipped sideways against the rippled metal wall. "Nice décor. For folks who got the latest and greatest weapons they left something out of that part of the budget."

"I highly doubt they purchased all these weapons of their own accord." Elden stood amidst the arrays, his feeds absorbing all the incoming information. Yes, they definitely had all approaches to the planet well-covered by observation satellites and dormant drones.

"Maybe you'd better ask your girlfriend."

Elden would have ripped the arms from any other Truppen who dared speak to him that way, but this was Goetz. He knew Elden as well as anyone alive—so to speak. And he would come closest to knowing what was on Elden's mind right now.

"Do we have anything else in orbit, Dave?" Marney looped her

M36 over the back of a chair and sat down. She pulled a brush from her camouflaged fatigues and ran it through her hair.

"Not a thing, besides their gigantic transport." Nolte stood before the hologram of the solar system, arms crossed, eyes locked on every motion of every object in view. "We'll keep watch for a spell."

Marney sighed. She must have caught Elden watching her, because she favored him with an impish smile. "It's a small luxury for a place like this. You wouldn't believe how the briars underfoot get stuck in a lady's hair."

"Mine's too short." Nolte ran a hand through his hairline and smirked.

Marney laughed. There was the sound, ringing clear as a bell, that flooded Elden with more memories than he could bear.

He locked them as deep in his storage as he could manage.

"So you say you're on a search and rescue," Marney said. "I have to say, there's been an assortment of starship activity over the past couple of months—hence our rather rude response. Sorry about that, Eldi."

"No apology needed," Elden said.

"Speak for yourself," Rett muttered.

His headpiece rang with the impact of Goetz's backhand.

"I assumed the people here were protecting their settlement against a potential threat," Elden continued, "though I was surprised by the degree to which they're equipped."

"I've done the best I could."

"You did all this?"

Marney nodded. Gone was the cheery, beaming young woman adorned in her wedding dress, waiting for her handsome Navy officer to whisk her to the altar. No, this Marney was tougher—her face showed the wear of deprivation, lack of sleep and probably lack of food, and her bearing was guarded. Yet, the mischievousness he'd come to love shone in her expression.

"Pretty blasted impressive," Goetz said.

"Thank you. I'm afraid I can't be much help, Eldi, when it comes to your lost friends."

"Comrades." Elden perched on the edge of a console, taking care not to crush its surface.

He rested his hands on the edge, amused at how much of his biological habits cropped up when he wasn't paying attention. "We scanned debris in your orbit that likely came from a Truppen ship."

Marney shrugged. "Truppen, Naplian, Audrian, Briddarri, Reittian—we've seen everything come through this way. The last two Naplian ships attempted to annex this planet for its mineral resources. There's precious few asteroids in the system, and all the heavy metals appear to be concentrated on one world." She tapped her boots against the floor. "You're standing on the proverbial motherlode, Eldi. But I've made it possible for the people here to protect themselves."

"One would think the CDF and Briddarri would be willing to invest their forces to protect such a valuable resource."

"Oh, would they? I asked our dear elected representatives the very same question and had infuriating conversations with military commanders. Their answers were the same: whatever mineral wealth this planet contains isn't enough to outweigh the cost of forces needed to hold it this deep in the Rift." Marney tucked the brush away. Her hair was burnished like fire under the holos' glow. "The people here had no one to protect them. So, I did what I've done on five other worlds: I gave them a chance."

"You keep saying this world," Goetz said. "What's its name?"

"I won't say it. Keeping it off my lips helps me not betray their location." Marney smiled again. "The local name means 'Flower in the Dark.'"

Elden found it poetic. Of course, he was preoccupied trying not to focus his optical sensors on her lips after she spoke the word. Steady, Elden. You're a cyborg now—and she's a married woman. "What does your husband have to say about this?"

Some of the bravado dissipated from her posture, and she twisted the end of her hair with a finger. "Tim ... he wouldn't understand. I told him about relief work that can make a difference in people's lives. He found it quite noble."

"I guess you could classify this as relief," Elden said, "though I'm curious how you came across such an assortment of heavy weaponry. I certainly haven't heard of any major incursions into this region by allied forces."

"Of course you haven't. Image how it would look for Father, if his daughter were known to be collaborating with aliens, criminals, and worse—Reittians—to buy weaponry for planets whose populations the CDF and Briddarri deem unimportant. My father is a resourceful man.

"Antiny Wester is a respectable administrator with myriad business contacts—but he also keeps quiet contacts with the less desirable segments of the galactic population. He passed me what he could, without drawing suspicion to himself, because he sympathized with my cause even if he couldn't outwardly support it."

"What kind of cause?" Rett scraped a claw down the wall. Paint flakes swirled. "This place is kind of a dump, even if it's well armed."

Marney rose from her chair. She put a hand on Nolte's shoulder, and the other on the arm of a woman seated at a portable communications array. "This is their home. This is why I'm here. I lost my home—the house in which I lived, the world I loved, the people I cared for.

Everything that made Baedecker Four what it was, has been taken away. We're all refugees now, and yes, many have settled elsewhere, or signed up for CDF service, but it doesn't change what happened. Well, I decided it wouldn't happen to anyone else. No one should have to become a casualty in a war not of their choosing. Anyone who comes near one of the worlds I've armed will find out the hard way."

Rett whistled, a low-pitched mechanical trill.

Again, Elden wished he could smile. What an asset to the Northern Alliance Marney would have been. He was more proud of her than he'd been of anyone in recent years. If only Governor Wester could see her in action. This was Marney's legacy. "You have my word, we will keep your efforts a secret, and do what we can to minimize enemy infiltration."

Marney stepped toward him and gazed up at his face. He couldn't detect any signs of revulsion; a quick bioscan confirmed she was exuding all the vitals of a happy person, without fear or anxiety in his presence. If he could have prayed for any single blessing, as old Abbott Jeopar had urged him, it would be this. "You're doing it, you know. Tilting your head, tipping your chin, Eldi."

Elden corrected the position of his headpiece so fast metal

clicked. Her soft chuckle simultaneously soothed and vexed him.

Something suspiciously like a Saarno fox's chortle echoed from behind him. Elden speared Goetz with an accusatory stare.

Goetz remained stiffly at attention.

"I have an idea about your missing Truppen," Marney said. "Dave, run back those scans from the past month. You know what I'm looking for—the anomalies."

"Check, Marney." Nolte manipulated the streams of data, hands waving with such rhythm Elden wondered if the bruiser had ever considered a musical conductor's career. "Got one. That was easy."

Goetz moved closer. "Time index matches a slice of the duration of Diaz's mission."

"It does indeed," Elden said. "What anomalies were you thinking of?"

"They were sensor glitches, and they made no sense." A red mark flashed on the scan readout. Marney stabbed a finger into the light display, freezing the image. "This, I believe, was your Truppen ship, though without your confirmation we had no way to determine. Eldi, could you …?"

Elden transferred the data from Goetz's scans to the console. Nolte swiped the new information into a stream and overlaid it on what he had.

"Confirmed," Nolte said. "It was the same ship." Goetz swore. "What was Diaz doing out here?"

"It was at least two parsecs from the transit points he was supposed to use," Elden said. "Something drew him out this way—or he was pursued."

"Here is the difficulty," Marney said. "The scans warp and distort for the next several hours. Dave has hazy readings that indicate another ship, but nothing conclusive."

"We do have a vector," Nolte said. "A possible trajectory. Problem: goes right through the Coalbin Front."

It was Elden's turn to swear.

"Weird name for a stellar formation," Rett said. "There's really coal out there?"

"No. Dark nebulae. Recent intelligence points to Reittian forces tangling with Naplians along a pair of sectors, with neither side budging. It's hotly contested." Elden shook his head. "I can't risk flying *Hessian* straight into a war zone without escort."

"Admiral Ergen's task force would be more than plenty to help us out, right?" Rett said.

"Not going to him for handouts," Goetz snapped. "Right, Consul?"

"You are correct, Goetz."

Marney frowned. "I do have a solution, but you'd have to bring a limited contingent. The transport we landed here is built for speed, and stealth. It can get us into the contested territory, and once there —well, I have a contact who's more than willing to do me a favor."

"Who, a gunrunner?" Rett snorted.

"No. A Reittian warship captain."

Elden finally let loose a laugh, not caring about its grating sound through his mechanical body's speaker. "Marney Wester, if there ever comes a day when you do not surprise me, I'm sure it will be when the galaxy collapses into a black hole."

Marney grinned, and Elden was reminded for a second of her brother. "Let's pray the day never arrives."

"I'll ready the ship for launch," Nolte said, heading for the door.

"You? But what about your people?" Elden asked.

"There's more than just people here. My wife Nancy runs the hydroponics shop and my daughter Tegan's working shifts in the comms station—only one who knows the Tessali language, if you can believe it. They can do without me for a spell." Nolte shook his head. "Besides, how do you think Marney wound up here? I'm her pilot."

***

Tag had several ideas in mind when Lira had said she needed different attire for their break-in—that didn't sound good, maybe he should term it "covert access"—to the Iriada skyhook. None of them involved the dress she now wore.

It was a deep, sapphire blue, with strands of sparkling material woven into the sides and flanks. Shined a great deal, and he swore there was a glow to it, maybe luminescent fiber from the moon-trees of Ryu-Talbot Six. He knew they were popular across this quarter of the galaxy.

The blue was even more stunning considering her hair was bound up short and re-colored white, and her skin blanched gray. A feline pattern of stripes reached up from the deep neckline, framing her throat and reaching behind her ears.

"Delianite female markings." Dyson's voice in Tag's ear was as unobtrusive as if the 'bot stood right next to him. "They are an insular species who live near the galactic center; however, this century is one of the few in which they have made greater contact with the empires of this region."

"Handy." Yeah, Lira's face definitely had a catlike appearance, right down to the piercing gold eyes with slit irises. "You're sure this will work?"

"Lira's access pin which she ... appropriated from the Iriada representative was sufficient enough to let her into their rooms at the expo. With the modifications I have made it is keyed to her false identity as Li'Raya'Faraya'Shi, a Delianite information specialist. Fortunately, the real Faraya'Shi is not due to arrive for two more days."

Tag nodded. The base of the Iriada skyhook hunkered in the darkness, a huge dome cast into a gold glow by the evening streetlights of Atterissage. Guards in standard police body armor, similar to the kind he'd seen on Colonial Police, were interposed around the perimeter fence. Sensor posts flashed orange at ten-meter intervals. A pair of Argus Omega guard robots rumbled inside the fence, triangular tread assemblies crunching across the paving.

"Let me speak with the guards, and for that matter, anyone else we encounter." Lira's voice had a definite purr behind the words.

"Why, you afraid I'll foul up your clever approach?"

She smiled. "No. As Ta'Grion'Faraya'Garr, you're one of my many concubines. You're forbidden by Delianite custom to speak with alien species when in my presence."

Tag grumbled and was surprised when the sound came out like a cat's throaty growl. Of course, he'd been altered, too—same coloration as Lira, a shade darker and more stripes. They rippled up and down his bare arms. His outfit was a simple, sleeveless brown tunic with matching brown trousers and shoes.

"Determine the location of the crystal lattice storage," Dyson said. "If you can obtain the module without detection, do so and return to the extraction point. I will stand by."

"Okay, sounds good, but be advised I'm not going to keep muttering to you." They were only thirty meters from the entrance, under the pulsing Iriada logo. One of the Argus Omegas stopped by the hatch. "Might make them suspicious."

"Point taken."

Lira walked right up to the human guard standing by the robot. "Good evening. I'm here at the behest of the Board of Directors."

The guard had a visor fixed over his face, hiding one eye behind a sensor module. He looked Lira up and down; Tag couldn't blame the guy. She was gorgeous.

Of course, then he did the same to Tag, so it must have been more of a scan than an appreciative perusal.

"The reception is on Level Six, Quadrant Two. The greenhouse." The guard frowned. "Need your identification."

"Certainly." Lira held out her arm. A bracelet of twin platinum rings spun around a black band, held aloft by a tiny anti-gravity suspender. Rubies—well, they were shiny red jewels—glittered on each ring. The Iriada pin she'd lifted was affixed to the black band.

The guard's sensor unit beeped. "Yes, ma'am, it checks out, but I'll need a DNA swipe to confirm against our registry. We've had a security issue and need to take precautions."

Novafire. Tag had wondered when Lira's theft of the pin would come back to hit them in the aft quarter. To her credit, her smile never wavered. "Oh, you boys and your *security*. Am I really so threatening?"

That got a grin out of the guard, one he had to work hard to suppress. "Ahem. Well, ma'am, as I say ... you know, it's not as big a deal as it seems."

"I'm only teasing." Lira plucked a hair and held it by the tips of her fingers. "All yours."

The guard took the hair in gloved fingers, still grinning. He used the same scanner; this time the results took longer. Tag held his breath the entire time. How long could Delianites do the same?

The guard nodded. "Okay, identity confirmed, Ms. Faraya'Shi. Now for your partner—"

Before Tag could even calculate how to get out of this mess, Lira shook her head and laughed. "No! My word, human, it's forbidden. He's one of my *rowai*—a servant to my bed and my body. What need do you have of his DNA? I can confirm everything you want to know."

"Oh. Right." The guard's eye went wide. "One of."

Lira stood nearly nose-to-nose with him. Her smile—and the pheromones wafting through the air—were intoxicating. Tag found it harder to concentrate than if he'd taken an EMP to his starfighter's systems and was hurtling through space without a nav screen. "There's always room for more, should one desire a career change."

"You're good to pass." The guard stepped out of the way, his face crimson. "Enjoy the evening."

***

Tag didn't relax until the cable car was halfway up the nano-construct wire, and he could see world below and stars above.

"You've got the scanner." Lira leaned in close to his ear when she said it.

Tag kept his expression studiously neutral. "Yeah. Getting away from the crowds will be difficult if we find the crystal."

"Leave that to me."

"So, what, I'm just here to look good?"

"Yes, and you're quite handsome as a Delianite."

Tag grinned. "Not as good as when I'm human."

Lira rolled her eyes, but there was still a smile on her lips.

The cable car was utilitarian, gray and white metals and plastics with two plas-glass ovals allowing a breathtaking view of their ride up to space. Lounge chairs of red fabric were arrayed in four rows of five. Straps as complex as any fighter cockpit were available in case of emergency.

A few minutes later, a chime sounded. The other passengers, of whom there were ten, got into their straps, so Tag followed suit. He was about to ask Lira what the deal was when something shot by their windows, a great gray lump, hurtling so fast the cabin vibrated like a badly balanced thruster. The thrumming subsided, and the chime sounded again. Off came the straps.

"Passing cable car," Lira explained. "There are actually two cables connecting each skyhook to the ground."

"Really? Huh. Missed that."

Lira tapped her ear. "Dyson's just a font of information."

"Yeah. He's great."

He must have put too much sour in his tone, because Lira asked, "Is that why you despise him? His general boringness?"

"Never said I hated him."

"You don't have to. If it was any worse, you'd have stripped him for spare parts to fix some of the more rattling bits of *Olivia Vy*."

Tag scratched at the edge of his seat. "Let's say his people and mine don't have a history of getting along. Leave it at that."

"If you insist ..."

"I said, leave it."

She shut down on him after that, cold as a comet, but turned on the charm for everyone else as soon as they disembarked. They followed a stream of guests down tan corridors lined with white tile, bathed in warm white light. Spiky russet ferns swayed in the breeze from life support vents. Serving robots rolled through the clusters on unicycle wheels, offering up a pale drink with amber swirls. Tag took one—only after Lira permitted it. After all, he was just a *rowai*. Not bad. Tasted like the local beers brewed in Vossberg City, without the bitter aftertaste of the stuff illicitly stowed aboard *Confiance* and other Navy cruisers.

The greenhouse took up the entire second quadrant on Level Six. A long, narrow viewport let the guests bask in the starscape, with thousands of different plants in bloom all around them. Tag had never seen so much greenery in one place, not even when he'd overflown a tropical rainforest in an unnamed system looking for Naplian weapons depots. The smell was heady to the point of almost being intoxicating.

Lira led them through the mingled guests, fully half of whom wore Iriada pendants or pins on their formal attire. She flattered the women about their looks and laughed at the men's jokes, seeming fully at ease in the social strata.

Tag, on the other hand, stayed stiffly obedient. He was supposed to be her plaything, seen but not heard. Wasn't easy for someone as used to voicing his opinion as he was.

"Scans confirm the presence of the radiation signature." Tag expected to see Dyson standing right behind him. "Three hundred meters behind you. I am overlaying the map of the facility."

A glowing wireframe layout of the Iriada skyhook appeared in Tag's vision, floating before him. It was so tangible he was sure someone would comment. But it was only a projection produced by the lenses he wore over his eyes, the same lenses that made him look like a Delianite.

"Do you have the location?"

A man nearby chuckled at something Lira said. *"Mm-hmm,"* Tag murmured. "I have informed Ms. Reen as well."

Lira looped her arm through Tag's. *"Rowai,* come with me. I need to see more of this magnificent jewel in space."

Together they followed a side corridor away from the greenhouse, past several lounges where couples and large groups ate, drank, and caroused. Tag grabbed a pair of glasses from a robot server as it rolled by. "Magnificent jewel in space? Wow. You're sure playing their game well."

"Please. What you call 'playing their game' I call casing my environment." She smiled. "I've already seen a handful of jewelry I would well make my own this evening."

"Maybe lay off in pickpocketing. We've got a bigger target to lock."

"Well aware of that, my dear. The storage room is the next left, up one flight of stairs."

"Yeah, so says the android." Tag didn't see any security guards in view; if they were around, they were behind closed doors. There were plenty of sensor pods mounted in the corners of the ceilings. "He'd better be ready to shut things down."

"I'm sure Dyson has everything ..." Lira's soft voice trailed off as they rounded the corner. *"Feurr."*

Tag had no idea what the Briddarri word translated as, but it couldn't be good—not with a quartet of men standing around the top of the stairwell, speaking in hushed tones and carrying tankards of amber ale. They were human, or rather, quite pale versions. Something about them seemed off.

Even more so when they walked down the stairs toward them.

"The radiation signature is moving," Dyson said. "Yet you have not changed position. How is this possible?"

Tag steered Lira back down the hall, toward the greenhouse. They needed cover, and up here that meant other people. "We got company."

"Your scans indicate the radiation is not being emitted by a crystalline storage lattice, but some kind of projector. Perhaps portable."

"They're following," Lira whispered.

Tag glanced over his shoulder. Yeah, definitely. All four were spread across the hall, still carrying the ale, but despite their loose-fitting formal garb, there was no mistaking their military training. Novafire, if they were any more in formation, they'd have wings and railguns. "Dyson, we're going to call you back. We've been set up."

"I believe I can be of assistance if you need extraction."

"Except for you being a gazillion miles away."

"Find yourself concealment and stand by." Great. Easy for the 'bot to say.

Back in the greenhouse, a band started playing. It was an odd wailing of musical instruments Tag had never seen before—of course, all five band members were Audrian, and Tag knew next to nothing about them save their kingdom was getting sawn in half by the Naplians. Each one played a long, spindly pipe with keys and levers spread up and down metallic red sides.

Good thing, though—all that racket only made the greenhouse even louder.

"Keep walking ahead," Tag murmured to Lira. "Make for some of those guys you spoke to earlier. I'll bank left and get in among the plants."

"Bank left?" Lira scowled. "This isn't a dogfight."

"Same principle." He hoped. Tag gave her a shove at the small of her back, and, when they rounded a curve in the path along the edge of the room, slipped in behind huge ferns.

Even with the noise, he heard the footsteps of the four men, walking in near unison. He also heard when two of them broke off from the formation and followed him. The other two sets of footsteps got quieter—so they must have gone for Lira.

"Now'd be a good time, Dyson," Tag said.

Lights flickered throughout the greenhouse. Then a handful of light banks died out completely.

The band stopped playing. Shouts of alarm went up.

Tag spun around. His followers were looking up at the ceiling, puzzled by the interruption, their attention drawn away for a pivotal second.

Good enough. Tag barreled into the nearest one.

They went down in a tangle of arms and legs. The guy slipped free of Tag's grasp, agile for a fellow dressed up for a formal party, and swept a kick at Tag.

He caught the guy's foot in midstrike and twisted, flipping him face first onto the floor.

The second guy had a device in his hands, small and round, with a red-orange glow at the end. Tag ducked as a burst of light flashed overhead. The weapon made less sound than a whisper. Were they trying to vaporize him?

Rather than hide, Tag reached for the guy he'd knocked down, and dragged him onto his feet. Just in time to intercept the next blast.

The guy he'd knocked down twitched, his arms and legs flailing in a macabre dance. He went limp.

Ah. Stun weapon. Good to know.

Tag elbowed the limp body forward, slamming into the shooter with his improvised shield. Both went down into the ferns, branches snapping and leaves tearing. Spray from the irrigation system got all three of them damp.

The second guy was up, his stun weapon nowhere to be found. He scrambled for it.

Tag caught him by the collar and punched him across the face. Blood spurted across his knuckles. He let the guy collapse, insensate.

Panting, wet from head to toe, Tag scooped up the stun weapon. He shot the second guy, just for good measure, then stomped on the gun. Sparks hissed where they encountered puddles.

He jogged back for Lira, wiping the blood from his hand as he went. Seemed really watery, not as thick as it should be. Maybe the irrigation had gotten them all soaked.

Lira was moving for the exit, seemingly none the worse for wear. People were still in a panic, and guards made their appearance, trying to calm the crowds.

"Hey." Tag caught her arm. "You all right?"

Her eyes widened. "Better than you, apparently. What happened?"

"Took care of two of our boys. You must have given the others the slip."

"Well, I suppose we can tell everyone they slipped." She gestured behind them, without so much as a backward glance.

The other two men lay sprawled at the base of the band. One of the red instruments was bent into an L-shape, and Tag guessed by the lumps on their heads and red marks on their faces they'd have huge bruises tomorrow.

"You're welcome." Lira kissed him on the cheek.

CHAPTER NINE

T ag had his hand in a bowl of ice. It felt good. Way better than the ache from when he'd decked one of the goons.

He frowned. Goons. What he wouldn't give to be back in a starfighter's cockpit. It was way easier to figure out: you targeted, you approached, you fought, you destroyed. This was parties and spies and false alarms.

Though he had to say, it was satisfying to get the drop on the people who thought they had you hemmed in. Like performing an Immelmann to put you on the tail of your pursuer.

"Iriada was a false lead." Dyson worked a tiny device, its scanning port aimed at a dish set on the kitchenette counter. A smear of red blood stained the white dish.

"Thank you for the obvious statement," Tag said. "We figured that out when the radiation was coming from four bad guys instead of the crystal lattice."

"More important is to dwell upon who the men were, and why they were waiting for you."

"I didn't see anything in the news about them. Whoever they were, they slipped the skyhook's security." Tag still had a slight headache between his eyes from perusing holo streams late into the previous night for any indicators about who had accosted them.

Now, he stood in the kitchenette with Dyson, soaking his hand and sipping from a steaming cup of the local equivalent of coffee. The liquid was a deep green, and carried a tang he couldn't identify, but the smell was close to what he'd expect from even *Confiance*'s mess hall. The entire room was bathed in reddish-purple light from the rising sun.

"Tell me you've got something in your medkit," Tag said.

"The scans are not conclusive, because of the degradation of the sample, but I have determined within eighty percent accuracy that this is Denic blood."

"Great. Humanoid spies for the Naplians." Tag scratched at the back of his neck. The blasted Delianite makeup itched, even more so now that the temporary adhesive had begun to wear off. Here's hoping he wouldn't get a rash. "They did a good job on their disguises. Looked like a group of humans descended from Eastern Europeans, as far as I could tell."

"There is no appreciable external difference," Dyson said. "However, the Denics' naturally clear blood does tend their complexion toward the very pale. It also makes it quite simple for their intelligence services to color the blood and alter skin color to match numerous other species and races."

"Denics sniffing around here, and drawing us into a trap," Tag said. "So, they knew what was on our scanners—knew we were after the crystals."

"It does. Since they were willing to expend the effort and risk public exposure, though, I can ascertain they have not obtained the lattice either. Why bother with us if they have the data?"

"Good point." It *was* a good point, so he didn't have to fake being polite. "Our next move—check out Pallas. That was the next strongest radiation signature."

"Indeed." Dyson abandoned his medkit scanner and activated his scroll. The map of Atterissage glowed, with the ten locations marked in red. Iriada's indicator blinked out, as did three more on the eastern edges of the city. "I was able to access several scanning points around Atterissage, and thus eliminate other possible sites. This leaves us with Pallas and five others."

"Any look more promising?"

"All exhibit the same radiation signature, though to varying degrees," Dyson said. "We will not be able to distinguish individual units until within personal range, and even then, it will take closer investigation to find the precise crystal lattice storage unit."

Tag folded his arms. "I don't suppose Terran Intelligence has any helpful hints on this one."

"As I said before, the file will be massive—likely more packed than any other."

"Otherwise, we'd have to guess."

Dyson's lips twitched into what Tag thought might be a smile. "I would prefer to avoid such an option."

"Yeah, me too." Tag went to the balcony, and the open doors. Atterissage was coming alive with aerial and ground traffic, the rumble of engines growing steadily stronger. One of those four-winged lizards squawked at him, hovering five meters away with the scraggly remnants of a large rodent clutched in its talons. Yeah, those guys were decent hunters.

Unfortunately, so were the Denics.

"The vehicle is back." Dyson stood next to him.

"Sure is. Every day since we've arrived, at a different time, never stops." It was a bulky transport, about the size of a ground-based delivery truck, shaped like a pair of upside-down bowls connected by a central spar. With its pale blue paint job, it blended well with the rest of traffic, as blues and greens predominated those kinds of vehicles. But it was definitely the same transport—the pilot flew with the same characteristic dip of the hull as he took corners and throttled back in the same way each time he flew down the aerial route two blocks from the hotel. "Can't get a look at the registry numbers."

"I have them." Dyson stared hard into the distance. "I have also recorded the company name written on the side."

"Nicely done. You got better than standard Terran eyeballs in that android head, I take it."

"Enough for our purposes. Though the windows are shielded to the extent I cannot penetrate them for a visual of the pilots."

"Don't worry about it. See what you can find out. The city's got to have some kind of listing, public or not, with everyone's registry numbers and flight licenses."

"I will run those numbers." Dyson cocked his head to the side.

Tag's scroll buzzed. He unfolded it from his pocket. It displayed a message from Amari Hadar, assistant to the very insistent sales representative for Pallas, Ranif Leroux. "Well, nothing new from our pals. Ms. Hadar assures me they're investigating the fighter malfunction to the best of their abilities. She hopes it won't affect my potential order."

"An order we can follow through to maintain our cover."

Tag raised an eyebrow. "How much money did TI approve for this mission?"

Dyson returned to his medkit scanner. "I am not aware of an upward ceiling for the budget line item."

Tag grinned—not just because of that piece of news, but also because of the rest of Amari's message. "I've got a chance to meet this gal for breakfast and dig up some more data in the process. You good here?"

"I am. I will let Ms. Reen know of your outing when she awakes—though I would exercise caution."

"You know me. First, help me get this cat getup off." He said in the chair by the counter. "Have to look presentable, and if she's expecting Tag Wester, that's who she's going to get."

As Dyson reached for a bag of equipment meant to strip away the Delianite masking, Tag glanced at the door to Lira's room. Still closed. He hoped she wasn't too high on alert from last night.

***

Lira was neither upset nor asleep. She was five blocks away, at a public communications hub, perusing the day's news net like any other citizen of Atterissage.

Her Delianite disguise was still in place, though if she'd chosen, she could have gone through the crowds as her Briddarri self. She'd seen a handful out on the streets, along with Audrians, humans, and dozens of other species. With nothing appearing on the news about the previous night's fiasco, she was certain it wouldn't hurt to stay hidden.

Now that the pain was increasing, she had better make contact.

The hub was a large, oval room with twenty-one booths arrayed around a central desk. A single robot, tall and spindly, accepted Lira's payment for time in a booth. She sat back in a chair as uncomfortable as her prison ship bunk and waited until the hub's privacy screen enveloped her. Good. She could see blurred outlines of people beyond the screen, but all they would see of her was a faint shadow.

No need to bother with the menu options, once she was logged into the public access.

Instead Lira detached one of the links of her bracelet—the fifth one from the clasp, to the right. The bracelet closed the gap, appearing as before, albeit narrower. She bent the link in half and pressed it against one of the data ports on the communications device. The link glowed green. Her holo display blanked, went snowy with static, and turned black save for a row of white text.

[Receiving.]

Yes, well, hopefully he would be able to converse, too. Lira wrote out a message with the stylus. [First attempt failed. Possible Denic spies were waiting. Naplians aware?]

Her gold text vanished. The reply was fifteen seconds later.

[Will investigate. Naplian activity confirmed in Union. Data location confirmed?]

[No. Another possible this evening. Will contact when it is secure.]

[You had better. The penalty for failure is high.]

Pain lanced through her side. Yes, she was well aware of the consequence—and the impetus to keep going. [Don't worry, Commander, I won't forget my job. Just don't forget your promises.]

[The agreement is intact. Get the data to us as soon as you can. Extraction will be available.]

The signal went inactive.

Lira snorted. Oh, she doubted it would. She snatched the bracelet link from the terminal. It fit easily back into her jewelry. Who did Commander Burrak think she was, a blind-marching cadet? She had her own way out well planned.

A tinge of regret interrupted her thoughts. Tag and Dyson seemed nice enough. But they were a soldier and spy, respectively. They had their own agendas. Dyson wanted the data to bring the Union into the war. And Tag? Well ... of the three of them, he was likely the least deceptive.

The ache in her side subsided. She rubbed at it. Didn't matter anyone's motives, whether or not they were kind to her ... or even worthy of friendship. If she was going to survive this, she had to have a plan. She had to look out for herself.

For Blue Kitt.

As always.

***

Round two.

That's how Tag thought of it. He flipped through the pre-flight list for *Olivia Vy*. Dyson sat beside him in the cockpit.

"Commercial Orbital Tracking doesn't seem too bothered by us departing in the middle of the night," Tag said.

"We are official representatives of Cavill Aerospace, affiliated with the Expo. Our transit certificate allows us—"

"Okay, I get it. They aren't asking questions. Good for us." Tag glanced behind him. Lira was back there, getting into something entirely different than her Delianite look. "This clouder. It had better work."

"You need to have more faith, Tag."

"Oh, I've got plenty of that. In my skills, in my family ..."

"In your team."

Tag snorted. "Us? We're not a team. I have a team. They're called Bronze Squadron. They've shot Naplians off my back, and I've done likewise. So how do you fit? How does it calculate in your artificial brain? I'm sure when you disrupted the power on the Iriada skyhook you did the math, and it was advantageous to get both of us out in one piece, so we didn't compromise a TI operation."

Dyson busied himself with the control board, his face lit pale green and blue by the holos. "I was safeguarding the two people who, along with myself, are vital to the success of this mission. If you cannot see past your anger at wrongs with which I had nothing to do, your concern about a team is misplaced. You have already sabotaged it."

Tag ground his teeth, but he focused his mind on the preflight. All the controls checked out. Fuel level good, core at full power ...

And the clouder. Said it was ready to operate. But it was equipment he'd never trusted before. Never even touched.

Maybe the 'bot had a point about faith. Neither of his parents had expressed any spirituality. Sure, Tag had visited the Hirrenhausen Monastery a couple times, and been impressed by the quiet determination of the abbots. Never stuck with him; though sometimes, if he was honest with himself—and when he was in the depths of space—he would wonder at it all. Wonder at what was holding together the universe.

Wonder at how in space he was going to get through this.

"Well, boys, my evening wear isn't nearly as lovely as our last outing." Lira stepped into the cockpit, clad in a jumpsuit so tight there wasn't anything about her figure Tag had to imagine. It was so black, so much like the darkness between the suns, he could feel himself falling into it.

Her face was uncovered, restored to its normal pale green hue. She must have caught him appraising her, because her cheeks got darker. "Meets your approval, Tag?"

Ahem. Tag started up the thrusters. A hum traveled throughout the entire ship, right across his body. "Not quite as nice as your dress, but it'll do."

"It should be more than adequate." Lira adjusted a control on her wrist, and the suit shimmered, like light glinting across a fighter's canopy. Lira pulled a mask down over her face, and she disappeared against the back bulkhead of the cockpit. Tag lost all sight of her until she shifted position and sat in the jump seat.

"Okay, turn it off. It's unsettling."

"Unsettling?"

"Creepy."

Lira laughed, but she deactivated the suit. Once more she was a black silhouette against the bulkheads.

"Okay, then. We're ready." Tag boosted power to the thrusters. "They cut us loose?"

"One moment." Dyson toggled the communications array. "Orbital, this is *Olivia Vy*, ready to depart."

"*Olivia Vy*, Orbital." It was a cheery female voice, not a robot, which answered this time.

Funny she'd be working the night shift, instead of an artificial controller. "You are cleared to depart Corner One along Ascent Route Three, with final destination of Diamantetoiles. *Bon voyage.*"

"*Merci, et bonne nuit.*" Dyson's reply was as flawless as the woman's command of the local lingo, with the same accent.

Lira propped her feet up on the side console. "Now there's a gift I would love to acquire—instant mastery of language, even if it's a primitive Terran dialect. Are you sure you can't give me lessons, Dyson?"

"Unfortunately, short of implanting a galactic translation module in the processing centers of your brain, there is little I can do to accommodate your request," Dyson said.

"My dear, was that a joke?"

"Let us call it a pithy observation." Then he winked. The blasted 'bot actually winked.

Tag flew them up through Kayna Two's night sky, into orbit, and on a vector toward Diamantetoiles, the only moon. It was such a distance away and such a small, gray body Tag imagined it a separate planet rather than a satellite. "Got a handful of traffic out here—couple of small transports, scattered shuttles. That one ahead, pushing greater acceleration, has got to be a patrol boat."

"I concur. You may cloud the ship at any time."

"Right." Tag touched the appropriate panel and muttered, mostly to himself, "Here goes."

Power levels fluctuated across the entire ship. Nav went down, so did Comms. If they lost the main drives Tag would have to deactivate the clouder and go for a cold restart. He pulled up the checklist on separate display—

Everything evened out. Lights came back, Nav and Comms were online, power levels restored to full. Their position on the displays looked correct.

"Take us to the Pallas skyhook, along the following coordinates," Dyson said.

"Roger that." Tag altered their course and accelerated.

Nothing from Orbital, or the patrol boat. In fact, every craft around them seemed ignorant of their deviation. Up ahead, the Orbital station loomed. Tag suddenly felt the urge for a greater demonstration.

"Your trajectory threatens to take us beyond the safe approach for the station," Dyson said.

"No kidding. I think I can judge the distance, thank you very much." Tag shut off the thrust, letting them race up to the station without the engines engaged. He'd set them on an arc to within a half klick of the solar arrays, which should set the proximity alarms screaming.

Olivia Vy breezed past without a whisper from anyone.

"They couldn't see us." Tag chuckled. "I'll be spaced. They couldn't novafired see us!"

"This is even more useful than foreign words," Lira murmured.

"I'll bet. You could steal a starship before anyone knew you were on the bridge." Tag applied thrusters to get them back toward the atmosphere, and guided them unpowered, until he could accelerate unnoticed. "Skyhook cable coming up."

"That's my cue." Lira headed for the hatch.

"Hey, Lira."

She glanced over her shoulder at him. "This is going to be pretty fast."

"I know. Dyson's told me all the approach velocities—twice—so I'm not concerned."

"Okay, well, just … be careful."

She blew him a kiss, then was gone behind the hatch. Tag frowned. Focus. Fly. Don't let her distract you. Yeah, way too late for that.

***

Alone in *Vy's* loading bay, Lira closed her eyes. She concentrated on her breathing. In, out. Rise, fall. She strapped on her grav-harness without looking. There was no need for sight. It was as simple as donning a tunic.

"Drop zone in one minute." Tag's voice was stern, full of worry—yet, she found it comforting, coming through clearly in her earpiece.

Lira stepped to the hatch. Her oxygen supply was limited, tied from her mask to a small reserve container affixed to her harness.

A subtle hiss told her the cargo bay had decompressed. Her wrist sensors confirmed it.

"Standby." Tag paused. "Good luck."

He was a kind soul. His words tugged at her heart, though not enough to make her reconsider the plan. Reciprocating his kindness would not end the pain, nor free her from Commander Burrak's grasp.

The hatch opened. Stars, and a double line of silver. The skyhook cable. It seemed she could reach out and touch it, no more than a virry scuttler's web.

She stood at the edge, the safe box of *Vy*'s cargo bay behind her, and the vast gulf of space ahead, with the sprawling curve of Kayna Two's atmosphere below. The cable car rose swiftly, a white capsule riding the lines from the planet's surface.

Lira checked her timers. *Vy*'s approach had to be perfect. If Tag couldn't pull it off, and if she couldn't be retrieved—

Oh, stop it.

Her view tumbled wildly. Lira's stomach churned as *Vy* changed course, swooping low, then coming back up the cable toward the skyhook. In seconds, the car was right there. Two hundred meters in front of her.

Two sets of numbers spun next to each other on her scanner— one for *Vy*'s velocity, one for the cable car's. Lira tensed, the grav-harness primed.

The numbers matched.

She leaped into space, hurling herself across the distance. For an instant she was floating, a glorious sensation of weightlessness. None of her dives had come close.

The cable car rushed at her with frightening speed.

Lira adjusted the grav-harness's output, flipped herself around so she was aiming feet first. If she'd done it right, the impact shouldn't be—

Her boots scraped the top of the car. Lira slapped for a handhold, found one of the maintenance rungs on the top of the car. She fastened a clip from her harness, tweaked its output once more.

She was on. She was safe.

"Locked." Her voice was a ragged gasp.

The whoop across her communications link left her ear ringing. "Nice! We're peeling off. I'm going to sit in a wide orbit until you're out."

"Thanks, Tag. Nice flying." She imagined his grin.

"Not too bad yourself."

When Lira looked back, all she could see was a faint flash of exhaust that could have been a star's glow. *Olivia Vy* was as invisible as they'd hoped.

Now for the hard part.

***

Tag put *Vy* into a circle, ten klicks away. "Anything on the scopes?"

"Negative," Dyson said. "All are clear."

"Okay, well, stay sharp. I don't want a Sunsaber pouncing on me in this thing. Keep Lira tracked so we can get her out quick."

"That was my plan."

Tag duplicated the nav display on his console. The cable car was a tiny point of light. The Iriada skyhook swallowed it.

Keep her safe.

***

The cable car docked inside a compartment barely large enough to accommodate both the outgoing and incoming vehicles. Lira pressed herself flat to the side of the car, having slipped down from its top. After reading Dyson's schematics—where had TI filched those, anyway?—she'd planned for the top being a tight fit where it anchored. Now, in real time, she was glad she'd paid close attention.

A handful of passengers disembarked, all of them Pallas techs. They were herded through an airlock tunnel, made of a clear material similar to plas-glass, and into an airlock. Both ends were firmly attached.

Well. There wasn't any way into the car, for easy access to the rest of the skyhook. Lira unlimbered her plasma cutter. Not quite the same as punching a hole in the roof of the sanctuary, and it would certainly set off more alarms.

The pink glow had no sooner lit up the dim environment of the compartment than everything was bathed in red light. Atmospheric loss. Feathers of air sprayed out around the hole she'd cut, becoming a torrent, then dying out as the whole tunnel vented into vacuum. She'd been lucky it hadn't explosively decompressed—thing was far sturdier than she'd imagined.

Lira pulled herself down through the gap, wriggling between the edges she'd cut. They closed in, the self-repair systems stretching the clear material, like a humanoid's cut healing in rapid time. Her feet slipped through as the hole pressed on either side of them. A tight somersault, and she was perched lightly on the deck.

The hatch at the end opened. Two figures, clad in EV suits, lumbered along the tunnel. She couldn't tell what manner of kits they carried, but they were definitely repair personnel, not security.

Lira held stock still. Her suit kept her blurred from their sight.

"Bioscan confirms two life forms closing on your position," Dyson said in her earpiece.

Such a statement of the obvious. She couldn't offer a pithy reply, because the techs were a bare ten meters away. Lira chanced shifting to the side and moving toward them. She'd landed right under the hole she'd made, and if she got stuck there—

They walked by, boots clomping dully. Lira felt the vibrations up through her legs. She thought she could hear the hiss and gasp of their respirators.

"Micrometeorite strike," one said, her voice buzzed with static. "Has to be. Self-sealer's got it braced up."

"Yeah, well, we'd better install a whole new section in case the integrity's lapsed. How'd one get past the bay shielding?"

The woman shrugged. "I'll pull the motion sensor logs. See what we get. Nothing set off the detectors, though."

Lira crept for the hatch. Any day now, Dyson …

The lights died.

***

Tag shook his head. Windows winked at him all across the curved hull of the Pallas skyhook, as if the hovering space station knew something he didn't. "Remind me not to let you anywhere near *Confiance*'s environmental controls. How long can you keep them in the dark?"

"I cannot keep them shut down permanently, nor can whole sections remain off," Dyson said. "The program I introduced via Lira's communications link will make lighting malfunction, but it will keep to a randomized pattern so as not to arouse suspicion."

"I'm pretty sure they're suspicious."

"No doubt. However, being humanoids trained to deal with such an emergency, they will follow two things without fail: their protocols and their emotions." Dyson nodded at his console, as if Tag could make heads or tails out of the huge data streams all over it. "And they respond on cue."

***

Lira found it funny that groups of people rushing about made her job easier. Certainly, she had to be more cautious, taking a roundabout route through the winding corridors to the location her wrist scanners indicated was the source of the radiation signature. But these techs made so much noise, barking commands, pounding their feet. Lira had never been enamored with Terran dogs—or Briddarri powndan, animals twice the size and with longer limbs—however, she appreciated the comparison.

The problem was at the destination itself.

Two guards stood outside a wide doorway—a human female in a black jumpsuit, and an Argus Omega robot. Like the one she and Tag passed on their way to the Iriada reception, it was a half meter taller than the human, all black body with four silver arms. Two ended in grasping hands, the others in stunpole emitters.

Lira was not about to kill the woman—the very idea, though the cold, rational portion of her mind suggested it, sickened her as always. If she needed to administer a beating, well, it was unfortunate, but a job was a job.

First thing was first. She stayed around the corner of the intersecting hall and turned the grav-harness to its greatest setting. Then she heaved it across the intersection. It cruised as steadily as a starship dropping from ripwave.

The Omega reacted as she hoped. It trundled forward, treads making a sound like a sticky substance peeling up. Red lights flashed across the top of its squat, boxy head.

"Bridge, I've got malfunctioning equipment in D-Hall." The

woman's voice was smooth, stern, full of confidence and command. Her steps rang out across the deck, a measured tread that told Lira of military training, a graceful body.

Not an easy mark. A pity.

When she was five steps from turning the corner, Lira ducked to the deck, braced with both hands, and swung up. Her feet impacted the guard's gut.

She heard the air expelled from her lungs with an *"Oof!"* Lira followed through with her motion, landing in front of the woman, and whipping her arm sideways.

The guard reacted quickly. She, too, had a stunpole, and a pistol strapped to her waist.

Electricity sizzled over Lira's head.

The robot wheeled after them both. Lira was well aware the 'bot would obey its programming to keep its partner safe and apprehend Lira without use of lethal force. She backed off from the female guard, hearing the rumble of the 'bot's treads and feeling the static from its stunpole arms.

She dodged sideways as the guard struck at her. The blow hit the robot instead.

The electrical discharge arced up and down the Omega's body, blue sparks rippling like waves of water. The guard was shocked— pun intended, Lira thought—by the outcome. Shocked long enough for Lira to put her down with a single hit to the side of her head.

The woman would survive. A quick bioscan showed only a minor concussion. Already, she groaned, even though she didn't make a move to get up.

"Our window is closing," Dyson said. "Move with haste."

Lira rubbed at the top of her mask, sweat sticking between her skin and the material. "I haven't been enjoying my tour," she murmured.

The door panel's security was quite sophisticated. But alarms began to blare, and Lira knew she didn't have the leisure of deftly cracking the encryption.

Instead she placed a small square of soft, pink and gray material to the center of the door. The detonator was programmed into her wrist scanner.

***

Dyson's console erupted with a shower of alerts and warnings, all of them dripping scarlet across his display. "Oh."

"Oh? What's oh?" Tag eyed a pair of distant craft. They kept on each other's wing, running a wide pattern, and abruptly shifted their trajectory. Not good. "If Lira's ready for extraction—"

"There has been a complication. She was unable to unlock the vault. But she has secured the crystal."

"Okay. That's good."

"Removing the obstacle required the use of explosives."

"That's bad." Tag kicked *Olivia Vy* toward the skyhook. "Hang on. I'll get us lined up to catch her."

"Wait. Do not accelerate without—"

Whatever he was going to say was interrupted by a shrill tone from the clouder assembly on Tag's console. More red lights. He hated those.

Those patrol craft shifted their aim even more, and the nav display showed them on a direct intercept.

"Novafire! Clouder's malfunctioned." Tag accelerated as fast as he dared to the skyhook. "Tell Lira it's now or never."

Dyson was silent. "She is on the move. However, she doubts she can reach the original extraction point at the landing dock and is instead returning to the cable car. She also mentions she has lost her grav-harness."

"Then what in blazes is she—?" Tag grimaced. He knew exactly what Lira had in mind. He'd read the TI dossier on her.

The proximity alert chimed. Sunsabers. Those patrol craft were each the same fighter he's just test flown. "They're scanning us," Tag said. "Any possibility they've made our ID?"

"No. I have disabled our transponder, and the clouder is coming back online." Dyson reached above his displays. Targeting brackets appeared in the nav holo. "Weapons are ready."

"Hold up! I'm not shooting those boys if I can help it."

"But our capture will result in failure of the mission, and Miss Reen—"

"Get the clouder re-engaged. Let me worry about the rest." Tag threw *Vy* into a steep dive. Good timing, too, because he just spotted something drop down from the skyhook along its double wire.

A tiny figure.

***

Lira hurtled through space, gravity dragging her down along the wire. She could have used her harness and been far more certain of her outcome, but there was nothing for it now. Another cable car had to be coming. She had the timing precise.

But no way to stop herself from smashing into it.

She knew her only hope lay with the human pilot and android spy. They weren't Blue Kitt, though. Surely, they'd already run to avoid detection. The very real fear of death crept through her, making her heart race.

Then she saw it—the wavy, hazy outline of *Olivia Vy*. A perfect rectangle of light opened on her underside, which Lira realized was angled toward her. The ship swept in, thrusters firing in reverse, the rectangle nearer and nearer.

The velocity had to match, or she'd be battered to pieces. Not that she had any other choice. Her suit was already warming like the inside of an oven, taking on an orange hue in places. Lira twisted herself, shooting to the ship like a comet.

Dyson was there.

They collided with such force Lira almost passed out. Everything was a whirl of limbs and netting and cargo containers. Over it all, a voice roared, "Go!" The single syllable was long and drawn out.

Gravity found her and slammed her against an unyielding body. The wind whipping around her suddenly cut off, and the silence in *Vy*'s cargo bay was stunning. She ripped her mask free, gasping.

She lay atop Dyson, who looked as unconcerned as a man reclining on a jump couch, even though his arm was bent at an angle that should have had him screaming in pain.

"Welcome back, Ms. Reen. I trust you were successful."

Lira laughed, and didn't stop, even as she dug into her pocket. The crystalline lattice floated inside a clear block cupped neatly in her palm. It twirled, a metallic violet snowflake.

"I have it, of course," she said. "And I made sure to leave behind a Blue Kitt."

CHAPTER TEN

Tag slipped Olivia Vy back into the flight route to Diamantetoiles and had them landed on Kayna Two's moon within a half hour.

Dyson, of all people, chose them a quiet, upscale restaurant set inside Diamantetoiles's Dome One, with a huge, curving transparent wall. Tag could see every inch of the lunar surface out to the bleak horizon, with the blue jewel of Kayna Two hanging in space.

Speaking of jewel …

He held the crystalline lattice in his hand. No worries about anyone seeing them—only reason Dyson had chosen the place was its lack of scanners or even optics to observe the diners. Sure, there was one at the entrance, but tucked back this far, with the high walls of their booth around them, the trio had as much privacy as in *Vy's* cockpit.

"This is what all the fuss is about?" Tag shook his head. "Hard to believe."

"Not so hard when one considers the sheer amount of data contained on it." Dyson had his scroll out, and a thin transfer cord connected to the center of the crystal. Not as simple as a signal connection, but then again, that was the point of these lattice things the Union liked to use. You couldn't hack into them unless you were hardwired.

Even then, it could be vexing, as the creases on Dyson's otherwise placid face attested. "If it's so huge, TI's going to be disappointed you don't just transmit everything right to them." Tag snapped his fingers. "We'll have to bring the crystal back."

"Of course. That is accounted for."

"Yeah? Did you account for how the Denics are probably scanning for its radiation signature just like we did? And how Pallas is going to check every ship for the same thing?"

Dyson raised both eyebrows, giving Tag the impression he was surprised the pilot could be simultaneously insightful and stupid. "All contingencies are planned for. Where complications arise, Tag, is where I rely on your skills. You have a talent for improvisation. Hence, Miss Reen's rescue."

Tag shrugged, though he couldn't play off the puffing up of his chest. "Won't deny, it was pretty amazing."

"What's even more amazing is there's still room in this booth with your ego swollen to the size of our transport." Lira returned to the table, dressed in a flattering dress of black and white patterns. Tag amended the description—no need for "flattering." Everything she wore fit the bill.

An Audrian waiter accompanied her, dressed in well-pressed grey pants, charcoal vest, and white shirt. The only spot of color was a blue cravat around its neck, which made an even bigger splash considering the Audrian had skin mottled dusty brown and gray. He carried a tray of three bulbous glasses and a bottle, one Tag stared at.

"You're not hallucinating. Crown and Scepter, 2677." Lira slid into the booth beside Dyson. Emerald eyes gleamed more brilliantly than Tag remembered.

"The last batch for sale," Tag murmured. "I didn't think any of it made the cargo ships out of Terran space. Has to cost a fortune."

"Don't fret. I'm sure our employers won't begrudge us a splurge on completion of our work." Lira nudged Dyson.

"Our budget is sufficient." Dyson watched the waiter fill the three glasses and set them on the table with the bottle in the middle. "Though consuming one will have no effect on my bearing, if that is what you're hoping to accomplish."

"Drink it anyway." Tag clinked glasses with Lira, and even with Dyson's, though the android hadn't bothered to pick it up yet. "Here's to our job well done."

"And to partners well chosen," Lira said.

No argument there. Tag savored his sip, the rum burning his throat. For a moment he was back in Father's office, worried about Marney's upcoming wedding and arguing with Father about getting Elden Selva away from Vossberg City before Reittian agents could snatch him up.

Now he was on a foreign moon, drinking to his successful heist with a Briddarri thief—Blue Kitt, nonetheless—and a Terran Intelligence android.

Dyson drank his rum in perfect imitation of his biological counterparts. 'Bot wouldn't even appreciate the taste; Tag was certain TI didn't waste money on giving them that sense. However, he was surprised when Dyson said, "The composition of the drink matches my database of flavors pleasing to humanoids. In fact, it is within the top ten."

Tag laughed. "Good to know. You could just say, it tastes great."

"If I were not among colleagues, I would resort to such duplicity, but honesty is best in this case."

Yeah. Honesty. Tag glanced at Lira. Where had she been? No way it had taken her so long to find the bar and lock onto a waiter. Hopefully she hadn't swiped someone's jewelry on the way back to the table.

"Are you in yet?" Lira peered over Dyson's shoulder. She had a hunger about her, one Tag doubted had anything to do with appetite for food.

"No. The levels of encryption are substantial, but the protocols our employers use should be able to penetrate them." Dyson expanded a bulk of code, yellow holographic symbols dripping as raindrops. "There is no doubt you did your work well, Miss Reen. This data file's contents are so massive any attempted transmission may crash a standard communications system."

"Crash a comms?" Tag paused his glass halfway to his mouth. "That isn't possible."

"Improbable, not impossible."

"So, this will do it, then. Whatever's on here will bring the Union into the war."

"Most likely."

Tag grinned. "I'll drink to that, too."

Lira sighed. "You boys and your war. Is that all you're concerned with?"

"Not all, but since I spend most of my days either stuffed in a bunk aboard a cruiser or blasting Naplian starfighters into atoms, yes, it's at the top of the list."

"And bringing the Union in will end it sooner?"

Tag shrugged. "Not my department. All I know is, the more allies in a Grand Alliance, the better chance we all have against the One-eyes. Especially if said allies bring a pile of Sunsabers to the fight."

"Dyson, what about you?"

He said nothing for a while, so long that Tag wondered whether he'd been so absorbed in the decryption he'd not heard Lira. "My role has never been on the front sectors of this war, as Tag's has. I have remained in the shadows—of planets, of cities, of people. My tasks are best accomplished as a being who can walk unnoticed among humans. However, there are many androids who have already sacrificed their lives in this war, and if more allies will aid in its conclusion, I will do my part to see it successful."

Tag snorted. His head buzzed from the beginnings of the rum's effects. He'd better get some food in him quick. "Sacrifice. They'll just build more."

"It is not a simple matter of fabrication," Dyson said. "Our cerebral matrices are individually built and programmed."

"Whatever you say."

"Don't breach your core." Lira laid a hand upon Tag's. "See? While you two sit here with war and destruction on your minds, I'm left enjoying the company of two fine men and admiring the beauty around us. Those palm fronds from the Kayna marshes—can't you smell them? The paintings by Joroc Baton are original watercolors, not prints or holos. The sculpture across from us, atop the divider of the next table—it's a Rutak Seventh Dynasty. There's far too many things to enjoy."

"The war cannot be avoided, if this is what you're implying," Dyson said.

"Oh, but it can. I've done it quite well." Lira placed something on the table. Where she'd had it hidden, or when she'd taken it out, Tag had no idea. It was a tiny statuette, no taller than his thumb, of a furred creature hunched on its hind legs. Kind of like the Banter squirrels from Baedecker Four, the stockier, bigger versions of Terran species, only with next to no tail. The statuette was carved from a lustrous blue stone, dark as deep sea around the edges but pale like an

Earthly sky in the center. "It's the goal of Blue Kitt—enrich yourself, at the cost of those who can afford to spare, without endangering others."

"I heard you've never killed anyone. Or your crew." Tag rubbed the rim of his glass. "The latest Blue Kitt is a pacifist, then."

"Hardly. I just prefer the beautiful things of life to the cold, ugly things of war. That's why I adore them so." She smiled. "Well, and the money. That's also lovely."

Tag smiled back, because having her look at him that way warmed him far more effectively than any volume of rum. But he also hid his discomfort. What kind of person was she, to ignore the suffering of the galaxy for personal gain?

And what had she been doing when she'd disappeared on them?

"Thirty percent remaining," Dyson said. "I shall make contact with my superiors when it is complete."

"Good deal," Tag said. "Then we all get to see if the Grand Alliance wins or loses."

***

Marney's transport was far and above what Elden considered adequate for her work. Yes, it had a voluminous cargo hold, large enough to accommodate four octants of Truppen, plus a half-dozen rows of crates and food storage units. It was also a decommissioned Terran strike corvette, its prow a tapered wedge and a bank of sublight engines primed for powerful acceleration.

The latter came in useful when *Vossberg*, as Marney had christened the vessel, emerged from its jump in the midst of a firefight.

"Five ships," Nolte said. "Two Reittian, three Naplian."

The nav display for the region showed far more than the helmsman's terse announcement. All three Naplian vessels were destroyers, eighty-four meters long, tossing out missiles from batteries on either side of the hulls. They were arrayed in a triangular formation, bringing their weapons fire to concentrate on their enemies.

Those enemies proved uncooperative. They were Reittian destroyers, diving straight into the Naplian flotilla at high acceleration. Against the graceful, curved wing design of the Naplian ships, and even compared to *Vossberg*'s angular hull, the Reittian vessels were ugly—a collection of four rectangles each, with hull plating overlapped like the armor of a hover-tank. Whatever defects they had in aesthetics, they made up for with sheer firepower. Elden counted discharges from eight railguns and four particle cannon turrets. Wave after wave of medium-range torpedoes came corkscrewing out of launch ports in segments of the ship he thought didn't have any.

The shielding of all five vessels flickered under their mutual onslaught. In terms of weaponry, the Reittians' two were an even match for the Naplians' three. But one of the Naplian destroyers broke formation first, in apparent panic. Its form twitched—telltale use of micro-jumps to avoid sensor formation.

The Reittian destroyers immediately pounced, redirecting their fire even as they shot straight for the other two Naplians. The frightened destroyer exploded in a brilliant white ball of a breached reactor.

"Bring us into weapons range, Dave, and let's see if we can lend a hand," Marney said.

"Will do."

Rett stood between Goetz and Elden, his head centimeters from the ceiling of the bridge. "Serious? This ship isn't even combat-rated anymore, is it?"

"We've got plenty of teeth remaining," Marney said.

"Targeting with medium-range torpedoes and firing," Nolte said.

Elden knew the Naplians hadn't spotted *Vossberg*—or if they had, they were far too concerned with the seemingly suicidal Reittians for it to matter. Nolte ripwaved them into the battle, running the generator for three seconds. Suddenly they were only 10,000 klicks from the nearer of the two Naplian destroyers. Four torpedoes streaked out from *Vossberg*, white lines on the mingled mess of trajectories tracked by the tactical station's holographic display.

The Naplian moved, and covered its aft with counter fire from laser turrets, but two of the four made it near enough to detonate. One of the explosions ripped apart the stubby wing on the starboard hull—the micro-jump array was blown to bits, Elden recognized.

It was all the distraction the Reittians needed. Within two minutes, the second Naplian was destroyed, and the remaining one jumped free of the star system.

***

"It is an honor to have you aboard *Dragonfly*. More warriors are always welcome."

The five of them—Elden, Goetz, and Rett, accompanied by Marney and Nolte—were aboard the lead of the two Reittian destroyers. The main corridor was spartan, deckplates and bulkheads the dreary gray and brown of that nation's fleets, but at least it was tall enough that Truppen could walk its length slightly hunched over. Captain Fyodor Zhivko's voice filled the space with all the thunder of sublight engines ignited in an atmosphere. He had thick black hair, moustache and beard shot through with gray that matched the streaks over his ears, and pale brown eyes sporting hints of green. His uniform was black as night, too, gleaming with silver piping, and he carried his gray cap under his right arm with the delicacy of a person cradling a newborn.

He was also a head shorter than Marney.

"Captain Zhivko, thank you for meeting with us on such short notice, and in the midst of what was apparently a well-planned operation," Marney said.

"Madam, woman as lovely as yourself, and who acquitted herself as hero of Baedecker, may call me Fyodor." He kissed her hand and smiled at the rest of her entourage. "Though I must say, I was not expecting so grand a party in your company."

"This is my colleague Dave Nolte, helmsman for *Vossberg*. The others—they are the reason we're here. Consul Elden Selva of the Truppen army, in service to the Briddarri Kingdom and the Grand Alliance."

Goetz shifted his stance, a subtle realigning of limbs. Elden knew he prepared himself to strike, and flee, because this was a Reittian ship—home of the people who tried to kidnap Elden three years ago. The same people who'd tossed his family away in concentration camps at the conclusion of the Second Consular war. To say there was no love lost was a gross understatement.

Yet, Captain Zhivko only examined them with curiosity. "Yes, I've heard your story as well, Selva. So this is what you've become. A demon machine."

"My mind and heart are still that of a Selva," Elden said. "And as such my tolerance for Reittian insults is as low as it ever was."

Zhivko chuckled. "Well put. I have no amity for Northern Alliance scum, but this is a war unlike any we've faced. If you are now a cyborg whose very name makes One-eyes soil themselves, so be it. You will make fine warrior for us."

His office was as opulent as the Baedecker governor's compound, with a pair of plush red velvet drapes framing a desk Elden scanned and found was real mahogany. A rug of intricate otherworldly designs formed the bright orange and yellow center—some kind of mythical alien creatures adorned it. A metal shelf rigged to the left bulkhead held dozens of liquor bottles, of myriad colors and vintages, ranging from near empty to unopened.

Elden must have performed the Truppen equivalent of staring, because Zhivko laughed. He dropped into a chair of shining red leather. "Naplians are not the only prey out here. Pirates and smugglers take advantage of travelers, supply ships"—he gestured at Marney—"aid convoys. My crew and I keep them suppressed."

"Not destroyed," Goetz said.

"Of course not! Captured for trial in Reittian space. All their property supports the war effort." Zhivko propped his boots up on the desk. "So, Marney. Your friends are here about their missing comrades."

"That is how they described their predicament."

"And you're certain they were in my realm?"

Elden nodded. "They were supposed to stop at several waypoints, one within a parsec of these coordinates."

"Our fortune is yours, then. I have seen ships operating quietly in this sector, ships which have no business in our territory."

"No one has claimed this portion of the Great Desert Rift."

Zhivko snorted. His moustache twitched like a live animal. "Surely you jest. Reittian ships patrol space between Reittian outposts, and you say no claim exists? Spoken like a true Northern Alliance terrorist."

"Fill in the facts we need, and stop wasting our time," Goetz muttered.

Zhivko seemed unfazed by the looming Truppen, his gaze settling instead on Marney. "The ships skulking about this sector are Briddarri, and I have sensor data proving they were in the vicinity of your men's waypoint."

Elden's thoughts spun. Admiral Ergen didn't say anything about patrols this close to Terran space, and Reittian strongholds. "You're not mistaken?"

"Let us pretend you didn't insult me by asking that." Zhivko waved his hands, as if to encompass the cabin. "I can tell ships apart well enough to capture pirates and smugglers. Whatever these were, though, they were not regular military. Custom designs. Yet, I see the Briddarri manufacture. They carry no identity codes. Briddarri insist I misidentify craft."

"We're counting on your expertise, Fyodor," Marney said. "Can you provide us with the sensor data?"

"Please. Three years now, I have fought against One-eyes and seen action with Briddarri in same solar systems. These vessels were of same hull lineage, I know this." He held up a data scroll. "Everything you need to know is here."

"Name your price," Elden said.

"My price is paid. Not all this comes from the capture of illegal goods. I make a decent profit from weaponry sales to—concerned benevolent parties." Zhivko smiled at Marney. "One can never pass up the chance to repay a valued customer."

Marney shook her head, her own smile crinkling the skin around her eyes. The blush on her cheeks made Elden wish he were the one provoking the reaction, rather than this borderline Reittian pirate. "Fyodor, my husband would greatly dispute your description of our relationships."

"Of course, of course."

"You'll take us there?" Elden took the scroll and uploaded the sensor reports into his operating system. Within seconds he'd passed it along to Goetz—but not Rett. Since Zhivko's revelation of possible Briddarri involvement, he'd rather just the two of them keep the information.

First new Naplian mechs, now mystery Briddarri ships. What in the rift was going on?

"An escort? Of course! We'll transit rough territory, winding us up along the Union of Planets border." Zhivko rubbed his hands together. "Much opportunity for plunder. Welcome to our flotilla, Elden Selva."

***

The Naplian battlecruiser *Fulnax* and the eleven warships of the 5th Colonial Squadron, IV Corps, jumped in threes to the edges of a debris field in a remote star system.

"The last signal from the trans-light pulse originated at this point," said the Tactical officer. "Triangulation confirmed."

Admiral Erassia frowned. "Their course is erratic. Do we have any way of ascertaining their destination?"

"No, sir. The pulse can only give us a fix on where they were, and while we can run estimates on an end point, you're right—their course has been erratic. The best I can do is give two handfuls of options."

"Six possible endings. Very well. Run your scenarios. I'd prefer to keep the squadron intact, but if we need to split off ..." Erassia turned toward the Communications station. "Signal the fleet captains. Tell them to standby for instructions by flotilla."

"Aye, sir."

Erassia tapped a panel on the arm of his command chair. The roster for the 5th Squadron sprang before him, green letters floating above his lap. Six battlecruisers and six heavy cruisers. Divvying them up by threes would present his captains with the possibility of independent operations, which would not only boost their careers—especially in Admiral Daviont's eye—but also improve their experience in combat.

He hadn't got halfway through when a chime sounded from the Tactical console. "Energy readings from the surface of the nearest planet. Small, substandard environment."

"A settlement?" Erassia stepped to the main holo display for *Fulnax*'s bridge. It sat deep in the deck, projecting a single orb surrounded by—junk. Broken rock and bits of hull. A red patch throbbed on the sphere. "Skirt the debris field. Spread formation to encircle this world. Shields to maximum deflection."

"Aye, sir."

"Give me a contact signal."

The Communications officer raised two of his three fingers when the signal was ready. "This is Admiral Gussan Va'Kur Erassia commanding the 5th Colonial Squadron, IV Corps, of the Naplian Imperial Fleet. Identify your settlement and respond. You inhabit space claimed for the glory of Naplia and her Emperors Bonante and Benaltep, all hail their Glories. If you do not comply you will be conquered. If you reply your annexation will be completed with minimal disruption."

Erassia waited, hands clasped behind his back. Major Gandraad appeared behind him, his footsteps so quiet Erassia hadn't heard him approach during his speech. If the man could operate his *ziurathal* with equal stealth, the Truppen wouldn't stand a chance.

"Sir, I'd recommend against wasting time with this planet," Gandraad said. "Anything we do to delay our search only maximizes the possibility of the Devastators escaping."

"I am well aware of that, Major," Erassia said. "Which is why I have no intent of wasting anything, including ammunition."

"Sir, I get no response from the surface," the Communications officer said. "There's considerable point-to-point transmission activity."

"Intercept and report."

"Trying to, sir, but it's encrypted. Terran military grade."

Military communication? Energy surges? Erassia swore. "Send to all vessels: break orbit! Prepare fighter squadrons for launch. Helm, ready ripwave for the following coordinates ..." The first blasts speared through space just as the Tactical officer sounded the alarm.

Hypervelocity shells. Erassia strapped into his command chair. Yes, the Terrans were overly fond of throwing rocks. However, those projectiles never dissipated, like Naplian energy blasts did, nor did they lose velocity unless acted upon by the gravity of a larger body.

"Multiple firing sites," the Tactical officer said grimly. "*Yirana* reports likewise from the opposite side of the planet. And—sir, *Tolondar* has suffered hull damage. Reports of breaches on several decks."

"I told those blinking dolts to move off from the planet! Target the nearest firing site and eliminate it!"

Streaks of green stabbed from the Naplian fleet visible on the holo display, lines drawn with precision to the planet's surface. There were eight firing sites and judging by the little amount of damage being done by Erassia's counterattack, they were buried deep. Erassia scowled. He should turn the entire surface to ash.

"Sir, fighter squadrons report ready to launch—thirty-six fighters prepped."

Long ago, upon being promoted to flag rank, Erassia had used what pull he had with Command and Admiral Daviont to retain captaincy of his own ship. As a result, he relished the control he wielded over both his personal flagship and an entire squadron. Far from finding it taxing, his mind felt fully alive in these moments, when tactical decisions threatened to assail him from every side. "Not yet. Withhold them behind our shields, until we can knock every last blasted projectile down."

The ships of 5th Squadron made it out into their defensive formations, forcing the planet's firing sites to spread their aim. Concentrated blasts from the battlecruisers hammered at those sites, and Erassia knew he would have to wait for detailed images from the surface to see the full range of the devastation.

One of the sites failed, then a second. But it was taking too much time. Still, he did not want to leave an insubordinate world at his back. Especially one with such high concentration of mineable metallic reserves, as the sensor data streaming across his console informed him.

A new set of alarms rang out. "Spaceborne contact!" the Tactical officer cried. "Bearing one oh seven, mark two five, coming at us from the debris field!"

Erassia cursed the Ascended Masters. So much for their infinite wisdom. Six small vessels, each twice the size of the largest Naplian bomber, raced up at high acceleration into the midst of this half of his squadron. They had to be unmanned, given the blistering g-forces exerted by their engines. Dozens of medium-range torpedoes arrowed among the formation, warheads exploding at far too close a distance for comfort.

"Launch fighters," Erassia said. "Stop those drones. And open another blasted channel to the surface!"

Three squadrons of Jarra Fols swooped out from their home battlecruisers, adding their missiles and energy blasts to the spreading fight. They quickly engaged the drones in a swirling dogfight, one in which the drones held their own with surprising skill—owed in no small part to the railgun bursts and laser shots adept at picking off Naplian missiles.

Fulnax shook under the impact of railgun projectiles, and a missile's antimatter warhead exploded near enough to make the starboard shield sections pulse red as dark as *shirish* blood.

"Sir, the surface installation is contacting us!"

"Put it through," Erassia said.

"Naplian vessels, you have been warned: leave our orbit and do not return. Your presence is unwelcome."

Succinct. The Terran accent was unmistakable. And three of Erassia's ships had suffered damage, two of those considerable. But if this *shirish* thought a Ffawe admiral would simply walk off after being given a bruised eye—"Your threats mean nothing," he snapped. "You will cease your fire, or we will target one of your civilian settlements for obliteration. Comply now or be destroyed."

No response came. The surface fire did not slacken.

Erassia's blood ran cold. So be it. Mining equipment could always be rebuilt. "Helm, move us into a lower orbit. Tactical, target the smallest of the mining establishments."

"Sir, the *shirish* have residences circling the pits and machinery."

"Do not make me repeat my order."

Silence, but *Fulnax* shifted her position in orbit. Red markings bracketed the smallest of the inhabited areas. Erassia noted the presence of one hundred eighty human life signs.

"Fire," he said.

Energy pulses coalesced into a constant stream from *Fulnax's* prow. The atmosphere roiled and steamed where the blasts cut the air asunder. Within minutes, the entirety of this small settlement was reduced to glassy rock.

The surface attacks stopped, and the drones shut down.

There were no cheers of congratulations, only the murmurs of communications and orders from Damage Control. "Sir," the

Communications officer said, "we've received a signal of surrender."

"As it should be. Signal Admiral Daviont and let him know this world requires a permanent naval presence, as well as transports for its wealth." Erassia glanced at Major Gandraad. He was staring at the display of the planet, eyelid narrowed, mouth pinched shut. "Problem?"

"If I may, Admiral ..."

Erassia spread both hands out, a gesture meant to encourage continuation.

"That was a battle lacking honor."

"Very true," Erassia said. "However, the *shirish* are not to be treated with honor. I doubt they will make the repeated mistake of challenging Naplia again. Select a contingent of soldiers to leave behind and secure the settlements. Those mines will produce for us now—it was lack of vision which left them untapped this long. As soon as they're in place, we'll depart."

To the Tactical officer, he said, "Destroy every weapon they have."

***

Tag grinned at Lira as she finished her tale of her most recent theft. "That was one blasted impressive dive."

"And done without an aircraft," she said, smiling back.

It was almost a perfect, relaxing evening. Somewhere deep in the back of the restaurant, music played, lilting string tunes. The soft lighting all around them made Lira appear even more beautiful. Not that the light had to work hard in that respect.

If not for Dyson's stone face bathed in holographic light, yes, it'd be perfect. But it must've been somewhat the rum at work, because right then Tag didn't mind the android's presence. They'd pulled off their mission. Tag could go back to his squadron, and Dyson to his spy work, and Lira ...

What did she have to look forward to?

"Completed." Dyson's pronouncement was as startling as a missile explosion. Tag swore he saw a smile flit across his face. "I have accessed the data files."

"What's it say?" Tag asked. "What's so novafired important the

Union's got it hidden on a crystal aboard a skyhook?"

"Something worth a great deal to them," Lira said.

Dyson was silent for far too long. "This ... must be in error."

"Why? Let me see." Tag spun the scroll away. Dyson didn't stop him.

He stared for a moment, and his jaw went slack. "I'll be spaced," Tag murmured.

"You're telling me it's bad enough the great Tag Wester has no words." Lira switched sides of the table, and slid in close to Tag, so their legs touched.

But not even that could quell the horror Tag felt.

"Yes," Dyson said. "If this is released, millions of people will die."

CHAPTER ELEVEN

T ag couldn't believe the numbers. Six million people. How many had died and also been evacuated from Baedecker Four? A third of that?

There was no guessing as to where the figures came from, either. Whoever had done the projection had determined the collapse of at least one skyhook, which would destroy Atterissage, and the release of a biological weapon capable of rapidly killing the civilian population.

"I don't get it," he said. "Why would the Leadership Board plan the slaughter of their own people? Are they hoping to knock out their enemies in the Riven Cabal in one shot?"

"If they were, it's a terribly expensive way to do so."

Tag would have teased her about looking greener than usual, but she probably hadn't any idea about human coloring related to physical symptoms.

"I don't think that's what this is."

"You are correct," Dyson said. "This is not a plan of action. It is a hypothetical situation, calculated to within ninety-two percent certainty, of what would happen on Kayna Two and elsewhere in the Union if the contents of this data were released to the public."

"Novafire," Tag muttered. "The contents have to be pretty bad for them to estimate destruction on that scale. I mean, we're talking full-scale civil war."

"Indeed. It appears our employers underestimated the scale of the Riven Cabal's infiltration of Union military units." Dyson shrank one display of data and enlarged another square. "This analysis indicates one-third to one-half of divisional commanders identify as Riven, with a plurality of enlisted personnel in their units supporting the same cause."

"Let me see this." Tag swiped aside display after display. Dyson wasn't kidding—the thing was packed full. The menu listing seemed infinite. One file in particular stood out as gigantic. "I take it I found the motherlode."

"Yes." Dyson paused. "A forewarning: the contents are disturbing, but I have calculated this is what my superiors wanted me to find."

Tag opened it. The first thing he got was a symbol made of overlapping, sharp-ended arcs. He couldn't tell what it meant but it was kin to the biohazard labels he'd seen stuck all over *Confiance* and other Navy vessels. Inside the file were vids, images, listings of dates and reports. Tests. Medical findings he didn't understand. Biological samples whose analyses confounded him. But as a whole, he knew what it meant.

"Tailored bioweapons," Tag said. "The Naplians are developing them."

"Tailored to what?" Lira asked.

"To who. Humans." Anger boiled inside him. "That's what the Union's been hiding. That's why the Riven Cabal's going to rise up against them and convince the population to back them in a civil war."

"You see," Dyson said in his predominant calm, "the Leadership Board has been selling humans for experimentation."

Lira made a face as if she'd been told the main course was the seat cushion upon which she sat. "That's revolting. Using their own people as *foorddar*?"

"What's a *foorddar*?"

"A *foorddar* is a tiny, hairless species akin to human *Rodentia*, though of greater girth and longer lifespan," Dyson said.

"Guinea pig, huh? Yeah, same in translation." Tag shook his head. "This is crazy. Dates of payments received—and through intermediaries, so at least they were smart enough to not deal directly with the One-eyes. Iriada. Pallas. They conducted the transport, according to this."

"It's no wonder they had this under top security," Lira said. "The Union Leadership has been neutral for years. The outcry would shake their worlds."

"Hence, the forecast casualties of an internal conflict," Dyson said.

"So, TI is banking on the Cabal taking over during a civil war and then pushing the Union to fight on the side of the Grand Alliance." Tag snorted. "I'd say their math is off. A civil war, especially one this bloody, would just make the people go even more neutral than they already were."

"Not necessarily, and please refrain from using our employers' designation in a public setting," Dyson said.

Tag ignored his rebuke. That was why they were here, wasn't it? No surveillance, and besides, the place was half empty. "Come on."

"The Cabal is estimated to push the Union into the war with Naplia precisely because of the nature of the Leadership's betrayal," Dyson said. "They have allegedly sold their own people into experimentation, for the purpose of developing biological weapons targeted to human physiology. They have aided in the death of Union citizens. But it is the Naplians who have carried out these experiments who have directly caused the deaths. They will be the target of Union vengeance—and I trust you see why, after viewing these records, the Union populace at large will clamor for such vengeance."

"Wars and more wars." Lira sank back in the seat. "It never ends, does it? And people treat me like I'm the one with something poorly wired. The Briddarri toss me out of society while everyone else finds more creative means of killing each other."

"Hold on." Tag touched her hand. "It makes sense, I guess, but if the Leadership's been up to all this, why in space did they write it all down? Why keep all these records?"

Dyson frowned. "Uncertain. Speculation points to an element inside the Leadership Board dissatisfied with their neutrality stance, and perhaps quietly allied with the Cabal."

"I'd say more than perhaps."

The three of them didn't say much for the next while. Food stayed untouched, partially eaten remnants getting cold on Tag's and Lira's plates. Sure, the smell was as tantalizing as ever, but those images—the numbers as cold as the food became—none of it put Tag in the mood to eat. Apparently, it didn't work for Lira, either, because she just stared at the blank cushion opposite her.

"Next step," Tag finally said. "We get back to Atterissage. We clean up. And then what—we drop this thing on the next transport to your bosses?"

"In a rough manner of speaking," Dyson said. "I have several tests I must run to confirm the validity of these files."

"Don't remember you saying that was part of the mission."

Dyson shifted his position in his seat. To Tag he seemed awkward, but he was a 'bot. If he was programmed with such quirks, were they put on for Tag's benefit? Or was he genuinely expressing discomfort? "It is not. Part of my parameters are to ensure the successful delivery of the data to our employers, and to see if the data is correct. If I cannot verify the origin of this data, how can I vouch for its accuracy?"

"Okay. Sounds good." Tag jerked a thumb over his shoulder. "I'm assuming you don't want to run those tests in the middle of Diamantetoiles's finest eating establishment."

"It would be counterproductive, seeing how the analysis will take far longer than the closing hours for the restaurant, not to mention the attention it will draw if I—"

"Never mind. I got it." He shouldn't have asked. Tag glanced at Lira. "How about you? This stuff gets to your bosses, you're off the hook."

She pursed her lips, the hint of a smirk at the corners. "Well, I would never say I'm off the hook as far as the Briddarri are concerned. But I'm certain I can find a way to wriggle free when they're not looking. I just ..."

Lira's eyes took on a glassy, vacant gaze. She clutched her side, and her skin paled. "Hey. Lira." Tag held her shoulder. Her palm felt clammy. "What's wrong?"

"Nothing. Just a bad spell." She smiled, but there was pain still evident. "It passed. I'm fine."

Tag caught Dyson watching them. The two met each other's looks, and Tag hoped the android was actually as concerned as his expression belied.

"You're right. You're both right. We should return to Atterissage, and take care of this—whatever this is," Lira said. "We should sell it off to the highest bidder and be rid of it."

Tag let go of her hand. "You can't be serious. If this got out—"

Lira stood. "It's going to get out, isn't it? Your precious government is going to make sure everyone knows about it, to force the Union into a war it doesn't want to fight! And what's that going to mean? More people will die. Things will be destroyed—museums and paintings and gardens. And lives! The most beautiful creations in the galaxy, all lost."

She started from the table. Tag was up in a flash and caught her arm. "Lira, the Naplians won't stop if we just give up. They're pulling this whole corner of Estra into their borders, and if we don't stand against them, they'll rule everything."

Lira shook her head. "It doesn't matter to me who rules, Tag. They're all the same. If you want a chance to walk away from it all, to live a life free from the conquerors—be they Naplian, Briddarri, or Terran—this is it."

She touched his cheek. "I'm sorry. You boys should have known I'd never be on board with your patriotism, or the Briddarri Kingdom's for that matter. I'll see you on *Vy*."

Lira left Tag standing there, hands useless at his side.

Dyson stood next to him. The scroll was tucked away somewhere, its displays gone from the table, as if the nightmare of information had never existed. "Captain, I understand what she is saying."

"Yeah? Find that hard to believe."

"It is not only the biological who mourn." Dyson walked away, following Lira.

Well, perfect. Tag fumbled for his ID, the one provided by Terran Intelligence, so he could settle up their bill. What a great evening.

Blasted war.

***

Elden knew it wasn't possible for him to feel human sensations like he used to, but as their ships hurtled through the twisted fabric of space via their jump drives, he swore his skin itched.

Ludicrous, of course. He didn't have skin, and it would have been folly to hook sensors to his Truppen frame's armor so he could feel things touching it. The whole purpose of keeping a Truppen's headpiece and nervous system separate from the frame in that regard was so a soldier wouldn't feel pain. Wouldn't stop fighting.

"On point for exit." Nolte's voice maintained its pleasant ring. "Thirty seconds."

"Thank you." Marney sat in the center seat of *Vossberg's* bridge, every bit the captain. Granted, there were only four more people she commanded on the bridge, and another couple dozen throughout the ship. The strike corvette had been retrofitted with as few crew as possible.

Which was of little comfort to Elden when the jump drive deactivated, and their destination appeared as light images in the holo display and magnified on the main view screen.

"Contacts! One station, one ship."

No wonder he'd felt his skin crawl. There had been something out here, in a blank space between star systems. An uncharted space habitat, thirty klicks long, nothing more than a monstrous collection of cargo ship hulls and transport containers welded into the rough shape of an asteroid. The screen's resolution was fine enough to let Elden see some of it did incorporate small asteroids, mostly buried among the containers. Likely they served as attachment points for the whole ensemble.

Of greater concern was the Naplian destroyer slinging energy blasts its way. "Their shields have failed," Nolte said. "Bioscan shows life aboard, but I can't differentiate. Can tell there's weapons fire aboard."

"They're trying to take it intact," Goetz said.

"Why bother?" Rett crouched near the holo display. He pointed a claw into the depths of the lights. "See here? Structural integrity's near collapse. A couple more blasts could break the whole thing apart."

"Obviously they don't want that, because their lines of fire are directed at the opposite end," Elden said. "What's Captain Zhivko's read?"

"I'm checking." Marney toggled a control on the arm of her chair. "*Vossberg* to *Dragonfly*. Fyodor, have you scanned everything we have?"

"Ah, Marney ..." Nolte gestured.

Dragonfly leapt from its coordinates, accelerating from where it had emerged from the jump. Sublight engines blazed as their outputs soared, the readings spinning up into red digits on the holo display. Long-range missiles slashed toward the Naplian ship, and a stream of railgun projectiles followed.

Marney sighed. "Elden, I suppose you'll want to join in the fray."

"Your man Fyodor seems to have the destroyer's attention out here," Elden said. "But I believe our octants can clean up the interior."

"Dave, take us around to the docking array at the following coordinates." Marney stepped to the holo display and touched a segment of the station less rundown in appearance than the rest. It pulsed gold under her fingers. "It's relatively shielded from the scrap they're starting."

"Roger that."

The communications array chirped. Marney took the call. "Fyodor, does restraint not translate into Reittian?"

Captain Zhivko's laughter boomed through the link. "These One-eyes are picking pieces off a garbage heap. They should know better than to leave their flank unprotected. Give me a few minutes; I will have their hulk for salvage. Or I can destroy them. Whatever your preference."

"I'll leave the Naval matters to you, but I won't lose any sleep if you turn their reactor into a sun," Marney said. "The Truppen are boarding the station. If you can't destroy the ship, at least hold it off."

"Can't destroy? You wound me. *Dragonfly* out."

It seemed to Elden that the Reittian ship doubled its attack.

***

The airlock mechanism was simple enough to override.

Goetz plunged his claws through the panels, tearing the control circuits apart. The malfunction caused the power relays to the hatches themselves to die. Then it was a simple matter of prying apart the double door.

"Deploy by octants," Elden said. "Eliminate all Naplian forces. I want officers alive—they will have information about why this facility was targeted."

"Yes, sir," Goetz said. "All right, boys, you heard the Consul. Move!"

The corridor ahead of them branched at a four-way intersection.

One octant each peeled off to the left and right, toward sounds of weapons fire. Elden, Goetz, and Rett moved ahead with the remaining two octants. Marney and Nolte accompanied them with a half-dozen mercenaries, men who were among the crowd that greeted them back on the planet. All eight of them carried Furta energy rifles, with the exception of the two largest men—they were armed with Kompton Arms Overwatch Series RG-18 SAAR railguns, person-portable weapons with enough power to cut even a Truppen in half.

They found the Naplians easily enough.

The One-eyes were ransacking compartments lining the corridors. Mottled-blue armor rippled as they moved from shadow to light and back again, adapting their camouflage to the colors around them. But they had to have been informed the station had been breached—by someone other than themselves—because they'd formed defensive bastions out of stacked furnishings and debris. Enough to repel small arms fire.

Elden shook his head. No matter how many times the One-eyes faced the so-called Devastators, they never learned.

He led the charge into sheets of energy bursts, the bulk of the shots gouging or reflecting from his armor. The Truppen closed the distance far faster than a humanoid could have managed, battering aside the flimsy ramparts. White-hot railgun projectiles screamed overhead in hissing streams, cutting apart the Naplians. Elden swiped aside the first defender he encountered, claws snagging the armor and slamming him against the bulkhead so hard it left a person-sized dent.

Goetz had two Naplians held in either set of claws and slapped them together as if he were clapping dirt off a pair of boots. He fired off a rocket-propelled grenade. It skipped over a trio of soldiers firing rifles and impacted at the feet of two Naplians laying down heavy bursts from a much larger gun set atop a tripod. Elden's scanners gave him the full readout on a Daish Kashiton-1010 "Garvu" pulse projector an instant before the grenade exploded, snapping it in pieces and incinerating the soldiers manning it.

The Truppen swept over the Naplians like a wave submerging rocks, not leaving behind any survivors. No officers were captured, however, because none were apparently in this corridor—the linked scan results from every one of Elden's men couldn't find them. Which meant only enlisted soldiers and noncoms had been left behind here.

Where were the officers hiding?

A pair of Garvu fired on them from the next intersection. Green flashes lit up the corridors, casting people and objects in a stuttering strobe effect. Bursts bracketed a Truppen alongside Elden, Private Jordahl, tearing apart his torso. Elden dragged him down.

It was nothing like the screams coming from one of Nolte's mercenaries, as Marney compressed a gaping wound in his thigh. Jordahl was Truppen; he felt no pain as his power core stuttered and died. The red lights of his optical sensors dimmed but stayed on—his headpiece was damaged where an energy blast had severed critical connections.

"Technician!" Elden fired his shoulder-mounted railgun, scoring hits on one of the Garvu as he dragged Jordahl into the shadows of an adjacent compartment.

Corporal Vingh bounded through the hatch. "I've got him, sir."

"Hold tight, Private," Elden said. "We'll get an aux power source to you, get those connections replaced."

"It's a ... lot of work, sir." Jordahl's voice was scratchy, as if partially jammed. "... can't get scan input. My ... won't start the box."

Elden knew the damage was more severe than it first appeared. The headpiece itself was close to failure, if Jordahl was spouting gibberish.

"I can't stabilize him," Vingh said. "The cortex is disintegrating."

"... won't let ... go with me away," Jordahl said. "... And ... end ..."

The optical port lights went black. Sparks sputtered from the base of the headpiece.

Elden rested claws on Jordahl's chest, ignoring for a moment the battle echoing around him. The true death of a Truppen. There was no return from it, no way to reboot. It was as final as a biological being dying.

What would Abbott Jeopar tell him? The soul was freed, gone to be at the side of God—or not, depending upon the soul's state. Something to that effect. Elden could only hope Jordahl found peace, and that peace was granted to him.

A thunderous explosion rattled the deckplates. "Way's clear through those guns," Goetz said. "Rett's onto something. Took off like a Saarno fox."

Elden gathered up Vingh and moved out into the corridor. Thick smoke blocked his vision, but once he switched to scanners it was no difficulty—Naplians stood out as bright yellow silhouettes on a deep blue background. "Prisoners?"

"None yet. No officers. Two men down. Urquart and Li."

Three indicators were blood red in Elden's listing of the octant. Li's was still lined with green; his headpiece had remained intact and was secured by a medic. They could get him a new Truppen form back on *Hessian*, if there were any undamaged still in storage.

"Are you all right, Elden?" Marney's body armor was stained with blood, and her face streaked with soot. She held her M36 with the proper ease and stance of someone who'd received considerable training; considering the last time he'd seen her she'd already been shooting in the midst of the Naplian invasion, Elden was glad to see she'd taken further instruction.

"I don't appear to be damaged," he said. "You?"

"We lost a man. Talbot." Marney's eyes were rimmed red, whether from tears or smoke, he couldn't tell. "But Dave tells me there's a way around this mess."

"Side corridor, through this antechamber." Nolte held up a scroll, its glowing hologram displaying a partial map of the station.

"I have it. Goetz?"

"Storing the data." Goetz stomped a Naplian rifle, mashing it to the deck. "Sir, Rett went that direction."

"On his own?"

"As usual."

"Blasted fool is going to get himself killed trying to prove his worth," Elden muttered. "Goetz, take the men straight on. Marney, Nolte, and their people will cut around. Meet us at the central command post."

"Yes, sir." Goetz bounded ahead.

"Let's go," Elden said to the humans gathered around him.

Nolte moved in front. "We've got it, Tin Man."

His mercenaries slipped into the antechamber, moving with unit cohesion Elden admired.

Nothing like linked Truppen, but impressive.

He vowed then to not let any of them die. Especially Marney. Every last One-eye would be ripped apart first.

***

The return flight from Diamantetoiles to Atterissage didn't raise any alarms with Orbital Control, though the security scans lasted twice as long. Dyson had the crystal lattice hidden away in a box Terran Intelligence rigged up special for the mission. It absorbed the majority of the radiation emitted by the crystal.

Tag had no doubt the authorities were searching for it.

"There is no chatter on the local bands about the theft," Dyson said. "Nor has the Leadership Board issued a reward for its recovery."

They were back at the hotel, seated on the couches by the balcony. Well, Tag was seated, with his shoes propped up on the table. Dyson sat opposite him, face distorted behind a transparent wall of holographic data. The crystal was inside a black box with gray trim perched on the center of the table.

"Of course they haven't," Tag said. "This stuff is top secret. I wouldn't go around broadcasting its disappearance. Novafire, I bet there's branches of their own government that don't know it's gone."

"It is unlikely; however, I am certain their own intelligence service is putting in long hours to investigate."

"Intelligence." Tag snorted. "If they were intelligent, they wouldn't have recorded any of it!"

"We have discussed the matter," Dyson said. "Not to your satisfaction, apparently."

"Will you two stop it?" Lira stood out on the balcony, arms braced on the railing. The morning breeze flung her hair like the flags whipping atop the expo center.

She hadn't said much else to either of them on the flight back, or their brief rest. Of course, Tag hadn't made a point to remedy the situation. She'd been so overwrought about the whole war versus life thing, he preferred to leave it alone.

But they were a team, of sorts.

Tag leaned against the open balcony door. Diving into this was harder than strafing a Naplian transport—and felt more dangerous. "I get why you're upset. Sooner we get this data back, the sooner we can push the Naplians out of this corner of the galaxy."

"You're so sure of that," Lira said. "Do you have any idea how long the Briddarri have been trying to do the same thing?"

Tag scratched the back of his neck. "Hadn't really thought about it."

"Nearly twenty years! Millions of Briddarri dragooned into service, countless dead, whole clans who haven't seen loved ones in such a long time that children have grown and married while the war was fought." Lira shook her head. "You humans think every minor advantage you gain will make you the ones to end the war for good. There's a reason the Grand Alliance will never stop the Naplians. They're relentless."

"So what? You'd rather we just surrender and become their next province? You don't know humans very well. We've got this terrible itch for freedom that makes us put up a fight every time a dictator comes around."

"I don't care about what your government does, or mine does, or what any other does. I only care about people, and their lives." Lira gestured out at the busy streets and skies of Atterissage. "Look at all of them! I don't want any of them to give up their dreams, their loves, for a conflict that's going to shred it all. I'm leaving it to the soldiers and their robots."

"I get what you're saying, Lira, but I'm a soldier." Tag joined her at the rail.

"No, you're a pilot. You love to fly."

"Yeah, well, right now that means I have to fight. There's no way around it. They took my home, killed my friends, and made me a refugee. I won't let it stand."

Lira's eyes glittered with tears. Space, why did she have to be so passionate about this? Why couldn't she see the war effort was important? She could always help with refugee relief, like his sister Marney was doing. Lira touched his cheek. "If we hand the data over, people will die, even before the Union joins the war on your side."

The idea made Tag ill. But it was a necessary cost. It was the best thing, in the long run. Right?

"Ms. Reen, Tag." Dyson beckoned them to the couches. "I have a reply."

They gathered around the table. "TI will have *Confiance* and her escorts waiting for us at the Yarbo System, in one week's time."

Tag ran the mental math. "We need to depart in three days, at the latest."

"Then you can all celebrate." Lira winced. She rubbed at her side. Her pallor worsened. "We should get you to a medic," Tag said. "You've gotten worse."

"I told you, it's nothing."

Dyson brought up a new image, a glowing outline of a female body. Internal organs, nervous system, circulatory routes pulsed a rainbow of colors. "If I may disagree, Ms. Reen, it is something. More specifically, it is a genetically-tailored poison slowly chipping away at your cellular structure. In the long term it will leave you crippled, and dependent upon machinery to live."

She stared at him, mouth agape. It was the most surprised Tag had ever seen her look.

Granted, he probably was just as shocked. "She's poisoned? How in blazes do you know?"

"Bioscan. I was concerned Ms. Reen's effectiveness had been compromised."

"I can't believe you violated my privacy!" she snapped. "And what does it matter if my effectiveness has been compromised? Our little job is done!"

Dyson bowed his head. Whether or not androids got ashamed, he was doing a bang-up job of aping the motions. "I apologize. I was concerned for your well-being. Regardless of the mission parameters, I have become … accustomed to your presence, and wish it to continue."

"At least we agree on that point," Tag muttered. "Lira, you should have told us you were sick."

"I didn't because it isn't accidental, or natural. The Briddarri did it to me as a way to ensure my compliance." Lira smirked. "Think they're quite clever, for a bunch of brutes."

"Let us help you," Dyson said. "We can make arrangements …"

"Sorry, boys. There's only one way I get out of this." Her eyes teared up again. She hurried to her room and sealed the door.

Tag rubbed his hand over his face.

"If you do not mind," Dyson said in a quiet tone, "I wish to take a walk."

"Be my guest," Tag said. "Just code lock the doors before you go. I'm taking a shower."

**

Tag let the steam beat on him until the bathroom was more fogged than the surface of Nimbarat Three. What could he say to Lira to get her to change her mind, about any of it? He had no clue.

All he knew was he couldn't stand the thought of her in pain.

He cleaned up and got dressed. Okay, Tag. Take it easy. No worse than a dogfight. "Lira?" He rapped his knuckles on her door. "Come on, open up. I need to talk to you."

Nothing.

"Lira?" Tag tried the latch. It was unlocked. He unsealed the door.

Empty. Even her gear was gone—stealth suit, wrist scanner, the works. Only thing left was a beige wash towel, with a word scrawled in lip liner.

Sorry.

"Novafire." Tag hurried to the living room.

The box containing the crystal lattice was gone.

It wasn't in Dyson's room either, nor was it among any belongings. The blasted thing had vanished.

Check that. It hadn't vanished. Tag knew exactly where it was. The thief had stolen it.

CHAPTER TWELVE

L ira didn't use the same public communications hub. She went the opposite direction, ending up at a local art museum which had a small café tucked off to one side. Four terminals were nestled in a far corner, near enough to the hiss of the steaming brew station that any words Lira had to speak would be lost. Helpful, too, that there were twenty people crammed into the place this morning.

She waited for the reply to her signal. The black box bulged from the inside pocket of the pale blue jacket she wore, digging into her ribs. Poor Tag. She doubted he was taking it well.

Their intransigence left her little choice. The Terrans wanted the data on the crystal for the same reason the Briddarri did, and when she'd signed onto this mission—albeit from a position of weakness, not negotiation—she'd thought it was worth the risk. Everyone wanted the war to end, didn't they?

Lira shivered in a way that had nothing to do with the morning chill and the frost on the edges of the circular window panes. Yes, well, ending a war by causing the deaths of innocent millions, to save the lives of billions, was no deal she wanted to make.

The terminal chirped.

<Value is extraordinary. We can provide transport.>

Lira smiled. Not since she'd grabbed the Seerrstone from the Sanctuary of the Revered Barad all those months ago had she felt so alive, such electricity in all her senses. They would come for her. She knew she hadn't been abandoned. <Will need a good rest. Very tired. Send me pickup time. Don't want to worry Mom and Dad.>

She sent the message. Within a few minutes, her contact codes would lapse, and her link would disappear. Hopefully they'd be able to have a decent medic standing by. Whatever the Briddarri had done to her to ensure compliance could be reversed, she was sure of it. But her people also needed to know that the Briddarri—Mom and Dad, as it were—probably had her traced.

<Will meet and greet soon. Wear your best.>

"Always ready," she murmured.

Movement beyond the crowd and the café's windows caught her eye. A pair of Audrians, in the midst of a heated argument, walked by. Their heads bobbed up and down. Streaks of deep purple marked their cheeks.

Lira had felt someone watching her.

There was no mistaking the sensation, not for someone like her who had spent years watching others, waiting for the right moment to move unobserved. A quick perusal of the species milling about the tables revealed nothing. Six languages overlapped, a rumble through which she could make out only a handful of words.

No one in here. Must have been someone outside, though not the Audrians.

She closed the communications link and headed toward the door with a sealed cup of jorva. The green liquid sloshed inside the clear container, and even with the lid shut to prevent heat loss, a sharp aroma greeted her. Steam condensed on the rim, finding its way around the lid. Her fingers were already damp.

Outside there were few passersby on the streets. Most were human of varying races. Lira was always surprised by just how many there were. Certainly, many humans were some shade of brown— tan, ochre, sienna. But some of the races were more sharply defined. People with hair as golden as the sun, or pale faces sprinkled with tiny dots as if they were diseased. Frackoles, or freckles, the humans called them.

The two men waiting down the street were pale, too, and she would have dismissed them soon after cataloging their existence, if she hadn't noticed their bruising. Both were blond. One had a long, crooked nose, and the other's was short and broad. They stood conversing over the images of local terrain projected from a scroll the taller, crooked nose man held.

She wasted a full five seconds figuring out she'd seen them before, then cursed vehemently in Briddarri. She walked quickly down the street, and crossed in the middle of traffic. Ground vehicles stopped, sensors for their automatic guidance systems triggered by her presence. A driver made what she took for a rude gesture.

Lira didn't care. Those men were of the quartet she and Tag had encountered aboard the Iriada skyhook. Denic spies.

The other two had to be near.

She caught the reflection of the blonds following her progress, on the opposite side of the street. No one else seemed to be around, but knowing as she did about Denics and their disguises, suddenly every human within several meters' radius was suspect. Especially those of paler complexion.

Lira consulted her wrist unit, mindful of the black box's presence in her coat. She could find a place to conceal herself, dig out the stealth suit from the bag slung across her shoulders, but as quickly as everyone was walking, the men could catch up with her before then. Instead she checked the building layouts on a commercial registry.

There. Half a block up, across the next intersection. The market went from this avenue to the next, allowing pedestrians to walk through the entire block, rather than having to traverse the streets to get to the other side.

She stayed with the flow, as more and more people joined the sidewalk throngs. A flock of Briddarri women exited a salon, jabbering excitedly in the native tongue. Lira smiled and strode into their midst. Some camouflage, for a moment.

Up ahead, the other two men—the ones she had beaten aboard the Iriada skyhook—rounded the intersection.

The market was thirty meters in front of her. The men, a hundred meters.

The women, all ten of them, moved at a decent clip, but she wished they'd move faster. The market entrance was so close, she could smell spices and the earthy scent of plants. Just a little farther ...

The blond men chose that second to duck across the street, at a fast walk. Vehicles lurched around them.

Lira shoved the nearest Briddarri woman at the precise moment she was in midstride. With a yelp, the young lady stumbled, careening off her companion, who in turn tripped on the legs of the woman in front of her.

Five of them went down in a tumble. The crowd around them reacted the same, everyone turning around to see what had happened. The people behind the girls stopped in their tracks.

The swift-moving current of people became a dammed-up river behind the wailing tangle.

Stopped the blond men in their tracks, though.

Lira sprinted into the market. Stalls surrounded her on all sides. Her shoes clacked across tiles like terra cotta. There was no stopping her run. She dove between couples, banked around families, sparing only a single glance back.

The two men, these with black hair, and the blonds shortly on their tails.

Up ahead, a melon stand. They stank, pungent with ripeness, each one with a soft white skin and gold flesh where samples had been cut open. The merchant was a fat Orgolon, waving six arm tentacles about and touting his goods in the songlike tones of his language. Beautiful, really, so much so Lira felt the urge to listen to Orgolon opera if she got free of this mess.

She grabbed a walking rod from the stand prior, hooked it around the melon stand's nearest leg, and pulled.

Fruit spilled and splattered everywhere behind her. The Orgolon's song became a strident shriek.

The first of the black-haired Denics to reach the mess slipped and fell, hitting the tiles with a crunch Lira found more satisfying than her first heist.

She didn't look back at the others, but didn't hear them fall either. Instead she kept running, lungs burning, breathing steady, every stride as practiced as walking across the kitchen for a cup of jorva.

There. The exit out onto the next block was a bright rectangle set among the dim orange and yellow lights of the market, framed by red curtains. Lira crossed the threshold—

A pale orange hover-truck halted in her path.

It was painted with Atterissage Emergency Services emblems, red wings on a blue circle. The side hatch hissed open, and the compartment beyond had two more men inside. They were bald, their complexions not as pasty as the foursome pursuing her but definitely on the chalky side.

She skidded on the pavement, veering left.

But the stun pulse cut off all her nerves. Lira toppled as if she were a statue cut from its base. The impact jarred her teeth, scraped her chin and cheek.

"We've got her. Load up." Hands seized her. Something pricked her neck.

Everything smeared when she tried to look around, as if an oil painting had been left out in a rainstorm. Colors dimmed. Sounds mushed together and turned to distant mumbles.

Tag. I'm sorry.

***

Where was she?

Tag jogged down one street, stopping at the corner. He tried his scroll, but it couldn't pick up any indications for him—no trace.

Novafire. He couldn't believe it. All the work, all the risk, shot down faster than a fighter-bomber flying without escort over enemy territory.

He had to find her. For a lot of reasons. For the mission, sure. But … If anything happened to her …

"Tag." Dyson walked toward him, as calmly as any man could who was an android out for a stroll. He even held a cup of jorva, steam trailing a miniature cloud behind him. Tag wondered how much he'd drank.

"Lira. She's gone. She took the cube."

Dyson nodded. "I surmised she would make such an attempt."

"Surmised?" Tag sneered. "Were you planning on telling me?"

"I know where she is going. The tracking signal is strong. Come with me."

Tag was so stunned he didn't fully process what was going on until Dyson was halfway up the street. "Hey. Hey!"

He ran after him, surprised it took a whole lot more effort to catch up with android. His strides weren't any longer than Tag's, but they were perfectly even, and so swift Tag had to work double-time.

Dyson, of course, wasn't winded. "Her position is 300 meters from ours. I suggest we move swiftly if we are to intercept."

"You have her tracked."

"Marked with a pulse transmitter, yes. It was arranged by the Briddarri. They provided me with the frequency. It was necessary to ensure—"

"Shut up." Tag grabbed the back of his collar. "You mark me with a transmitter, too? Did you inject me with something while I was sleeping, or put something in my food? Listen to me, blast it all!"

Dyson wheeled on him. Tag collided with him as solidly as with particle shielding. Suddenly two hands held his collar with a grip as tight as any weapons clamp. Tag couldn't breathe.

Dyson's face was implacable as ever, but it was also devoid of any simulacrum of human emotion. There was nothing—though considering his position, Tag wasn't at all certain there wasn't real anger behind those dark eyes. "You will listen to me, Taggart Wester. I have no desire to hurt or kill anyone. I have never betrayed my human superiors, nor have I ever betrayed my oath to the Terran nation. Lira Reen is one of our team, our band of three. Likewise, I will never let anything happen to her. Her presence—and yours—are now a part of me. With my artificial mind, none of those memories will lapse, not even long years after the two of you have succumbed to old age. We must act swiftly to save her. I will not fail her again."

"When … have you …" Tag coughed. Something snapped into place. "Her? Olivia."

"Yes." Dyson released him. "Olivia Vy. She was a counterpart in my Terran Intelligence work. We were—efficient. I valued her presence, too. There was no one I trusted greater. And in an instant, in the detritus of one mission gone wrong, she was gone. Destroyed. Nothing was left but parts."

Tag stared at him, grateful for the lungs full of air he gulped. Whatever animosity he held against Dyson, for being an android like the beings who'd killed his ancestors, he found it dissipating like dew on a fighter's wing in the sun. "Okay. Let's keep moving."

They were near to some kind of open-front market, similar to the ones Tag remembered from late summer in Vossberg City. Smelled great. He could have eaten anything from every stall they passed— fruit, fish, vegetables, cooked meats of a dozen animals he didn't have a chance of identifying without a scroll.

Speaking of which, Dyson was following a blinking red indicator on his. "Ahead, 150 meters."

"Got it. Someone else's been busy here." A sanitation 'bot hovered over smeared melons, using pincers to pluck unbroken fruits from the tile paving. The 'bot's body, round as a planet and gleaming brass, reflected splotches of squished fruit and shattered rind. An alien with tentacles and a voice that grated on Tag like an unbalanced thruster screeched in obvious displeasure.

"Indeed. There is a vehicle ahead." Dyson squinted toward the opening on the opposite end of the market, facing the street on the next block. Tag wondered how good a magnification those android eyes could accomplish. "And Ms. Reen is not a willing occupant."

Tag swore and put on a boost of speed. He wished he had a gun, or any kind of weapon.

Well, whatever worked. He hadn't needed one aboard Iriada.

Two men stood on the curb. Beyond them was the hatch of the vehicle, some kind of delivery wagon. And in the instant the hatch hissed shut, Tag saw two guys bundling Lira up in heavy straps. Her eyes stared blankly at the ceiling.

"Hey!"

Four men turned around—two at the front of the truck, and two just inside the exit into the street. Tag recognized all of them. How could he not? Two of the goons still had bumps on their faces, courtesy of his fists.

All four had stun weapons, small, grey and gold devices the size of a drinking glass. Each one was wrapped around their wrists and extended out over their hands. Even without android vision Tag could see the air rippling around the discharge ports like summer heat on a tarmac.

No way he could dodge all four, even as he barreled straight on for his targets.

Good thing Dyson was faster.

He was a blur that slammed into the first two guys, black-haired bruisers. Both of them went down so fast Tag swore he heard the air crack—or maybe it was just their heads.

It didn't stop those two from firing their stun weapons. Flashes of miniature lightning left spots in Tag's eyes. Dyson and the black-haired goons were a tangle of limbs.

The other two, the blonds, fired on Tag at the same time, but he was ready. He snagged a tapestry woven with the greatest care, gold and green designs so intricate he felt a pang of guilt when he stole it from a merchant's rack. Tag swept it across his path, as sure a barrier as if he had personal particle shields. The stun bursts fizzled out upon impact, though the hairs on Tag's head and arms rose at the touch of their static.

Tag threw the rug aside and caught the nearest blond Denic with a right hook across the jaw. He slammed him against the side of the hover truck, bashing the wrist equipped with the stun weapon repeatedly until sparks and tendrils of smoke signaled its demise.

The second blond slugged Tag below the ribs, blowing the air from his lungs. Tag wrenched out of his grasp and planted a kick in his sternum. Bones broke—hopefully the same ones as would snap on a human.

Dyson was having much better luck with his opponents. The android was up on his feet, facing both. The first struck at him with a chopping martial arts motion so fluid, so fast, Tag knew anyone else wouldn't have had a prayer of dodging. Dyson, though, was simply not in the same space the next instant. Instead he had the attacker by the back of the shirt and belt of the trousers. He threw him a good ten meters down the sidewalk.

The second one was smarter. He twisted and fired into Tag's melee.

Tag let go his two blond Denics and tried to make himself as small a target as possible. Upside, the blast was misaimed; downside, it skittered across Tag's right leg. The limb buckled, as if he had a landing strut minus all its power.

The blond Denic who he'd hit into the truck pummeled him with blows. Tag absorbed them best he could, gritting against the pain, until he had the timing down. Took a few seconds. When the fourth punch hammered down, Tag grabbed the fist, twisted with both hands, and rammed his head into the Denic's gut.

The second one's shadow shifted—lining up for a stun shot? Tag yanked on his puncher's arm, slinging him into the line of fire. The stun weapon buzzed, and tiny lightning bolts arced from the first guy's back up and over his arms, down his torso.

Tag put everything he had behind his operational leg and lunged.

But the second guy must have anticipated the move. He slid aside, leaving Tag to fall atop his stunned companion. No sooner had they thudded onto the sidewalk than he kicked Tag in the side.

The blow was worse than a gunshot. Tag rolled off clutching his side. He waited for stun that would put him down.

Nothing. Instead, clothing rustled on pavement, and the hum of the hover truck's lift engines increased. It pulled away from the curb, headed down the street.

"They have boarded and are escaping." Dyson hurried past Tag. "I am in pursuit."

Sure enough, the blonds were already aboard and the black-haired Denics were helping each other into the hatch. Tag didn't know how fast the hover truck was moving—maybe 25 kph, in the vehicle traffic—but Dyson closed the distance with next to no effort. Rather than boarding, he grabbed onto a collision guard on the back end of the truck and planted his feet.

The truck's progress slowed. Dyson's shoes started leaving streaks on the pavement, then started shedding pieces.

Tag grabbed onto a light pole and hauled himself up, dragging his foot. If Dyson could just hold the truck in place—

But even the android's strength had its limits. The hover truck's engines raised in pitch, and the chassis vibrated with the added exertion. There was a squeal, a sound of materials rending, then the collision guard ripped free of the truck. Dyson staggered backward, his legs and arms stiff. The truck shot off down through traffic and disappeared around a corner.

Tag limped to the end of the block, following as best he could. Dyson walked behind him, his legs seemingly damaged from the strain of trying to hold back a couple of tons of vehicle on his own. By the time they reached the corner, looking the most ragged pair Tag had ever seen, the truck was well gone. Worst of it, there were three emergency services trucks going to and fro, making it impossible to figure which was which.

"You can track her," Tag said. "Lock down her location."

Dyson shook his head. He held up a tiny object, small as a grain of rice. His fingertips were stained red where he touched it. "They removed it. It is possible to trace the radiation emitted from the crystal lattice, but I cannot guarantee it will work."

"Of course not. Because it's in that blasted box." Tag wiped sweat from his forehead. With the adrenaline of the fight fading, he was suddenly exhausted, and thirsty. And starving. "Okay, so, next steps."

"The next step, gentlemen, is you come with me."

The voice came from a short alien, only a meter tall. Tag had mistaken him for a kid, but by the way he stood, and the depth of his bass voice, he had to be an adult. He was humanoid, stocky, with rusty orange skin and a flat face. The nose was two long, deep slits, and the grinning mouth full of flint-colored needle teeth. His eyes were glossy gray, and ridges of spikes framed a round, armored face. His outfit was casual—brown boots and trousers, long gray shirt without sleeves, and two sets of white cloth bands around each arm. He had three broad fingers and, judging by the shape of his boots, the same number of digits on his feet.

One of those hands held a gun, half the size of a DK-40 pistol favored by CDF.

"Who the blazes is this?" Tag muttered.

"A Shikasta," Dyson said. "Generally an unsavory people."

"You think? The gun was my tip-off."

"My name is Akro Nuvish. Less talk out here," the Shikasta said. "We have much to discuss, and little time to find Lira."

"What? Okay, spill it, short and orange," Tag said. "What makes you think we even know what you're talking about?"

"Because I'm Blue Kitt." The grin widened. "And we've been watching you all."

***

Elden's small group encountered only one squad of Naplians through the side corridor.

He eliminated four of them on his own, before any had time to so much as widen those blasted single eyes.

Nolte stabbed one from behind, hand clasped over its mouth. It let out a muffled warble, but the sound died in a gargle as yellow blood soaked his blade. He let the Naplian fall, and Elden saw the blade was more than any military-grade combat knife—it was sixty centimeters long, akin to a machete. Nolte squeezed the handle in a deliberate pattern of finger presses. The weapon shrank down to fit easily in a twenty-centimeter sheath on his belt.

The corridor turned twice more, through dark patches. Elden led, his scanners making up for the lack of light. Marney, Nolte, and the five mercenaries—the sixth being taken back to *Vossberg* under the care of Elden's medics—stayed close behind, in a staggered formation.

"Fyodor's taken care of the Naplian ship," Marney said. "He's inquiring how many weapons you want salvaged from the wreck."

Strange that the death of an enemy starship should go unnoticed, Elden thought, but inside a windowless space station, there was no way to determine the nature of anything beyond the bulkheads. "Extend Captain Zhivko my congratulations. I think we'll pass."

The corridor opened up into a 100-meter wide chamber, open to a tall, curving ceiling, and a deep, sloping floor with a depression that mimicked what was above. With primary power knocked out the only illumination came from sickly green lights inset along structural supports arcing up to the ceiling and down into the center of the room. Dozens of alcoves were set in the walls, at regular intervals, with pipes, storage tanks, and monitoring computers set on either side. All of them were broken, the plas-glass shattered and scorched by energy blasts.

All of them contained humanoids—fit, muscular, large men. Each had been altered.

Limbs had been removed, replaced with crude weapons or blades. Some had scanning devices implanted in place of eyes. A dozen had cybernetic legs.

Everything about them offended Elden. It was as if a deranged child had played at making cyborgs, without any notion of the complexity, yet there were enough elements of Truppen construction through the dozens of subjects the sight and scans chilled him.

One of Nolte's men gagged. Marney's complexion paled, and she held her hand to her mouth.

Elden was thankful his Truppen frame no longer afforded him the sense of smell. "One-eyes," Nolte said.

There were, but only eight. Each one was dead, shot or stabbed. Rett slumped against a holographic tank, his armor dripping yellow blood.

"Rett, are you damaged?" Elden checked him with a cursory scan even as he asked.

"No. No, I'm okay." Rett shuddered, armor rattling. "They'd killed them all by the time I found the place. Even the workers. Tried to stop them but … I had to shoot back. Didn't leave anyone to question."

No one to question? As Marney and the mercenaries fanned out around the room, Elden inspected the nearest Naplian corpse. Yes, an officer. All eight were officers.

The very ones he'd wanted alive.

"They shot at me first," Rett repeated.

"Don't worry about it," Elden said. "We'll find another way."

"Elden?" Marney called to him from across the room. "You'll want to see this."

She and Nolte were standing behind a row of mainframes, the sides of which glowed yellow. At their feet, four more bodies slumped in a row. They'd been lined up, backs against the bulkhead, and shot in the head.

Nolte knelt. "Looks like One-eye blasts."

"Their lab coats are unmarked," Marney said. "I can't find insignia on anything in this place."

Technicians. Elden stared at them, and at the experiments stashed in the alcoves. The giant room was a charnel house, a place of death and torment—with none left alive to tell what had happened.

"Sir!" Goetz emerged from a corridor opposite where Elden's party had entered. "We found him!"

Colonel Diaz's headpiece was in a room just outside, hooked to a bewildering array of machinery. There were more computers and holo displays in this room than Elden had seen even on the flagship *Winter Scourge*.

"Where's his body?" Elden's claws trembled, not out of fear, but a growing anger, dark like a storm front.

"We found pieces," Goetz muttered. "In a replication shop down the corridor. Shoddy job of copying."

"Technicians?"

"Five. Dead."

"... S ... Sir." Diaz's voice emitter sounded fragmented, damaged. "... Help."

"Hold steady, Colonel." Even as he said it, Goetz quietly shook his head. Blast. Diaz was one of his most trusted advisors. Elden would be spaced before he'd leave him to die in this godforsaken wreck. "Your headpiece is gravely damaged. I won't chance moving you until we can secure ..."

"... too late. You can't ... stop. Them." Static washed through his words. "... Army readying ... prepare ... Harvest."

Something beeped beneath the headpiece, buried amidst a tangle of wiring. Sparks sputtered, and electricity arced with such amperage the lights in the room dimmed and died, leaving only a cluster of tiny green emergency beacons.

Diaz's headpiece died along with it.

The small group was silent. Marney rested a hand on Elden's arm. His scanners registered the transfer of heat, and he was grateful for the gesture. "Package him up, carefully. We'll want to recover everything possible from his memory."

"All right, but the surge probably fried him." Goetz swore. "What is this place sir? What were they playing at?"

Elden saw another body sprawled in the corridor, half buried under collapsed ceiling plates. He scraped them away with his clawed feet.

The body was a woman's. Like the others, she wore an unmarked lab coat. Like the others, she was Briddarri.

"That, Goetz, is a question for Rett and Admiral Ergen," Elden said.

CHAPTER THIRTEEN

It was the only time Elden had seen Admiral Ergen quiet.

The evidence laid out before him was striking enough on its own: the desolate space station; the dead Briddarri researchers; the sickening attempts at cyborg soldiers; and, of course, the remains of Colonel Diaz. This alongside the fragments Goetz had identified from five more Truppen, soldiers who had been missing for months. Their headpieces were long since ruined, experimented upon and dissected with such cold precision, Elden couldn't fathom how Ergen could stand there in his office without any outward display of emotion.

"Is there a point to all this, Consul?" Ergen lacked even a stub of a cigar, though judging by Elden's scans, wisps of smoke clung to the corners of the room from a smoke not a half hour prior.

"The point? I want an explanation, Admiral. I want to know why the remains of my men were found in a Briddarri research station. I want to know why it is both you and Rett were aware of this installation as I was making inquiries to the location of missing Truppen."

"Wait a sec!" Rett stood off to one side, his stance as forlorn as a discarded puppy. "I didn't know what was going on! All I knew, the Admiral had some place marked on charts and—"

"You gave out classified information from my records?" A sneer curled Ergen's lips. "Typical snake of a spy."

"I wasn't spying, Admiral. Consul Elden's on our side, and he needed help. I thought—"

"You thought, what? You'd secure yourself more favor from his side?" Ergen shook his head. "I should have known better. There isn't a scrap of Briddarri left in that frame."

"Leave Rett aside," Elden said. "I'm much more interested in this base."

"I'm much more interested why you've brought a bunch of

terrans onto my ship, without my permission," Ergen said.

Marney and Nolte stood close to a broad viewport beside Ergen's desk. The room was large enough to accommodate them, Elden, Goetz, Rett, and Ergen, with plenty of space for more individuals to sit. But no one was sitting. Not even Ergen, who leaned against the front of his desk, as if this were a coffee chat instead of an interrogation.

"They were instrumental in our capture of the facility," Elden said. "More than you were."

"You're all as blinking blind as a One-eye," Ergen muttered. "With talk of cyborg monsters and Truppen bits ..."

"It isn't talk!" Goetz snapped. "We saw them. Diaz died. There's no bringing him back, not with his headpiece rigged to be fried. Explain that, Admiral. Explain how your greenbloods got ahold of our men and ripped them apart!"

"Easy, Goetz." Elden put a clawed hand on his shoulder. The words were the exact ones he wanted to use, but the anger much hotter than Elden preferred.

"Greenbloods. So that's how it is, eh?" Ergen snorted. "Let's get one thing straight: this was obviously some kind of privately funded operation, a corporate-run station involved in illegal research. Considering all the people involved are dead, thanks to the Naplians, I think we can call it resolved. We'll have the Bureau for Law and Discipline look into it further. Meanwhile, I've got a war to run, and we lost a repair dock at Aladro while you were prancing around the aft end of the sector."

"Admiral, please," Marney said. "Whatever was happening at the station had to be part of something bigger. It was in the middle of deep space. Where did they get their equipment? How was staff replenished? A probe or two left behind to scan could reveal lines of supply."

Whatever Ergen thought of Marney and her escort, he was obviously nonplused by her astute observations. "I get what you're doing. Governor Wester's daughter, fighting the good fight since her planet's gone. I applaud that. But this is out of your hands now. Out of mine, too. Me blundering around with a battleship and a squadron won't help matters, especially if I'm dragging around *Dragonfly*."

The Reittian destroyer was easy enough to spot out the viewport, a tiny model of itself suspended among the stars, as was *Vossberg*. *Hessian* formed the third corner of their triangular formation, having rejoined the Briddarri fleet upon their rendezvous. They were amassing quite the ragtag task force, Elden thought, but it wasn't a disparaging realization. The more ships he had that were not beholden to the Briddarri, the better.

He glanced at Rett. The more personnel he had, likewise, was better, too.

"Look, what more do you want me to do? Thank the gods it wasn't the Naplians who were doing this kind of research, and that you all were able to destroy them." Ergen shook his head. "Naplian Truppen. That's the last thing we need right now."

A comm panel on his desk chirped. Ergen pressed its surface. "What is it?"

"Sir, we've got the latest intel from sector reports."

"Give me the holo in here. I'll be out on the bridge in a moment."

"Aye, sir."

Ergen motioned for Elden and Goetz to vacate the center of his floor. It took a firm grasp, but Elden got Goetz to move, though he sensed from the latter's sullen silence that the tirade Elden had quashed was merely the beginning. A ring two meters across rose from the floor to ankle height. Its rim glowed white. A ball of stars and lines appeared as suddenly as a bubble, suspended in midair.

"The One-eyes have been busy," Ergen said. "They've got one of Daviont's lackeys pushing across the sectors from the supply route through the Great Desert Rift. We've been slashing across that same route, but we need more ships—and more men. Every move we make gets countered. Thanks to your Truppen we've put some major dents in their serjaum supplies, which helps clog the funnel, but they're still moving a bunch of materiel into Terran space."

He waved a hand, fingers brushing the edge of the stars. A long red line, sinuous as a stray thread, cut across the dark blue expanse of the Great Desert Rift. Numbers shifted, a chronology of the past year. Star systems blinked from red to green, to white, some back to red. The green space was gaining, Elden saw. The past three months had been times of significant gains for the Briddarri and Grand Alliance forces.

Terran space was being severely squeezed, though the blue lines appeared to barely budge.

"Last two weeks were rough," Ergen said. "This squadron, the 5th Colonial of IV Corps, took three star systems—two of ours, including Aladro, and one neutral. They'd be easier to stop if they had a blasted pattern to their conquests, but they've been following a bizarre route, right up until they dropped off our scans."

Elden's sensors had no trouble finding the pattern—because it was the same route he'd taken on *Hessian*, then *Vossberg*.

Marney gasped. She stepped near enough to the holograms for her face to reflect its glow. "That system, the neutral one you said the Naplians took—" She pointed.

Nolte swore. "Home. Blast it."

Ergen raised a bushy eyebrow. "You know it, then. I'd send a task force out to retake it, because the scattered reports I received indicate it could be worth our while, but I don't have the ships to spare."

"You'd better find someone to get back there," Nolte snapped. "My wife and daughter—I have to get word to them."

"Not a chance, unless you want the One-eyes pouncing on us when we send off your love signal."

<They're tracking us, sir.> The signal from Goetz to Elden was clear. <Don't know how but we have to consider ourselves compromised.>

<I agree. Get on it.>

<Why bother? Rett's the problem.>

<What would you have me do? Eliminate one of our own?>

<Still a Greenblood, sir.>

<Out of the question.> There had to be another way. No matter what Ergen said, Elden had to find out who was behind the deaths of his men. The haunting demise of Diaz's headpiece replayed in his memory banks. "Admiral, since you've given us nothing to go on, I have to continue our search."

"Out of the question," Ergen said. "I need your forces more than ever."

"That is for me to decide, as Consul of the Truppen."

"Look here, Consul, I won't get dragged into the debate again—"

"Admiral!" The sounds on the end of the intercom were jumbled. "We have ships emerging at the edge of the system. Preliminary scan indicates squadron strength. Naplian."

"Confounded cursed One-eyes," Ergen muttered. "And I'm sitting here with barely a squadron of my own. The rest are all off dousing hotspots. All right, send battle alert to all our ships. Move to intercept."

Elden gestured for his people to follow him from the office, as more reports flooded through the intercom.

"Consul," Ergen said. "You'd better get your forces ready for the tussle. And I'd recommend the civilians sit it out."

"Exactly my thoughts, Admiral," Elden said. Though he planned to do far more than that.

***

Admiral Erassia paced the tactical display, admiring the poise and determination of his enemy.

They'd stumbled upon a single squadron of enemy ships— fourteen Briddarri vessels, plus a trio of Terran and Reittian craft. Erassia was not concerned about the outcome. With *Fulnax*, he had twelve vessels to field against them, all warships. His only minor qualm was the presence of three Briddarri battleships.

The lead was designated *Winter Scourge*.

Erassia smiled. Admiral San Sett Ergen. A far finer prize than the leader of the Truppen *ziura*. Though truth be told, he'd be happy taking home the heads of both.

A klaxon howled. A wave of torpedoes crashed against the first line defenses of his squadron. Counterfire missiles and particle weapon bursts took down the bulk of them; a handful made it amidst the ships, but damage was light, limited to shield stress.

"Sir, the Briddarri are splitting off into lines," the Tactical officer said. "Six vessels on direct intercept for us, two lines of four taking long arcs to opposite vectors around our formation."

"Signal the command: break by threes. *Hannark* I want to block the center strike. Send *Vedor* after the farthest line."

"Yes, Admiral."

The helmsman glanced over his shoulder, large eye wide with anxiety. "Our course, sir?"

"Circumvent the nearest of the Briddarri lines." Erassia brushed his fingers through the Tactical hologram. The gesture highlighted three vessels drifting slowly away from the main group. *Fulnax*'s deck shuddered as a new salvo of missiles raced out from the Naplian formation. Indicators flashed in rippling waves across the display from the entire squadron, hurtling across space between Erassia's ships and the Briddarri fleet.

"I have the coordinates you indicated, sir."

"Plot a ripwave leap. Comms, advise *Sardin* and *Napriad*—concentrate fire on the largest of the three vessels, the one identified as a troop transport. Disabling shots only." Erassia smiled. "We need not injure our prize."

***

Back aboard *Hessian*, Elden watched as the Briddarri fleet spread out for combat maneuvers. The incoming Naplian ships ripwaved into the area, twelve ships spread out in trios. There was no attempt at communications from either side. *Winter Scourge* opened up with torpedo salvos, leading the Briddarri attack. The Naplians responded in kind, until the hundreds of thousands of kilometers between the forces was filled with projectile tracks.

"We should stand off from the battle," Goetz said. "We're not much good, though *Hessian* can take the beating and dish out some of her own in response."

"I agree," Elden said. "The only question remaining is in which direction we should stand off, and at what distance."

Goetz chuckled. "Such as, measured in parsecs?"

"Exactly so. Hail *Vossberg* for me."

The link opened, and the pleasant lilt of Marney's voice offered to take Elden from the silent horror of the tactical display. Every wink of light was either a weapon or a warship—right then, only the weapons were disappearing. "You're not going to float there and wait for Admiral Ergen to whistle, are you?"

The words cut at his pride, but there was enough of the familiar teasing that Elden knew they weren't intentionally meant that way. He recognized the steel behind them, too. "I certainly am not."

"Neither am I. We have a world to rescue."

"Indeed. There's more, however. Such as the coordinates Goetz recovered from the research facility."

Rett had been standing silently at the back of *Hessian*'s bridge. Now, though, he sprang forward with the energy of a young child. "What? You didn't tell the admiral anything about it! I didn't—"

"You didn't need to know," Goetz snapped. "Stand down, soldier." Rett's armor plating creaked, but he waited in sullen silence again.

"We'll help you get the Naplians off your world, Marney," Elden said. "But I have to follow this trail first. I'd like your help—and Captain Zhivko's—to do so."

"Fine. Let's make it work. Transmit the coordinates to me and Fyodor."

"Consider it done. *Hessian* out."

Elden watched the display. They had to time it well. If they could jump with Ergen's attention diverted by the Naplians, there'd be little time for him to backtrace their route. Of course, he'd be able to ascertain it later, though it would require a great deal of analysis, and the region of space would be littered with debris and radiation from the brawl.

There was always the possibility the Naplians would win the fight. Elden coolly observed Ergen's death as an advantageous outcome.

Three of the red indicators vanished from the hologram.

"Blast it," Goetz muttered. "We've got One-eyes incoming. Ripwaved right out of the middle of their formation."

"You're certain they're headed for us?"

Goetz sighed, the sound ragged with static. "I'm going to pretend you didn't ask that again, sir. Vector analysis estimates them in ten seconds."

"Okay, forget what I said before," Rett said. "Forget it all. Let's get out of here right now."

"As much as I would love not to be a lumpen target for Naplian missiles, Rett, we are limited by our run-up time for the jump drive." Elden triggered the comms himself this time and set the signal for both companion ships. "Marney, Captain Zhivko, we're going to have company very soon."

"More spoils." Zhivko sounded cheery, and possibly a tad inebriated. "Perhaps I shall share with you."

"Three Naplian battlecruisers are hardly easy pickings. Marney, I must insist, get out. Jump to the first set of coordinates."

"We will, as soon as our drives our up," she said. "Good luck and be careful."

Elden wanted badly to smile then. He caught his reflection in a tracking monitor. Yes, his headpiece took on the habitual tilt. "You may count on it."

Vossberg's image on that monitor flickered, stretched, and vanished. A trio of battlecruisers took its place.

***

The ripwave leap was done with such precision Erassia made a mental note to append the helmsman's record with a commendation. They were no more than 10,000 klicks from the two enemy ships.

Two. One had jumped just a blink before they exited ripwave. No matter. It was the largest transport he wanted, the great lumbering bulk that rivaled even his heavy cruisers.

Hessian. Home of the *ziura.*

Green lines lanced out from his triangular formation, stabbing at the transport. She certainly packed dense shields, for at this range, what should have been damaging blows were inflicting only irritating rattles. "Close the distance," Erassia said. "Shift disabling torpedoes into Tubes One through Four."

"Aye, sir."

The smaller vessel, a Reittian escort of some kind, lunged at them with the tenacity of a *jolar* hound. Despite being hopelessly outclassed in tonnage and weapons loadout, the destroyer swept the Naplian flanks with stunning speed. Before Erassia realized what had happened, the battlecruiser *Napriad* registered collapsing shields in one key sector, despite cutting apart the Reittian's shields like gauze.

"Cursed vermin," Erassia muttered. "Launch torpedoes! Tell

Napriad to keep that *shirish* away!"

Orders and responses overlapped in fluent *Ffawe-aul* technical dialect. There was a musical quality to the speech; Erassia mused about intercepted Terran reports classifying the language as just that.

The torpedoes streaked at *Hessian*, and Erassia wasn't surprised by the railgun tracks that shredded the formation. Enough of the torpedoes would get through, no matter the counterfire.

Besides, they were not his only option. "Target with energy weapons and fire."

Green bursts bracketed *Hessian*. The transport shuddered along its course projection, causing the line etched in the hologram to waver—and Erassia suddenly realized the projection was dead on for *Fulnax*.

"Sir! The transport is charging us!" the Tactical officer said. "She's maxing her acceleration!"

***

The alarms echoing around Elden confirmed that it was a foolhardy plan. Perhaps the proximity to *Dragonfly*'s potentially suicidal run at the One-eye battlecruisers had inspired it.

Elden suspected he was tired of fleeing. "Shields are … not happy," Goetz muttered.

"So I gathered."

The lead battlecruiser loomed on the display, magnified as it was across less than 8,000 klicks' distance. Elden longed to sever those garish jump sails, ripping the wings right off the blasted One-eyes. He'd do it by claw if necessary.

Railgun and Briddarri plasma cannon fire would have to suffice.

Hessian cut apart most of the incoming torpedoes, and accelerated through the remainder, outracing what he'd assumed from technical specs were time-delay explosive triggers. A few simply caromed off the shields.

Two detonated.

Lights flickered wildly across *Hessian*'s bridge. "We're losing main power!" Rett said. "I'm bypassing the reactor safeties."

"What? You idiot! Are you trying to blow us all up?" Goetz said.

"Relax! If it works, we'll have enough juice to jump out of here."

"If? I knew it." Goetz reached for Rett. "Ergen's planted pet, ready to take us down."

"Enough!" Elden didn't need a brawl between them, not in front of the rest of the crew, and especially not in the middle of a running ship-to-ship battle.

Every monitor died.

For a second, the bridge was bathed in dull emergency lighting. Elden was sure they would hurtle on, powerless, engines dead, weapons deactivated. Then everything flared back to life in a blaze of riotous colors and sounds.

Rett slapped a console so hard the monitor shivered. "I knew it! See?"

"Shields stayed intact." Goetz sounded more relieved than Elden knew he'd ever admit. "Still taking direct fire from the lead battlecruiser. We're good to jump whenever you're ready, sir."

Elden watched the battlecruiser with a new hunger. "Let's give them a proper send-off."

***

The *Hessian* wasn't stopping. "Evasive!" Erassia snapped.

Fulnax tumbled starboard, rolling over and over in a maneuver designed solely to get her free of an onrushing projectile. Erassia was fully aware it meant she was taking more hits from those cursed railguns. Shield overheat alarms clamored for his attention. *Fulnax*'s weapons should have gutted the transport by now, yet they'd been unable to penetrate its shields. Even the torpedoes had failed to do the job, when they'd detonated, no less!

"Cut them off us!" Erassia said. "Concentrate all cannon!"

Fulnax and *Hessian* were bound by streams of particle weapon fire, energy blasts, and railgun projectiles as the two slugged it out at close range. Erassia knew the limits of his flagship's shield capacity, and he had vague sensor readings hinting at that of his enemy. Which would falter first?

"*Hessian*'s port dorsal shields are in flux," the Tactical officer said.

"Failure imminent."

"Helm, shift us eight degrees," Erassia said. "I want all weapons brought to bear—"

The flare of light overwhelmed all the visual monitors and sent a burst of static through the main holographic displays.

Hessian was gone.

A flash from farther across the battlefield signaled the Reittian's departure, too, leaving *Napriad* limping with a torn starboard jump sail.

Erassia swore. Their prey had slipped the net. And the Briddarri were pounding away at the rest of his forces. So far, no ships had been lost among the loyal Ffawe. The Briddarri were down a cruiser but blasted if that didn't make them fight all the more viciously.

"Signal all units," he said. "Withdraw to pre-plotted holding coordinates. We'll regroup and continue the hunt."

Elden Selva would have to wait until another day.

***

Lira winced at the sharp sliver of pain in her side. Hadn't it gone yet? She'd tried to wait it out. For hours. Many hours.

Everything was pitch black, except the blinding white light stabbing down. She was strapped to a stanchion, some kind of support beam, left standing alone.

"Where is it?" The voice echoed to her right. She couldn't see its owner.

"We know you hid the crystal." This time it came from her left. Had he moved? Or was it an audio trick? Whatever the case, she couldn't get her bearings. The room threatened to spin out of control.

The pain cut at her again, the same place. It triggered the aches, courtesy of the Briddarri.

Not fair. She wanted to get as far away as possible, from the Briddarri, from Denics, from the humans ...

Tag. Dyson. Surely they had to know by now she was captured. She only hoped they'd be able to recover the crystal before the Denics found it.

Or before they broke her.

The pain crescendoed until the only way she could sustain her resistance was to scream. She cried out until her throat was raw, and the pain never subsided, never dimmed.

But she'd be shredded alive in a black hole before she told this scum anything. "Shut it down," the voice commanded.

The pain cut off as suddenly as if it had never existed. Lira gasped. She couldn't have been more out of breath if she'd climbed to the top of the Sanctuary of the Revered Barad.

Memories of that night drifted through her mind, and she seized them. They helped her ignore the tears dripping from her chin, the sweat soaking her clothes, the bindings digging into her skin.

"Listen, Briddarri. We know you stole the lattice crystal device from the skyhook. We know you had it on you at the market, before those Terrans showed up." Irritation crept into the voice. Good. If he could get angry, he could make a mistake. Lira would wait for any error she could take. "You must have hidden it somewhere there."

"I won't tell you a thing," Lira's voice rasped.

"You will. You'll beg to tell us everything."

"If you're so intelligent, surely you can find one box." Lira smiled as boldly as she could manage, with no idea who was watching her from what angle.

The blow hit her jaw with such force she swore it was dislocated. But she worked it, and for now, at least, she could still talk. "Oh, did that make you feel better? A bunch of strong, clever Denics with one girl tied to a post, and this is all you can manage?"

"Tell us where you hid it."

"Show me your cowardly face and I will."

The Denic was one of the bald pair who'd grabbed her from inside the disguised hover-truck. He had a short, stubby nose, broad face, high cheekbones, and gleaming pale blue eyes. A puckered scar shone pink under his left eye.

He leaned inside the circle of light, too far for Lira to touch—well, if she had been able to get an arm or leg free. She itched to break a bone.

Instead she spat in his face.

Saliva dripped from his jaw. The muscle there clenched, but he didn't lash out. He didn't move at all. Oh, he wanted to—Lira could see it in the glare, the tension of his arms. He'd already done it once, she realized. Even though his hands were held behind his back, she spotted the collapsible baton shining silver.

He shook his head. "Again," he said, over his shoulder.

The pain stabbed deeper than before through Lira's side, until she felt she'd be sawn in half. Caught as she was in its throes, she managed to look down. Her body was completely intact. There wasn't a mark on her clothes.

But stars, she thought her insides were going to explode like a supernova. It shut off again. Lira sagged against the restraints.

"My time is important to me, and you're wasting it," the Denic said. "It hurts. And so I'm hurting you. I'm going to keep hurting you until you give me what I want. If you refuse, you will die, and then your team will die, and then anyone else who gets between me and the crystal will die. Consider that while you rot."

His footsteps were so soft, he could have been a specter.

Then Lira was alone again. Alone with her plans, her schemes. None of which would do her a bit of good if she couldn't get free.

Her only hope was in her team.

But which one? Surely Blue Kitt would come for her. She'd been extracted before.

Barely. That was because she was a valuable thief. If she were left imprisoned, she'd cost the organization money.

No one had come for her when she was trapped on the Briddarri prison ship, though.

Could she blame them? The risk would have been too great. Besides, what worth had she as an individual when compared to Blue Kitt and its profit?

As for Tag and Dyson ...

She'd stolen from them. She'd betrayed their trust. No way in space they'd forgive her for what she'd done.

Well. She could rely on herself, until the situation changed.

A cold, hard knot formed in the pit of herself. It was the way it had always been, no matter how deep into Blue Kitt she'd gotten.

Nothing entered the blinding light, and she couldn't leave. Alone. Always.

CHAPTER FOURTEEN

Tag paced up and down the alley. How many novafired hours had they been there? He'd left any electronics back at the hotel, per the insistence of their new orange buddy, Akro.

"Are humans always this fidgety?" Tag couldn't see the alien's face, not in the blackout conditions between two tall storage buildings, but he guessed those razor-sharp teeth were revealed in a sneer.

"Yes." Dyson's voice came from the left. Eerie as all get out that there was no breath from him. "I have found the species, when confronted with an inability to resolve a potentially dangerous situation, is compelled to expend energy. It is especially pronounced in males."

"If you two are done analyzing my species' traits, how about we get back to the whole watching for the bad guys thing?" Tag gave Akro a good shove on his way to the front of the alley. The streetlights were dim out there but revealed enough of the identical storage bins and parked delivery hover-trucks that Tag could tell nothing was knew. Figured.

"Get back here!" Akro's fingers dug into Tag's arm.

"Move it or lose it, Orange," Tag muttered. "I don't care if you've got a gun at my back or a missile targeted on my location."

Akro growled something in unpronounceable words as pleasant as grinding gears, but let go. Tag brushed off his arm. So far, the supposed Blue Kitt had told them next to nothing, except that they were to stake out this location until a target appeared, someone Akro surmised could lead them to Lira. Okay, fine by Tag.

"Blue Kitt," Tag said. "I take it you're what, Lira's replacement?"

Akro snorted. "Hardly. I'm a thief, like her, though most of the time I provide extraction. Ships. Shuttles. Hover-vehicles. Even got her out of a barracks with the eight-winged poaraxa, in the Languan worlds, once. Me and another Shikasta, we're the best at that."

"Another? Lira has two accomplices?"

"Accomplices?" Akro laughed. "Our organization's got far more membership than either of you can dream up. There's only a handful of active thieves at any given time, and we rotate people into and out of supporting roles when the authorities get wise."

"Seems complicated," Tag said.

"It's worked well for a century or so," Akro said.

"If it's a big secret, you sure blabbed about it awfully quick." The realization made Tag grateful he had a knife stashed away in his boot.

Akro shrugged. "The odds of you two surviving this mess are slim. Who are you going to tell? The Terrans? They don't care. The Briddarri?"

"It is within our prerogative to inform the relevant authorities," Dyson said.

"So, do it." It was more a challenge than a suggestion.

"To reveal the nature and extent of your organization would be— detrimental to our rescue of Miss Reen," Dyson said.

"You spies are always looking for an advantage," Akro said. "You'll keep this for when you need something good in return. Besides, when this is over, I'll disappear, and you'll never find a trace of Blue Kitt again."

A hum grew steadily. Some kind of vehicle, approaching from the right. Tag backed deeper into the shadows, pressed close to the wall so he could see at an angle into the street. The building's cold seeped through his jacket. The night shed temperature fast enough he could see wisps every time he exhaled.

"On schedule," Akro murmured. "He's made a handful of other stops over the past few days, following a terribly predictable grid around the city. I'll hand it to you Terrans—your Intelligence randomize way better than most. The Denics? Awful."

A compact hover-car slid up to the sidewalk opposite the alley. White panels were suffused with amber and gold by the streetlights. The windows were opaque, and when the right side hatch folded open, the passenger who exited kept his face toward the building. No hair, pasty skin, grey jacket. He walked up a ramp to the unmarked door inset on the right half of the building's front.

"What's the plan?" Tag asked. "Since you've been skimpy on details."

"We take the car," Akro said. "Quickly. Silence anyone inside and kill the onboard nav. One of us will follow the Denic inside at the same time."

"That's me," Tag said. "Come on."

"Wait …!"

This time Tag moved quickly enough Akro's fingers missed his elbow. He was out in the alley, without pretense of concealment, moving as quick as he could without running. He'd got to the front of the hover-car when the driver's hatch opened. A blue glow from the nav systems seeped into the night, putting the driver into the same shade.

"Stop where you are." The man's voice was flat, carrying a peculiar accent unlike any Tag had heard. Of more interest was the pistol he carried, a small sidearm of unrecognizable manufacturer but not a stun weapon. Definitely as capable of killing as a DK-40.

"Hey, no problem, I'm headed inside." Tag grinned and kept walking, tossing off a salute.

"Stop now!" The click and buzz of the safety mechanism disengaging was faint, but familiar enough Tag almost paused.

But he didn't, because the stutter step of Dyson behind him was clearer. A muffled *whump*, and a sharp *crack*, were the only other sounds that followed.

Tag glanced back from the bottom of the ramp. Dyson had the Denic draped over his arm as if he were carrying foodstuffs in a bag. Akro helped him shove the spy into the back seat of the hover-car, then slid behind the driver controls. Lights died out within seconds.

Good enough. Tag took the ramp as swiftly and silently as possible.

The hatch whisked open. White lights illuminated portions of a huge storeroom in stark white circles, with the rest of the space hidden in darkness. The tang of new plastics stung Tag's nose. Containers were stacked in neat rows, up two stories of burnished red racks. Some were blue, others white, but all bore labels for a furniture brand.

The brand burned itself into his memory when the nearest

container, large enough to conceal a table, hurtled down off a rack.

Tag dodged the impact, the sound as loud as an explosion. He'd only just found shelter down an adjacent aisle when energy blasts lit up the room with a garish green. So this guy was armed with something more advanced than a slug-throwing pistol?

Footsteps. They clanged on the racks overhead. Tag couldn't see the man, but he hauled himself up a ladder on the side of the rack. More blasts scored the red metal, charring it black and brown.

He had to be across the aisle. The shadows contrasted with the brightly lit portions of the storage building made it difficult to determine where.

From below, a gunshot of a different tune rang out. Tag saw orange flash by the door. The Denic, hidden among the racks, shifted aim and fired back.

Akro. His shots were meant to draw out the spy. But the gambit failed. For a moment, silence filled the room as tangibly as fuel. Tag crept down the rack's upper level, squeezing between the containers.

Blasts scorched a container in front of him. He shielded his face from hot bits of plastic, turned molten red by the energy discharge. A few burned through his sleeve.

The pain angered him enough that he forgot all about staying discreet and emptied an entire magazine of ten mm ammunition from his DK-40. Amidst the crashes of gunfire, he heard the faint echo of footfalls.

Those stopped when Dyson appeared in the middle of the aisle, a wide-open target. "Look out!" Tag shouted.

The energy burst caught him square in the chest, knocking him to the floor. Steam rose from a ragged wound, blackened and slick with residue Tag couldn't identify. Tag's heart jumped. First Lira, now Dyson. He couldn't believe the android exposed his position.

But the attack was enough he finally pinpointed the Denic's hiding spot.

Without waiting for support, Tag sprinted for the edge of the rack and hurtled across the space between. Air rushed around him, the containers growing larger.

More gunshots, courtesy of Akro, startled him. They must have startled the Denic, too, because he appeared from behind one of those containers toward which Tag flew.

He slammed into the spy, their bodies colliding with enough force to blow the breath from Tag's lungs. The Denic cried out, his back bent awkwardly against a box.

Tag didn't give him time to do more than that before he cracked the butt of his pistol across the man's jaw, knocking him out cold.

"Do you have him?" Akro asked.

Tag kicked a curved, steaming energy pistol to the floor. "Yeah. He's napping."

"Good. Get him down here."

"What about Dyson?"

"There is no need for concern." Dyson waited at the bottom of the rack, standing erect and seemingly none the worse for wear, despite the ugly hole in his chest. "The blast missed my vital systems. Self-repair routines should suffice until I can affect a more permanent fix."

Tag tried hard not to grin. No sense in the android getting an overinflated sense of his importance. Instead he dragged the unconscious Denic down. It got much easier when Dyson lent a hand. "Well, I'm glad you're not dead. Let's get out of here and get some answers from our sleeping buddy."

***

Tag had never interrogated a prisoner in the plush living area of a downtown hotel before.

But he figured there were a lot of things one did in war that went beyond the war. Such as sipping Crown & Scepter while a diminutive, spiky-faced, orange Shikasta growled at a bruised Denic strapped to a reptilian leather lounge seat.

Dyson had restraints among his kit. At this point Tag wasn't the least surprised. What didn't the android have on him? Though Tag would have preferred a squadron of Warhawks, maybe even Sunsabers, to their limited supply of offensive weaponry.

"Where is the container?" Akro's growls were insistent, a constant rumble beneath his words that occasionally cut through a syllable. How he managed to snarl and speak at the same time was beyond Tag; Shikasta vocal cords must be set up with more versatility than a human's.

The Denic said nothing. His bald pate gleamed like a city streetlight. Bruises marred his forehead. They didn't affect his bearing, however—stiff as a stanchion, that one. Not a word out of him.

"Answer me." Still nothing.

Akro grabbed the Denic's shoulder with a three-fingered hand. Tag made a face. Really? Holding the guy's arm like a buddy would make him talk?

The thought bemused him right up until the slender, needlelike black claws jabbed out.

The Denic grunted, his face screwed up with pain. He shifted in the seat, pressing against the restraints, but Akro held him back with a hand to the chest. "We're not interested in you playing loyal spy. You've got our person, and you've got the data box. Tell us where both are, and you get to leave with all of your limbs."

Akro twisted his fingers. The Denic groaned, sweat glistening across his forehead, but he didn't let any articulate words slip.

Didn't matter. Tag had had enough. He poked Akro on the shoulder. "Okay, that's it. Let him go."

"Not until he tells us where the data is." Akro twisted the claws again. The groan escalated into a shout.

"Hey! I said knock it off." Tag jerked Akro back. The motion ripped the claws free of the Denic's arm. Blood dribbled down his sleeve.

Akro sneered at him. "You humans. You think because you speak nicely to these pretenders, they'll be grateful for your mercy and give us the data? They have one of my own captive. They'll torture her with every method at their disposal to get what they want, and we'll be lucky if we find a fragment of her DNA, let alone a corpse."

"Shut up," Tag snapped. "I've had it with the lectures about the right way to do things. Guess what? I know we have to find Lira. I know we have to recover the crystal. But we're not going to do it by torturing this guy, because it makes us just as bad as him."

"You'll never win this war," Akro muttered. "The Naplians will stomp over your Terran people the same way they've trampled everyone else in their path."

Tag glanced at Dyson, hoping for a wingman in this verbal dogfight. The android sat on the couch, staring across the room.

Great. Of all the times for him to mimic daydreaming ... "Akro, I'm not going to tell you again. Shut. Up. Go downstairs and get something from the vendors if you want something to stab your claws into. It isn't going to be our prisoner."

"Then what's your great plan?" Akro asked. "I can't wait to see what the vaunted human has in mind to force this Denic scum to speak."

Okay, fine. That was it.

Enough of these games, this sneaking around, this risking his neck with no backup for information that was going to make a planet bleed and add more bodies to interstellar war.

Tag grabbed the Denic by the front of his shirt and started hauling the man and the chair. The legs moaned against the floor as he dragged them.

Dyson sat up straight. "Tag, I would not recommend that course of action."

"Then I'd recommend you lend me a hand, because I'm pretty sure this guy and the chair are more than I can hold up." Tag shoved the balcony door open. A blast of cold night air hit him. Already the sky was reverting to deep blue as the early morning sun crept up, still beyond the horizon.

Tag thumped his cargo over the threshold and banged to a stop against the railing. The Denic looked around, eyes wide when he saw just how high up he was.

"Here's the deal." Tag put a hand under the seat, and another at the top of the chair. "Tell me where she is, or you fly."

He lifted them both up and over the railing.

There was a brief moment when the Denic and the chair were heavy, weighing near a ton, then a second after when they were light as a feather, teetering on the railing. All he had to do was tip his right hand, let go with his left, and the guy would be a tiny, pasty smear a bunch of stories below. Tag wanted it. He wanted the guy dead. Why was that so hard to overcome? He wanted the Naplians dead when he shot down their starfighters, right? Wanted every One-eye burned for what they did to Baedecker Four and its people.

He let go with his left hand.

But the Denic and his chair didn't move. Not even when he yelled.

He stayed immobile, tipped over so his head angled toward the empty space between the edge of the balcony and the street far underneath.

Dyson's grip anchored him in place.

"Tell me where she is, or he drops you," Tag said. "Simple."

"I will! I will. Pull me up."

"Nope. You don't understand my language? Lousy spy." Tag nodded at Dyson.

"No, wait, wait!" The Denic's breathing was labored, his face so pale he could have been completely drained of blood. "I'll tell you. All right. I will."

"Keep talking, because all I hear is a bunch of whining. Bores me."

"She's being held in a decommissioned agro-tower to the south of Atterissage. One seven oh five Southwest Radial Spur, Section Six."

Tag grinned. "You got that, Dyson?"

"I have the coordinates entered," he said. "They do match with an agronomics center."

"Good for you." Tag patted the Denic on his cheek. "Okay, Dyson, let him go."

The spy cried out, a pitiful sound that was cut off when the legs of his chair hit the balcony floor. He gasped, drawing in ragged breaths.

"For that, we don't kill you." Tag slammed his head against the railing, putting him out cold.

He stalked inside the living room, the sounds of the city awakening to morning fading away. Akro waited, crouched on the edge of a chair.

"Effective," he said. "Thanks a bunch."

Dyson deposited the bound, and now unconscious, Denic in the center of the room. "Thanks for your help, too." Tag flopped onto the couch. He felt as if he could let his body evaporate. He needed food, and drink—something other than the Crown & Scepter. Probably a bad idea this late at night. Or early in the morning. His stomach turned.

"You knew I would not let than man die."

"I had a good hunch. Plus, I wouldn't really have dropped him."

Dyson eyed him but didn't agree or argue with his statement.

"Look, it wouldn't have been necessary if stab-hands over there hadn't pained him into shutting up, and if you hadn't been locked in your daydream."

"It was not a daydream," Dyson said. "I was running through all the scans I conducted at the market when we attempted to rescue Ms. Reen. Lira."

Tag tried not to think about the *attempted* part. "So?"

"So, I have ascertained the location of the data. Our Denic was telling the truth—they do not have it. And they do not believe we have it."

"The robot's right," Akro said. "If they thought we had the data, they would have made a ransom demand, or an exchange. And they didn't kill Lira. Not yet. Your boy there wouldn't have given up the location of a corpse. If she's dead, they don't get the data."

Tag frowned, but both of their comments tracked clean. "So, you think she hid it, before she got grabbed."

"I do," Dyson said.

"Can you take us to it?"

Dyson gave Tag a look that was a perfect replica of the withering stare he'd given the android.

Tag grinned again, and this time he felt it, clear down into his gut. "Let's go."

***

They passed the market, mingling with the scattered groups of shoppers this early in the morning. Tag kept as leisurely a walk as he could, but his senses were sharp. So far, no sign of any Denics.

"Our opponents have doubtless been combing this area before our arrival," Dyson said, his tone soft.

"But you don't think the crystal's here. Otherwise you'd have come back long before now."

Dyson nodded.

"As long as it is where you think it's been stashed," Akro muttered. "The sooner we get it and leave, the better."

They went three blocks past the market and turned down a side street. Dyson entered a white building lined with blue trim and broad windows of smoky silver glass. There were no identification marks, save for large characters emblazoned on the second floor: OWR-017.

The stink inside was enough to make Dyson gag.

"Can I help you?" A technician, long and lanky, with deep dark skin, had a scroll in hand. Data dripped through a hologram hovering over its surface. He wore drab gray coveralls lined with the same blue shade as the building, and he wore both a white safety helmet and a visor which covered half his face. "This area's off limits to civilian visitors."

"Sorry about that." Dyson grinned, and gave an effortless shrug. Tag shivered. Yes, the grin was as familiar as his own. "We're new to Atterissage. I heard about your OWR plants and wanted to show my companions. Akro?"

The diminutive alien rolled his eyes in very human fashion—a gesture barely noticeable, Tag realized, because his eyes were all one color. He dug into his pocket and tossed a pouch at the tech.

He caught it. "What's this?"

"Our thanks for letting us have a peek at this facility."

The tech opened it. Tag thought his jaw would literally dislocate and hit the floor. Couldn't blame him. Tag had seen how many jewels were packed into the bag. "I ... ah ... Right. Of course. We can make exceptions. Be glad to let you through. Just need to authorize it. One moment."

His hands flew through a series of displays floating over the scroll. He smiled. "You're all clear to have a look around. Just, ah, leave through the side exit, okay?"

"No problem."

Soon as he was gone, Dyson led them on a direct walk down a corridor lined with hatches. The floor was wet, with the smell of having been recently cleaned—sharp chemical odors. There was still an underlying stench of rot Tag couldn't place. "You'd better have this right."

"Is there any doubt?" Tag caught a ghost of the faked grin on Dyson's face. Dyson stopped before a hatch on their left. He reached for the handle.

"Hang on." Tag crept in front of the access mechanism. Somewhere in his boot … ah. He drew out his knife and gingerly pried up the edge of the mechanism's cover.

"What is it?"

"Alarms. Checking for them." He peered around the underside. "It's clean."

"Not in the strictest sense." Dyson opened the hatch.

The compartment inside was about the size of the shower stall back at the hotel. It was half full of fruit peels, vegetable skins, and plants, all in varying stages of decay. The smell was enough to make Tag's eyes water. "Okay, that isn't disgusting. Not at all." He gagged.

"You humans and your giant noses." Akro sniffed. "It isn't any worse than a composting pile."

"You're kidding right? The restroom cycler on *Confiance* has less of a stink."

Dyson stepped into the muck, sinking up to his knees. He plunged both arms deep amongst the refuse. "This is one of thirty Organic Waste Reclamation buildings throughout Atterissage. From here composted organics are redistributed to agronomic compounds outside the city perimeter, for a decent fee."

"You studied up on farming?"

"Only when I reviewed my memory banks of our arrival at the market," Dyson said. "The sanitation robot which cleaned up the collapsed melon stand would have brought the remnants to this facility, as it is the nearest such. Each 'bot is assigned a designated hatch for deposit. It was a simple matter of reviewing the city's records as to which robot was assigned which hatch."

Tag smirked. "After you hacked in."

"I accessed all records utilizing Terran Intelligence tools at my disposal."

"Like I said …"

Dyson froze. He turned toward Tag, his expression unreadable, and for a moment Tag thought he was about to get into a fistfight with an android.

Then Dyson held the crystal's box aloft. It was still smeared with the same color juice as the melons smeared across the market tile.

Akro made a chirping sound. "Well done, construct! Now let's get off this rock."

"Off this rock?" Tag frowned. "No. We go get Lira."

"Are you kidding? She'd want us to get this data box of yours to the highest bidder as fast as possible." Akro bared his teeth. "That is what she was doing when this whole mess started."

"We are not abandoning Miss Reen." Dyson joined them in the corridor, seemingly oblivious to the muck clinging to his trousers and shoes.

"This is absurd."

"What, you want to leave her to get questioned by the Denics instead?" Tag said. "You want them finding everything about Blue Kitt they can dig up?"

"Lira would never tell them! She's loyal to us all."

"Better than she'll get from you, apparently."

Akro shook his head. In that moment, he drew his gun. Great. "I don't have the patience or the time to argue with you. Give me the data."

"You've got to be kidding. You saw what a gunshot did to Dyson, right? Absolutely nothing." Tag grinned. "He's still got the hole in his chest to prove it."

"Yes, but you're not similarly protected."

Akro's stance shifted, but Tag had him marked from the moment he'd started up this little spat. He'd aimed for Tag's head. Bad data for Tag if the shot hit, but it was better than having the gun pointed at his center of mass. Tag grabbed the gun and shoved it aside as hard as he could, twisted with all his strength.

The gunshot was as loud as a cannon in the corridor, and Akro's yelp of pain was lost behind it. Tag latched on like a vise to the gun, and punched Akro in the throat. At the same time, he swept his foot behind Akro's ankle, dropping him onto his back. Tag brought his knee down on Akro's chest in a blow that popped the air from Akro's lungs with the force of an airlock cycling.

"Effective." Dyson knelt beside them. The box bulged in a sealed jacket pocket.

"Thanks." Tag breathed hard. His left ear rang like an emergency klaxon from that blasted gunshot. Good thing Dyson spoke to him on his right side. "This guy strike you as not entirely trustworthy?"

"Your understatement of this mission." Dyson frisked Akro with a swift deliberate method Tag figured was borne of long experience. "I have had my suspicions."

"Cold, even for a thief."

Akro groaned but made no attempt at motion. His eyes were squeezed shut.

"Here is something of note." Dyson held up Akro's arm, and let the sleeve fall back. A thin band of black metal, stamped with intricate designs, was clamped around his wrist.

"Local artwork?"

"The writing is Shikasta. The band is a pledge to honor his people with his earnings."

"Nice. So, he shares."

"The metal, however, is not standard for such a band, but rather is improvised from military leftovers. Specifically, an alloy used by the Briddarri for missile casings."

Novafire. Tag leaned back from Akro, letting him gasp for air. Blue Kitt—or a Briddarri spy. At this point he didn't put his faith in a blasted one of them.

"I suspect our mission has been more closely monitored by our allies than we first suspected," Dyson said softly.

"Speaking of understatements …" Tag shook his head. "Let's boost before the authorities show up. You have any of those restraints left?"

"No." Dyson looked over his shoulder. "There is a more appropriate place to stow this refuse, I believe."

CHAPTER FIFTEEN

The agro-towers which fed Atterissage spread out in a broad, deep crater, one with weathered edges long overtaken by savannah grasses. Gold blades waved in the wind, contrasting with the transparent towers that showed off green bounties. There had to be forty towers, arranged in concentric circles. Some were only a few dozen feet tall, and wide, while the majority topped out at twenty stories and were quite slender.

Tag steered the hover-car across a dusty track, hard-packed rock that had been laser shorn to a perfect surface. The vehicle was a perky four-seater, twin boosters, quad grav panels, and a smooth, aerodynamic shell making it a prime candidate for their raid.

Also helped that Tag was breaking every speed limit across the plains.

"I would recommend we keep this vehicle in optimal condition for its return to Pallas," Dyson said. "We would be hard-pressed to explain any damage."

"Well, we did tell them we required a car for sight-seeing." Tag goosed as much acceleration out of the boosters as he could. Topped out at 200 kph. Not too shabby. Not a starfighter, but hey, not everything was. "Besides, whatever it was we paid them for a flight of Sunsabers should cover any damage."

Dyson was immersed in holographic readouts on his scroll. He swiped through diagram after diagram of the agro-towers. Each one teemed with plant life, and very few had human biosigns. They'd better find a Briddarri and some Denic ones. "I doubt TI will be pleased to learn of the purchase."

Tag rolled his eyes. "Give me a break. I had to do something to convince them we were legitimately interested in arms tech. Us sightseeing wouldn't cut it. Besides, the money was there for us to use."

"Yes, but TI did not expect us to actually spend it."

"So, send the bill to Pallas. Now, if you don't mind, how about you narrow down our target?"

"I have the coordinates provided by our … temporary guest." A smile quirked the corner of his mouth. "I am routing them to your navigation console."

"Nice." Sure enough, the onboard computer marked off one of the shorter, stumpier agro-towers on the left side of the crate. Tag skimmed the access road winding down the rim, watching the data stream by. "Vegetables."

"That is what it once produced. However, it was decommissioned two years ago following an introduction of Vastose Blight. Standard quarantine period for agronomic centers on Kayna Two is three years."

"No interruptions for us."

"No. However, this decommissioned tower is showing periodic low power spikes, despite behind unhooked from the city and outskirts grid. I am also reading nine life signs."

"Nine? Novafire. Let me guess, only one Briddarri."

"That is correct."

Tag blew out a breath. He ran his hand through his hair. "Okay. This plan of ours might have hit some atmo."

"Indeed. I have marked the primary entrances into the facility. Stealth should have been our primary objective, however …" Dyson indicated their surroundings, blurred as they were by Tag's speed. "We seem to have negated that advantage."

"Let me worry about that. You have Lira's location?"

"Pinpointed."

"Good. Just point me to the front door."

Tag put the hover-car on the straightest road through the center of the agro-tower complex and pushed it past the red line for the boosters.

***

Shouts echoed around Lira.

Were they yelling at her? She couldn't tell. She roused herself from sleep—a shallow sleep fragmented by nightmares and the very real pain cutting into her side.

Think. *Focus.*

More shouts. Footfalls. Boots on metal, and dirt.

Blood caked her left eye so much it took effort to pry it open along with the right. At least the wound on her forehead had stopped bleeding. She looked around just in time to see two Denics go sprinting by. Their weapons were Terran—probably M36s. Heavy artillery for spies.

So that was two of them. Lira heard three more voices arguing upstairs ... so, five. A hatch trundled aside, metal squealing against metal. Light blasted all around her.

Suddenly she had a clear view of the room in which she'd been held captive—circular, with storage lockers and large pipes clustered at every quarter of an X. The hatch ahead of her was huge, inset in the floor, and with it open she found herself looking down a long, broad ramp. Lira was seated far back on the circle.

She realized the noise she heard was more than the shouting and the footsteps. It was an insistent hum, one rapidly growing to an angry sound. Something was coming their way, getting louder.

Good. She was tired of being stuck here. She didn't much care what was happening, but if it gave her even a microsecond to get free, she'd take it.

Lira scraped the nail of her right ring finger against the bindings, where her wrists were strapped together. They must have scanned her and searched her when she was brought in, she had no doubt. But beneath the benign polish coating her fingernails, the nails of her ring fingers were not hers—they weren't even natural. Each had been replaced with a reinforced alloy sealed inside a sturdy polymer, and when she held it at the right angle, they were sharp as any knife blades.

More men. Different voices. Brought the count up to eight. Lira smiled, even though the expression made her cheek hurt where it was bruised. She'd been right. Eight Denics. Now she knew where they all were.

Well, all except ...

"No one's taking you out of here." The voice hissed in her ear the same instant a gun pressed against her ribcage. Her interrogator, the scar-faced Denic with the stubby nose. He was no less intimidating in the sunlight setting the room aglow through the windows opening below them. "We don't have what we came for."

"You'll never get it, either." Come on. She was halfway through the bindings.

"We will if you're endangered."

Lira stopped sawing, not afraid he'd felt or seen her imperceptible motions, but frozen by the recognition of what he'd said.

No one would care if she were endangered. No one but Tag. And Dyson.

They were walking into a trap.

The noise rose to a thunder, and the men by the hatch below them raised their weapons. Suddenly the front door exploded, the flimsy plas and metal ripping free from either side. The center buckled as deeply as if it had been punched.

And it had. By a hover-car. Some maniac had driven the sleek vehicle dead center, bashing the door in like a battering ram. Two Denics were flung aside. The rest scrambled for cover, stunned enough only a couple remembered to open fire.

The Denic holding Lira swore. "Who in space is that?"

Lira sawed the last centimeter. The restraints went as limp as noodles. She grinned. "Those are my friends."

***

Ow.

The crash landing onto a lake outside Atterissage in a malfunctioning Sunsaber fighter hurt less than this collision. Tag reconsidered the wisdom of his plan.

Only for a half-second. Then he was out the driver's hatch of the hover-car, his DK-40 in hand.

The front end was crumpled, but not as badly as one would expect. The plas-glass canopy wasn't even cracked. Thank goodness for whoever designed the thing with a micro-trigger force shield, a miniaturized version of the same screens deployed on starships. It absorbed and redirected the majority of the kinetic energy, leaving the occupants unharmed, save for a bad case of whiplash.

Gunfire rattled all around him. M36s. No mistaking the sound.

Tag didn't think, or plan, other than to find cover, which he did behind a toppled container. Dirt spilled out where the lid had bent in.

Sparks sprayed along the top of the box from the impact of flechette rounds. Bits of shredded material showered him. The stink of burnt plastics filled the air.

He had one target already.

At the first pause in the onslaught, he popped over the top, aimed, and squeezed the trigger. Four rounds took down a Denic advancing on the container—all four to the chest.

The automatic fire resumed, and Tag felt the rounds breeze across his hair as he hit dirt again. He had a couple magazines tucked in his belt, but they hadn't come prepared for this type of action. No TI tricks available besides standard sidearms.

Tag grinned. Well, almost no tricks.

Another Denic had made his way around the passenger side of the hover-car. Dyson remained upright and stiff in his seat, staring straight ahead. The Denic kept the barrel of his M36, the muzzle steaming and white from the heat of expelled flechette rounds, pointed at the open door.

Of course, he should have asked himself the question, if the door was open why was the guy still sitting there?

By the time the thought penetrated the Denic's thick skull, Dyson was out of the vehicle, the M36 was bent at an angle that impeded its further use as a weapon, and he had the same skull gripped between his hands. He flung the Denic up and over his shoulder faster than a missile fired from a Warhawk.

Dyson sprinted for his next victim before the first Denic hit the wall.

By now the goons had figured out which of the two attackers was the greater threat. They shifted their fire, ripping up the dirt and chipping the concrete around Dyson. A few shots ripped holes in his clothes. Tag saw bits of what he was sure was android flesh go pinwheeling. Didn't stop Dyson's onslaught in the slightest.

"Okay," Tag muttered as he gripped the top of the container and hauled himself up, "Remind me never to get on your really bad side."

He slid over the side and pushed off. The nearest Denic was moving in toward his fallen partner, the one Tag had killed, but had let himself be distracted by Dyson's charge. By the time he returned his attention Tag shot him down. The blood was the same strange viscosity as the samples Dyson had examined in his pristine mini-lab back at the hotel.

Not nearly so clean now. Especially not where it stained Tag's clothes. But he didn't let sight of it penetrate his mental defenses. There'd be time for nausea and regret later. Right now, he had a mission. Targets.

Same as in the cockpit.

The pain in his neck spiked, so much so that his vision swam. Forget it. Tag shoved his DK-40 into his waistband and scooped up the M36, without breaking stride.

Someone cried out. Another Denic. A body slapped against the crumped door so hard it rebounded like a kid's ball. Dyson had a third Denic's neck twisted between his arms, and his hand clamped on the guy's mouth. Within a few seconds he'd passed out.

Five down. Good work.

Tag skidded behind a support column just as flechettes pierced the air—and his right arm. He gritted his teeth, imagining the biggest, meanest wasp ever to sting him when he was a youth magnified a hundred times slicing through his skin. Blood soaked his sleeve.

He returned fire, but the Denic came from a different angle than he'd expected. All his shots went wide. The Denic bashed the stock of his M36 across Tag's right shoulder, driving him to his knees. Tag's back erupted in agony, the injury caused by the collision all the worse with this new damage inflicted.

Tag swept his leg under the Denic's ankle, flipping him onto his backside. He aimed his M36 but the guy was quick, he kicked Tag's weapon clear aside. A second blow slammed Tag against the pillar.

Blast it!

The Denic got back to his feet and had the M36 pointed right at Tag's gut. Not quick enough, though. Tag pushed the barrel aside with his left hand and hooked his right around it even as the Denic fired. Heat singed Tag's shirt, but he now had the gun immobilized, and the part of it sure to kill him tucked away from his body.

Tag punched the Denic insensate.

When Dyson caught up with him, Tag still had the gun tucked under his arm, and the Denic's blood on his knuckles. His chest heaved with each breath.

"There are two remaining, near Miss Reen's position." Dyson could have been announcing a sunny afternoon in Atterissage's parks for the lack of strain behind each word. Of course, skin was ripped free along a trough over his left ear, and Tag swore he saw something blink beneath a tear in Dyson's shirt.

"Yeah. Counted." Tag sagged against the pillar. He checked the magazine for the M36.

Twenty rounds remaining. Good enough.

Dyson's hand rested on his shoulder. Warm, not like he'd expected from a 'bot. Could have been any pilot's. Could have been Scrape's.

The thought of his long-dead co-pilot and RIO fueled Tag with renewed indignation. Novafired Naplians and their war. Where would he be now if not for their invasion? If not for their blasted war? Home. With friends.

Of course, he'd probably be in trouble, and fighting with Father. He wouldn't be where he was, with the responsibilities he had. Tag shook his head. "Come on. Let's go get her."

"Exercise caution." Dyson gestured above their heads. "Both Denics are on the next floor."

"That was my plan," Tag said.

They crept up the ramp, weapons ready—Dyson had finally drawn a DK-40. Tag wanted a clean shot, prayed for Lira to be unhurt. He didn't expect an answer.

He also didn't expect her to be free of her bonds.

She wore the same outfit in which he'd last seen her, sans jacket and with bare arms—arms that now bore bruises. The device attached to her left side pulsed with a red light, black and ugly in design and with tendrils stabbing into her skin. Dried patches of dark green blood smeared her face, her throat, and her leg.

Tag and Dyson cleared the top of the ramp in time to watch her double one of the two Denics over her leg. The hit was so hard the man's feet left the floor by a couple centimeters, before he dropped like a deflated weather balloon.

The second Denic, a bald one with a huge bruise on his jaw, scrambled up from behind a support column and seized her by her long hair. He pressed a pistol to her head. This one Tag recognized, too—Naplian energy blaster, a DA-14 Hassai. Could throw twenty of those deadly green bolts. The charge indicator was yellow, meaning the guy had half that many available. Only one would be needed to boil her brains.

"Let her go." Tag didn't bother with pretense. He kept the M36 at his side.

"You think I don't know what's going to happen to me?" The Denic scowled. "I'm walking out of here with the data, or you're walking out with a corpse."

He really had no idea, did he? Tag shook his head. "You're in no place to negotiate."

"Are you blind, Terran? I have her! She's mine."

"No." Dyson held his gun down by his side, too, but his posture was ramrod. He could have been another of the support columns. "She belongs with us. We are not leaving without her, nor will we surrender the data."

Lira's eyes were fierce, her expression pained, and there was a furiosity Tag had never before seen in her stance. She was a Saarno fox ready to be unleashed. "Last chance."

The Denic pressed the gun so hard Lira winced. "No, yours."

Tag never took his eyes off the man's face. He wouldn't look away, not now. "Dyson. You have this?"

"I do."

The Denic's eyes flicked to Dyson, and back to Tag. Tag braced himself. "Lira … duck."

She snapped her head forward as far as she could. The Denic's attention shifted to her for a moment, bewilderment evident, a bewilderment that froze with the sound of a single gunshot and the appearance of a neat red hole in the center of his forehead.

His head snapped back so hard Tag thought it had disappeared. Then he crumpled like a demolished building, folding down on himself.

Dyson stood there, as rigid as ever—only his gun arm was up, the pistol aimed, and smoke curled from the muzzle.

Tag shivered. As much as the android had earned his respect, he was not the least bit comforted by his ability to kill.

Lira sagged to her knees, shoulders shaking. Tag hurried to her, knelt with the M36 rested against his leg. "Hey. Hey, we're here. It's all right."

Lira's face contorted; she shoved the Denic's body aside, a growl escaping her lips. She kicked it, over and over, a yell rising from her lips.

Tag took her in his arms and held her tight. "No, hey, enough. Let it be. Come on, Lira. We've got you."

Her kicks subsided, replaced by wracking sobs. She buried herself against him. Tag didn't have any intention of letting go.

"We should leave." Dyson's shadow covered them. "The authorities will no doubt be alerted by the weapons discharges. I recommend an immediate withdrawal aboard *Olivia Vy*."

"What, I don't even get to pack?" Tag quipped. Dyson actually smiled.

Lira lifted her face, tears streaking grime. "I'm sorry. You didn't deserve this."

"Don't worry about it."

"I stole the data from you both. We were … a team, and I betrayed you."

"Hey." Tag held her chin. "We *are* a team. That's why we came for you. No one gets left back. Ever."

He couldn't stand it anymore. Tag kissed her, and she kissed him back.

The warmth flooding him made him forget about his four or so injuries, the dead bodies strewn about, and the overall mess they were in. Made him want to never step into a fighter ever again.

Well, almost.

***

Elden was used to Truppen forces getting stares from or being avoided by biologicals. The Briddarri weren't as bad. They'd grown accustomed to the cybernetic soldiers among their units. Humans reacted with downright hostility—little surprise, given the Truppen role in dragging out both Consular Wars.

But he had never been to a place where he was completely ignored.

The main corridor of Doan Skere Rock was packed to its laser cut walls with trading booths, drinking establishments, lodgings, travel kiosks, and every imaginable service under any number of suns. Elden could have procured female companionship, a gun, and smoked tunnel otter in that order, had any been of interest to him. There were thousands of people milling about beneath the soft glow of yellow and orange lights meant to mimic a planetary sky; the ceiling was painted a pleasant eggshell and blue among support struts the same color. Anything and everything had been added—right down to trees both coniferous and deciduous—to make the inside of this asteroid resemble a world.

Dozens of species passed him by: humans of every kind, Rutak, Audrian, Briddarri, Shikasta, many more Elden couldn't identify. There were even some artificial pedestrians: android or cybernetic, it was unclear, but they had the appearance of silver and brass statues in motion.

"This doesn't feel safe," Goetz muttered.

"If you haven't noticed, this is the only place in which we're not complete anomalies," Elden said. "Don't worry. We won't be on the street long."

Goetz glanced back at Marney and Nolte, followed by Rett. "You and the rest will be inside, true, but I'm keeping Greenblood outside where I can keep both optical ports and all sensors on him."

Elden laughed silently. Strange that on this journey, so far from what he considered home and so removed from what had been a normal life, Goetz was still with him.

So was Marney, for that matter.

The chapel was a hovel by comparison to the lodgings on its left and glassed-in restaurant on its right. The front panels were worn brown plas, edges fading and chipped, and a single window of stained glass allowed a broad oval of multicolored light for illumination. The hatch was propped open. Elden ducked inside, Marney and Nolte with him. Goetz took up his post and pointed a sharp claw to indicate to Rett he'd better do likewise.

There were a handful of pews made from cargo containers cut down into crude metal benches. At the far end, a desk, with a raised pulpit, and a huge collection of books crammed into shelves dug out of the rock wall. A second hatch, this one closed, led to a back room.

Elden didn't care about that. His scans showed it to be living quarters. He was interested only in the older man seated at the desk, gnarled fingers twitching as he took notes on a glowing scroll with a stylus. Abbot Damal Jeopar wore a white shirt with a red collar, and khaki trousers adorned with pockets. A tan cloak was draped over the end of the desk. He had a face that exuded calm, serenity. Dark eyes flicked back and forth to notes as he transcribed. He had a thick bushy beard of wiry gray hair and had shaven his head to a thin silvery stubble.

"Good day, Abbot."

At the sound of his name, Jeopar pursed his lips in thought. "Of all the manner in which I thought I would see Elden Selva again, this is the furthest from it."

The thoughtful expression became a smile that sent creases across tanned skin. "Welcome, my friend, to my humble sanctuary. It does a soul good to see you again."

"Thank you, Abbot. Forgive me if I do not sit."

Jeopar laughed. "No, comfort is no longer chief among your concerns. The last I heard of you, the Truppen were engaged against Naplian forces halfway across the Rift. What brings you and your—companions this deep among the searching?"

"You of course remember Marney Wester."

Jeopar stood and gave a slight bow. "Miss Wester. It is an honor to have the governor's daughter with us."

"There is no governor of Baedecker Four, Abbot, but I appreciate the greeting," Marney said. "We're here for your help. We're tracking the whereabouts of a group of Briddarri who have conducted experiments regarding cybernetic soldiers."

The joy seeped from Jeopar's face. He looked drab. "Ah. The rumors."

"Rumors?" Elden asked.

"Rumors of silent shipments through this sector. Privately run, well-armed ships loaded with all manner of advanced technology.

Ships whose final destination is unknown. A few people have made attempts to find out." Jeopar shook his head. "I have heard nothing of them to this day."

"We have already found one such destination," Elden said. "I had hoped General Baessler would be—"

"Erich is gone."

"Gone. Where?"

"I do not know. I have prayed for both his safety and his swift return, but it seems the Lord's will is not mine." Jeopar accompanied his statement with a wry smile. "Erich was heartbroken by war; you must know this. That is why he left your unit and his Truppen behind for a life of quiet, in a place of contemplation. Erich was not wholly convinced of the nature of his soul."

"I won't speak of souls with you, Abbot. You know my feelings on the matter."

"There it is: your feelings. If you were truly just a collection of programming and parts, Consul, there would be no feelings to take into consideration. You were given a second chance at life, an opportunity to extend your stay among the living when you should have been dead. Is that not gift enough to make you rejoice?"

Elden scratched his claws against his palms.

"Please, Abbot," Marney said. "These ships. Where were they departing from?"

"They stopped here only to refuel and resupply. No one was allowed aboard them but maintenance robots." Jeopar smiled again. "However, Erich was able to alter a few such robots to report what they saw to him."

"And?" Elden was beginning to feel—to compute—that he never should have come here. "What did they find?"

"Abomination," Jeopar said. "Men's bodies turned into machines. These have no recollection of their lives before. Their souls, gone. Nothing remains but a cruel mockery of mankind. They are trained only to kill, programmed only to destroy. These are no Truppen like you and your ilk, Consul, but weapons. Monsters. Whomever has wrought them has no regard for life, only death. That is what drove Erich to his decision. He left soon after."

Elden glanced at Marney. "We are on the right course."

"We are. Fyodor—Captain Zhivko—assures me he can take us the rest of the way, without attracting greater attention," Marney said. "Neither the Naplians nor the Briddarri appear to have tracked us."

"Not yet." Elden turned from Jeopar. "If Erich returns, tell him his presence and his leadership are missed. There's no shame in resuming his duties."

"Erich's only duties are to the people of the galaxy." Jeopar stood and touched Elden's arms. "Please—you must promise me you will stop this."

"Stop what? The destruction of my kind? Yes, Abbot, I can guarantee that."

"No. That, but more so, turning back the tide. There is a wave building, Consul. I have seen it, visions granted to me, and never before have I despaired so. You must destroy the abominations before it is too late. Before the galaxy is consumed."

Elden stared at him. "Perhaps, then, it would be prudent for you to include us in your prayers."

Jeopar took his seat. The glow of holographic Scriptures illuminated his face, gaunt with age and weariness. "I have never ceased."

CHAPTER SIXTEEN

I t turned out, despite Tag's humorous question, they did have time to pack.

Dyson did not want to leave a trace of their operations on Kayna Two. Tag didn't get what the big deal was—there were doubtless dozens of people who knew Taggart Wester, former CDF AES pilot and war hero, was in town.

Of course, Dyson wasn't the one who had to explain why the Pallas hover-car was in such rough shape.

"Really am sorry about the damage," Tag said into the comm. "The way that truck swerved out on the plains road—I thought onboard nav systems were supposed to autocorrect for that kind of stuff."

"It's a testament to your piloting skills no one was hurt." Amari Hadar smiled at him from the other end of the link, her face just as beautiful in miniature holo as in real life. "Don't worry about it. Pallas has a huge motor pool, and our vehicles are insured for just such an emergency. Though I must say, we've never had such a strain on our resources in a short time as you've exerted."

Ah, right. How could he forget the Sunsaber's pancake onto a body of water? Tag shrugged. "What can I say? I'm hard on tech."

"You are that. Will you be joining us at the banquet this evening?"

Out of the corner of his eye, Tag felt Dyson's stare as keenly as a missile's target lock. "Sure will. Unless something else comes up, my colleagues and I plan to be in attendance."

"Very good. We look forward to seeing you. I'll make sure to save you a few seats at our best table. There's a delightful set of wines to which I'd be happy to introduce you."

Blasted shame he'd be a couple parsecs away by then. "I wouldn't miss it."

He shut down the link and blew out a breath. "You know, that's the worst part. Lying to people who haven't done anything wrong to me."

"It is a necessary evil of this work." Dyson stacked a travel container atop its larger cousin. One more remained to pack.

"Yeah, another reason I preferred being a pilot."

Lira exited her room, two containers in hand. "I'm all finished."

"The transport will be here soon. I have signaled ahead to *Olivia Vy* and put all operating systems on standby," Dyson said. "Tag should be able to achieve orbit with minimal startup time."

"Best thing I've heard all day." Tag sat on the couch. The ache in his shoulders and back wasn't getting any better—if anything, the muscles were stiffening up worse than iced wings.

The gunshot wound, where the flechettes had sliced through his arm, was healing nicely thanks to some well-placed dermal stitching.

Lira moved about the living space of the hotel as if the entire ordeal of the past day had never happened. Her stride was as confident and fluid as ever; only the bruises tattooing her skin were in evidence.

"You had no idea the Briddarri were shadowing you planetside, huh?" Tag asked.

"No. Though I'm not surprised. Commander Burrak struck me as the controlling type." Lira scowled. "It was clever of him to try using a Shikasta to fool you two into thinking Blue Kitt was looking for me and the data."

"There's Shikasta among your crew."

"There are. By virtue of—well, that's neither here nor there, as you humans say. I could have saved us all the trouble by telling you Akro, or whatever his name is, was not Blue Kitt because the true Blue Kitt never would have come looking for me or the stolen data."

Tag frowned. It sounded reasonable enough, and after all they'd been through—plus that kiss—he was inclined to take her at her word. Still ... "But you took the data and meant to get it off-world, right? So there had to be a plan."

"Oh, yes. The extraction was in the works." Lira sighed. "I'm sure they scattered as soon as I was picked up. There is no doubt someone from Blue Kitt was monitoring me, but who it was, and where they were, I have no idea. It's the beauty and curse of our compartmentalization, which allows the organization to survive at the expense of individuals."

She sat by him on the couch and touched his hand. "But you two didn't leave."

Tag's cheeks burned. "Hey, we couldn't do that. Besides, Dyson would have been all weepy even though I thought we should boost."

Lira made a face and socked his arm, playfully. Tag chuckled. Felt good to do so.

Dyson raised an eyebrow. "If you two have completed your courtship ritual, I suggest we move from this location. We have already tarried long enough."

"Hey, you're the one who wanted to pack," Tag said.

"The logistical and operational reasons for our cleaning this place —"

"I'm teasing, Dyson. Let's get to the ship."

***

All joking aside, the ride to the hexagonal landing pad at Corner One seemed to take forever, as tense as they all were. Lira sat in the middle, hands folded over her lap, hair blowing in the wind. Tag leaned up against the side of the transport, arm across the back of her seat and the other lazily tapping on the frame—within easy reach of his concealed DK-40. Dyson's eyes flicked from object to object, apparently cataloging everything that could be a potential threat, though Tag thought he worried too much when he started marking every lamp post they passed.

The landing pad was buzzing with activity, literally. Shuttles lifted off and landed every half minute. Ground crews of mostly humans and a few Audrians bustled between ships, conducting scans, making repairs, and overseeing squads of maintenance 'bots that bore greater resemblance to upright spiders than anything humanoid.

Ranif Leroux, erstwhile Pallas Industries rep, was there. His moustache and hair gleamed as slick as a freshly polished cockpit canopy. He wore a white suit of a different cut from the one in which he'd shown Tag around the Pallas booth at the expo, and didn't seem the least bit bothered by the grimy attire of the ground crews. In fact, there was a great deal more color to his cheeks as he read out orders from a scroll casting various images and text in the air.

"Make certain the Sunsabers are on the next transport to orbit," he said. "Mister Wester has issued a notice that the Terran CDF will take possession in the Yarbo System, across our border on the Rift. Do try not to invert the coordinates like were mistakenly entered on the last shipping run."

Tag frowned. So much for telling Pallas he'd be at the banquet this evening.

Leroux's face broke into a broad smile when he spotted the three of them disembarking the transport. "Ah! Mister Wester. I trust you're feeling well after the accident?"

"Yes, we're all fine." He helped Lira out of the transport and grabbed a couple of the travel containers.

"I wasn't expecting to see you here today."

"Our companion, Ms. Raddock, is a bit unnerved by the crash, so we're taking her to meet family out-system," Dyson said. "It shouldn't be a long trip, but we need to make sure she's well."

"I'm sorry to hear you won't be joining us at the banquet, then, Ms. Raddock," Leroux said.

Lira smiled. "I regret missing it, sir, but the incident has left me shaken."

Tag wondered how much of the nervousness emanating from her was an act, and how much was channeled from her actual feelings. "Best get aboard."

"Yes, of course." Leroux took him aside. "I have a transport ready to meet in the Yarbo System as per your instructions, though I have not made contact with your designated fleet representative—at least, they have not responded to my hails."

Tag smothered a grin. He'd have given both arms so he could have been present when the purchase communique reached Commodore Ram. The look on his face would have been worth it. "I wouldn't worry. We'll hash out the details."

Leroux nodded. "Anything else we can do for you, please, don't hesitate to ask. Your endorsement of our Sunsaber fighters is already boosting sales. We've seen a twenty-five percent spike beyond what we'd anticipated from the expo, and it's attributed to your performance evaluation alone!"

Which was funny, because no one had ever explained the malfunction—though Dyson considered it intentional. Probably the Denics, or that Shikasta double-spy. So Tag had figured it only fair to shine a spotlight on the starfighter, because it really was one of the greatest planes he'd ever piloted.

Given Akro's involvement, though, Tag put even odds on the Briddarri and the Denics as possible saboteurs. "My pleasure, Mr. Leroux. You take care."

They shook hands. "Pleasant flight," Leroux said. Yeah, well, here's hoping.

True to Dyson's word, power was already routed to *Olivia Vy*'s primary systems. Tag could feel the heat from her ascent boosters, the air shimmering around exhaust ports. Inside, he stowed his bags, pausing for a moment by the empty cabin which had served as his home away from home during the days spent journeying to Kayna Two. The beginning of their mission had been full of promise, optimism at the goal of upending Naplian dominance in the war.

Tag thought of the data they'd recovered, as he slid into the pilot's seat and started his pre-flight checklist. How many lives would be saved if the Union joined Terra and the Briddarri's Grand Alliance? He already had a hint of how many lives would be lost—the files promised that much.

He didn't see a way to outmaneuver the circumstances.

Dyson and Lira were quiet as they secured their gear and sealed up *Vy*. Dyson took his seat at Navigation, keying into the comm frequency for Commercial Orbital Tracking. "Tracking, this is Dyson Aster with *Olivia Vy*. Requesting confirmation of clearance to depart."

"Confirmed, Olivia Vy. Sending course for Departure Route Four. Please do not deviate until receiving your assigned outbound vector from Kayna Two. Hope you enjoyed your stay."

Tag snorted but didn't offer any quip in return. He eased *Vy* up on her boosters. Within seconds the city dropped away, a miniature of itself in sharp relief against the sprawling savannah. Dozens of ships and shuttles fell and rose, flocks of man-made avians.

"I have the coordinates for the Yarbo System input," Dyson said. "Jump drive is winding up. We should be ready to transit in ten minutes."

"Sounds good." Tag didn't know what else to say. One minute he wanted to chuck it all and fly off into the depths of the galaxy. The next he wanted to strap on the nearest starfighter and dive headlong at a Naplian battlecruiser's batteries. He clenched his hands around the controls as *Vy* rattled up through the fringes of the atmosphere, relaxing only when the air thinned out to the smooth ride of solar space.

"This isn't right," Lira said.

"What isn't?" Tag glanced over his shoulder. "I'm pretty sure I followed the departure course within centimeters. I've got a laser marker in the back; you can measure if you like."

Her smirk told him her humor was still intact. "No, not that. The data crystal. The fate of the people of the Union. Are we really going to hand it over to Terran Intelligence and their Briddarri equivalent, so we can plunge an entire people into war?"

"I believe we have discussed this," Dyson said. "Our mission is clear."

"This was never a *mission*, Dyson, not for me," Lira said. "This was always a job—a job on which I bargained my life, in more ways than one."

"Your condition is unfortunate, yet I believe we can parlay the data encased in the crystal to receive advanced help from TI."

"Please! Do you honestly think anything but my incarceration will happen? I'll be thrown back in a cell, to rot and most likely die, while you two go back to spending your entire lives fighting."

Tag didn't want to think about it. Everything he'd been holding back these past few days boiled to the surface. Irritated, he turned his attention to the orbital sensor scans. Commercial Orbital Tracking loomed, its familiar oval a bright sun in the gleaming rays of Kayna Two's star. He didn't recognize many of the ships berthed there; most must have been new arrivals, and the ones they'd seen when they reached the system had gone. A huge freighter, which could have easily swallowed a Briddarri battleship, eased into a dock. The Denaxa Starman liner was still there, somehow looking even more elegant. Tag surmised it must have put into port for a cleaning and overhaul.

"Our duty is to deliver the data." Dyson's tone sounded flatter, more robotic, than as of late. It reminded Tag of the lifeless state he'd remembered when they first met.

"And that's all that influences you. Duty. Programming." Lira unstrapped from her seat and stood between the two of them. "Programming made you come back to rescue me, when you could have left with the data and succeeded in your mission."

Dyson said nothing. He stared through the tangle of course estimates and ship positions floating on the nav console's holographic displays.

Tag wondered if *Olivia Vy* was on his mind right then. "Look, Lira, I don't like this one bit. People are going to die either way."

"Sounds to me you're justifying your involvement."

"I don't want it to turn out this way!" Tag snapped. "But there's not a lot of choice left to us."

"There's always a choice left to us. Like the one I made."

"Yeah. You stole from your friends."

"It … was the wrong way to do it. But I wanted the data out of TI's hands."

"What were you going to do with it? Sell it to the highest bidder?"

"Of course not!" Lira scowled. "Blue Kitt would have sold it back to the Leadership, through intermediaries, so they could hang onto their dark secrets."

"You'd hide the truth."

"If it kept millions from dying, yes."

Dyson shook his head. He seemed weary, a funny thing for Tag to think about an android. "Our dissension gets us nowhere. We have a rendezvous to keep, and seventy-two hours in which to keep it. The coordinates are set. The jump is prepared."

Tag met Lira's eyes. "I'm sorry. We've got to do this."

She folded her arms but didn't respond. The plea in her expression was plain enough.

She returned to her seat and reattached her restraints.

Tag reached for the jump drive controls. One way or another, this was going to end soon. He only hoped he hadn't fouled up the chance to do what was right.

Tag threw the controls, and *Olivia Vy* winked out of the star system.

***

It was bound to be a long journey. Tag spent a lot of time in his bunk, or the cockpit, or buried in the coffin-like access tunnels of *Olivia Vy*'s drive systems. Tinkering for hours with the power systems passed the time over the next three days and helped focus his thoughts. He had long stretches in which he could truly ponder what he was doing, and for what reasons. He and Lira and Dyson steered clear of each other. They didn't even eat together.

That last part irked Tag, and not for the most rational of reasons.

So much for the kiss.

He was on his back, hands deep in the acceleration compensator's third nodule when the comm chimed. *"Tag, we're coming up on the Yarbo system. It's about a half hour away."*

Hearing Lira's voice, tinny and distorted over the intercom as it was, lightened his mood. "Be right out." He finished his work, marveling at how the TI techs had crammed major military hardware into every hidden nook of the repurposed freighter. Maybe they'd let him fiddle with a job like this. It was a soothing change from blowing things up …

Tag shook his head. Forget it. He was a pilot, and a squadron leader. He'd lost sight of his command responsibilities, and here he was, minutes away from zipping on the uniform and doling out salutes again.

Assuming that's what he wanted. "Novafire," he muttered. "Quit moping!"

Dyson wasn't in the cockpit, nor was he in either cabin. Lira sat in the co-pilot's chair, watching as space rippled by in eerie, pulsating purple and blue waves streaked with rainbow spirals. Jumping always gave Tag the sensation he was hurtling somewhere incredibly fast, while simultaneously standing as still as a parked fighter. "Mind if I join you?"

"Of course, Captain." She smiled at him. Tag leaned back in his seat. "You okay?"

"As well as I can be. Ill, yes, but comfortable." She didn't appear comfortable. The lines on her face had deepened, and her expression was gaunt.

"I'm not mad, you know." Tag fidgeted with the straps. "This isn't easy for any of us."

"I know. I'm sorry I pushed at you both."

Tag touched her hands. "If there was a way I could help you, and a way to avoid all this, you know I'd take it."

She smiled again. "I know."

They sat in silence until the timer counted down the last minute to their destination.

Dyson joined them, settling quietly into the rear cockpit seat. He held the data crystal's container in both hands. "I must speak my mind to both of you."

Tag touched the jump drive controls. "Hold that thought for a second."

They hit their mark precisely. Space flattened black, and hundreds of thousands of stars speckled the gloom. Lira ran the sensor check; five marks lit up.

"Olivia Vy, *this is TSS* Confiance." Commodore Ram's cultured voice was unmistakable. Tag felt the warmth of reunion. *"Good to see you on time and intact. Was your mission a success?"*

Tag held the gazes of Lira and Dyson in turn. He couldn't resist a last look at the box—and as he did, Dyson opened it. The lattice sparkled in his hands. "You better believe it, sir. It's good to be back."

"Roger that. Commander Ess will move his flotilla into escort posture, and we'll move in for docking procedures. Standby, and well done."

"Thank you, sir." Tag signaled Lira to mute the feed. "Dyson, you want to say something, now's the time."

"It needs to be said to Commodore Ram, as well."

"All right, open her up." Tag cleared his throat. "*Confiance*, Captain Wester here. Our Terran Intelligence operative has an immediate report to—"

Static shredded the signal. Lira cursed and turned down the volume. Displays went haywire. "Of all the things to malfunction!"

"That's not a blasted malfunction." Tag kicked power to the drives, aiming directly for *Confiance*, and Tim Ess's gunboats. They were still a good five minutes away from rendezvous, even with a ripwave kick, and that generator had to spin up for a while. If he was right ...

The proximity alarm bellowed. Red pips flashed across the nav display. "Naplian ships," Dyson said.

Lira switched places without another word. Six Naplians. Two lines, led by a battlecruiser. "Perfect," Tag muttered. "Way to end a trip."

***

The planet was remarkable only in possessing one side which always faced away from a distant, feeble dwarf star. Ice and snow sheathed a rocky surface. There wasn't a trace of liquid water until one scanned down a good three klicks. Elden was thankful he wouldn't be able to feel the biting cold of temperatures that hovered well in the dozens of degrees below zero.

"No orbital traffic," Goetz said. "No satellites we can determine, either."

"We couldn't spot anything at her world," Rett muttered, indicating Marney.

"It's a risk we'll have to take." Elden magnified the view of the stark white and gray planet. "I won't have us bombard the planet with our scanners. It could tip off any inhabitants to our presence. We've chanced that enough using ripwave to close the distance from the outer system."

Goetz nodded. "Landers for the final approach."

"Correct. Assemble twenty octants and include heavy weapons units."

"Yes, sir."

Elden traversed the ship to the equipment cabins, where he found Marney, Nolte, and the mercenaries fitting out in cold weather survival gear—padded white jackets and trousers, mottled gray and white ceramic armor, thermal adjustors, and respirators. All of them carried Naplian Furta rifles now, along with Naplian pistols.

What Elden found less surprising than their choice of weapon was he'd given no order or permission for them to join his raid. "You're staying aboard *Hessian*."

"I am most certainly not." Marney frowned. "You're going to need help. That's why Dave and I brought our people over from *Vossberg*."

"From a squad of humans? I have 160 Truppen for the assault."

"And eight more people won't hurt. We're coming down with you. I don't care if we have to hang on the shuttle's hull. *Vossberg* will move off under *Dragonfly*'s protection—"

"So, you're acquiescing to one of my orders."

"Only the one. And it isn't an order, Elden, because I'm not one of your soldiers." Elden separated himself and Marney from the rest. The way she glared at him now, sapphire eyes ablaze, reminded him of their more heated arguments from the old days. Days he really didn't want to think about. "Marney, I understand your drive for revenge, but it's only going to get you injured or worse. You aren't a soldier."

"Don't you think I know that?" Marney said. "Neither is Dave. He's a mining consultant, helping FEGG set up access to his world's wealth, who fell in love with one of the first settlers. Not a warrior, just a man doing anything necessary to protect his family. You're right, I'm certainly no soldier. But neither am I a governor's daughter studying agriculture. The Naplian invasion took away everything I was, and I had to reshape my life. Nothing is left."

"That isn't true. You have your family—your brother, your father." Elden wanted to delete the next words but spoke them anyway. "Your husband."

"None of them understand. That's why I've had to use relief work as a cover, so I can take the fight to the Naplians." Marney shook her head. "Tag would understand, perhaps, but he'd want to keep me safe. Tim … I love him dearly, and he loves me, but it would be the same situation. Father is the only one who sees things the way I do. He sees the need for action outside the chain of command, to make the Naplians pay. You see it too, don't you?"

Elden was about to protest; however, he was all too aware of his borderline insubordinate behavior in search of first his missing comrades and then the cybernetic laboratories. Marney had a point, and besides, human soldiers could be just as capable as Truppen, if more fragile.

Who was he to deny her the moment to strike against the One-eyes when it was the very thing he'd rededicated his life to do?

"Very well. Your team can accompany us. But stay close to me, and Goetz." He leaned in, lowering his audio emitters to keep the conversation between just the two of them. "Mind Rett. He hasn't convinced me fully of his loyalty, yet I refuse to let him out of my scans."

Marney nodded. "Thank you, Elden."

He returned the gesture. "For you, Marney, and no one else." Elden considered himself a blasted fool.

***

Crosswinds ripping through the mountains made for a rough ride to the surface, so much so Elden was thankful for the internal gyroscopes of his Truppen frame. Marney and her human companions had to strap themselves in with shock webbing. Even so, a few of them got sick.

On the plus side, no one opened fire.

The landing craft swept in low to the valley floors, kicking up so much snow with their jets it was impossible to see out the tiny portholes. Elden didn't know they'd landed until the hull rang out and came to an abrupt stop after making several sharp turns.

<Keep Marney and her people between us,> he linked to Goetz. <And make sure Rett is watched at all times.>

<Already locked onto him, sir,> Goetz said.

A full force blizzard raged around them. The Truppen clustered close together, with the humans in their midst, outside the landers. They climbed a short ridge to a section of rock Goetz pinpointed on their sensors as abutting concealed tunnels of the facility.

<Blasting through here should get us into a maintenance shaft.> Goetz affixed a plasma cutter to his right claw. <Course it will alert the entire base to our presence.>

<Glad to hear you've taken that into account.>

<Always thinking, sir.>

Pinkish-red light flashed all around, sharp contrast to the blinding white of the snowstorm. Steam roiled where the plasma beam superheated the air and chopped rock. Soon Goetz had sliced a hole large enough to admit a hunched over Truppen into a dark, quiet space.

Elden ducked inside first. His octant slipped in behind him, spreading out both directions in the unlit corridor. Marney and Nolte were orange silhouettes tinged with gold in Elden's scanner output.

No reaction so far to their entry. Elden didn't like that. Surely there was some kind of alarm system in place, unless the operators were so assured of their concealment they found it unnecessary.

He ordered the entire group of 160 Truppen to move inward along the corridor, sharing Goetz's sensor scans made from orbit. Scouts with more powerful onboard sensors ranged a few strides ahead. No sign of biological life, though indicators showed a heavy concentration up ahead.

<Main chamber's in 100 meters,> Goetz said.

Elden glanced down at Marney. If she was afraid, it was hard to see it, with most of her face concealed behind the respirator. Her eyes were wide, though, reflecting the scant light let in by their breach. That same light vanished as the rearguard of the Truppen forces blocked off the entry Goetz created.

Up ahead, the Truppen scouts rounded a bend. Their claw steps stopped.

<Movement at our backs,> Goetz said. <Seems to be automated patrols coming up the corridor.>

<I can take some men, draw them away,> Rett said.

<I appreciate your eagerness, but I want the unit together.> Elden had no intention of letting Rett wander off again, not after those Briddarri researchers turned up dead.

All thoughts of the troublesome Briddarri-turned-Truppen vanished from his thoughts when Elden turned the same corner as the scouts.

The chamber before them stretched out a kilometer long and wide, divided up every hundred meters by support beams and grated metal decks rising five stories. It reminded Elden of a massive version of the berth decks of *Hessian*, where the deactivated Truppen had been stored. Dim orange lights revealed these decks, too, were crowded.

Hundreds of cyborgs were spaced throughout the cavernous room. Each one rested in a socket, lined with power couplings and monitored by sensor posts. They were a hideous amalgamation of crude weapons, clunky sensors, and cannibalized Truppen gear attached onto and inserted into humanoid forms. Most were Briddarri and a few were human.

A soft sound pervaded the room. Elden thought it was the life support systems, until Marney said, "Can't you hear them breathing?"

Goetz stood there, claws limp at his side.

Elden contemplated his orders for the Truppen, all the time, Jeopar's warning about abominations echoing in his mind.

Then, they stirred.

CHAPTER SEVENTEEN

The shouts echoed from the farthest end of the building, working their way along the walls in concert with pounding footsteps. Elden switched to thermal scans. Humanoid life signs. Briddarri? The body temperatures matched.

It didn't matter, because dozens of the sleeping cyborgs stumbled out of their resting booths, taking their first steps as a cohesive unit. Steps they already had synchronized.

They were armed. Every last one of them. Be it with blades or energy weapons or projectile weapons—some with a combination of the three—the cyborgs turned to meet the intruders.

Elden didn't need to give orders. The Truppen knew what to do, how to react. Octants split off from the main body and bounded into the deep chamber, headed for spaces where they had cover—cover their sensors had pinpointed within seconds of the first scans. Automatic weapons fire shattered the silence, made into a roaring flood by the man-made cave.

Elden grabbed Marney with both claws and hurtled across fifty meters to an assembly of crisscrossed support girders. Midair he returned fire with the railgun mounted on his left shoulder. Frame indicators warned him as the heat index spiked.

Marney managed one wild and ill-placed burst of Naplian energy fire with the Furta rifle. She broke from Elden's grasp and huddled alongside the girders, propping her gun against them. "How many are there?"

"More than there are Truppen." Elden's sensor count clicked north of 300 and added a few more in the intervening seconds. The cyborgs he could stop. He tried sending them a communications link, using the same frequency his onboard systems told him the cyborgs utilized to maintain contact, but they didn't respond. "They're inexperienced, however—taking too many risks, remaining exposed to our fire. We should be able to hold them long enough."

Nolte and his mercenaries joined them, lugging heavy knapsacks. "Charges are all accounted for," he said. "Show me where to do the most damage."

"There are twin power cores for this room," Elden said. "One midway, one at the far end. Ring both of them with charges and that will be enough to turn half the mountain to slag."

"The charges have timed delay, with a remote override, but I wouldn't bet on the remote's signal penetrating all this rock once we're back at the entrance."

"Then we'll rely on the timers." Elden shifted aim with his railgun and stitched a line of projectiles across two advancing cyborgs. The impacts ripped them apart, leaving little recognizable of their original forms. <Goetz, what's our status?>

"Here, sir." Goetz slammed down from an upper level of the room, his feet leaving clawed imprints in the metal floor. He had a cyborg by the neck.

Marney and Nolte aimed their rifles, but Elden waved them off. "A prisoner?"

"Source of intel." Goetz squeezed his claws around the cyborg's neck. Pinpricks of blood welled red.

For all Jeopar's admonition, there was still human life in this one. "Name, rank," Elden demanded.

The cyber said nothing. He was young, taller than both Elden and Goetz had been when they'd possessed human bodies, with shock blond hair buzzed near to his scalp. One blue eye was gone, replaced by a flat grey sensor module. Both arms were also removed —a cybernetic appendage with a blade formed the left and a thick, wide-bore gun the right. Those weapons, though, had been crushed and rendered useless. Elden surmised he had Goetz to thank for that. Elden searched for an access point, and found Goetz already holding a breach in the cyber's security system open. <Name your superiors.>

His onboard operating system visualized the cyber's electronic defenses as a series of glowing, transparent domes, like nested shielding for a starship. Goetz's attacks shattered them one by one, allowing Elden deeper into the cyber's memories. Finally, he found the core of his consciousness. <Our orders are to protect them.>

<Who are they? I need names.>

<I am not authorized to give them.>

<You can and you will. I know you have the data. I can sense it behind your barriers.>

<I am not authorized.> The cyber's personality quaked. Elden's digital footing trembled.

<Not going to be able to hold the breach much longer, sir,> Goetz signaled. <He's going into rapid decay. Safety protocol.>

<Tell us who is commanding you and we'll cut you loose from them,> Elden said to the young cyber.

<I am not authorized. I will follow the orders and destroy the enemies.> It was like dealing with a basic 'bot, only the will, the drive, far surpassed any sort of combat AI. But the level of complexity Elden got from communicating with a Truppen—or an android possessing human thought like General Erich Baessler—was missing. The cyber was a shell of whomever he'd been.

Warnings slashed red across Elden's displays. He felt queasy, a sensation which worsened the deeper he got into the cyber's personality matrix.

<Back out!> Goetz's voice was a bizarre echo. <Losing the connection … will get caught … fragmenting the …>

Elden withdrew the link as fast as he could and emerged so disoriented he neglected to reconnect his audio inputs. Gunfire and explosions crashed over him. Marney was there, knelt beside him, hand warm through his frame's feeds.

"What happened?" she asked. "Goetz brought that prisoner, and you froze up."

Elden's internal chronometer informed him that four seconds had passed. He thought he'd been trapped inside the cyber's mind forever.

The cyber lay on the floor, body twitching, eye rolled back until only white sclera showed. Goetz shook his head. If he could spit, Elden knew he would have. "Fried his network. A backup against coercion. Brutal."

"I found what little he knew," Elden said. "The Briddarri have a lab at the far end of the chamber, past the second power core. If we want any of the men who did this as evidence, we need to get down there."

"Consider it done."

Their group hurried along the right side of the room, dodging ricochets and energy blasts. Elden relayed orders to the Truppen through their network. Octants split apart and reformed with the fluidity of schools of fish, coming together to take out a group of targets, then peeling away to engage individual cybers. Heavy weapons units fired long-range railguns down the far end, taking down the cybers armed with modified plasma throwers. Dozens more engaged the Truppen hand to hand, slashing at their armor with blades whose edges did far more damage than Elden expected.

Twenty cybers poured into their path, swarming through the gap ahead of Elden, Goetz, Marney, and Nolte, the human mercenaries, the other eight Truppen ...

Rett. Where was Rett?

<Blast it,> Goetz grumbled. <Rett! Get back in position!>

<I'm right here.> He was, indeed, standing in front of them—with the twenty cybers at his back.

"You'd better have an explanation for this," Elden said.

"Take a wild guess," Rett snapped. "You think you and the Truppen are undefeatable? You think you're the only ones who are going to have this power while the rest of my people struggle and bleed against the Naplians? Not a chance."

"Greenblood scum!" Goetz lunged for him.

Rett took the impact head on, grappling with Goetz, and shouted a command. The cyber surged into their midst, blades and claws slashing.

Elden took a swipe across his left shoulder, and the blade severed not only his railgun's mount but took a sizeable chunk out of the armor. Circuitry sparked where it was exposed. The shock of a weapon doing that amount of damage up close made him hesitate, only for a second.

Then he drove his claw through the chest of the cyber and tossed him aside with no more effort than swatting a fly.

Elden pressed forward, clashing weapons with the cybers. The Truppen did likewise, firing from mounted railguns only when they were clear of any friendly fire—such as the humans.

Marney scorched the side of a cyber's torso with a blast from her rifle, then smashed the stock across its face. It slashed the air near her head, only missed because she was fast enough to dodge and Nolte's aim with the Furta rifle was sure enough to take the back off the cyber's head.

Rett managed to shove Goetz aside, though not without taking a kick that opened a gash in his armor. Self-sealant foam oozed across the wound, and Elden's sensors dutifully informed him to the presence of repair nanites hurrying to close the gap.

They'd pushed the cybers back and killed ten. But more flooded the area.

<Jump out!> Elden sent this to Goetz on their private frequency. Rett still had access to their communications bands and it would take too long to reconfigure them while he was around.

<Get to the far end! Take as many of Marney and her people as you can!>

Goetz's only acknowledgement was to scoop Marney under one arm, and a scowling Nolte under the other, before leaping up two stories.

The remaining Truppen—in the blur of battle Elden realized two of his men were dead, Vike and Satorama, both their heads severed and mangled—followed suit. Soon they'd all jumped up to the catwalks, carrying the mercenaries. The humans fired back down into the midst of the cybers, with seeking grenades that adjusted their descent with tiny thrusters.

A trio of searing explosions gave Elden the added boost by way of their shockwave. He flailed up to the third story, landing heavily in a crouch with a resounding *clang*.

Not dead yet.

He'd better move fast, or he would be.

***

Switching from his several days' work of pretending to buy starfighters and skulking around Atterissage on Kayna Two looking for hidden data back to flying in combat proved a cinch for Tag.

As soon as the Naplian ships appeared on *Olivia Vy*'s scopes, the line of six vessels disgorged four squadrons of Jarra Fols, the ubiquitous plane that reminded Tag of a clawed hand.

"Dyson, you'd better not have been making it up when you told me she's got offensive weaponry packed away."

"I was not. Shields are primed." Dyson swiped his hand along the right side of his navigational displays with a chopping motion of his palm. The holographic images shrank to two-thirds their original size, pushed over by an array of targeting icons. They presented enhanced scans of the six Naplian warships.

Tag grinned. Good deal. Nothing like catching some One-eyes flatfooted. He flipped over the chipped panel Dyson had showed him when he'd first inspected *Vy*'s cockpit. Now those looked familiar.

"Railgun is charged and ready," Dyson said. "Targeting array at your command."

"All right, everyone hang on." Tag kept the ship on her course toward *Confiance*. The Terran heavy cruiser was angling her vector toward the Naplians, crossing an invisible T, to bring the most weapons and narrowest profile to bear. Meanwhile, Tim Ess's four gunboats burst out of their formation in a spray of missile salvos and drone launches.

The Naplians responded with long-range torpedo strikes, the projectiles fast outstripping the speed of all the fighters on the battlefield. Unfortunately for the Terrans, the enemy fighters spread apart into two groups of two squadrons each, circling around the ships.

Fortunately for Tag, no one had paid *Vy* any notice, until a flight of four Jarra Fols peeled off one squadron and made a run for them.

"They're not coming for escort purposes, I assume," Lira said. "I'd recommend we get out of here, but that doesn't seem part of your plan."

Tag shrugged. "Not my plan. Dyson, how about you?"

"I would suggest misdirection and ambush." Dyson's slight smile was enough to get a chuckle from Tag.

"Right. Let's see how they do." The missile rack was indeed full of six. Nice thing, two were disabler warheads and the other four packed with flechettes. Tag queued up one of the latter.

"Range is 50,000 kilometers and closing."

Tag nodded. "At the speed they're cooking, it won't take long. Stand by for countermeasures—assuming we have those."

"Besides the clouder? With the shields engaged and the railgun active, I would not advocate putting significant strain on the power core."

"Don't be such a baby." The targeting sensors gave him a beautiful detonation point dead in the middle of the formation. Just a bit nearer ...

Missiles exploded around the distant *Confiance* as her railguns and particle cannons knocked them down one by one. But there was no way she could continue to swat them, not with six warships sending salvos her way. The gunboats proved adept at sweeping missiles and torpedoes, however, as they spread fields of scattering debris between the onrushing parties.

More Naplian missiles burst well before their intended targets.

Meanwhile *Confiance*'s torpedoes outmaneuvered the repulsing fire from the Naplian ships. Tag smirked. After three years of war, it was nice to know Terran Research & Development maintained their edge in electronic countermeasures.

When the Naplian fighters were twenty seconds from intercepting *Olivia Vy*, Tag launched the missile.

The tactical display showed him an immaculate 3-D rendering of the ship, including the aft shielding that opened up, revealing the hidden launcher in its compartment. The missile raced off in a blinding glare of its drive, streaking ahead of *Vy* and into the midst of the Naplian formation.

The starfighter pilots were no slouches, Tag had to admit; they broke ranks and scattered.

Two of them fired green bursts at the missile.

They weren't paying attention when Tag boosted *Vy* to her maximum acceleration and cut apart the nearest fighter with a perfectly placed railgun blast.

The missile detonated seconds later, its rudimentary but dedicated onboard targeting brains sending the greatest yield of flechettes toward the remaining two fighters. Razor-sharp fragments hurtled forth, carried by the missile's acceleration and their own explosive charge. They glittered in sparking fury where they weakened shielding on all three fighters, though two suffered the worst—one exploded as its core was breached, the other lost a wing and both drive engines.

The third one, well, Tag had it bracketed and punched clean through its cockpit before he figured the pilot had half a clue what had happened.

"Fighters launched." Dyson enlarged a corner of his displays. Sure enough, *Confiance* had scrambled a squadron of Warhawk starfighters and Raider fighter-bombers.

The sight of the distant specks and the enhanced imagery on his sensor readouts was enough to make Tag wish he were back in the command seat for Bronze Squadron. But *Olivia Vy* was a decent second. "Give me a tight signal to their lead out there. I don't want to get blown away by the good guys when I'm here to lend a hand."

"I have put you through to their commander, I believe."

The female voice that rang through the comm was cold, brusque, and so familiar Tag couldn't help but laugh. "Olivia Vy, *this is Bronze Squadron, Lieutenant Wyss commanding. Or should I say, temporarily commanding, sir.*"

"You miss me, Princess?" Tag racked up two more missiles.

"Hardly, sir, since your absence has given me more command time than I'd otherwise accumulate. But it is nice to hear your voice again."

"Blasted right it is. I'd love to get back aboard *Confiance* and buy the Bronzes a round of whatever moonshine Ryoshi's been cooking up between the jump drive cables, but we've got this minor problem of a One-eye task force to tackle. You have anyone in particular you'd like me to sock in the nose?"

"It wouldn't hurt to see if you can distract the war destroyer on the flank nearest Confiance," Princess said. *"Seems she's trying to do an end run around our formations, and the gunboats are preoccupied with the frigates the One-eyes brought to this soiree."*

"Consider it done. Hold a glass for me." Tag cut off the signal. "Okay, Dyson, concerns or not, fire up the clouder."

Dyson nodded. "Commencing."

The clouder's monitoring systems aside, Tag could tell when it went active, because a pair of Naplian fighters zoomed by them, ignoring their presence. Perfect. Tag boosted *Vy* toward the destroyer, the vessel easy enough to pick out even without scanners because of its distinctive single broad wing. Princess was right—as the Terran starfighters engaged their counterparts, *Confiance* dueled with the battlecruiser, and the gunboats grappled with the Naplian frigates, the destroyer was making a broad loop around the Terran flanks.

"I infer the vessel is lining up for a broadside salvo," Dyson said.

"You think? How's my acquisition look?"

"Target is locked. Two disablers and two flechette warheads, ready."

"Yeah, got them racked." The destroyer grew larger in the cockpit viewport. Tag had no idea how effective this clouder would be—it fooled scanners of Union skyhooks, but this was a Naplian warship, not some civilian model.

Well, guess he'd figure it out if they shot first. "Range is optimal," Dyson said.

"Space, Tag, if you're going shoot at them now would be a fantastic time." It was the only thing Lira had said since the battle commenced, and every word was drawn tighter than a cargo cable.

Tag glanced over his shoulder. She was pale, sweating, and trying her best not to cringe where the straps pressed against her. Novafired Briddarri. Whatever they'd done to her, they'd better be able to fix it.

He waited until he could see the registry number etched out in Naplian script before he launched.

The missiles shot away, and Tag peeled off, using the drive's full thrust—no point in hiding behind the clouder anymore, as the missiles' flare would instantly alert the One-eyes to his presence. Guided by Dyson's programming coupled with his sensor readings, the disabler missiles struck first, slamming into the destroyer's shielding at a weak point under the dorsal fin—home to the ECM and communications arrays—just above the main drives. Dyson's displays flashed in wild colors as the shielding cut out, the generators overwhelmed by the sudden, pinpoint strain.

The flechette missiles exploded in that gap with the force of bullets punching through a flimsy scroll.

The dorsal fin was gone, and the drives sputtered, intermittently boosting the destroyer on a vector Tag was sure its captain hadn't anticipated. Green energy blasts lanced out, thrashing wildly for whomever had inflicted the damage, but Dyson re-engaged the clouder.

Tag slapped the console. "Now that was a stab! Nicely done."

"It is not a 'stab' we can likely repeat, given the strain on the core," Dyson said. "We will have to disengage the clouder in a few minutes."

"Way to take the charge out of my jump sails." Tag shook his head. "And we're still outnumbered. Okay, time to get creative."

Light flickered at the edge of his vision, something quite different than an explosion, of which there were plenty. It was a vessel completing a jump.

"Class Five light freighter, minimal crew, full hold," Dyson said. "I believe your delivery has arrived."

"The Sunsabers? Huh. Isn't that interesting." Tag cranked *Vy* around onto a new vector, spraying railgun projectiles at a pair of Naplian fighters winging past. One of them exploded; the second spun about and peppered them with shots that rattled *Vy* terribly, but he was going so fast the opposite direction he'd have no chance to intercept.

"Tag …" Lira shifted in her seat. "You can't be serious."

"I am entirely that." He unstrapped from his chair. "Dyson, you fly this boat. Where do we keep the EV suits stashed?"

"Second locker, cargo hold." Dyson switched seats with him. "Miss Reen, would you deign to be my co-pilot?"

She sighed, and shook her head, but sat beside him at the co-pilot's station. "We don't have to do this. All three of us—we could jump from this system."

"Not one of my options," Tag said. "Get me near enough I can pick up our purchases courtesy of Pallas Industries."

***

Elden dropped down beside the first of the two power cores, depositing Marney and Nolte at its base. A pair of his Truppen followed, planting four mercenaries, who immediately took up defensive positions. Their stolen Naplian rifles lit up the chamber with green flashes as they held off the incoming cybers.

"Plant the charges at those conduits." The core was a six-meter-wide cylinder, three meters tall, covered with black panels and segmented by pulsing yellow lights. Four conduits branched off from each quarter, diving into the deck.

Marney strapped her charges to two of them, activated the transponders, and checked the wrist unit on the sleeve of her jacket. "They're ready."

"Detonators are synced," Nolte said.

Good enough. And no sign of Rett, though he couldn't be too far behind if he was still gunning for them. Elden was just about to gather them up for another leap down the hall when a tremendous explosion shook the entire chamber. Marney and Nolte went to their knees; even the Truppen staggered off-balance.

"What in space was that?" Goetz said.

"Neither of the power cores, thankfully," Elden said. "I'm not getting anything from the other octants, only the same question as yours."

"If Rett decides to blow this place and get the researchers out, this whole trip will have been a waste," Goetz muttered.

"I had thought of that, yes."

Elden grabbed his passengers and leapt down the chamber, then bounded up to the second level. A pair of cybers came at them, one firing a mounted flame weapon, the other slashing with extendable claws not dissimilar to a Truppen's.

From whose corpse did they sever those?

The thought enraged Elden. He put his back to the cybers, shielding Marney and Nolte as fire scorched his armor. Using himself as a barricade gave his passengers time to disengage from him and fire on their attackers. Marney cut down the bladed cyber with a flurry of shots to the torso; Nolte's pair of quick bursts seared the head from the flamethrower's owner.

"Are you hurt?" Marney asked.

Critical temperature indicators declined, and coolant systems did their best to alleviate the overheating Elden suffered. "I wouldn't say hurt. I can't be hurt. But the repairs will take a while. I'm still able to fight."

"We can't have you dying on us, after all."

"You won't."

"Sir, we're getting a priority signal through from *Hessian*," Goetz said. "One-way. Sounds like she's moving off from the planet."

"What? I gave no such order."

Instead of arguing, Goetz linked the transmission.

"A Naplian squadron has entered the system. Transports are on their way to the surface of the planet. As per instructions to withdraw, we are doing so to preserve Hessian *and will await reinforcements. We will rendezvous with* Vossberg *and* Dragonfly *at their prescribed coordinates."*

So that was the instruction. Naplians.

And if Elden hadn't sent the order to withdraw ... "Lock Rett out of our comms."

"Been trying, sir, but a little busy with these cybers."

"Keep on it. We're apparently going to have more company."

More explosions, these accompanied by the distinctive keen of Naplian energy weapons. Troops flooded out of the entrance at the far end of the chamber, the one the Truppen had used. Elden swore.

It was the Naplian mechs they'd fought on an earlier raid. He and his people were trapped.

CHAPTER EIGHTEEN

A ll Lira could think of was Tag's death, and how he was going to leave her with nothing but free-floating particles to mourn.

But as soon as the Sunsaber fighter soared free of the freighter's hold, she breathed more easily—at least until she focused more on her possible death. The thought cheered her even less.

"It is possible Tag overestimated our chances." Dyson rolled *Olivia Vy* through the onslaught of three Naplian fighters, her shields shaking them so badly Lira was convinced she'd lose a tooth.

Indicators flashed red across her board. While her expertise did not extend to piloting or weapons, she did know enough about shipboard systems to reroute power from the core to places where it was needed most. Blue Kitt made sure its thieves were skilled in more than merely grabbing pretty trinkets—or high value data. "I can't imagine that," she said. "I'm surprised he didn't go after the Naplians with bravado alone."

The Sunsaber was the only one of the six Tag had purchased to fly into battle. Had Pallas actually sent one loaded to fight? Well, apparently the railguns were functional, because he tore through a Naplian plane with twin streams of white-hot projectiles. She didn't see any missiles underneath the tiny, distant fighter, and a quick scan confirmed it didn't have any offensive weaponry besides the guns.

This didn't appear to hamper Tag.

"*Stay on my wing,*" he said through the communications link. "*With only two missiles between us we'll be hard-pressed to take down another ship like I crippled the destroyer, but we can make a merry mess out of their birds.*"

"Your pilot friends are cleaning up the destroyer well enough," Lira said. "By the looks of it the Naplians have lost a frigate and the destroyer, but one of the Terran gunboats has been destroyed."

"*Tim?*" Tag swore.

"No, Commander Ess's vessel is intact, though damaged. Frankly all of our vessels can carry the description," Dyson said.

"Yeah, it looks like Confiance *is taking a beating, but I'd wager Commodore Ram isn't ready to give up quite yet."*

Lira had never met the human forces' leader, but she agreed with Tag's assessment. The way in which the Terran heavy cruiser practically pirouetted through its maneuver bespoke a helmsman with impeccable skill and a commander with tactical ability. No sooner had she thought it than *Confiance* bracketed a Naplian frigate with particle cannon blasts, while tumbling end over end through the most bizarre dance Lira had ever seen. Its gracefulness was only marred by the brilliant flash of the frigate exploding, its core having gone off like a nova and the remaining hull fragment spinning away in cometary fashion.

The communications link crackled as a new signal came across. "Olivia Vy, *this is* Confiance. *As much as I enjoy taking a beating from our One-eye friends, our best chance at survival appears to be a strategic withdrawal. How soon until you can jump?"*

"Our core is significantly drained by our exertions." Dyson tore apart a Naplian fighter with the railgun, scattering dying embers of debris. "It will take us time."

"Time is something we have little of, at this juncture. We will screen you as best we can, but unless I can seriously injure our battlecruiser adversary ..."

***

An explosion cast a brilliant flare throughout the cockpit. Lira shielded her eyes. Tag's Sunsaber spun away from one of the Naplian frigates, trailing a frenzy of energy bursts and a pair of missiles. He left in his wake a shattered jump sail. "Our enemies won't be making much of a retreat, either, Commodore."

"Your help is appreciated, ma'am, but these are Terran military matters."

Lira glanced at the chronometer inset in the board. If they could hold a few moments more ... "We're better off not running."

Dyson raised an eyebrow. "This is not your usual assessment. Nor was it your suggestion when this ambush was sprung."

She smiled. "Let's say, I'm skilled at leveraging the odds in our favor."

"I'd rather I had an explanation than cryptic responses," Ram said.

"I have one." Dyson cycled through a holographic menu, a listing of outgoing communications signals. Ah, so he'd noticed. Lira was quite proud of him. If she'd been able to pull one over on Dyson she'd have been severely disappointed. "You signaled your compatriots prior to our leaving Kayna Two—discreetly, yes, but not unnoticeably. I had assumed the piggybacked transmission was an error."

Lira had no idea what a "piggyback" was—didn't humans have a genus of Suidae they used as a food source?—but he'd pinpointed the method. "I did. They should arrive shortly. And when they do, Commodore, they'll expect payment for their services."

"I've already had to deal with TI burning about a purchase of six starfighters, five of which are now spinning in space."

Lira hadn't noticed the freighter's departure. Possibly it had done so when she was distracted by the weapons fire and the explosion Tag caused. But Commodore Ram was right; the other five Sunsabers drifted from where they were jettisoned. She cringed. Hopefully they could be picked up—such a waste of money.

"So whatever services they'll offer, they had better be worth my while."

Space lit up with a trio of flashes, not explosions, but the telltale signs of a jump completion. Three ships accelerated from the source, two of which were stout, brown vessels with three drive engines mounted on stubby pylons halfway down the hull. They were ugly cousins to the already ugly Terran gunboats.

The third vessel was completely their opposite: massive, gleaming, and gorgeous.

Tag's voice cut across the comm. *"What's that novafired Denaxa liner doing here? Sightseeing?"*

Rather than answer, Lira relaxed into her chair as the Denaxa Starman opened fire with six sets of particle cannon. Intermittent blasts from two concealed plasma projectors—of Briddarri design, lamentably—scattered the Naplian forces before the ship as it dove into their midst at great speed.

Dyson stared for a long spell. "This was not calculated; however, it is welcome."

Lira laughed. The tension bled out of her, and for the first time in days, she felt something other than despair. Her people had come for her. They would not let her die.

They had another chance.

"When this is all said and done, I suspect I shall have a very different assessment of Blue Kitt to keep on file," Ram murmured. *"If you wouldn't mind giving me a hailing frequency for your friends out there, I'd be happy to direct them to a place where they could do maximum damage."*

"Gladly, Commodore." Lira punched in the code from memory and sent it. "Please prepare yourself for some rather intense negotiations, as well. Payment will be required."

"I'll empty my operating budget if I have to. Ram out."

The Blue Kitt vessels soon split up, with the twin gunboats joining their Terran counterparts, and the Denaxa Starman pummeling the battlecruiser from the opposite side as *Confiance.* Lira was no strategist, but she could read people and situations. The confusion on the part of the Naplian formation was plain to see.

Dyson pulled *Vy* out away from the battle, seeking a gap in the swarms of fighters still dueling. Tag's Sunsaber stayed with them, following the wide arc around the other ships. "We will be able to jump within four minutes."

"Four minutes and this show'll be over," Tag said. *"I don't know about you, but I have a squadron to run, no matter how much Princess is going to complain."*

Lira watched the tide of battle turn. There was no mistaking it—she'd thrown in her lot with the humans. Even if she could slip away at the end of this, would she want to?

Could she turn her back on Tag and Dyson, when they refused to do the same to her? "I think, Dyson, that Tag needs an escort to his command," she said.

Dyson smiled, without looking away from his displays.

"Right then," Tag said. *"Let's show the One-eyes how to dance." Olivia Vy* and the Sunsaber dove back into the melee.

***

The Naplian *ziurathal* piloted mechs swarmed both the cybers and the Truppen scattered throughout the chamber in their running fight. Major Gandraad didn't care which was which—the cursed *ziura* were his primary targets, but he was equally happy to showcase the might of his Ffawe by slaughtering these hideous cybers. They were worse even than *shirish*, some half-finished amalgamation of the humans and their Truppen warriors.

His *ziurathal* lashed out with two extruded tentacles, the claws skewering two cybers and pinning them to the floor. The mounted Furta rifles on his mech kept up a steady stream of automated fire. One of the Truppen, itself wounded by the cybers and bleeding hydraulic fluids, charged him. Gandraad withdrew his claws from the cyber bodies and put up a whirling defense that sloughed off armor from the Truppen slice by slice.

They grappled, pinwheeling off a column, slamming against crates. Gandraad felt a spike of fear he wouldn't be able to handle this *ziura* one to one, but managed to stab it in the back with two of his claws. He dragged the cybernetic warrior off his frame, then blasted it point-blank.

The Truppen lay in a heap on the floor. Its optical ports flickered, dull red. Red like *shirish* blood.

"Clean out this nest," Gandraad ordered his men. "But I want Elden Selva alive. Not necessarily in one piece."

He swiped the head off the *ziura* with one stroke.

***

In orbit of the snowy planet, Admiral Erassia paced a circle around the tactical display. His squadron spread around the world, watchful for any ships leaving the surface. They'd missed *Hessian*, blast it all, and he knew the heavily armored Truppen transport was hiding somewhere in the system.

"Send to commanders of *Yirana* and *Tolondar*: Sweep for the enemy transport. Cripple and board if possible. I want as many Truppen prisoners as we can seize for dissection." Erassia smiled. "If the ship is destroyed instead, I will not be distraught."

"Yes, Admiral."

A chime rang from his console. Major Gandraad's initial report —scores of *ziura*, as well as some new form of cybernetic soldiers heretofore unseen. Gandraad suspected Briddarri involvement.

Of course. Who else would dog his steps and make his mission all the more complex?

Erassia typed an encrypted message back: Get me Selva. Destroy the rest and bring samples of everything you can find. Whatever the Briddarri want in this place, we will take.

For Naplia and her Emperors Bonante and Benaltep, all hail their Glories.

**

The doors sealing the lab from the chamber were the toughest nut to crack, but with Nolte's demolitions expertise, they eventually folded—or rather, were weakened enough Elden and Goetz could tear them open.

"Scans indicate the main corridor of this facility leads out from the lab, to the left," Goetz said. "I recommend that for our extraction point."

"Signal the landers." Elden dropped a three-by-three-meter chunk of hatch onto the floor, where it rang with the resonance of a gong. "Have them fly low, barely out of hover. If they get shot down by the One-eyes in orbit we're going to have a very long stay on a very cold world."

"Not once the mountain blows," Nolte muttered.

"The power core's in here," Marney said. "The more detailed scans have it beneath the deck, not in the main chamber like we'd thought."

Elden was about to answer her but was struck by the scene before him—the Briddarri and humans floating in pale orange suspension, tucked in transparent tubes; the handful laying on operating tables, cybernetic limbs attached and in various stages of assembly; the personnel only now looking up from their work, green and red blood smeared on white frocks.

The fear in their eyes was apparent.

<All Truppen, converge on my location,> Elden signaled. <Hold this door. Repeat, regroup on my location.>

There were far fewer Truppen remaining to receive his orders. Yes, the bulk of the cybers had been defeated, or driven back into concealment from which they sniped at his soldiers, but Elden had lost forty Truppen.

He knew the number would not be nearly so high were it not for Rett's treachery and the arrival of the Naplian mechs.

The lab personnel dropped everything they were doing, some of them literally, and scurried for the very same exit Goetz had just mentioned. Unfortunately for them, the human mercenaries were faster. They shouted and shoved, putting the fourteen people onto the deck, face down, hands behind their heads.

"Those mechs are coming in hot," Goetz said.

"I know." Elden stomped across the deck, leaving clawed imprints with each step. He swept up one of the researchers so fast he heard the man's back muscles groan. Elden brought the terrified, green-skinned face close to his. He could see the reflection in the irises of the man's eyes—a featureless Truppen face, red eyes glowing, devoid of outward emotion. "Whose project is this? Tell me everything."

The man shook his head so fast Elden considered the possibility he was having a seizure. "I can't! I can't! Orders are against …"

His eyes rolled up into the back of his head. Pale green foam frothed from the corners of his mouth.

Elden swore. "Poison!"

"Put him down!" Marney hurried over, dragging a medical kit from her jacket. Together they did their best to stabilize the man's condition, but as soon as his body stopped twitching, Elden knew it was useless.

But Marney and the mercenaries stabilized two of the others, even as the rest of the researchers died trembling from whatever toxin they'd introduced into their own systems.

Weapons fire spiked through the open hatchway. Truppen had taken up defensive posts around and inside the hatch, but the Naplian mechs were still advancing. Elden shielded Marney from a blast. "Get the final charges around the core!"

"Already on it." Dave shimmied into an opening in the floor, pushing aside a panel he must have wrenched up. He was down far enough Elden couldn't see the top of his head. Yellow light flickered through the opening.

Elden joined Goetz at the front line. A hundred Naplian mechs, as far as his scans could discern, fighting and pursuing his Truppen.

Smashed and torn bodies of cybers littered the chamber, as did crushed mechs and broken Truppen. He got no signals from any of the downed soldiers—no surviving headpieces. Elden would have ground his teeth, had he any remaining. Whoever the Naplians were, they knew how to permanently destroy a Truppen.

"Get our people through the corridor to the extraction point," he told Goetz. "We'll hold as many of them as we can here."

"Don't wait too long," Goetz said. "I'd blow the hatch."

"That is part of my plan, thank you."

As Goetz ushered the humans through the corridor, as many Truppen as could withdraw followed them through. Several pairs had to haul injured comrades.

Elden rallied three octants of the remainder and crashed headlong into the Naplian mechs. They wanted to face the Devastators? He would oblige them.

Major Gandraad couldn't believe how broadly the Gods of Eternal Fortune smiled upon him. Elden Selva was his primary target, and here came the *ziura* commander himself, leading two dozen of his men into the waiting guns of Gandraad's *ziurathal*.

Only it was not the lizard shoot he imagined.

The Truppen had no sooner emerged en masse than they flew apart with the fury of atoms released in an old-style fission weapon. Gandraad had his men in clusters, by sixes, spread out to encircle the charging horde, but in such formation, they couldn't stop what was an individualized assault. Naplian rifles lit the room with a lightning storm of green blasts, banishing shadow from every corner, and scored a few hits. Several Truppen went down, their headpiece still intact.

Yet the *ziura* fought with astonishing coordination. Three Truppen moving in separate directions—one straight, one at an angle up two catwalks, and one at the opposite direction over Gandraad's head—fired simultaneously on the same *ziurathal*. The mech had time to aim but nothing else before it exploded, its power pack gone critical.

"Fan out! Draw them out of their patterns!" That was all the semblance of order Gandraad could make of the frenzy, as another Truppen landed at his feet.

Selva.

Gandraad whipped his pincers around, hoping for a clean strike, but Selva dodged the blows. He wrapped his arm inside one of Gandraad's tendrils and wound it tight. Gandraad fired at close range, the heat from the Furta rifle bleeding through his own armor. The shot tore a black, blistering gouge across Selva's already damaged shoulder, severing half the connections to the arm.

Not enough.

Selva chopped through the first tendril, then swung the remnant back at Gandraad, cutting armor with his own severed pincers.

More Truppen were streaming out the entrance. How many had managed to retreat from his *ziurathal*, only to counterattack? "Fall back!" he signaled his men, even as he countered and parried Selva's blows. "Regroup at—"

A pair of explosions drowned out his orders. His mech's sensors were functional enough to extrapolate the location of several charges, which had been planted in his wake. Whether intended for the cybers or the Naplians, Gandraad couldn't tell. All he knew was a dozen *ziurathal* were gone, obliterated in a pair of powerful, short-range blasts. And the sensory data feeding back told him it was a human designed weapon.

"You should never have hounded us." Selva's voice cut through the gunfire. "You took everything from me. Now you strap on that can of metal and think you can challenge Truppen warriors?"

Gandraad smashed a pair of pincers through a fold in the armor at Selva's torso. He pulled, tearing circuits and crumpling armor. "Not one *ziura* will be left before the Naplian conquest!"

Selva swiped the tendrils off and stabbed through the front of Gandraad's mech with astonishing speed. The Naplian officer didn't have time to register the magnitude of the damage done to his suit because of the fiery pain in his midsection. Blood dribbled from his mouth, hot and yellow. His thoughts swam, and his vision tunneled.

His final thoughts were for his men, his *ziurathal*, until they too faded to blackness.

***

Another pair of explosions rocked the chamber. Elden, dazed by the damage inflicted on his frame, let Truppen herd him back to the lab. They smashed the broken lab doors back together.

"Go! The timer is running on both sets of charges!" Elden hurried through the corridors with them, watching as the digits in his heads-up display ran down. The exit wasn't far off. He'd heard nothing more from *Hessian* or the landers, but it didn't matter if they weren't ready to make the extraction. He had to get everyone off the mountain.

Ahead, the dark corridor terminated in a blinding white square. Elden burst through, his optics adapting to the swirling maelstrom as fast as they could process.

One of the landers was crumpled against the long, broad slope down to the valley below, smoke billowing in thick black clouds from its hatches. Elden's onboard systems told him another twenty Truppen were gone. Wiped out. No chance at restoration.

As much as it grieved him, to see so many red indicators on the list of green that denoted his ten octants of soldiers, he was more horrified by the immediate sight before him.

Goetz was down, his legs severed by the same explosion that had taken a chunk out of the mountainside. Nolte and his mercenaries were buried under the rubble; their life signs showed up on Elden's scanners as weak, but present.

Rett was there, with a bedraggled group of thirty cybers, and he had Marney clenched in his claws.

"Let her go." Elden's quick count showed fifty Truppen, gathered around him and spreading down the slope. The other landers were coming—their transponders pinged clearly, even through the interference of the storm. "The Naplians ... once they find out we're all here they'll wipe us out."

"I'm leaving here without you on my tail, Consul." Rett spoke the title as if it were a curse. His frame had been damaged in the fighting, too; large chunks of armor were missing, his right leg was twitching, and there were ropes of exposed cabling on both arms.

"Did you know this place was here? Did you know what the Briddarri were doing?"

"I knew something was happening—something that would change the outcome of the war. Face it: we never trusted you, not even after Baedecker Four and especially not after your Truppen mopped up so many of the Naplians there. Soldiers as powerful as you could be turned against us, if they were ever duplicated by the One-eyes. It made sense for the Briddarri to do the duplicating first."

<I'm still operational.> Goetz's signal was as strong as ever, no matter how battered his body.

<Can you take him?>

A digital snort.

<That was unfair of me.> "Rett, she has nothing to do with this."

Marney, if anything, looked furious rather than afraid, though tears streaked the grime on her face. Rett shook his headpiece. "Sure she does! She's following you, and you won't let anything bad happen to her. Will you?"

<On my mark.> Elden sent this to the rest of his men. They in no way appeared to be in formation; several were damaged and undergoing self-repair. But all had their orders.

By now the thrum of the landers' engines was audible over the roar of the blizzard winds.

Rett moved closer to the edge of the slope. "Last time, Consul: stand back while we ride these landers out."

"And where will you go? *Hessian* won't let you back! And neither will the Naplians, even more importantly."

"We can get as far as the girl's ship," Rett said. "And once I kill everyone aboard *Vossberg* there'll be plenty of room."

<Now,> Elden signaled.

Goetz launched a grenade into the midst of Rett and his cyber accomplices. Damaged as he was, he completely broadcast his move, giving Rett enough time to dodge. The explosion injured a handful of the cybers.

But the distraction offered enough time for Elden to spring forward, and Marney the opening she needed to tear into the wires and cables on the exposed portion of Rett's armor. Hydraulic fluids sprayed brown specks everywhere, a hideous smear on the bright snow. Rett's arm froze up, malfunctioning to such a degree Marney— her survival suit slick from the fluids—wriggled free.

It was the few seconds' opening Elden needed to run Rett through with his claws.

Weapons fire shattered the air around him as the Truppen engaged the cybers and cut them to pieces with little opposition. Whatever these cybers were, they were not yet trained to par with seasoned Truppen.

"Don't ... I ... they can rebuild me from my headpiece, can't they?" Rett's murmur was fragmented by static. His optic ports flickered.

"They can, but you won't be left to betray anyone again." Elden yanked a claw free from Rett's midsection and plunged it deep into his headpiece.

The lights died, and the voice faded in a warble of electronic noise.

It soured Elden to kill another Truppen, something he'd not done since he'd had to wrest control from a rebellious general. So many others had died in the war, on this and Elden's other missions, that they could spare few. They weren't recruiting to their ranks.

That might have to change.

Elden helped Marney up off the ground. His soldiers removed rubble and got the injured Nolte and mercenaries ambulatory, as the landers soared into view at the bottom of the slope. "Are you hurt?"

"Bruised, but otherwise fine." Marney wiped snow and grime from her face. She shuddered. "I'm sorry."

"Sorry?"

"I know he was one of your people."

Elden considered the crumpled, lifeless Truppen frame. "He was a Truppen, but he was never one of us."

"Sir!" Two Truppen were hoisting Goetz to the edge of the cliff, for all the good it did them. He seemed determined to drag himself along, even missing his frame's legs. "Got word from *Hessian*. There's more ships coming into the system. Briddarri. Looks like Admiral Ergen's out to play."

"Signal back to *Hessian*. Have her remain with *Vossberg*."

"I doubt Captain Zhivko will keep *Dragonfly* out of the fight," Marney said. "Besides, even Ergen may need help."

"Not likely," Goetz said. "Word is he's brought three squadrons."

Elden glanced up at the sky. No way he could see beyond the

white smear of wintry weather, though he imagined pandemonium amongst the Naplian vessels at the sight of thirty-six Briddarri warships. "Happy hunting to them. Let's get out of here."

***

The double detonation of the mountain facility's power cores was visible as an energy spike from orbit. Erassia swore he saw a pinprick of light on the viewscreen imagery, though without magnification, it must have been a trick of his eye.

The three Briddarri squadrons were no illusion.

"What word from Major Gandraad's men? Anything?"

The Tactical officer shook his head. "Nothing, sir. Not since they engaged the *ziura*. Vital stats are coming back negative. And our landers report no contact."

Erassia slumped in his chair. Gone. All his *ziurathal*, and their best officer. How many Devastators had they taken with them? Was Selva killed? It hardly mattered, not with the *Hessian* still hidden somewhere in the system. With Briddarri warships bearing down on him, it didn't matter. "Recall the landers. Run up the jump drives and prepare to depart."

"Sir, we have a contact at bearing two oh seven mark five six! ID comes back as Reittian—the destroyer from our ambush, Admiral, *Dragonfly*."

Erassia squinted his eye. "Break us from formation and engage."

He had grudging respect for these wayward Terran offshoots— the Reittians fought with a ferocity that would honor even the basest Ffawe. No matter how much *Fulnax* threw at the tiny *Dragonfly*, the destroyer kept coming. Three, five, seven waves of missiles—what kind of weapons magazines did they possess? *Fulnax* hammered at her shields until they were near collapse.

Then the greater threat arrived.

"Incoming fire from the lead Briddarri elements!" Tactical sang. "*Winter Scourge* is hailing us."

"Deploy counterfire," Erassia snapped. "Break pursuit of *Dragonfly*. Are the drives ready?"

"Landers have returned to the fleet, and yes, Admiral, the drives are prepared."

"Very good. Standby."

"Do you wish to respond to the hail?"

Erassia scowled. "The only response I will give is the backside of our jump sails. Take us out of here."

As the squadron fled, Erassia sank into his chair, a deep dread mounting. He'd failed his mission. He'd lost valuable resources.

Admiral Daviont's ire was assured.

***

"Form on my wing and follow me in!" Tag spun the Sunsaber onto a new vector, and for the umpteenth time reveled in the speed, power, and endurance of his new ride. Whether or not his comrades in Bronze Squadron were jealous of the display, well, he'd leave that up for debate.

Their Warhawks swept together, closing ranks until they were each only a few hundred meters apart, then concentrated their fire on the Naplian frigate that was their current target. A railgun would do little in the way of damage against a capital ship, but twelve, combined with a handful of plasma projectors, were enough to pound shields until they fizzled and failed.

"They're down." Princess wasn't any more impressed by the fact than she would have been announcing the weather forecast. "Launching."

She, along with Bronze Five and Six, fired two missiles each. The squadron flew so close to the frigate, and so near to each other, their shields overlapped into one reinforced screen.

Counterfire from the Naplian had little effect; the missiles exploded in rapid succession. Seconds later the frigate was a dead hulk, spinning on its axis as it trailed dying plumes of flame.

"Get free of the defensive radius and come back for a second pass," Tag said. "Finish her off."

"Negative, Bronze, the enemy is withdrawing, repeat, enemy is withdrawing."

In the blur of battle, Tag had forgotten Commodore Ram was monitoring their communications. He was right; the One-eyes that could flee, including the wounded battlecruiser, were jumping out of the region. Three Naplian ships were crippled. *Confiance* and her escort gunboats limped along, burgeoned by the ships Lira had brought.

Blue Kitt with warships. Tag shook his head. The woman never stopped amazing him.

"Once the area is secure, we'll get you and your people aboard, Captain," Ram said. *"Our Briddarri colleagues are awaiting the results of your mission."*

Yeah. The data. Tag steeled himself against the litany of death he remembered. Time for the toughest call.

CHAPTER NINETEEN

I t was, Tag realized, as if their first meeting's tension level had been cranked up higher than a booster running over redline.

Everyone was there: Ram, bulwarked by his antique desk; Vollan, standing beside him; Tag, Lira, and Dyson seated together in a cluster of chairs; Timothy Ess seated to their right; Commander Burrak of the Briddarri's version of TI seated to Tag's left, across from Tim Ess.

The container sat open on the table between them, crystal lattice shimmering. Tag thought Burrak's hunger for it was bad enough the guy might literally eat it. Tim seemed perplexed. Dyson, as always, was a stone-faced enigma, while Lira—well, she leaned against Tag, in a way he knew the others couldn't see. But he propped her with his shoulder as subtly as he could.

If he sat on his hands, he'd have a better chance not pouncing on Burrak and forcing him to cure her of whatever contagion was ravaging her body.

"Well, ladies and gentlemen, there it is." Ram poured water from a carafe into the base of his violets' pot. Blasted things bloomed even more brightly than when Tag had last seen them.

They were certainly the most cheerful faces in the cabin. "A great deal of effort and expenditure, for something so simple."

"Simple," Burrak said. "You speak the words as if this unit could not change the fortunes of our war. One firm push in the correct direction will have the Union of Planets add their fleets to our own."

"I don't believe Terran Intelligence ever planned to simply hand the lattice over to you, Commander," Tim said. "Our agreement was joint study and dissemination of information to the Union Leadership."

"Blackmail." The word came out with sharper bite than Tag intended, but there was no retracting it.

"It's negotiation, Tag," Tim said. "We give them a chance to sign up, otherwise we can release the data and let things take their course."

"Cowardice," Burrak said. "We release the data contained here for all the Union's warriors to see. Let the Riven Cabal marshal their forces and remove the inept Leadership, replace them and guide the people with a strong hand."

"I would be remiss in not pointing out releasing this information will result in the deaths of millions of Union citizens," Dyson said. "Such an outcome cannot be tolerated. It is ruinous for the Union and will give us a damaged ally."

"If we do nothing, we have no ally."

"I disagree, Commander. I project the Union growing amenable to our efforts over time with—"

"There is no time!" Burrak snapped. "The Naplian Empire slices off more and more of our systems every day. We have barely the resources to strangle their advance into your backwater stars, Terran. The sooner the Union can cut out its excess fat, the faster it will become a lean soldier in our ranks."

"This is crazy," Tag said. "I didn't go traipsing into somebody's backyards to steal a secret that was going to kill people."

"The mission came with risk," Ram said. "We did make that clear."

"Not this kind of risk! Not regular people dying." Tag glanced at Tim. "You really think the Union will negotiate? What if they call your bluff, and say no? Is TI really going to make this stuff public?"

Tim shifted in his seat. He had the expression of someone who'd swallowed a sour bite. "That isn't my call."

"Of course it is. The novafired thing's sitting right here." Tag snatched the lattice from its container.

"Put it down, Captain Wester." Vollan's only words so far in their conference were colder than deep space.

"I don't think I should leave it there for him to take." Tag jerked his thumb at Burrak. "He'd condemn all those people to die in a heartbeat—however long that is for a Briddarri. Meanwhile his own agent is dying right now!"

"Tag ..." Lira sat as upright as she could. "This was never going to end with me getting a parade and a medal."

"Doesn't make it right." Tag glared at Burrak. "You heal her of whatever's wrong."

"I don't see how that is relevant."

"It is relevant, Commander, in this joint operation." Ram's tone was stern enough to make Tag stiffen his spine. Judging by the way Burrak lifted his chin it had the same effect on the Briddarri. "There was no mention of harm being done to the lady."

"I sure didn't hear about it," Vollan said.

"This is a thief and scum. Whatever cure can be available, it isn't mine to give."

"You mean you don't have it?"

"I mean, I withhold it until I have what I came for. The data." Burrak didn't retake his seat.

"Yeah, about that." Tag held Lira's hand. "We've come to a decision."

"Dyson, what is he talking about?" Tim asked.

"Captain Wester is correct. He and I and Miss Reen concur in the course of action which must be taken."

Tag handed Dyson the lattice, his muscles tightening worse than if he were stepping into the cockpit for a sortie. There wasn't any turning back. If they were going to back out, now was the last chance. He knew he wouldn't—but Dyson, and Lira, they weren't obliged by any decisions he made. They could still make their own choices.

Dyson cradled the lattice gently in his right palm, as if he were trying to hold a snowflake without it melting. "We cannot allow the deaths of millions of innocents and accept full responsibility for our actions."

He crushed it.

Vollan gasped. Ram stood swiftly, hands splayed on the top of his desk. The violets spilled from their container, dirt and mud mingled, water trickling across the surface.

Tim went pale, paler than Tag had ever seen him.

Burrak's cheeks and neck darkened a dangerous shade of green, perfectly fitting his ramrod posture.

Tag exhaled. That did it.

Dyson opened his hand. The lattice was mashed, crumpled far smaller than any human's hand could reduce it. He tipped his palm sideways. Eight pieces, mingled with tinier fragments, rained into the open container.

Nobody spoke. The only sound Tag noticed was his own breathing, and the gentle rumble of the life support systems.

"The data on the lattice may be recoverable," Dyson said. "My estimates put such a feat at sixty-five percent chance of success—if I were involved in the recovery efforts. This allows our government time to negotiate with the Union of Planets, without any real threat to its people."

"That was not your decision to make." Ram's voice was quiet, so quiet Tag had to strain for his words. "This operation was sanctioned —"

"Sanctioned by Terran Intelligence and the Briddarri Espionage Directorate's Forecasting Division, neither of which will admit involvement in the theft of the data. I suspect this was the reason for involving Miss Reen."

Burrak nodded, teeth clenched. He didn't speak. Tag liked it that way.

"Sorry to disappoint you, Commander," Lira said, "but there was no way you'd ever give up a prize like me—Blue Kitt, apprehended by your sterling law enforcement officers. That became abundantly clear when you poisoned me. This was the most profitable option."

"You were never going to see an ounce of payment, be it in money or freedom," Burrak muttered.

"All the better. Some things are of greater value than either."

Commander Vollan cleared her throat. "Commodore, sir, I can have Marines in here to arrest them all."

"For what? Destroying the fruits of a classified mission which no one will ever affirm took place, for the purposes of blackmailing a neutral nation?" Ram snorted. "I think not. Commander Ess, you have been the one in contact with TI. I am open to suggestion."

Of all the people in the room, Tim was the one Tag wanted least to disappoint, and by the pained expression on his face, Tag figured he'd failed. "I understand why you did what you did. But this doesn't bode well for your career, Tag, nor does it for your operational status,

Dyson."

"On the contrary, my status is not in jeopardy." Dyson smiled. "My memory banks are backed up at an undisclosed location."

Tim swore. First time Tag had heard him do so since he'd shot One-eyes away from Marney during the Naplian invasion of Baedecker Four. "That's a breach of protocol!"

"It seemed prudent to expand my options, when the actions of my so-called allies"—Dyson glanced at Burrak—"were questionable. I will not release those memories, unless provoked."

"This is outrageous. I demand the delivery of the data." Burrak reached for the box.

Tag grabbed his wrist. "Hold on, Commander. That's Terran property, no matter how beat up."

"Captain Wester is right." Ram rounded his desk. "Your division has not operated with full transparency in this matter, Commander Burrak. We will, of course, share whatever is recoverable from the lattice with our allies, but this is a Terran matter. How we proceed with the Union is up to us."

Burrak's lips compressed into a line so straight you could level a laser. "Of course. My superiors will hear about this and take appropriate action." He pressed the communications unit on his belt.

The hatch to Commodore Ram's office slid open. Two hulking Briddarri in dull gray body armor took up positions behind Tag, Lira, and Dyson. "In the interim, I am taking Lira Lin Reen back into custody," Burrak said. "As per our agreement."

Tag stood, but Lira's hand was on his arm. "It's all right," she said. "I knew this was coming."

"Doesn't mean it's right. You gave up a lot to try to help everyone —and you're left with nothing."

Lira smiled and kissed him on the cheek. "Do me a favor: win the war. Drive the Naplians out. And save as many innocents as you can. I'm proud of you, Tag Wester."

She let the guards bind her and lead her from the room. Just like that, she was gone.

Burrak leaned in near enough his sour breath sickened Tag. "Interfere again, human," he murmured, "and you'll join her in whatever black hole we cast her down."

Tag bared his teeth. "Looking forward to it, Commander."

With the office cleared of Briddarri, Tim sealed the hatch. "What now, Commodore?"

"Now, I make inquiries with TI as to what in space has transpired, and what the Briddarri think they're doing." Ram folded his arms. "If we'd known what was in that data, I doubt TI would have authorized cooperation."

"If I may make a suggestion, Commodore," Dyson said. "Ms. Reen proved most valuable as an asset and ally. Far more trustworthy than her handlers. She could prove so again, were she ... available to freelance."

"Yes, but she can hardly assist us from a cell ..." Tim's voice trailed off.

Tag clapped Dyson on his shoulder. "You've still got the comms logs backed up on *Olivia Vy*, right?"

"Of course."

"Good. We've got a call to make."

Ram joined them by the hatch. "Commander Vollan, check in with the hangar chief. Have *Olivia Vy* prepped for departure. Quietly."

She nodded. "Will you require a plot of all the ships in the area? The Denaxa Starman and its pals are still awaiting their payment."

"Oh, I remember. TI may take some arm twisting to empty their account." Ram raised an eyebrow. "But before we arrange payment, I have a feeling Captain Wester has one more use for them."

"Blasted right I do," Tag said.

***

Commander Burrak stormed through the bridge of the battleship *Jade Knife*. None of the crew spoke to him; he knew none would dare. They'd seen him in this mood before. They knew to skirt the storm.

Burrak preferred it that way.

"Get me a tightbeam link to Admiral Ergen," Burrak said. "Encrypted, Code Zero."

"Yes, sir."

He could hear the communications officer entering the commands as the hatch to his ready room shut. Within five seconds, a blue holographic display lit up his desk. Burrak sat before it, let the retinal scan from his control panel confirm his ID. Three seconds after, Admiral Ergen's face took up the screen.

"If you're calling me Code Zero, I assume it's bad."

"The Terrans broke the lattice. Ruined it."

Ergen's moustache twitched. "How bad?"

"Bad enough we cannot retrieve anything from it. The chances of them doing the same are slim."

"Blast it all. They still have it?"

"They were not about to turn it over."

"Then there goes our prime route for dragging the Union into the fight," Ergen muttered. "All right. Fine. We have the backup option."

"Yes, sir. The units are in place. I can be there in six days."

"Good. Sweep it clean, you hear? The sensor records can be prepped within hours of you getting me the results."

"I will do that."

"You'd better. I've got my hands full as it is. Blasted cursed humans and their Truppen spawn," Ergen muttered. "Cost me years of data and far too many resources. You get me what I need, and we'll take the fight back to the One-eyes, understand?"

"Yes, Admiral."

"Don't foul this up."

"I won't."

The screen blanked.

Burrak blew out a breath. He hadn't asked about the thief, the Blue Kitt. It didn't matter. The instructions from Forecasting were clear. She was a liability. The Terrans wouldn't divulge what had happened on the mission—the Denics, the idiot Shikasta, the attempts at sabotage.

But she might. She owed no allegiance.

Space was vast. Once they could drag from her every piece of information, everything she'd seen and done, every location of everything she'd stolen from the Briddarri people, they'd find some distant sector and leave her.

Accidents were frequent.

***

Lira let her head rest against the cabin wall. It wasn't a cell, no, not with a bunk and a private restroom and a tiny viewport of diamond-studded space. But it might as well have been, with the boxy green and gray guard robot parked outside the open hatch. The hatch, too, was an illusion—the telltale flicker of a force screen lined the gap.

She watched as Burrak's battleship disappeared in a flash of light. Jumped, and gone. The transport in which Lira traveled was next. It figured. After all this, she would be taken away into the dark, never to be seen or heard from again. Already, she could feel the vibration in the deck plates as the transport wound up its drive for the jump.

Her body ached. They would never give her any cure. Whatever pain this was, it would linger, intensify, until she died. Or until they questioned her. Why couldn't she just be rid of it?

There was a blur of motion outside her viewport. Another ship?

Power blinked, then died. Orange emergency lights filled the room, and the corridor ... The force screen was gone. She couldn't feel the distant static from it.

[Do not attempt to leave your cell,] the robot said. [This is an emergency status. Do not attempt to leave your cell.]

"Wouldn't dream of it?"

More noise—clanging metal against metal, footsteps, muffled shouting. Silence. More footsteps, greater numbers. Hatches sliding open, then slamming shut. Fewer steps. Only two sets.

Lira pressed into the darkest corner of the room. She had no weapons, but really, she didn't need any. In this poor light she could make do with her hands and feet.

The robot trundled on treads away from the door. [Present identity. Your presence is unauthorized.]

"Friendly guy."

The robot made what Lira could only describe as electronic

gargling. The footsteps bypassed its position, and she heard no further attempts to stop the intruders.

The lead intruder poked his head around the corner. "Hey," Tag said. "Did you miss us?"

***

Olivia Vy nestled against the Denaxa Starman. Tag watched as the green lights lit up on *Vy*'s airlock indicator. "Clean seal. We're good to use the walkway."

He led Lira and Dyson across the transparent tunnel. Except for the silver ribbing, and the grey footpath beneath, they could have been strolling through space unprotected.

"We have limited time. The Briddarri transmissions will no longer be jammed, and even now they are attempting a restart of their 'malfunction.'" Dyson held out a hand to Lira. "We wish you well."

She flung her arms around him and kissed him on the cheek. Tag laughed. He'd never seen the android so befuddled, though he did return the hug with a reasonable facsimile.

"Thank you, for all you've done." Lira let go.

"Of course. I hope to see you again, and in not too great an interval." Dyson left for *Olivia Vy*.

Which meant Tag was without a wingman. He scuffed his boot on the footpath. "So, I don't even have your comm signal ..."

"And you won't. You can't."

"I guessed." Tag smiled. "You take care of yourself."

"You took care of me, when I didn't think anyone else would." Lira pressed a hand to his cheek. "I won't ever forget."

"Good. Because it'd be a shame to go through all that trouble with nothing to show." Tag winked and brought her in close for a kiss.

He didn't know how long the kiss lasted, but it was apparently long enough for them to attract an audience—a Briddarri woman, and two Shikasta, neither of whom looked a thing like Akro Nuvish.

"Sorry. I have to leave. They need to start treatment for the Briddarri's ailment as soon as possible." Lira shouldered a bag and walked toward the group, and the Starman's hatch.

"See you around, Blue Kitt."

At the name, not only did Lira glance back, but all three individuals with her gave him the same look. "Likely not, but we can hope."

It was a lonely walk back to the cockpit. Tag leaned back in the pilot's chair, and watched as the Starman jumped away, another speck disappearing among the stars.

"Are you well?" Dyson said.

Tag shrugged. "Like the lady just told me. We can hope."

***

Elden Selva hadn't seen or heard from Admiral Ergen in twenty-four hours. He counted that as a blessing.

Instead he spent the time reviewing every scrap of data he'd gathered, checking in on Goetz's progress as the techs installed a new set of legs—"Cheap parts," Goetz muttered—and gathering what forces he could spare for Marney.

"With Captain Zhivko's help, there will be plenty of force to allow you and Nolte to kick the Naplians off your world," Elden said. "Especially if you can parlay the planet's mineral wealth to the Reittians' benefit. But I'd urge you to get to real relief work, no matter how much effort you and your father have put into this. The risks are too great."

"Everyone knew the risks," Marney said. "It isn't your fault the Naplians found the planet and conquered it. We know that now."

They stood in a maintenance bay aboard *Hessian*. It was a spare, dark room lit by two white beacons and lined with equipment lockers. Rett's mangled body lay on one of three worktables.

A scanner, fixed to a long, dangling arm, highlighted a trans-light pulse. It magnified the tiny transmitter into a holographic wireframe as large as a Truppen's torso.

It was how the Naplians had followed them to Marney's world, and the Briddarri fleet, and to the hidden laboratory on the icy planet below. However, it had been missed by *Hessian*'s onboard scanners. Rett had to have known it was stashed in his frame. When they'd triggered his self-diagnostics, even though he was deactivated, the onboard systems had pinpointed the pulse with a single deep scan.

Small wonder Ergen's squadrons found the planet with equal ease.

"He must have known, this whole time, or at least soon enough he passed the information to the Briddarri," Elden said.

"What will you do now?"

"I promised we will free those people, and we will. As for the Admiral, he does not appear to be in any hurry to move against me."

"It'd be foolhardy for him to do so," Marney said. "The Briddarri and the Truppen are a key part of the Grand Alliance operations in the Great Desert Rift. They can't look divided, not with the Naplians pressing."

Captain Zhivko rapped on the open hatchway. "Marney, my dear, I am ready to depart, so I am asking if my warrior friends are ready to take their fight the next step."

Elden nodded. "We are, Captain, and many thanks for your continued support."

"I should thank you! Have you seen what was hauled from the Naplian base's wreckage? And the technology scrounged from orbit?" Zhivko chuckled. "If you were designed to eat, you would be feasting with me soon, after I sell my new treasures. I will await your signal."

He left, with Dave behind him. Marney followed, but Elden stopped her, claws gently touching her back. "Marney, please—go find your husband. Leave the war to the rest of us. If these cybers are truly tied to the Briddarri, and not just a rogue civilian operation ..."

Marney turned. "No. Once we free Dave's planet, I will find time with Tim, but this war is mine to fight, too. I'll do it any way I can."

"Tim—Commander Ess should know what you're doing, then. Promise me you will tell him."

She deflated a little. "You're right. I should, and I will. But don't presume to tell me again to stop, Elden. Because I won't. I'll work around you and the Briddarri and the entire Terran fleet if I have too. Good luck with your crusade, and be safe."

Marney left him alone with Rett's body.

Yes. His crusade. Elden knew if he didn't confront Ergen, his time was limited. And whatever cybernetic experiments the Briddarri had planned would continue.

Elden wouldn't allow it. He owed his dead.

***

"Sir, *Hessian* is moving into jump orientation," the Tactical officer said. "*Vossberg* and *Dragonfly* are joining them. Shall we intercept?"

"Negative." Ergen tugged on his moustache. "Let the blasted things go. Selva's no fool; he'll go after the One-eyes at that resource-rich planet, then he'll come find me. No, let's get back to operations. We have a rendezvous to keep."

And, he mused as the three ships bolted from the star system, a new war ally to collect.

***

Six days later, Commander Burrak found the perfect world.

The environment was harsh—greater gravity than humans found comfortable, wild temperature swings, and extreme tectonic shifts. Why the Union of Planets chose to sponsor a colony there was beyond him. All he knew was it had four hundred people, none of them warriors, and all of them dependent upon shipments from space for their survival.

The harvest could begin there.

The orbital bombardment *Jade Knife* laid down was enough to cripple the atmosphere processor. All it took after was to set eight landing craft down, with a squadron of starfighters to pick off any ill-conceived defense. They weren't needed. Burrak's soldiers were enough.

It took him less than twelve hours to round up every man, woman, and child from the colony. He didn't have to be there for the screams, for the gunfire. It was all very tidy, when handled from the bridge, amidst consoles and holograms and hushed murmurs of the crew.

The only thing he let himself do was go to Cargo Bay Three and view the stinking masses he'd harvested.

Their scans came up clean. No major ailments, no major injuries. A few had been killed in the raid. But it was a good start.

And he had it all on crystal clear scans.

Burrak lined up the available data on his scroll and sent it via

Code Zero encryption to Admiral Ergen. Let the Terrans hem and haw about the Union of Planets. In less than a day, it wouldn't matter.

The Grand Alliance would have more ships.

And the Briddarri would make their own Truppen.

EPILOGUE

Two Weeks Later

Tag climbed free of the Warhawk, stripping off his helmet and sucking in the dry, recycled air of Confiance's hangar bay. After a few hours breathing his own stink, it was a sharp contrast. Also reminded him he badly needed to shower. Three back-to-back patrols would do that.

"Captain." Princess called to him over the clamor of the bay from her fighter's cockpit. "Would you be so kind to paint those two kills on my fuselage?"

"I'd tell you what to do with your fuselage, but it isn't gentlemanly." Tag slapped the side of his fighter as he slid to the deck, forgoing the ladder rolled over by a technician.

Princess laughed, and Tag felt lighter on his feet. Lighter than he'd felt in days. They'd hit several convoys and run escort duty on their own. Nobody lost. Tankers of serjaum hulled.

Yet, something gnawed at him. He couldn't put words to it. It didn't bug him until he was alone, without the noise of the hangar bay or the constant input of the fighter cockpit. When he was in his cabin, feet up on the bunk, Baedecker Home Jazz murmuring through the sound panels in the bulkhead.

Lira. And Dyson. And the data they'd ruined.

"Tag."

He was in the corridor through pilot country. Rows of cabin hatches and storage lockers lined both sides. Pilots and technicians in rumpled jumpsuits hurried back and forth. Commodore Ram stood out as glaring as a solar flare.

"Sir." Tag whipped off a salute, helmet still clutched in the other hand.

Ram returned the salute. "You haven't heard, since you just got back aboard. The Union has declared war on the Naplian Empire."

Tag blinked. "I ... wait. The data. Was Dyson able to recover it?"

"Sadly, it appears your android comrade exaggerated his abilities in the matter. The crystal lattice was damaged beyond repair. Even if it could be physically reassembled—and we are speaking of a substantial 'if'—the likelihood of retrieving the data is not as great as he stated."

Dyson lied. Tag decided chuckling in front of Ram would have been his worst idea in a line of bad ideas. "But if the data's lost ..."

Ram held up a scroll. "Tandesh. A minor colony on the western fringe of the Union of Planets, abutting the Great Desert Rift. Naplian forces overran its meager defenses and scooped up every person. Very similar to the supposed Naplian taking of Union citizens for experimentation."

Tag watched the sensor records streaming across the scroll's surface. The sight of One-eyes herding people—even kids—aboard transports at gunpoint chilled him. "No wonder. Did the Leadership actually do it?"

"They did. Gave them a temporary reprieve from the pressures of the Riven Cabal. The Union has already struck at a listening post inside the Rift, quite successfully."

Something didn't feel right. Ram was stolid, and the whole situation seemed—off. "This happened right after our mission."

"Yes."

"And we get an ally."

"Not exactly. They cast in their lot with the Briddarri, and the Grand Alliance. Which we, of course, have yet to formally join. But my sources further up the Admiralty chain tell me it will happen in less than a year."

"You're thinking something about all this."

"Whatever makes you say that, Captain?"

"Because, sir, we're discussing this in a crowded hallway with a whole lot of noise around us. Because you came and got me right after I came down from the flight line."

Ram smiled. "Aside from your combat skill, it is your frankness I value most. There are rumblings from TI, through our mutual friend Commander Ess. The recordings were provided by the Briddarri to the Union. It was a Briddarri scout which supposedly discovered the raid and chased off the Naplians. They were unable to affect a rescue."

"Real shame. You think—?"

"I think our allies have been less than forthcoming. I think the number of people I trust on this matter are few." Ram handed Tag a small, sealed container. The gray identification plate was addressed to Captain Taggart Wester, Bronze Squadron, TSS *Confiance*. "Keep in mind, you may be called upon again, for work farther afield from routine fighter patrols. Dyson Ashteo sends his regards."

Ram left him in the midst of the corridor traffic, turning the box over in his hand. Tag pressed his thumb to the plate. [Identity confirmed. Serial number authorized,] a tinny voice said.

The lid unsealed. Inside were two items—a folded piece of vellum, and a Blue Kitt statuette.

Tag lifted it from the box. The sapphire stone wasn't any carving; it was the same one Lira had shown him in Atterissage. He unfolded the vellum.

"Greetings, Tag. I trust you are well. If this message reaches you in timely fashion, know our mutual acquaintance has recovered well from her illness. She looks forward to seeing you in the near future, as do I. Our triad was an effective, and pleasing, one I hope to renew, especially regarding recent questions of alliance. Your service is greatly appreciated. Sincerely, Dyson."

"That old 'bot." Tag chuckled and stuffed the box into his flight suit. Yeah, Ram was right. He would be called upon to get his hands dirty. Tag didn't mind. War as it was, he'd have to adjust. After all, the Naplians he could deal with. The Briddarri, well … they were more dangerous than he'd like to admit.

Fortunately, he knew the right people to reach if he needed answers. Time to give Father a call.

***

Admiral Ergen had left Elden alone for far too long. The Truppen had received no orders and executed no missions for days. So, when he did finally summon Elden, it was all Elden could do to restrain from gouging the Briddarri's moustache from his smug face.

"How'd your little excursion to the human planet go?" Ergen blew cigar smoke at him.

It had to be a snub—though a foolish one, as Elden couldn't smell anything, nor could his senses be bothered by the literal smokescreen. "The Naplians left behind were a token occupation force. Their defeat was embarrassingly simple."

"But you enjoyed it, no doubt. As did your lady friend."

"Marney Wester is no concern of yours, Admiral. She's returned to her family for rest." And a serious reexamination of her principles, Elden hoped.

"Good to know." Ergen tapped ash from the end of the cigar. "So, we haven't had a good talk for a while. Care to enlighten me on what your detective work found?"

Enough of this nonsense. "I know what you and your people did."

"Not sure I understand."

"The cybernetics installations."

"Run by mercenaries working for a corporation, I understand. Private enterprise. That isn't the jurisdiction of my command."

"Don't lie to me, Admiral. I saw what was done to those people. They weren't human any more. Nor were they Truppen. And I've seen the reports about the Union colony, the one the Naplian forces conquered. Everyone is gone."

"That is a shame. I've got no intel as to where the One-eyes took them." Ergen smirked. "You want to go hunt for some more missing persons? Be my guest. I've got new naval elements from the Union of Planets to work into my command."

"The timing is suspect."

"It's interstellar war, Selva. Lots of things are suspect." Ergen leaned in. "Let me tell you what isn't suspect. My loyalty to the kingdom. My commitment to win this war. My willingness to do whatever it takes. Don't be a fool. You and your kind are the greatest benefit to this conflict. Since you won't produce more of yourselves for our armies, my superiors want another route taken."

"You can't. These experiments … they're not right. You're melding a person and a machine by brute force, in ways that strip their souls out piece by piece. The Truppen transfer is a complete merger."

"And expensive! I've seen the numbers. Best we can use Truppen for is special operations. But to build an army to crush the Naplians? Don't be so naïve. That takes conscription. It takes a harvest."

Elden stared at Ergen, too stunned to respond.

"You really do think yourself high and mighty, don't you? The great Truppen, on their holy mission to knock off the evil Naplians." Ergen laughed. "Please. You're products, built by the humans when they were too cowardly to do their own fighting. You all barely survived the end of your petty local war. But the way you fight—like no others. If we can duplicate that, we can slaughter the One-eyes, drive them out until we show up on Bonante and Benaltep's palace steps with a cyber's blades for their necks."

"The blood of innocent people is on your hands, Ergen," Elden snapped. "It'll never be washed off. When the time comes, the galaxy will know what you've done."

"Of course! They'll blasted thank me for it. Mind your place, Selva. There's the Alliance, or Naplia. No in-between. Get out of my office and await your next orders—unless you think you'd have better luck with your human enemies."

No in-between. It was all Elden could do to restrain from ripping Ergen's head off in a splash of blood and splinter of bone. Instead he thundered down the corridor. Marney was right. So was Jeopar. The Truppen were held in check, but the technology that bred them, that brought new life to people like he and Goetz and even Erich Baessler … there was a balance to it. A terrible balance.

What mattered now was only one thing: How much further would he be willing to go to stop it?

STEVE RZASA

ABOUT THE AUTHOR

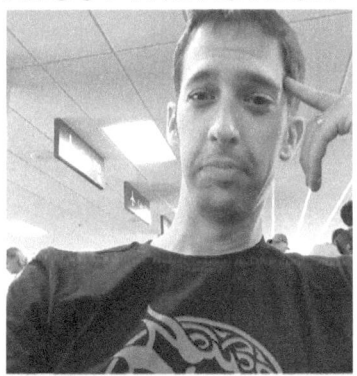

Steve Rzasa is the author of three Takamo novels. He has several other science-fiction, steampunk, and fantasy novels, with a bunch more in progress. He was first published in 2009 by Marcher Lord Press (now Enclave Publishing). His third novel, Broken Sight, received the 2012 Award for Speculative Fiction from the American Christian Fiction Writers, and his debut novel, The Word Reclaimed, was nominated for the same. The Word Endangered was recently nominated for the Realm Award presented by Realm Makers.

Steve grew up in Atco, New Jersey, and started writing stories in grade school. He received his Bachelor's degree in journalism from Boston University, and worked for eight years at newspapers in Maine and Wyoming. He worked as a librarian for fifteen years, earning his Library Support Staff Certification from the American Library Association in 2014—one of only 135 graduates nationwide and a handful in Wyoming. Steve now devotes all of his time to writing.

He is the technical services librarian in Buffalo, Wyoming, where he lives with his wife and two boys. Steve's a fan of all things science-fiction and superhero, and is also a student of history.

Takamo Universe Books

www.takamo.com

The Emperor's War Series

Empire's Rift by Steve Rzasa

Strife's Cost by Steve Rzasa

Counterstrike's Ruin by Steve Rzasa

The Ice Cold Heart by KS Augustin

Aeon Project Series

Aphelion by AR DeClerck

An Enduring Sun by AR DeClerck (Aeon Project Book I)

Dark Star by AR DeClerck (Aeon Project Book II)

Decaying Orbit by AR DeClerck (Aeon Project Book III)

Resonance Factor by AR DeClerck (Aeon Project Book IV)

Escape Velocity by AR DeClerck (Aeon Project Book V)

Ammanian Origins Series

For God and Mars by Shona Husk

Last Run of the Ice Duchess by Shona Husk

Muto Chronicles Series

Rhats! by Kerry Nietz

Rhats Too! by Kerry Nietz

Rhataloo by Kerry Nietz

Rhats Free by Kerry Nietz

Omiata Chronicles Series

Degara's Mark by Amber Draeger

Degara's Bane by Amber Draeger

Also by Steve Rzasa

Mercury Hale Series

The Face of the Deep Series

Vincent Chen Series

Deception Fleet Series (with Daniel Gibbs)

Galaxy Bridge Series (with Daniel Gibbs)